The Hidden Door

The Hidden Door

ACROSS TIME & SPACE
BOOK FIVE

M. Marinan

Silversmith PUBLISHING

First published in New Zealand in 2019
This edition published 2023
by Silversmith Publishing

A catalogue record for this book is available from the National Library of New Zealand

Original cover paperback ISBN 978-0-9951196-4-2
This cover paperback ISBN 978-1-99-001426-0
This cover hardcover ISBN 978-1-99-001427-7

Dedication

*For Kate, my editor, a dear friend and one
of this series' biggest fans.*

*Also thanks to Anne-Marie for helping to
shape and polish this story.*

Contents

Prologue

Somewhere, not too far from the busiest cities, the most windswept beaches and the quietest forests, there is a wall. It shoots up high into the air, higher than any person or even any rocket can reach, and as far in each direction as the eye can see, or as far as any person could ever travel. It is, in fact, a complete barrier.

It shines like gold, like a thin layer of cellophane that sparkles in the sunlight and glows at night. It looks thin, looks weak, but it's the exact opposite. It's the rift between realms, the separation between the Other realm and the normal realm, and it's impenetrable.

From one direction, anyway.

On the human side, the barrier goes unseen. People walk around it and near it and even brush over its surface again and again, yet most of them will never know that it exists.

But for the ones on the Other side? It defines their existence. It shows them the boundaries of what they once had, and what they lost. It's their prison, their weakness, and always their target.

Breach the boundary. Take back what's ours.

Or take back what they'd been grasping for at the very moment the boundary was created.

Because if they can't come through to us, then they'll bring us through to *them.*

Somewhere else, entirely in the normal realm, someone was going for a walk in the forest. It was a walk with a purpose: they'd identified an object of power was somewhere in the vicinity, and they were determined to find it.

It better be something useable, they thought. As a Halfling, with one parent human and the other supernatural Creature, some objects just didn't work for them. There were objects of power left, right and centre if you knew where to look for them. Those made in the Mountain of Glass, those made in the Other underground cities, and those made out in the human realm.

And this one…

The person felt the faint hum of alter-power intensify, but it was so faint that they thought it must be hidden deep underground. And then when they stepped on a small, black, rock-like item hidden in the thick grass, they concluded the object must be practically worthless. Otherwise how would it give off so little signal?

But when they bent down and picked up the item, and saw what it was, they realised how wrong they'd been. It wasn't worthless at all – it was possibly *invaluable.*

The question was, could a Halfling like them use it?

In the distance, they heard the faint sounds of someone traipsing through the greenery, and so they closed their fist around the item, their eyes narrowing. This was a perfect chance to test it out.

Less than an hour later, the question had been very clearly answered. Yes, a Halfling could use the object of power – but only for half of its intended purpose.

Even more interestingly, when in possession of this

particular object, the Halfling's own innate abilities had warped. They could no longer create supernatural links to individual humans in order to leach life-force – instead they got all that power in one go, so to speak. But the outcome had been messy, and decidedly fatal for the human.

The Halfling studied the now red and green scene around them thoughtfully, their hand opening and closing on the object. While they never claimed to be a saint, they'd just become far more lethal than they ever intended to be. The *new* question was; did they still want to keep the object, now knowing what the outcome would be?

Just then a certain town came to mind; one they'd visited decades before, and had been rather unpleasantly ejected from. A smile curved their lips.

They might just pay Erastus a visit.

HOME AGAIN

"Brilliant! It's just *brilliant.*" George leaned forward, an enormous pair of goggles sitting fly-like on his beaming face. He looked rather like a mad scientist off TV, Ash thought, especially with the way his curling blond hair had been blown upright by the forceful spring breeze. "Have you seen this, Ashlea?"

"Mm…yeah. It's cool, I suppose."

"Cool!? It's *marvellous.*" George's jaw fell open. "Ooh. Ooh, look."

"Has he never seen a kaleidoscope before?" Karen O'Reilly whispered in an aside. "We bought it for the baby…"

"No, he hasn't," Ash replied honestly, resisting an affectionate eye-roll. This sort of thing happened often when George was here in her time. "Mum, I told you his upbringing was very…old-fashioned." Like, two-hundred years out of date, old-fashioned. Literally.

"Hmm. Well, he *is* very well-mannered. Where did you say he was from again…?"

Ash coughed a little into her hand. *1819.* "A little Anglish town in Leister County. Nowhere, really."

Sort of like the Anglish equivalent of where they were now. They'd gone for a picnic on the riverbank. It was one of those early spring days where the sun showed its face, and so she'd pulled out a wide-brimmed hat, startling her mother who'd never thought she'd see the day Ash voluntarily wore such a thing. They sat on large smooth rocks at the riverside, with a bag of fresh bread rolls, a bottle of fizzy drink, and some deli salads and meats.

Yep, this was luxury alright. George was even wearing jeans with his light woollen sweater, and in Ash's unbiased opinion he looked very good indeed.

Fine, so they didn't have any servants, or multiple courses, or the meticulous social rules from George's time. But they did have the natural beauty of this green, damp, mountainous land, the convenience of everything being made for them, and of course…kaleidoscopes. Even this sort, which was fancy enough to be in the shape of binoculars.

George was still oohing and aahing, so Ash turned back to her mother. "The baby is the size of a broadbean, Mum. I don't even have a proper baby belly yet! It won't be able to appreciate anything like this for years. But at least someone does."

"Hmm. Well, have you thought of a name? Time flies."

Ash bit back a giggle. *Yes, it does when you're a time traveller.* "We've had a few ideas, but haven't yet agreed on anything."

"Horatio," George said suddenly, thus proving that he was listening after all. He lowered the binocular-glasses, smiling at her so that a dimple appeared in one cheek. "Or if it's a girl, Horatia. Now that's a strong, noble name."

Eeek. But Ash's mother came to the rescue. "Perhaps a little dated, George dear. And besides, children can be so cruel with nicknames."

His strong brow creased in confusion. "What kind of nicknames can come from Horatio?"

Now Ash did roll her eyes. "Just say the first syllable by itself, and you'll see."

He actually mouthed it out, then she knew he'd got it when his cheeks flushed pink. "Oh. I say, that's a bit much. My brother's middle name is Horatio."

"Edward Horatio Seymour," Ash murmured.

"Wow," her mother agreed. "That's a really Anglish name, isn't it?"

"Sounds like some kind of lord," Jacob O'Reilly said from where he stood ankle-deep in the river, a long-handled net in one hand. "Ha. Lord Edward Horatio Seymour, at your service."

Ash's father's Anglish accent was dreadful, but he'd been so close to the mark that she and George exchanged alarmed glances. But no, it had just been a coincidence, she realised. Her father had gone back to focusing on the water and the cockabillies he was trying to catch. He planned to donate the tiny fish to the local kindergarten's aquarium.

"By Jove," George murmured, sidling over to Ash. "Do you think he suspects…?"

"He suspects *something*," she murmured back. "That's the kind of guy my dad is. He's been looking into conspiracy theories my whole life. Political, alter-power, man-never-walked-on-the-moon, you name it. But I doubt he'd guess the truth on this one."

The truth being that George didn't just act like a regency gentleman, he *was* one. And when Ash went to visit his family at such short notice? She was actually stepping through a gateway in time and space, one that happened to have a supernaturally-charged midpoint now. In fact, their exit was just up the road from this very location. Not that Ash's parents knew about it. They thought the two had made their way here from the airport.

Lies were ugly and difficult, Ash mused once again. But in this case, the truth would be even more difficult.

"You need a classic name," her mother said thoughtfully, having missed their whispered conversation. "Something that would please George's family, and still fit in here. How about…Anne?"

"Mum, that name is dated," Ash argued. "It's practically medieval."

No, really. Anne of Covington was a good friend of theirs, and she was practically medieval.

"No, I meant *Anne.* Isn't that your little red-haired friend walking towards us right now? The one you flatted with last year in Angland. I didn't realise she'd come with you."

Ash followed her mother's pointed finger, and saw that indeed, their quiet, green spot on the riverbank wasn't quite so quiet. A petite figure was strolling towards them on the little-used path, her long, paisley skirt just brushing her ankles. Her red hair was tied loosely behind her head, and she wore a zipped-up hooded sweatshirt. A sparkly, purple pair of shoes sat on her little feet, and that was how Ash knew it was really her rather than some creepy, evil copy.

They'd met more than a few of those. Whenever Anne would travel through time, her clothing would change to fit the time period. But since recently, one thing would never change – those eye-popping shoes.

"Anne!" Ash cried, jumping up out of her seat and running over to give her smaller friend a hug. "What are you doing here? Is Elspeth here too?" Elspeth was Anne's half-sister, last seen in the Mountain of Glass. Ash lowered her voice. "Did *Amaranthus* send you?"

"Squeeze me that hard and you may regret it," the redhead replied tartly, widening her brown eyes. "I've just eaten." Then she smiled. "'Tis good to see you too, Ash. But no, 'tis just me today. Amaranthus did send me, and 'tis for a matter of grave import."

Ash paused, mentally translating the old-fashioned Anglish into something logical, then decided it didn't sound good. "What's happened?"

Anne turned towards where the others sat or stood near the picnic blanket, watching her curiously. She smiled again, waving, but this time her smile was tight. "Good day, Mrs O'Reilly, Mr O'Reilly. I trust you are well?"

"Well enough, thank you Anne. And nice to see you again in person," Karen replied politely.

"Lord, she speaks like he does," Jacob muttered, but Ash saw him studying Anne curiously. "Sounds a hundred years out of date."

Try five hundred, Ash thought.

"I do apologise for interrupting your leisure, but I bring news. George, if we might speak privately?"

George stood, his eyes widening, and followed Anne off to a space away from the others. Ash followed, because…if it was for him, then she could hear it too. Right?

"'Tis your brother," Anne said finally. Her expression was sombre. "You must come at once."

Mountain of Glass, time irrelevant

Elspeth, formerly of Covington, was on fire. And 'twas not in a manner of speaking, as some might say. She was quite literally on fire: covered in the silvery flame that would destroy evil, but leave anything else untouched. For her, she found it merely tickled.

She stood in a hollow at the inner Mountain's base. There was smooth rock underfoot and on three sides around her, creating a sort of stone alley. On the flat rock wall up ahead she had painted a simple target with concentric rings. She took a deep breath, let the fire build up until it felt white-hot within her small hand, then launched it towards the central ring.

A silvery stream shot out in front of her, then splashed harmlessly off to the left of the target before dissolving into nothing. "Oh, z'wounds!" she swore crossly. A moment later she recalled she was not alone, and glanced guiltily to one side. "My apologies for my language, Jon. I quite forgot myself."

"Er…what language?" Jon looked up at her from where he'd been seated nearby, his brown eyebrows raised. When she'd met him some weeks ago, he'd been as pale as milk, but since then his skin and hair had been slowly darkening to more natural shades. 'Twas a most odd change, but to her surprise, she rather liked the darker version.

"Z'wounds. I said z'wounds." Elspeth repeated, then felt her cheeks heating. "Oh, and now I have said it yet again!"

"Have you? What does it mean?"

"Er…" Elspeth paused. If he hadn't been offended by her language, it seemed of little value to explain to him why he ought to be. "'Tis of little import. I was merely disappointed at my own lack of aim once more. You would think that if Amaranthus gave me a gift such as this, then I would also have the means to use it correctly!"

"Don't worry, Bets," Jon said casually, using his usual nickname for her. "It'll all work out with your, er, invisible flame." Then he sighed.

She was mildly offended that yet again, he could neither see nor acknowledge her gift, but pushed that aside. She'd been born crippled and illegitimate in sixteenth-century Angland, and merely being overlooked was normal enough, even now that she was healed and well away from her birthplace. Even so, she felt irritated. But because she was quite infatuated with Jon, she focussed on his sigh. "What ails you? Have you seen something new in the viewing pool?"

At the top of the Mountain of Glass's own glass city, there was a pool. 'Twould show one literally anything, which Elspeth found quite disconcerting. But Jon spent a great amount of time there, peering at images which she could not see.

"No." He paused, then sighed again. "It's something else. Something…from home."

Elspeth was silent a long while. She burned with curiosity, but she knew well that if she were to ask about his home, he would simply change the subject once again. So instead she asked delicately, "If you cannot tell me of your home, then might you tell me of your travels instead?"

"What do you mean?"

She shrugged, spinning a ball of silvery flame in one cupped palm. "How did you come to arrive here in the Mountain of Glass? You know that I left my home by means of the Eternity Stone, which allows travel across time and space. If not for that, 'tis certain I would either be buried in the Iversley graveyard, or else working in some low, servile position without my sister's help. We used the Stone to travel to the Other realm, then after much confusion, we fell through a secret entrance into this place."

Jon's serious expression faded as one side of his mouth quirked into a grin. "Heh. It still makes me laugh to think of your expressions as you came in."

Elspeth recalled it well. She'd feared for her life, then had found herself in a place of unimaginable beauty, with this most comely, pale young man awaiting them…and laughing like a loon. It had been their first meeting. Her sister Anne had been offended, but Elspeth had seen past the laughter to the person beneath. "So did you fall in also?"

"You know I was brought by alter-power," Jon replied dismissively. "But tell me more about the Eternity Stone. Where did it come from? Where is it now?"

'Twas a clear deflection of her question, but she found herself answering anyway. "Forsooth, 'tis a question that burns me still, yet I always forget to ask Amaranthus. I understand that 'tis from this place, yet he and his People cannot touch it. I forget the reason why-"

"Oh look!" Jon cut in suddenly, pointing across the garden to where a short, balding figure moved by, heading towards the main city itself. "Isn't that Amaranthus? Why don't you ask him?"

Elspeth glanced over long enough to see that 'twas in fact their host, then turned back to Jon with narrowed eyes. If he wished to be alone, or to change the subject more thoroughly, she thought, he might merely have said so. "Indeed I shall," she agreed with dignity, deciding not to be offended. Taking offense would be easy, and would in time be the death of their friendship.

She bid him farewell and moved quickly after their retreating host, who had slowed as if expecting company. Elspeth knew him well enough that he would not have been seen if he did not wish to be, so was confident in her welcome. "Good morn," she said cheerfully, her spirits lifted merely by being in his presence. "Where do you go today?"

Amaranthus's dark eyes crinkled with a smile. He wore the plain form in which she'd first met him, the one where he could easily be mistaken for an ordinary, somewhat elderly man. "Here and there, dear Bets, but for now, the Tapestry Room. Will you join me?"

She already had, Elspeth thought, but agreed happily anyway. She glanced back over her shoulder to see if Jon might like to accompany them, for he was still within earshot, but he had almost vanished from sight. Her heart sank.

"He will be returning home soon," Amaranthus said mildly. "He cannot stay here. Most cannot, as you know, not in these mortal forms. It weighs upon his heart."

"But *I am* here, sir," Elspeth pointed out, her shoulders

slumping in dismay. Jon would be leaving. She'd known it must be coming, and yet it saddened her. "And you promised Anne and I should not ever have to return home. Do you not remember?"

Amaranthus smiled at her, a secretive glint in his dark brown eyes. 'Twas as if he knew some jest that Elspeth did not. "Indeed you are right, dear one. You *are* here, and you and your sister do not ever have to return to your place of birth. But you shall make yourself another home, and it shall not be here."

Elspeth sighed in relief, and a moment later her imagination pulled up an idea; that of her going to wherever it was that Jon called home. She would arrive at his front door, wearing some lovely local garb and bouncing with excitement. Then when he opened his door to see her standing there, he'd beam with unexpected happiness at the wonderful surprise, and say....

Ah, here we are, Amaranthus cut in, speaking straight to her mind.

Well, I do not think he would say that, Elspeth thought, but dismissed the fantasy. While she'd been lost in thought, they'd somehow moved from outside in the Garden, into the Tapestry Room without her even noticing. By this point, such supernatural things bothered her not at all. Her host did not follow the usual rules, even those relating to time and space.

They were now inside an enormous round room, with its walls filled with one enormous tapestry in shades of grey. She knew the grey was merely an illusion. In truth 'twas fine threads of black and white, interwoven to create a pattern. Or so one might think. To Elspeth, it had always looked like a right mess.

The pattern is on the other side.

Amaranthus had vanished from his place next to her, and she looked about in surprise before spotting him in the distance, at the other side of the room. He crooked a finger, indicating she should join him. She took a step towards him, then *whoosh*. Her head spun a little as she found herself right next to him once again. She'd crossed half a mile in one step.

"Now," he said aloud. "Let me tell you about the Eternity Stone."

Erastus, north border of the
Secular Republic of Lile, 2598 AD

Kamile sat under the shelter of a spreading pine, watching as her sort-of husband muttered unhappily and tried to grab back the large hammer-gun he'd been using. But the flying tree, a copy of the very one she sat under, had caught the tool in its tangled, hanging roots and was currently in the process of floating off with it.

Aras let out a frustrated huff, then grabbed a handful of the tree roots and dug his feet into the ground, trying to pull the thing down. Enormous, muscular man vs overactive, supernaturally charged pine tree? Guess which one was winning. Hint: it wasn't the man.

"Do you want a hand?" she called out.

Aras flicked her a brief glance, blowing aside the lock of blond hair that had fallen over his scowling face. His gaze settled on the bundle in her arms, and one eyebrow raised. "I'll pass."

She'd known he'd say no, and didn't bother arguing. Even if she'd been big and strong like him, instead of literally half his size, and if she hadn't been recovering from a life-threatening injury, he still would have said no. Besides, what would she have done with Isla?

The baby in her arms blinked as if in surprise, then scowled. Her face might be tiny and squished just like any other one-month-old child, Kamile mused, but somehow she still looked like her father…

Kamile looked up again just in time to see the pine tree give one last burst of strength and literally soar up into the sky, with Aras still hanging onto its dangling roots. Her jaw dropped, and a moment later so did he. He let go, landing heavily on his feet, then fell backwards with a shower of dirt over his head. He swore again.

Kamile bit back the words 'are you alright', since the answer would be 'grunt'. Judging by Aras's behaviour, tough men didn't show emotion…except when someone died.

"It was a nice idea to create a grove of trees outside our new house," she said instead. "But I think that particular pine didn't want to cooperate." Even though Erastus was still in the normal realm, the very atmosphere of this small area was so charged with alter-power that flying trees were the least of the weirdness. On the upside, someone like her with Other blood could also live quite comfortably.

When she and the others had arrived three months earlier, the locals hadn't been unfriendly. Aras had found a place quite quickly, since he looked strong and capable and so forth. More recently he'd been hired by the town's mayor to contain the many flying trees that were becoming a nuisance. It was easier said than done.

Aras climbed to his feet, gesturing at the tree she sat beneath. "I got that one. I'll get another, once I can find a new hammer-gun."

He'd quite impressively nailed down the first tree just this morning, creating shade on an otherwise too-warm day. "Maybe it warned the others, and that's why they gave you trouble," Kamile joked.

There was a long silence, and she added, "Just kidding. I'm

pretty sure the trees aren't sapient." She *hoped* they weren't. They'd not been here for long, and no doubt there'd be more to see.

The tiny town of Erastus was set in a quiet valley, a bit dry except for the wide river that ran down its length. In certain areas the trees had a tendency to roam, and there were odd doorway/portals set randomly around the valley. They mostly looked like stone doorframes or archways, and Kamile could sense the alter-power emanating from them even from a distance. She didn't know what was on the other side. Something supernatural, she knew, but it could be anything.

Just then a shadow passed over her. She looked up and saw the escaped pine tree, back for a second pass. She could just make out the hammer-gun hidden in its dangling roots. Was it loosening? "Hey…"

Then the tool fell.

"Look out!" she cried.

It seemed as if it would hit Aras right in the head – in which case she'd *definitely* say the tree knew what it was doing – but he moved at the last moment and it hit him on the shoulder instead. She heard the crack of the impact from here, and gasped. "Chaos, are you alright!?"

Isla let out a startled wail.

Aras shook himself, then with a grunt, bent down to pick up the hammer-gun. "It was my left arm."

The metal prosthetic, that was. "Oh. Good."

"But if it had hit you or Isla, you'd be dead."

Probably. Kamile warily looked up at the sky again as if there'd be a whole flock of travelling, violent trees. "Maybe I'll sit inside," she suggested.

He grunted again in what sounded like agreement. Then he nodded at her, turned and walked away.

She watched him go with something like longing. She didn't know where he was going. It didn't really matter, but the fact that he hadn't told her just confirmed they didn't have a relationship. Just a baby, a shared history, and two dead friends that had meant a lot to them in different ways.

Well, Coryn had meant a lot to both of them. Kamile was pretty sure Aras didn't give a jot about Trennan, except that Coryn had been in love with him, and therefore *not* with Aras. That was how they'd got into this whole situation, in fact.

One hundred years ago…or actually just under one year, but it felt like longer…they'd been living with the Chosen, a group of people who'd made their home on the borderlands between the normal realm and the Other, supernatural realm.

It had been a dangerous lifestyle since they'd been living in a stringent secular republic, but back then, they'd thought it was worth the risk. The custom among their people had been to handfast with the intention of having children. One year of faithfulness, no unpleasant long-term attachments. Except, presumably, for the children.

Kamile had never questioned the idea, not until she'd found out that the leadership of the Chosen – both Other and human – were very, very wicked. Oh, yes they were. Then she'd decided that if the people making the rules were actually evil, then she oughtn't to be following those rules. That had led to a whole lot of nastiness, a near-death experience, and ending up…here.

She got up carefully, shifting Isla to one arm as she did so. The movement made the wound at her throat tug again. In these last months it had progressed from 'horrendous and almost fatal' to 'horrendous and uncomfortable' which she figured was a step up. Even here in Erastus, where some of the locals were *weird,* she still got a few strange looks.

Although she was almost alone here at the edge of the valley, she still shifted her scarf to cover her neck. Her straight, mid-length brown hair wasn't nearly enough of a shield.

Her house was built of huge sheets of metal. It had three small rooms, plus a primitive bathroom detached from the house, and the whole of it was raised up on an enormous, thick metal pillar. Cheap. Mostly safe. Apparently the river was prone to flooding every ten years or so, and raised houses were standard.

The inside of the house was sparsely furnished, since they'd literally arrived with the clothes on their backs, but given enough time they'd make it nicer. Or she would, Kamile thought as she carefully climbed the metal steps. She didn't know about Aras, or even if he'd still be here in two weeks' time when their year of handfasting was up.

She wondered if they were still keeping to those traditions. Well, he hadn't said that they *weren't*. All she knew was that at the last Summer Solstice, he'd wanted to handfast with her dear friend Coryn. But Coryn hadn't been so keen – for some reason not finding the giant, impressively muscular Aras as attractive as Kamile found him – and so Kamile had stepped in. She'd offered to handfast with Aras for a year instead, and he hadn't pulled out. No double meaning there, even though the one time they'd slept together, she'd got pregnant.

And then she'd discovered that the Fey weren't the only Others. There was another place, one full of life and purpose. Oh, and then the Chosen Elders had killed Trennan and tried to murder her, and a helpful sort-of-Creature called Shulamithe had possessed her body just long enough to keep her alive. And then she'd been rescued, sort of, and Coryn had been killed too, and then…

Kamile sat down with a bump on the edge of the house's metal frame. Isla's tiny face screwed up again, and she let out a hearty wail.

"Ooh, is she hungry? Can I feed her?"

Kamile glanced behind her to see one of the house's other occupants. "Oh, hi, Poli. I thought you were still out with Magdalene."

Poli came to sit beside Kamile, stretching out her arms towards the baby. She was only fourteen, auburn-haired, freckled and round-faced, but she was several inches taller than Kamile. But wasn't everyone? "I was, but she wanted to go see her friend." The redhead screwed up her nose, but kept talking as she took Isla. "She met him after school the other day, but I didn't see who he was. Then today, when I asked if I could come to meet him, she acted all cagey. Said they had plans."

Magdalene, or Mags, was also fourteen, although shorter than Poli and brunette. She was also a refugee, just like Kamile and Aras and many others, and she was dealing with the upheaval in her own way. They'd done their best to fit into this new town, enrolling in their version of school and living here with Kamile, who they'd known for a while.

They visited the River frequently too, but it was still hard. Kamile could see it in Mags' moodiness, and Poli's clinginess. But they didn't have anyone else. Even before they'd fled their old home in Lile's capital city, they'd been orphans in the care of the state. Along with Aras's son Ric, that meant a very full house right now.

"We'll ask her about it when she comes home," Kamile said instead. "Shall I get a bottle?" Part of the issue with her almost-dying, and so forth, was that bottle feeding seemed a darned sight easier than the alternative.

Poli leaned over the baby, making cooing noises. "Do you want a bottle, Isla Coryn? Do you- *urgh*." The baby had made another scowling face, there was an intense noise somewhere around the other end of the parcel, and then her expression settled. "I think she needs her nappy changed."

Which Poli was rather less happy to do, Kamile thought wryly as she took her daughter back. And she'd had another realisation. "She looks grumpy when she needs the toilet," she said with some humour. "Perhaps that's why Aras always looks grumpy too, hmm?"

Poli laughed, and Kamile set herself to finding the washcloth. She had to take her fun where she could find it.

The Mountain of Glass, time irrelevant

The Eternity Stone is a piece of the bedrock of the light-world – the place that I and my People came from; the place that will be many humans' ultimate destination. It was shattered away from its origin when the realms were forcibly separated, creating a barrier between the human world and what became the Other realm.

Amaranthus pointed at a little patch of white somewhere near the end of that tangled mess. *This is where the Eternity Stone first entered your realm,* he continued, speaking straight to Elspeth's mind. *Near the end of time, as you'd see it. Here, let's follow its journey.*

Just then, a shining golden thread lit up, tracking its way across the greyish tapestry like an odd sort of map. Elspeth let out a gasp of amazement as her host began running his finger along the thread, sending images shooting up into the air as he did so.

See how few people recognised this object's worth, Amaranthus whispered into her mind. *So it spent so many centuries sitting alone and ignored, or even at the bottom of a privy.*

An image sprung up of Elspeth herself dropping a cloth-wrapped item into that very place, but rather than feel embarrassed, she found herself giggling at the memory. Forsooth, how very different her life had been. How very different *she* had been.

She moved forward to run her finger along the golden thread, trying to see where it came into the hands of different people along its journey. Ooh, *here* her friend Ash dug it up from the old privy, and *here* she travelled to find George, Anne and Elspeth herself. Then they had travelled *here, here* and *here…*

"Oh," Elspeth said in surprise. "I remember now. We lost the Stone when we entered the Other realm." She recalled someone – mayhap 'twas Jon – saying that it could not enter the Other, and must stay in the mortal realm. She wondered why 'twas that way.

For many reasons, dear Bets, but perhaps the simplest reason is this. The Eternity Stone must be returned to the place it came from, and once returned, the eternal, timeless bedrock of that place will once again be complete. No immortal hand should touch it in the meantime, and the Creatures least of all. They cause enough trouble merely by existing, let alone having such power and freedom from time.

Causing trouble. That was an understatement, as Jon would say. Elspeth finally found the golden thread's trail again. It sat unused for a long while after her own group had misplaced it, and then suddenly 'twas picked up again, but its use seemed at odds with how she'd seen it previously…

"'Tis not being used to travel across time," she realised. "But only from place to place. Who then is this person who uses the Stone thus?" She ran her finger a little further along, then let out a cry of outrage. "Amaranthus! I do think this person is using the Stone for villainy!"

He moved up beside her, and the villain's face came into clear relief. Elspeth couldn't help but shudder a little, for that was a face of such ugliness that one would not soon forget it.

The tapestry shows what is really there, Amaranthus explained.

Other people will not see this 'villain' in such a way. But the Stone has been used for evil many times, just as often as it's been used for good. Humans have a tendency to misuse objects of power. He looked at her solemnly. *One day someone will have an opportunity to return the Stone to its origin instead of using it for their own gain.*

Elspeth watched him wide-eyed. "Will they do it?"

He smiled, then patted her on the cheek in a fatherly fashion. *Of course. Everything on your world comes to its end eventually. And no matter how deep and dark the evil, there will always be someone or something to defeat it. No matter how terrible the surroundings, there will always be a way out.* He winked at her. *I've made sure of it.*

Hmm. Elspeth was left confused, but with a vague sense of happiness and hope, as was often the way with her host. Oddly enough, she'd noticed her sister Anne had begun to talk in a similar manner. Speaking of whom…

Anne has just returned. You'll find her through there. Amaranthus waved a hand behind him, and a gateway opened in the air, leading directly back to the Garden.

"Oh. Thank you!"

You are most welcome. And Elspeth…

"Yes?"

Don't forget to look for opportunities. He smiled, his warm, dark eyes crinkling in that way that made her want to smile back. *You never know when you'll trip over one.*

"Thank you?" Elspeth tried. But she could not make heads or tails of what he meant, so instead of trying to understand him, she simply left.

Mayhap Anne could translate for her.

Before the Rift

The sun was rising. From up here, the planet below looked like an enormous, dark blue pearl, with the cloud cover swirling in pale curls on its surface. The early light shone along one part of the curved horizon, highlighting its outline with gleaming gold. Mixed with the natural glow from the alter-power saturating this world, it was stunning. She had seen it before – every twenty-four hours in fact – but she never got tired of the view.

"Look, here it comes," she breathed aloud.

Then the planet turned, and she let herself be pulled with the gentle orbit. And then, mere moments later the sun 'came up' in earnest, an intense bluish-white light streaming over this previously darkened area. It lit up oceans and continents with green and brown and gold. If she squinted, she could just make out the details of forests and tiny figures moving on its surface.

"Beautiful," she announced with satisfaction. She moved one arm gently to the right, turning her whole body to face her companion where he floated next to her in the increasing light. "Isn't it beautiful, Bright?"

Bright shrugged one faintly speckled, shining shoulder. He gleamed like a tiny sun himself, or like the burning metallic heart of the planet below. But his gleam was all alter-power, not physical matter like these others down below. That was how they were made. "It still doesn't compare to home, Peaceful."

"It's not home," Peaceful said in confusion. "So of course it's different. It's *new*." She glanced behind her, at the rectangular doorway open in the starry space behind them. It led directly to home, to their universe that shone far more brightly than even the small sun of this world, and they could return there quicker than a thought. *But why would we do that? We chose to come here with our master, for the joy of it. For the joy of discovery, obedience, of aiding these weak ones here-*

No.

That one thought shot straight from Bright's mind to hers, quiet but clearly heard. It was so contrary to everything she knew, everything that was true, that for a moment she was speechless. She gave him her full attention, probing his consciousness gently for more information. But except for that single syllable, he was silent.

Strange. No one's mind was ever silent. How had he done that?

"Is all well?" she asked aloud, thinking even as she said it that it was a…*wrong* question. How could anything not be well? Bright was the most beautiful, most powerful Person she knew, except for the Master, of course. He had honour and authority, and everywhere he went, others smiled and bowed. His position was second to only their master, and she'd loved and honoured him as a brother and a friend for aeons.

She floated around him, trying to catch his golden gaze. *Bright?*

But he wasn't looking at her. "Do you see that creature down there, Peaceful? The one that looks like me."

Peaceful followed the line of his thoughts, right down to the world's surface, through a thick layer of damp green foliage. There, on the forest floor, lay a made creature. It was four-legged and long-bodied, with a thick coating of orange and white fur striped with black. Its ears were round and set on the top of its head, and it had a long, lushly furred tail that twitched as it playfully rolled onto its back.

"I see it," she agreed doubtfully. "But it is like you in shape only. You do not have fur, and it has stripes where you are spotted." Spots that each shone like tiny gems in his metallic hide, in fact. Peaceful stretched out her own blue arm, faintly marked with horizontal lines of darker blue. "You might say that *I* look like the creature also."

That was intended as a joke, since with her waving tendrils, fins and differently placed limbs, she looked the farthest thing from the furred creature.

But Bright didn't smile. "Why has he made these weak things, Peaceful? Their minds are so simple. They're messy and pointless." He nodded at another area on the planet below. "And let's not mention those ones."

But he already had. The *other* made creatures also looked nothing like Bright. They had four limbs, but they stood upright on their two lower legs, and their two upper limbs functioned as arms like her own. They were straight and tall, with egg-shaped heads sitting on strong necks, and faces that didn't resemble either hers *or* Bright's.

Odd forms, which were very physically capable, even if they did lack supernatural abilities. Even now, they'd taken the pieces of the planet around them to create themselves a home – along with the aid of the Master, of course. It was a stone building she'd heard referred to as 'the castle'.

But while those odd two-legged creatures didn't resemble herself or Bright, they did look like someone else. The Unfading One…their Master.

If the Master was the colour of dirt, with the barest hint of power or light, Bright said derisively, directly into her mind. *He could have done a better job. How about* this?

Then after a few seconds his form molded and changed into something different. Something like the creatures below, and like their master, only not. The two-legged, two-armed form was shining and beautiful and a little speckled, and when Bright raised a new eyebrow, she could see a hint of fang through his parted lips.

"Ooh. I don't like that at all," Peaceful said vehemently. "Change back, please."

Bright shrugged, and a moment later he was in his usual form. "You didn't know I could do that. If those dull creatures can be like the Master, then so can I. Only better."

Peaceful couldn't disagree. Bright was superior to the dirt-beings in every way...except one. The Master had chosen them quite deliberately. He'd made them to look like him. And because they looked like him, they had value just as did Peaceful and Bright and all of the others who came from their home, and who still lived there. And that meant that something about Bright's attitude felt...wrong.

Wrong? How could he ever be wrong? He'd never been before, she mused. But before she could dwell on that any further, she heard the Master's voice, speaking their names in the old language.

Shulamithe(Peaceful), Beraht(Bright).

She straightened, forgetting her friend and eagerly focusing on the call. *Coming.*

And she never saw how behind her, Bright-Beraht hadn't followed. And within his shining chest there was a patch of darkness over his heart, one that was growing...

DEATH AND TAXES

Te Waiwai, Southern Isles, 2013

"But you just got here," Ashlea's mother was saying, sounding baffled. "I understand that George's brother has been injured, but is he really going to fly all the way back to Angland, right now? It's such a long way! How will he get any flights?"

"Mum," George heard Ashlea begin, then he and Anne moved out of earshot and he didn't hear the rest of it. He couldn't have focused on it regardless. All he could think of were Anne's words. *Edward has been severely injured. Possibly fatally. Come quickly.*

"Thrown off a horse?" he said aloud. "I don't understand how he could be thrown by a horse. He's a *good* rider."

"No one is perfect," Anne replied as she walked along beside him, her smaller steps extra fast to keep up with his longer ones.

"But he can't be…*dying*, surely?" he persisted disbelievingly. "Edward's not even thirty, and he's a viscount!"

"Everyone's end comes at some point. Kings, dukes. Viscounts."

By Jove, that response wasn't precisely comforting! "Death and taxes, the only inevitable things in life," George said sarcastically. He still couldn't comprehend what she'd told them. All he could think of was his stronger, handsomer, invincible older brother apparently…on his way off this mortal coil. *Severely injured.* "But he can't die. He just can't."

"I did not say he would definitely die from this," Anne said in a small voice. "In truth, I do not know the outcome of this injury. But I *do* know that this is a matter of most grave…"

"Import, yes," George agreed sharply. Somehow the fear of losing his brother had also made him angry. "So what can be done now?"

Anne didn't respond. Instead she turned a sharp corner. To those behind them, they would have appeared to have moved out of sight behind a block of grey stone lavatories. But instead they were heading for a faintly shimmering patch of air near the pipe out back, just by an enormous, fat-trunked tree. It was one of the remnant gateways left behind when a time-travelling device called the Eternity Stone was used, and it had been left here purposely for him and Ashlea to use so that they might visit her family.

George stepped through it even before Anne could, feeling the faint tingle as he moved across time and space. Then he was inside a hallway full of doors, having just stepped out of one. He barely paused, spotting the gateway to 1819 AD which looked rather like an enormous, red leather-bound book. He was an inch away from stepping through that too when he felt Anne's hand on his arm. "Your clothing," she said.

He looked down, and suddenly his rough blue jeans and Millennial garb changed to his more usual beige trousers, high brown hessian boots, and neat jacket. "How…?"

"'Tis a new trick I have, now I am immortal. I use it for special occasions only."

Like the possibly imminent death of a loved one. George paused, feeling tears burn at the back of his throat and prick his eyes. Anne *was* immortal, was she not? Something had happened to her, something fantastical that he still didn't know the whole of. Ash had dismissed it as nonsense, but George saw the change. Anne wasn't who she used to be. She was better. And she was rather close friends with Amaranthus, also known as the Unfading One, or the Eternal One…or Deias.

"So you've truly become immortal," he choked out, barely believing he was saying such a thing. But it was true, was it not? "How?"

She stared at him solemnly, her eyes dark in her pale, oval face. "I died, George. I was burned at the stake in 1558 AD. But because my passage to immortality had already been paid by Amaranthus, I moved through death into this new life."

George sucked in a breath, closing his eyes briefly. He recalled the time he'd read about one twice-wed Lady Anne of Covington being executed in such a manner, either for heresy or witchcraft. He'd been so terribly concerned for her, but she'd assured him that while the history books might report such a thing, in truth she was quite well…except that she could not return to her home time.

He hadn't asked further questions in that conversation, but now he saw the real answer so very clearly. Anne could not return to Tudar Angland because as far as they were concerned, she'd been executed. She *had* been executed, and was quite, quite dead. Yet here she was…

"Was it painful?" he asked, hearing his own voice echo oddly through his ears. "Dying?"

"For a while, I believe it did. But I barely recall it now. 'Twas like…being born for a second time." She smiled just a little. "Most uncomfortable, but most certainly worth it."

"I see." But George didn't really understand, except to see that Anne was…*dead*…and now she was alive. To him, that made the whole process of mourning somewhat pointless.

"So...Edward...he could be like you?" he asked hopefully. "He might be severely injured, but perhaps...he'll be born again into an immortal form, and just...carry on?"

George felt a warm hand on his shoulder as Ashlea came up behind him. "What's this about Edward being reborn?" she asked curiously, and he heard that same mix of confusion and hope in her voice. "Is he going to be OK, then?"

Anne's lips tightened, and she answered Ashlea's question. "Most people do not get to simply carry on after death," she answered finally. "Most go on to their final destination. I'm rather a special case, you see. But as for Edward, I do not know if he will live or die this time. Only Amaranthus knows that, and he knows the future to its very end. But I do know that...that Edward's passage is...not paid. Not yet."

Not paid. George didn't entirely understand *that* either, except that it wasn't good. Not at all. He stared at his redheaded friend blindly for a moment, then shook his head, his heart wrenching inside his chest. Then he stepped through the second gateway.

On the other side, Lunden 1819 was foggy and dim in spite of the early hour. The sea fog had rolled in early. He could feel the cobblestones of the merchant district with each step but only paused long enough to gather his bearings, then turned in the direction of his family's townhouse. He'd hail a hansom cab, if one of those horse-drawn buggies was about, or else he'd run the whole way. He mightn't have long...

"George!"

He turned, and there was Ashlea, suddenly in the middle of the empty footpath where he too had appeared. She now wore the clothing typical of Anglish gentry – a high-waisted, full-skirted blue gown with a matching pelisse jacket. A small bonnet sat over her dark hair, looking somewhat out of place as it always did. Clearly Anne had helped her too, since that wasn't at all what she'd just been wearing.

George swallowed, realising he'd not even stopped to see if she was following. "We need to hurry."

His wife nodded, running forward to take his hand. "Pray for a cab."

Thank Deias they found one, Ash thought. Barely pregnant or not, she wasn't up to running the whole way, especially not in this corset, even if it did feel a bit looser than normal. Didn't these people know that corsets could cause miscarriages as well as being damn uncomfortable?

But then she heard George suck in a deep breath where he sat next to her in the rattling hansom cab – AKA this era's 'taxi' – and she tightened her grip on his hand. She wanted to comfort him, to say that it would be OK, but that could be a lie. Things weren't always OK. People died from illness, or from getting turned to ash by very modern weapons, or from getting thrown from a horse and landing on their head.

Urgh. That last part sounded particularly awful. Ash swallowed and tried not to think of how tight her stupid corset was, but instead focused on how her husband must be feeling. If something happened to Edward...she meant, if he...*died*...then George would be an only child, as well as the new Viscount Morley. And that would make Ash...

Oh, *collywobbles*.

Fifteen minutes later George and Ash pulled up outside the tall, pale stone house. It was sculpted in the most modern design for this time, but Ash barely noted the pillars and carefully created architecture.

George let go off her hand, practically throwing himself out of the carriage door. "Pay the man, Prowd!" he shouted at the startled butler who'd opened the townhouse's front door, then charged inside.

Ash gave the hansom cab driver a polite smile. "Family emergency. Sorry."

"Yes, ma'am," he replied, but his expression said he didn't care as long as he got paid.

Fair enough.

She waited only long enough to ensure that he *was* being paid – although not by her – then followed George. The house was identical to how they'd left it two months earlier, when she and George had showed up very late one night to convince her in-laws that yes, they *were* time travellers. It had worked, but Ash still looked at this building with its dark wood and fancy carpets and too many paintings, and felt out of place.

But today there was a pall over the house that went beyond her feeling like a misfit. It was in the hushed movements of the few staff she passed, in the very absence of anyone or anything. It was like everyone knew what had happened, and was waiting for Edward to die.

So Ash prayed as she walked down the hall, following after the maid who led the way. *Please Amaranthus. I know you can hear me.* And he could, right? Even though there was silence within her mind – well, just her own messy thoughts – she felt like he was there. She wasn't alone. *Don't let him die. Fine, he's a bit of a douche at times, but he's young. You helped us save Elspeth, right? And you helped Janeus, and he was a murderer! And you helped Coryn...*

Ash felt herself slump as she realised that Amaranthus's version of helping Coryn hadn't been to stop her dying. It had been to take her to the other side of dying, to take her to a bright, golden place that was seared into Ash's memory. It had been beautiful, and surreal, and…

…And then Ash was at the doorway of the master bedroom. The door had been left open, and in the dim interior she could see George crouching beside the high four-poster bed. On the other side was a blonde woman wearing something off Pride and Precipitation.

Olivia, the Viscountess Morley, was usually pretty, and usually not very friendly. Today she just looked drained, her eyes reddened as though she'd been crying for a long time. She looked blankly at Ash, briefly acknowledging her arrival, then turned back to the bed.

Edward Seymour, Viscount Morley, was six or seven years older than George, she forgot how much. He had the same blondish curly hair, and there was a resemblance, but his features were slightly more delicate. Pretty, not like George who was just handsome (said Ash). But today he lay on the bed, with his face far too pale and his arms by his sides. There was a shadow over one temple, and he was so very, very still…

Ash swallowed. Barring one ancient great-aunt at a funeral, she'd never seen a dead person. Well, not anyone she'd known and cared about, anyway. And if Edward wasn't dead, then he was at death's door.

It'd be OK, she reminded herself. That golden, glowing place where people went? That wasn't a place of suffering. If Edward went…*when* he went…he'd be OK. Really…

But even as Ash told herself that, she felt a hollowness inside, like she'd been repeating nonsense. Like she was trying to convince herself it was sunny when it was obviously raining.

That, a quiet thought whispered, *is not true.*

But he's not that *bad*, Ash thought desperately inside her head. *He's just…ordinary. He hasn't killed anyone. He's polite to his mother, even if he cheated on his wife before. He might even pay his taxes…*

But the thick, dark, horrible atmosphere couldn't be shaken, and it was so unlike her experience before with Coryn. If he wasn't going to the golden place, Ash suddenly wondered, then where was he going?

"George?" she whispered.

He must have heard her, but he didn't respond. He was standing next to the bed, staring down at his brother with a hollow-eyed expression she'd never before seen on his face. His hands were clenching and unclenching at his sides, and he leaned over Edward, staring at his chest, his mouth. Ash couldn't see Edward moving. Then George reached out and pressed two fingers against Edward's neck, on his pulse, and-

Suddenly Edward's eyes shot open, and he sat bolt upright, almost smacking George in the face. They all screamed, and it seemed like Edward had too, since his mouth was wide and round in the same shape. But then George let out a horrified laugh, and Ash found herself laughing too in a startled, semi-hysterical way.

"You scared us, old fellow," George was saying. "By Jove, I thought you were a goner!"

She'd thought he was already dead too. But Edward didn't answer the question, didn't speak. His mouth opened and closed a few times, his blue eyes wide and unresponsive.

Olivia whimpered. "Edward...?"

Then the viscount's eyes rolled back in his head, and he slumped back onto his pillow. This time Ash could see his chest rise and fall a little, but otherwise he looked as nearly-dead as before.

There was a long silence. "Where's Mother?" George asked finally.

"She might not have been notified yet," Olivia replied, her voice sounding small and hoarse. "I didn't think you'd have come

so soon, except…" She waved a hand, the gesture encompassing all the strangeness surrounding the two of them. "Can't you *do* anything?"

There was a pause, then both Olivia and George turned to stare at Ash. Her eyes widened. "Me?"

"You're from the future, are you not?" Olivia persisted. "You've showed us these strange devices for…writing, and for capturing images. Can you not heal a simple knock to the head?"

"Actually, concussion and brain damage of this level…" Ash's voice faded out. It wouldn't be helpful to say they were pretty much unfixable by the doctors of her time. "Um…not me. But Amaranthus could." She looked at George. "The healing pot. That saved *everyone* until it ran out, and the Mountain is only half an hour away. If we could get some more…?"

George moved as if he'd run towards the door, then stopped, his face twisted in anxiety as he looked back at his brother. "I don't want to miss…"

Edward dying. "I'll go," Ash quickly offered. "It's not far, and I've got my mobile phone and the medallion." George had insisted she keep the protective medallion on her at all times once they'd discovered she was having a baby. Before that, they'd played a game of hiding it on each other's person, but not anymore. Baby Broadbean was more important now. As for the phone, it had a weird habit of working when there was only one remnant gateway between them. She didn't question it.

As for George, he didn't even say 'oh no, you can't go alone', so she knew how unsettled he was. She paused, then decided to ignore Olivia's presence long enough to give him a quick kiss. "I'll be back in an hour."

Erastus, 2598 AD

Magdalene sat on the summer-dry grass with her knees tucked underneath her. She barely noticed the mild discomfort, since she was so caught up in her conversation. "And then Coryn warned us that we'd been discovered. She didn't say it like that since we were in public at the Mall, but we knew what it meant, so we ran for it. We knew we didn't really have anywhere else to go except here, and back in Lile they'll execute you for the kind of thing we were doing."

"And what were you doing that was so bad?" her companion asked.

She shrugged a shoulder, not meeting his eyes. Chaos, he was *soooo* gorgeous! The best-looking male she'd ever seen, and his *hair*… Every time she met his eyes she'd blush, and that was the worst. So she just didn't look at him. "Well, y'know that the Secular Republic has forbidden all use of alter-power. Anyone who uses it or talks about it, even if you're religious or pagan or just too sciencey – they get grabbed. And me and my friends – and Kamile too, at the end – we were talking about it *all* the time. You'd understand."

He nodded, sending his golden hair shimmering over his shoulders as if it had a life of its own. Magdalene rather suspected that it did. But then yes, he *would* understand why everything Sec was dry, and dull, and extremely boring.

"And we'd also been hacking into other people's virtual reality sessions for ages," she added when he was still silent. "And that's just illegal. We knew it, but we didn't care. We thought we'd got away with it." She sniffled a little, thinking of what she'd lost. "Until they killed Coryn. Boom, just like that, and we had to leave everything."

And everyone. She'd just started seeing someone, a guy called

Karl who'd worked at the same Mall as she had, but that was over now. It didn't matter, anyway. He'd been just a boy. Not like her new friend.

"I thought you said it was someone else who killed your friend. A vigilante."

"Yeah…" Magdalene knew it had been someone else, someone completely wicked and crazy, but she still blamed the state. It was easier that way, especially when the actual killer was as dead as Coryn. "But dead's still dead. She's gone, and we can't get her back. I mean, we were super glad to have Kamile 'cos we thought *she* was dead too, but then we found her here and she wasn't! Just all, you know, sliced up. But Coryn's still gone, and that's terrible 'cos we'll never see her again."

"Never…?" He sounded unconvinced.

Magdalene shot him a startled glance. "You mean…after death? I know that'll happen. Kamile said some girl told her she saw Coryn in some other, shining place. Dead, but not really dead. Kamile seemed to believe it, so I suppose I do too-"

"Yes, after death. But you don't have to wait until then. There's a faster way."

Now her attention was caught. She stared at him, for once not feeling so imperfect and embarrassed when comparing herself to his almost flawless features. He was perfectly formed, except for those slightly shaggy eyebrows above his warm, dark eyes. "How?"

Her friend stretched out one hand, gesturing at the rectangular shape surrounding him, then pointed in each direction. There were doorways on either side too, she saw, looking like empty doorframes standing in the middle of the plain. They weren't far from the River which Magdalene knew to be safe, but she couldn't see through these doorways. All she could see was a grey haze, or in some cases, darkness.

"You've been here in Erastus for some time, Magdalene. Haven't you noticed how people go in through the doorways, then come out different?"

"Yes, but…" Kamile had said not to go through, and Poli had agreed with her. They'd said how except for the River itself, they didn't know what was on the other side of those other doorways. It wasn't safe.

"And the unknown is always dangerous," her friend prompted, raising his eyebrows.

He'd been reading her thoughts, she figured, and that embarrassed her because he would have known about how she liked him, how she admired him and quietly wished that she could grow up faster so they could…be together. And then she knew he would have heard *that* too…

But he just watched her with that same kind patience that showed he wasn't judging her, and she ducked her head. She knew what he meant. "Not necessarily dangerous," she hedged. "But it could be, if you didn't know what you were getting into. Especially around here, when there's the Other, and Kamile said there are definitely dangerous things inside. Killers."

"Could say the same for out here with you lot," he said lightly. "Forget the lawbreakers who make it dangerous for you to walk in some areas or at night. How many has the government itself executed? You know that your towns aren't always safe, and yet you can live in them freely if you know how to be careful. The doorways are the same."

Magdalene didn't know how many had been executed, because those figures weren't publicized. It would be hard for the Sec Republic to claim that everyone was happy if they were killing loads of their own people for sedition, treason and so on. "Do you mean…some doorways are safer than others?"

He shrugged one perfect, white-clad shoulder. "If you're with the right person, they are. But don't take my word for it. Watch those who go through, and see what they look like when they return. That'll show you the truth."

He was offering to take her through, she realised. Her heart leapt with excitement and nervousness, and she found herself checking to see if anyone was currently using the doorways. There was no one in sight, though.

"But not now," he continued. "You're supposed to be home, aren't you? We wouldn't want to upset anyone by making you late. Your friends care for you."

Yeah, she supposed they did. But she looked again at that ordinary, stone-edged doorway, and wondered. "I'd better go home," she agreed, glancing up at him once last time. He was watching her, smiling, and she ducked her head, a blush warming her cheeks. "See you tomorrow?"

"See you tomorrow."

But as Magdalene got up to leave, she turned and slammed straight into someone. A woman dressed in white, and with silver hair like an old person. But her skin was smooth and almost as pale as the white dress she wore, and her full red lips definitely didn't belong on an old person.

"Careful, sweetheart," the woman said with a laugh.

It was a nice laugh. A very nice one, in fact, the sort that made Magdalene want to smile back in pure friendliness. But then she realised that this too-attractive woman was visiting *him*, and her smile abruptly faded as a wave of dislike washed through her. Had he noticed that, too? Jealousy was never attractive. So Magdalene lifted her chin and gave the silver-haired woman a polite smile, before quickly walking away. Ooh, and it took everything she had not to turn around and see if they were watching.

But then she gave in after about twenty steps. She turned, and the woman *was* watching. She lifted a hand to wave at Magdalene, and so did he.

Magdalene's lips tightened, but she waved back before continuing on her way.

How embarrassing...but she still knew she'd be back tomorrow. Some people were worth a little embarrassment.

Lunden, Angland 1819 AD

Ash reached the gateway outside Tolliver's bookstore in excellent time. She paused to check that no one was watching, then quickly stepped through. A moment later she was inside the hall of doors, as she thought of it.

Just across from her was the door leading to Te Waiwai in her own time. To her left the hall stretched out into the distance, impossible to see its end; to her right the hall opened into a grassy plain, speckled about with houses, and with an enormous leafy tree shading its entrance.

She could smell hotdogs.

Ash faltered. That smell probably meant Anne was outside, manning the odd little food cart that always served just what you wanted. The redhead had a direct link to Amaranthus, which also meant a much shorter trip to find the healing pot, or whatever it was that would save Edward. After her first trip here, Ash had always been a little hesitant to leave this hall for the valley outside. Erastus was...strange. Still, it was one of the few places where she could fly and not have anyone stare.

But Edward was more important than her nerves, so she steeled herself and headed for the large tree guarding the entrance. As she left, the scent of hotdogs became even stronger.

Then she glanced back and saw that the hall had vanished, leaving a view across the dry valley and scattered houses. That was OK; it'd do that whenever she left. You didn't even know it was there until you were practically tripping over it.

The food cart was to her left just up ahead, its bright, striped awning stretched out to provide shade for the couple of kids lingering there. One held a bright green ice cream in a purple cone, and the other sipped at an old-fashioned milkshake. Both looked at her curiously as she ran up to the cart's serving counter. But the man behind the counter wasn't Amaranthus, and he definitely wasn't Anne.

"Oh…sorry," Ash began when he looked at her in surprise. Then out of the corner of her eye she saw something copper-red. She turned to see a petite redhead in a neat blue tracksuit. The girl was some distance away, but Ash recognised her in the brief moment before she vanished behind a building a good five hundred metres away. "Anne!"

But Anne mustn't have seen her, because she didn't reappear. Ash called her name again, then set off at a run towards where she'd vanished. Deciding that flight would be faster, she raised her arms and felt her whole body lift several feet into the air. At her best she could zoom, if not quite like a speeding bullet, then pretty darn fast. It seemed to be connected to her state of mind…but today, she felt slow. Too slow, and-

Suddenly gravity reclaimed Ash, and she collapsed to the ground, almost grazing her knees. "Ow!" She sat up crankily, looking around to see if anyone had noticed her fall, then met the eyes of a woman standing nearby.

"It's the doorway," the woman said apologetically, her red lips curving into a rueful smile. "You just passed one, see? For some reason some gifts are affected in these spots alone. Steer clear, and you should be fine."

Ash hauled herself to her feet, dusting off her dirty knees, and briefly assessed her helper. The woman was perhaps in her late thirties or forties, but if so, age had been very kind. Her skin was flawless, her prematurely grey hair shone like freshly polished silver in its loose bun, and she wore a simple white trouser suit that flattered her excellent figure.

Ash spent a second debating whether to be impressed or jealous, and decided to settle on the first. The woman had a friendliness about her that would have made jealousy seem extremely petty. Or so Ash told herself.

"I'm Joy Silver," the woman continued. "But people around here call me Mama. Who were you chasing so ardently, sweetheart?"

"Um…" Suddenly Ash was befuddled, and she took a moment to remember. "Ah. A friend, and I'd better go after her now…"

"Or you'll miss her," the woman agreed. "But if she's gone through a doorway, you'd best be wary of following her. Some of those lead to great good. Others to great danger." She shrugged. "And some are simply boring. You're new, aren't you? You won't know which is which."

Startled, Ash looked at Joy more clearly. She'd been spot on, and Ash hadn't expected to be understood so quickly, and by a complete stranger. "Er…"

Then Joy laughed. It was a lovely laugh, the sort that made her more beautiful and made Ash want to laugh back, even in spite of that lingering envy. "Yes, yes. You'd better go. But I'll see you around, no doubt. I'm always here."

Ash nodded, then finally managed to focus on her task. Anne, who'd disappeared somewhere over…there. She ran – since flying now seemed dangerous with all these odd, high-gravity doorways scattered about – and then finally reached the point where she'd last seen her friend.

But the space behind the building was empty except for a stone archway, set in the tiled ground like some kind of sculpture. It was smooth and plain and made of pale stone blocks, and was just tall enough for Ash to go through if she ducked. Inside was darkness. A doorway to another time or place, or even another realm – but where?

"Umm…" Ash stopped in her tracks, studying the archway in dismay. She could feel a sort of thick, uncomfortable atmosphere emanating from it even though she stood ten feet away, and that darkness did *not* look welcoming. Or perhaps that was her childhood fear of the dark coming through. The remnant gateways she so often used to travel through time weren't even visible to the average person, since they looked more like shimmering hot air above a subway vent.

But here in Erastus, the gateways were literal doorways or archways that apparently anyone could walk through. She would be OK with that, especially if Amaranthus or Anne had led her through one. That way she knew they were safe.

But no one had told her *these* particular stone doorways were safe, and she definitely didn't feel that they were.

"And I didn't actually see Anne go through," Ash reasoned aloud. Hades, she hadn't actually *seen* for certain that it was Anne at all. For starters, Anne didn't usually wear pantsuits.

So her choices were to go through a scary-looking super-natural doorway to an unknown place, just because her friend *might* have gone through…or to turn around.

Ash had made her fair share of mistakes, but she wasn't a complete idiot.

She turned and headed back the way she'd come.

Ten minutes earlier

Aras stretched out his prosthetic arm, wincing at the ache where the metal joined with his shoulder. He'd had his original arm shot off in a battle three years earlier, and that had been it for him. He'd taken the prosthetic offered by the army and had retired early. War was fine – it served its purpose – but he'd rather not die bit by bit.

As for this place? It might have more supernatural power floating around than he'd ever experienced before, and it might have dangerous (and vindictive) trees, but it'd do for now.

But damnatus, that blow had hurt…

"Need a hand?"

Aras barely kept himself from jolting in surprise, and he turned on the newcomer with a scowl. He'd chosen this quiet room inside the council chambers for a reason – so he could wince without an audience. But then he saw who'd spoken, and straightened. "Ms…Silver."

"Call me Mama, everyone does." The woman smiled at him, her golden-brown eyes seeming to sparkle with merriment. In fact, everything about her seemed to sparkle, from her silvery hair to her teeth to her skin…

Wow. She did *not* fit his idea of a mother. Not his, anyway. "Ah…thank you, but I'm fine." His voice came out gruffer than he'd intended. And were his cheeks heating? He wasn't a boy anymore!

"I've seen you around," she continued, "but never had the chance to be formally introduced. I understand you're one of those from the recent Lile exodus, and the council has hired you to deal with our flying tree problem."

What was there to say to that? Aras nodded, but couldn't take his eyes off her. Her voice was beautiful, like silver bells. Could a woman have a voice like music? 'Cos she sure did…

"They don't mean to, but they do get rough at times," she said, stepping forward and setting her hand on his shoulder where the hammer-gun had hit him.

'They' being the trees? he wondered. For a brief moment he felt terrible pain, but then it receded entirely. He pushed back the collar of his shirt and glanced at the skin – the bruise had almost vanished, and his metal arm gleamed as if it had been freshly polished. "Did you heal me?" he asked in amazement.

Mama stepped back, just a little, and winked at him. "There are a few benefits to living so close to the Other realm. You've heard I spend a lot of time through the doorways, no doubt?"

"Ahh…" No, he hadn't, but it made sense now. She had a gleam to her that only came from alter-power, and it was remarkably attractive. Or maybe that was just her…

"Well, I do. My friends and I – they're the others with silver hair you've no doubt seen around – we spent a lot of time in other realms." She leaned in again, and this time it seemed her smile was distinctly flirtatious. "I'll take you through any time."

Aras swallowed, and his mind blanked. What was she offering? Two long seconds ticked by, then he choked out, "Maybe later."

She moved back again, shrugging a shoulder and smiling at him. "Whenever you like, Strong-Man. I'll see you around."

Aras watched her leave with a raised hand of farewell, then the moment she was out of sight, shook himself. He almost felt like he'd gone into a trance when she'd been talking to him. It was more than just looks – Mama Silver had something about her, something wonderful and seductive and special…

"Maybe later, huh?"

He wasn't alone after all. Kamile stood in the doorway, one eyebrow arched above her expressive brown eyes, and with Ric half hidden behind one shoulder. With her petite height, and Aras's son taking after him in size, Ric wouldn't be able to hide behind her much longer. But although Kamile's eyebrow might be saying 'humour', her eyes were distinctly less happy.

That made Aras feel as though he'd done something wrong, which made him feel irritable, and he briefly wondered if he *had* done something wrong. Nah. He covered that worry with a shrug. "She offered to take me through a doorway. It might be a good opportunity."

"Or it might leave you stuck right in the middle of the Fey, er, *Creatures* that we'd just escaped." Kamile didn't need to touch her scarf-covered throat to prove that point, but he looked anyway. Her scar was thick, red and not quite raw-looking, but it was nasty.

"The Creatures like to watch us," Ric piped up suddenly. He was six and looked like a small, dark-haired version of Aras, and he was disturbingly in-tune with the Other realm. "They like to meet people who come through the doorways."

For a moment Aras and Kamile both just stared at the boy, then her mouth twisted into a rueful smile. "Point proven, huh?"

Point proven indeed. Aras hadn't bought into his handfasted wife's spiel about Creatures/Fey bad, River good, but he'd seen enough to now be very wary of anything Other related. He finally shrugged in agreement. "So what brought you here?"

Kamile forced her most relaxed expression on her face. She knew how things were between them, and she wasn't going to make it awkward by getting jealous. Really. "I was coming to pick up Ric from school, and he wanted to look in on you. Watch you chase down the trees." She said the last with distinct humour, because really, it was funny. Weird, occasionally scary, but silly enough to be funny. "So here we are. Did we miss all the fun?"

Aras glanced at her, and he blushed. Just a bit, just a faint touch of pink on those stubbled cheeks, but enough for her to notice.

Damnatus, what *had* she interrupted?

"There are dozens more flying trees out in the valley," he answered finally. "Ric can come watch, if he wants. Where's Isla?"

"Back at the house with Poli."

Aras grunted – the sound probably meaning 'OK' or 'I understand', or maybe 'You terrible mother, how dare you leave her with a mere girl?' – but Ric took it as encouragement. He began to chatter about his day as they followed Aras out of the room and into the valley. He'd lost a lot of his shyness around his father these last few months, Kamile mused. That was one good thing that had come from all this mess.

Finally Ric skipped ahead, and Kamile picked up her own pace to match Aras's much longer steps. "It's good we've got a little privacy," she said, forcing her tone to be light. This subject was painful, even though they'd never discussed it. But then she'd never been in this situation before, not with a baby and such a history between them. "I was wanting to ask what your plans were after the year is up."

He looked down at her, eyebrows raised. "What year?"

Kamile blinked. "The handfast year. You know, we tied a red ribbon around our wrists at the last Solstice, and pledged to be faithful for twelve months? That's up in two weeks." He didn't comment, and she persisted, "So are you going to be staying at the house still? Because if you're not, then we'll need to make our own plans." She'd need to get a job for starters, which didn't sound like much fun when Isla was so small.

There was a brief silence. "You thought I would leave you.

Right after the year was up."

Was he offended? She sneaked a glance but couldn't tell – he always looked cranky. "I don't know. Maybe. You haven't made any promises otherwise, and…"

"And what?"

She shrugged. "You said 'maybe later' to that woman. Do you mean two weeks later, when our time's up? You have to admit you're thinking about it."

Now Aras definitely looked angry. His straight brows had drawn low over his eyes, and he'd stopped in his tracks to glower down at her. Ric skipped on ahead, oblivious to the undertones between the adults. "We're not with the Chosen anymore, Kamile, and we don't need to keep their rules. Did I ever say to you that I was going to leave? That I wouldn't look after you and Isla?"

Kamile held her ground, although internally she was disconcerted by his strong response. Was this good or bad, and did she care? "Um…maybe?" Nope, she was definitely flustered. "Or maybe not. Are you saying that you were planning to stay?"

There was a long silence, then Aras turned away and picked up his pace, following after his son. It seemed their conversation was over, and nothing had been achieved except for an unexpected argument – one of their first. They'd been getting on so very well, Kamile thought desolately, even though they'd been living like flatmates rather than proper handfasted partners. Definitely not like they were handfasted. Perhaps if she'd filled that gap for him, he wouldn't have been *blushing* when a certain silver-haired woman flirted with him…

They came out from the town's centre to the more open spaces where the doorways were scattered around, in between small houses and elaborate tiled areas dotted with occasional bench seats. Up ahead Kamile could see the food cart that marked the entrance to the River of Life, with the enormous spreading tree just to its left. (It wasn't flying, that was an important point.) She should invite Aras through that particular Other entrance again, she decided firmly. A new visit would do her good too, and if he agreed to come this time, perhaps he'd drop the idea of visiting any other unknown doorways, with any other woman.

Maybe.

She paused ten feet away from a different doorway; a rough, wooden arch sitting in the middle of the dry dirt. That was why she had a good view for what happened next.

THE BLACK FISH

One moment it was just Kamile, Aras and Ric, plus a few other Erastus locals doing whatever it was they did. The next an enormous black *thing* burst out of the wooden doorway, seeming to squeeze out like toothpaste from a tube; too big to fit through and yet it had. In that brief moment Kamile saw what looked like a sort of enormous catfish: charcoal grey with a colossal mouth, blubbery lips and tiny eyes set high on its blobbish shape. It was as big as a small whale, as big as the food cart nearby.

What the…?

But as blob-like as it was, it sure moved fast. Now free, the black fish skidded across the dry ground, scraping a trail of destruction behind it, its huge mouth gaping wide and letting out a wailing noise as it went. It was heading straight for Aras and Ric up ahead…

"Look out!" Kamile screamed, but Aras had already seen it. He grabbed Ric around the waist and leapt aside, just out of the fish-thing's path. The fish barrelled on through and smashed straight into the River-entrance food cart.

Kamile saw a few people run screaming, and then it came to rest against the broad trunk of the tree. Then the fish-creature began thrashing around, trying to force itself up on spindly legs that she'd first taken for being catfish-like whiskers. It let out a roaring wail and turned away from the tree, its enormous mouth open wide – a mere metre away from a stunned-looking Ric…

But then suddenly Aras was on its back, riding it like the world's most unfortunate cowboy, and he had a knife in his hand. Up went the knife, and then down into the creature's hide – and then Aras slid down to the ground, dragging that blade with him as he went.

Ugh. *Ugh.* Kamile automatically stepped back as if the thing would spray offal everywhere, but it didn't. Instead it let out one last wail, flopped onto its side, and began to deflate like an ancient balloon. Ric's eyes were open wide, staring at it, and she rushed forward towards him. "Are you alright!?"

But the child kept staring at the now much smaller shape. It looked rather like when a tent was let down and someone had left their luggage inside: a big, wrinkled form spread over a smaller, long shape… "Daddy saved me. But Bob is dead."

Kamile wrinkled her nose as a waft of stench reached her, and she took Ric by the arm, pulling him into fresh air. "Who's Bob?" Not someone from inside the food cart, she hoped. That whole thing looked absolutely wrecked, and the stinking carcass was right over the entrance to the River! What was she supposed to do now?

"Bob." Ric pointed at the carcass.

Kamile frowned, but then she couldn't focus on what he was saying. They'd gathered quite a crowd, and the stench from the black fish was becoming overwhelming.

"What do you think it was?" she mused aloud. "Fey aren't supposed to be able to come out of the Other." Creatures, she meant. The immortal, extremely unpleasant beings were trapped in that realm, although they could see and influence the normal realm through people, objects, or various doorways…

"What makes you think it was the Other?" someone next to her said. "It could have been any realm."

Feeling irritated, Kamile turned to study the speaker. It was a boy in his mid-teens. At first he looked old, since his hair shone like silver, then she realised he must have coloured it – he was gorgeous, bronze-skinned, and absolutely unlined. "What other realms are there?"

"Many. An infinite number." He grinned, revealing perfect white teeth. "Take a look through the doorways some time. You might be surprised."

He reminded her of Joy Silver, Kamile realised. His voice even had that same musical echo to it. The comparison didn't please her, and she shrugged a shoulder. "There's an entrance behind that tree. I know what's on the other side, and it's good."

"That tree?" The youth pointed towards it, and as if on cue, the tree groaned and tipped slowly sideways, landing right over the smashed food cart and the black fish carcass.

Kamile groaned in dismay. If the dead body wasn't bad enough, now the whole thing had been blocked off! Seriously, how was she supposed to get to the River now?!

"Wherever you were trying to go, there's always another way," he commented mildly. "Sometimes many."

She didn't answer, instead just stared at the destruction for several moments. "If there are," she began finally, then realised he'd walked away. She could see his silver head moving off into the crowd, his white clothing making him shine like a beacon. He seemed to float...

Wait, he *was* floating! She could now see his feet didn't touch the ground, and as he moved, the crowd seemed to part for him. It was very impressive, and she wondered where he'd got that kind of power. Through the doorways, maybe? She looked again at the rough wooden arch that the black fish had come through, and resolved *not* to go through that one. If she saw the silver boy again, she'd ask.

Coming from the kind of background she had, Kamile was very cautious about everything Other-related. If it was connected with the River and Amaranthus, then she'd accept that it was safe and good. As for the rest? She simply didn't know enough, and she didn't dare risk going near it. Having her skin turn green from the alter-power was the least that could happen. Then there were the Creatures…

She'd called them Fey once; all the Chosen had. She'd even had a couple of occasional visitors: two adorable miniature ponies, one perfectly black, one perfectly white. She'd spoken to them several times in childhood when she'd cluelessly visited the Other, and they'd told her things that had defined her life for a long time.

Halflings are an unnatural race, she remembered their sweet voices saying. *It's not your fault, Kamile Greenskin, but you have a responsibility not to breed. Stay away from children. Let your unnatural blood die out with you…*

They were liars, Kamile thought fiercely. She didn't know what their plan had been – to make her miserable? – but she now knew the Creatures/Fey were not on humanity's side. And in spite of her unusual heritage, she *was* human. Enough. Then there was her precious Isla, who never would have existed if she'd taken their advice.

Just then a hint of movement caught her eye, and she turned to see a nearby stone doorway. This one was simple and grey, with a view of the town beyond it, but was that a flash of black and white she'd seen?

Suddenly her breath was coming short, and she stopped for a moment, her hands fisted at her sides as she stared at the doorway. It looked so innocuous now; nothing except dirt and buildings to be seen through it. It might even be one of those that led to another part of the town, rather than to the Other, but…it wasn't the first time since arriving here that she thought she'd seen something Other-based. At the time she'd put it down to Aras's stupid Fey-made prosthetic arm, which unfortunately he couldn't remove. But now, when he was nowhere in sight?

"Show yourself!" Kamile ordered, her voice trembling a little with the fear that something would actually respond, and that it wouldn't be nice at all.

But the doorway stayed clear, and finally she shook her head. It must have been her imagination. She *wanted* it to have been her imagination.

She turned her back resolutely on the doorway and left.

Before the Rift

"Shulamithe. There you are."

Peaceful's heart jumped joyfully at hearing her name in the Master's voice, just as it always did. And as it always did, that was followed by an intense feeling of relaxation. Hearing her name spoken in the Old Tongue would always cause that effect, because such words were laden with power. "Yes, Master. Why did you call me?"

She'd followed the sound of his voice straight from one location to another in an instant, in the manner that she and the others often travelled. Now she was inside an unfamiliar place. She could feel that it was part of the Master's palace, but it was like a long, narrow hall, with the other end fading into the distance. There were many shelves and alcoves on either side, but most were empty.

"I'm making something new," he replied. "A hall of treasures, gifts for my new children."

"Ooh!" Peaceful *loved* new things. They were always so exciting, because you never knew what you were going to get. And the Master was the only one who could ever make anything truly new. "What are they?"

"That depends on what they need," the Master answered. He held up one five-fingered hand, and a shining little bottle appeared in his palm. It gleamed as though carved from diamonds – which it probably was – but it appeared empty. "What are they lacking, Shulamithe?"

She tried not to screw up her nose too obviously, remembering Bright's scorn for those dirt-made, powerless creatures. "Well...the two-legs can't do very much," she ventured cautiously.

"How do you mean?"

She knew he was asking because he wanted her response, not because he didn't know. "They can only crawl on the surface of the earth," she suggested. "And they don't know things unless you tell them aloud. They can't see through solid objects, and they're constantly surprised because they don't know the future." *She* didn't know all the future either, she allowed, but she definitely wasn't startled at every falling leaf.

"But the crawling thing is a true disadvantage," she continued enthusiastically. "What if one was to fall into a deep hole? They might be there for quite some time before someone else found them and got them out. Whereas if *we* fell into a hole..." She shrugged. They couldn't fall – it didn't make sense. "Or they might wish to cross a ravine or a river. They'd have to crawl around it."

There was a brief silence where Peaceful realised the Master was smiling. *They walk on two legs rather than crawl, my dear.* Then aloud he said, "Indeed you are right. It would be unfortunate if one was to fall into a hole and not be able to get out, or if they had to walk around something." And then something appeared inside the little bottle; some kind of liquid. A moment later, scrolling text appeared on the outside.

"Flight," Peaceful read aloud, thinking of the winged creatures the Master had made on the dirt-planet. They were even simpler than the special creatures, but quite lovely in their own way. "Will they grow wings too if they drink this?"

He smiled slightly and set the bottle on the otherwise empty shelf. "I don't think that will be necessary. If they were to drink this, they'd have the ability to ride the air like you or Beraht." He lifted up his hand and another little bottle appeared. A moment later it too was full, and its label read *Far-sight.* "So that they won't be startled by every falling leaf."

Ooh. He was turning her ideas into reality, and she loved it. "Will they all drink it? Will they all become like us?" It would be quite nice to have a few extra People, she decided. There was always room for more, especially back home.

The Master set that bottle on the shelf too. "No, and not straight away. We'll let them learn and grow, and eventually…"

He didn't finish his sentence, but Peaceful got the idea. Something good would happen, and the new two-legged creatures would join them up here.

The Master kept making little bottles, each with something lovely and useful inside. In truth, more than a few of them didn't make any sense to her – why would anyone need 'purifying fire'? What was there to purify? But she figured if he had made them, then there was a purpose.

So she watched in fascination, admiring the way the alter-power shimmered and bubbled inside the liquid, its colour constantly changing, and the way each bottle was subtly different. Heh, he'd made one labelled 'Peace'. That was practically her name!

Shulamithe.

Peaceful looked up immediately. *Yes?*

He smiled again, and there was something in that smile that she didn't understand. A...sorrow? *You always listen when I call. That is a very valuable trait.*

She frowned. Why would she not listen? She'd only not listen if...if...if he stopped calling her!

Exactly. He set aside the bottle he was working on, then stepped towards her, reaching out his hand. She didn't move as he cupped her cheek, then kissed her gently on the forehead. A warm, powerful affection swept through her, and she smiled up at him. He was so very beautiful, so very brilliant. More than anyone else in existence. Oh, she was so very happy to be favoured by him!

No matter what happens, you'll always listen. And I'll always call you...eventually.

Peaceful wrinkled her nose in confusion. Well, yes. That was how things worked. But she didn't argue, because surely he'd said it for a reason, even though she didn't yet know what it was.

Huh. Perhaps she was more like the two-legs than she'd realised.

Bright.

Peaceful could feel him nearby, down on the dirt-world's surface. No, *underneath* the surface. He was somewhere between two rocky layers that provided the framework for this area of forest. A cave? But he didn't respond, and he didn't show himself.

Bright? She tried again. *Where are you?*

Ooh, there he was. She could sense his presence, so strong and powerful, almost as much so as the Master. Why was he hiding himself? She wanted to tell him about the new gifts, and about how the Master had listened to her! It was all so very exciting.

She lowered herself through the layer of foliage that was the forest's canopy, and gently touched down on the damp forest floor, making herself solid enough that her fins would rest on it instead of slipping through. "BERAHT!" she shouted aloud. "I know you're here!"

Psst.

Peaceful turned to see…nothing. Then she felt a touch on her lower fins where they rested on the ground. His touch. It turned her from solid to insubstantial, and she didn't fight as she was pulled through the ground for quite some distance, and then finally released.

She was now in a cave far below the dirt-world's surface. The space was only twice her own height, and it stretched into the distance until the roof lowered into nothing. She could hear water somewhere down here, but couldn't see any.

What she *could* see was Bright, once again wearing that wrong-looking, two-legged form. On either side of him were two familiar higher-level beings, also in the same two-legged form, right down to the five fingers. Like Bright's, their particular physical traits had carried across into these new forms.

Truthful was still shining white, with the feathery topping on his head still in rainbow colours, and his eyes were large and black. But his beautiful butterfly-like wings were gone. Strong was bigger than the other two, more muscular, and his own skin was still a warm blue colour. But his tusks now seemed enormous as they curled out of his mouth to rest decoratively against his cheeks.

They'd come down here to this unseen place, Peaceful realised, and had made themselves look like the Master.

And she'd been going to tell them about the wonderful new treasures…

Why had they done this?

Because we can, Bright said in response to her unspoken question. *You can too, if you want.*

Peaceful's brow furrowed in confusion. She still couldn't shake this feeling of wrongness. Not about the change of forms, but about something else, something she couldn't pinpoint. *But I don't want to. Why do you?*

Bright exchanged glances with the other two, and there was also something in that glance that she didn't understand. "Let me try this again," he said aloud. "We want change, so we're going to make it happen. Are you with us, Peaceful? Or are you against us?"

Now that made even less sense than the rest of it. If they wanted change, they should go ask the Master rather than skulk around down here. He probably wouldn't even mind these new forms, even though she didn't like them. "You know I follow you in all things," she ventured. "And I am here. So I am with you, yes?"

She doesn't understand, Truthful said, studying her with those now almond-shaped black eyes, so very dark in his white face. He too looked beautiful in this new form, but just...wrong. *Do you know what would happen if your Master saw us down here, Shulamithe?*

A wash of peace fell over her as her name was spoken in the Old Tongue, and she replied lazily in kind, "You tell me, Veritas. You are truthful in all things."

But he didn't answer, and Peaceful turned to the other. "Strong? Geburah, old friend, what is going on here?"

But he didn't answer either. Instead Bright stepped forward and set his hand on Peaceful's. His skin was so very gold and speckled next to her own striped blue hand – but then that was the way they were made, and it was good. "I will tell you the truth instead," he whispered, and his claw-tipped fingers tightened on hers. "You follow me in all things, listening to my directions and advice, except when the Master calls. Then you leave me."

This was true, and it was right. She didn't know why he'd bothered to say it, though. "Of course…?"

"You've been a dear friend, a faithful one, except for that matter. And that's why I've brought you down here, right before the change."

Change? What change?

His fingers were gripping hers so tightly, and she was beginning to feel strange. Weak, like something was being taken from her. And she watched stupidly as a golden glow of alter-power, her own life force, trickled from her hand to his like a shining cloud. Her stripes were fading, and she could see them reappearing on Bright's hand and spreading up his arm. Stripes and spots and claws, and a growing darkness beneath his skin…

What are you doing…?

Gathering strength for what is coming next, he said into her mind. *You might survive, or you might not. It would've been better if you'd followed me wholly, Shulamithe.*

And then the weakness spread until it consumed her entire body, and right before it took her consciousness she touched his, and saw what he intended.

Mutiny.

Oh, *dear…*

Lunden 1819 AD

"George." His sister-in-law's soft voice caught his attention. "He's awake!"

George was startled from his half-doze, and he turned

towards the bed with hope rising in his heart. Olivia was right, he saw. Edward *was* awake, his blue eyes heavy and blinking as he turned from his wife to his brother.

"Georgie? Livvy?"

"Yes, yes, it's us!" George replied hurriedly, moving closer to the bed. "How do you feel, old chap?" Being awake was a good start, but he wouldn't forget how his brother had had that awful fit just an hour earlier, right after he'd arrived. George had spent that time alternately worrying about Edward, worrying about *Ashlea* and wondering if he should have let her go, and begging fervently in his mind: *Amaranthus, please don't let him die. Please, please...*

Plea answered. Or so far, anyway.

"Where am I? What happened?"

"You're in the Lunden townhouse," Olivia answered. She held his hand between her own smaller ones, and she was almost as pale as he was. Despite their significant troubles in the past, it appeared she still loved him. "Your horse threw you, and you landed on your head." She swallowed back a sob. "Except for brief moments, you have been unconscious since yesterday."

"My horse threw me?" Edward retorted, sounding more like his old, arrogant self. "Impossible! I'm an excellent rider. Besides..." But he didn't explain the 'besides'.

"Precisely what I said," George pointed out. He felt almost faint with relief. "But it appears your horse stumbled. Such things happen."

"Nevertheless," Edward muttered, scowling. "And why is it so ber'lody dark in here? Someone open some curtains!" But then as if he couldn't wait for his order to be followed, he pushed his way out from under the covers and stumbled over to the drawn drapes, then began tugging at them. "What are these infernal things!? It's so...*dark.*"

"Leave it Ned, I'll get it." George rushed over to help him, pulling at the cords, then swore under his breath when in fact the curtains *were* difficult to draw, and perhaps even a little infernal in design. Finally one came down off its railing, falling heavily to pile into George's arms as light streamed in. "Oh. My apologies."

But Edward had moved to stand in front of the now uncovered glass, clad in only a nightshirt, with a pair of stockings half falling off his hairy ankles. He was shaking his head, his eyes wide as he stared out of the window. "Lunden townhouse. I'm in the Lunden townhouse. It was merely a nightmare…"

"What was a nightmare, Eddie?" George asked, finally giving up on replacing the curtains. The servants could do that; it was their job, wasn't it?

"The hole in the ground," Edward replied, but then his lips tightened and he shook his head more firmly. "It was a nightmare. Merely a nightmare …"

"Hole in the ground?" Olivia echoed. To George she murmured, "He must mean the hole his horse tripped in. I understand it threw a shoe."

"By Jupiter, no! It was a crater. An absolute chasm. And so very, very dark…" Edward shivered, his eyes widening until the whites showed clearly, and he wrapped his arms around himself. "But it was a dream, wasn't it?"

"Yes?" George ventured, since he still didn't know what his brother was talking about. A chasm in the ground? That sounded most unpleasant. Then when Edward looked anxious at George's uncertainty, he amended, "Oh yes, indeed. Very much so."

Edward nodded, but he didn't relax his tense posture or his too-wide eyes. After a few moments of him standing there silently, rocking, Olivia approached him carefully and set one hand on his arm. "Eddie?"

"Do you know," he said conversationally as though she'd not

touched him, "it's a good thing it was merely a nightmare. It's a good thing that I didn't...*die* when I fell on my head. Because upon my word, I could have sworn..." and here he paused, "...that the place I visited in my nightmare...was something like Hades."

He'd said it so casually, but George felt a shaft of dread shoot through him. Surely not. Surely not! He exchanged shocked glances with Olivia. For several minutes there they *had* thought Edward was dead...

But Olivia spoke first. "It was just a dream," she said firmly, although her face was also pale. "Now get back into bed, darling, and we shall get you a nice hot posset."

So Edward was wrangled back into the big, be-curtained bed, albeit with much more light this time. But George couldn't shake the memory of Edward's pale face, couldn't shake the feeling of dread sitting in his stomach. He really, truly had thought his brother was dead, at least for a moment. And Edward had had a nightmare about a chasm in the ground.

It was something like Hades...

Erastus, 2598 AD

Ash saw the destruction as she turned the corner from the town's centre, having given up on following someone who might have been Anne through the dubious gateway. She stared blankly for a few moments, noting the smashed building and the strewn, striped cloth and the big black thing in the centre. Oh, and the crowd surrounding the carnage.

A moment later she realised what it was – Amaranthus's food cart, and the entrance to the hall of doors.

"Oh, *nooo!*" She ran over to the edge of the crowd and began pushing her way through. Or tried to, anyway, because the crowd was thick and not so easily moved. "Let me through!"

"Careful, Miss," a man in the Council's tan robes said. "The carcass is likely toxic, and you'll want to be extra careful, what with the baby."

Ash paused momentarily, glancing down at her baby bump. No, it still looked like too many pies rather than an actual pregnancy, which meant he may have picked it up through some other supernatural means. Erastus locals were weird that way. "Thank you," she said tersely, "but I need to get through there *now*. There's a gateway-"

"No access until we've cleaned up," the man interrupted, sounding rather less friendly this time. "No exceptions."

"Yes, but this is life or death!"

"No exceptions," he repeated, then turned his back on her, moving away to…whatever he was doing.

Ash was just about jittering with panic, and she would have gone after him except for a light touch on her arm. She glanced down to see a familiar petite brunette with a pale yellow scarf around her neck. "I wouldn't test him," the girl warned. "The ushers tend to react strongly to challenges, and they don't like repeating themselves. They're like the Lile enforcers in that way."

The girl was referring to the extreme police force of the neighbouring country, Ash knew, as she'd run into them herself a few months earlier. But then she also recognised the girl's face. "Kamile?"

"That's me. And you're…Esh?"

"Ash," Ash corrected, realising belatedly that it sounded almost the same in her Southern Isles accent. "Or whatever. Um…I realise I haven't seen you in a while – nice to see you're healing up well! – but I really need to get through to *there* right now…"

Kamile kindly didn't comment that the last time they'd met, Ash had had a brief sob session about the death of a mutual acquaintance, Coryn, and had revealed how she'd seen Coryn in a beautiful golden place. She now knew for certain that there was life after death.

Kamile also didn't comment that the time *before* that, she'd been sort-of possessed by a sort-of Creature called Shulamithe, who'd also saved her life. Kamile's, not Ash's, that was. But Ash was thinking of all of that, and thinking of poor Edward on his deathbed, and how *he* didn't seem to be going to that beautiful golden place. She couldn't say why she knew that, but every time she'd thought it, the thought had seemed *wrong*. Just so wrong.

Life or death was a lot more than just a moment. It was for eternity.

"I suppose you'd be heading for the River," Kamile said. She had a pretty, youthful face that looked as if it smiled a lot. Right now she wasn't smiling, and there seemed to be a green tinge to her skin. "There's an entrance just past that tree, past where the food cart was."

"The River?" Ash paused, then recalled that the River of Life ran from the Mountain of Glass, which was where she was hoping to go. That, and then back to 1819 AD. The hall of doors and the River entrance were practically in the same place, except it appeared that people couldn't see the hall of doors unless they'd been gifted access. "Ah…yes. Yes, I suppose it is."

Ash looked again at the chaos in front of her. The people in tan uniforms had backed off, and even the rest of the crowd had moved away. Someone in a black full-cover suit was spraying something like a dust cloud into the air right over the destruction. Another in matching black was tracing a line around the edge of the mess, around the tree, the smashed food cart, and the wreckage. As the dust cloud touched the line it seemed to solidify and lighten, forming a translucent wall around the entire area. "Hey…"

"You won't get through that now," Kamile told her. "That's a protective barrier. Keeps things in and keeps us out, at least until they've done whatever they wanted to do."

Of course Ash had to test it. She touched her finger to the shimmering cloud that blocked her way, then quickly jerked back when her skin burned. "Ow!"

"Told you." Kamile shrugged. "There was another entrance to the River on the other side of the valley, but it was destroyed too. Sorry."

"But…but…" Ash felt on the edge of tears. She didn't even know the entrances *could* be destroyed! How would Amaranthus allow that? "But I *need* to go through! I wouldn't have come out at all except that I thought I saw Anne, but then I lost her…" If she'd just gone straight to the Mountain like she'd told George, skipping straight through from the hall of doors without entering Erastus, then none of this would have happened.

Just then her mobile phone rang. It was the distinctive ringtone she had set for George, and she rushed to answer it. If there was reception, then the gateway was still intact through there. She just needed to get through. "Hello?"

"Ashlea!" George said urgently from the other end of the phone. "I have good news. Edward has woken."

Ash's heart skipped a beat, but in a happy way. Not a cardiac-arrest sort of way. "Really? Like, woken up and walking about, or still looking at death's door with greyish skin, or-"

"Up and about," George interrupted, his voice sounding as clear as if he stood next to her. He didn't sound entirely happy, though. "Not greyish. A bit shell-shocked, talking about nightmares of holes in the ground."

Ash was so relieved by the news that she ignored the 'nightmares' bit. "That's great! You know, I really thought he was a goner."

"As did I. But…well, I suppose it wasn't yet his time. Did you see Amaranthus?"

Her shoulders slumped, but she forced on a cheerful tone. "Er…not yet."

"Perhaps you might thank him for me when you do," George continued through the phone, "and ask him what…" Then his voice faded into silence.

"Are you there? Hello? Hello?"

"Yes, I'm here!" he snapped. There was another silence, then he sighed. "My apologies. Would you please get the healing pot, if you are able, then return at once? I wish to speak with you at length. Something about this whole matter just feels wrong."

"Yes, well…" Now Ash was silent for a moment.

"Ashlea…what has happened?" George's tone was low and clearly displeased.

"The gateway home is temporarily blocked and I'm in Erastus," she replied rapidly.

"WHAT!?"

"I saw Anne, or at least I thought I did, and I followed her into Erastus," she explained quickly. "And then I fell over and she was too far ahead, so I lost her, and then when I came back the whole entrance to the Mountain and the hall of doors had been smashed and it's now blocked off by men in black – not like the movie. I can't get through 'til they clear it. It's not my fault, I swear."

There was a heavy sigh from the other end of the phone. "By Jove, you have the worst luck at times," he murmured. "At least Edward isn't in such urgent need as we'd supposed. How long before you can return?"

Ash turned to Kamile, who'd been watching with interest the

whole time. She probably thought Ash was mad for speaking into a brick – here in this time period, they had far more advanced ways of contacting people. Or so Ash figured. "Kamile, you said there was another entrance to the River that was damaged. How long before it was reopened?"

"It was a month ago," Kamile replied mildly. "But I said it was destroyed, not damaged. It's still closed off."

Damn it! Damn it, damn it- "Wait," Ash realised suddenly. "There's another gateway to Lile City somewhere around here. It comes out by Aras's apartment. And then there's another gateway from Lile back to Tolliver's. Do you remember, George?"

"I remember the gateway was shut when we tried to go back for your blonde friend," he replied thoughtfully. "But I also recall the way we fled while under heavy attack from the local police force. I'd rather you didn't risk going through."

"But I have the protective medallion," Ash argued. She said that just for the sake of arguing, as she didn't actually want to risk the Lile enforcers herself. They had been scary, especially with the weapons they'd carried. One shot would turn someone to dust – from their clothing to their bones.

"It won't stop you being captured," he retorted. "Don't go through, Ashlea. Promise me you won't."

"Fine, I promise I won't use that gateway. But I'm not hanging around here forever! You're eight hundred years away, George!"

"Please don't mention that," he groaned. "Look…I'll call you back. Wait for me, will you?"

"Alright…" And then the phone shut off. "Huh." Ash looked down at the ended call, bemused. "That was abrupt. Good news though, Edward isn't dead."

"That's good," Kamile commented. "I always like it when people aren't dead. Who's Idwid?"

"Edward," Ash corrected, then realised that also sounded the same with her Southern Isles accent. "My husband's brother." She quickly explained how she'd ended up here in Erastus, since they knew each other (kind of) and she'd need any friends she could get. She finished with, "So it seems he wants me to wait here. It's not like I can do anything else."

"Hmm."

"What?"

Kamile shrugged. "It's just there are so many gateways around here, and there *were* at least two to the River. Surely there are more leading to where we want to go." She gestured around them. "We just need to find the right one."

"Yeah, I just met someone who said that," Ash said thoughtfully. "And I thought I saw my friend go through one across town, but I didn't want to risk being wrong. I could swear it's the Other realm on the other side."

"What's the worst that could happen?"

Ash just stared at Kamile, and the shorter girl rolled her eyes. "Oh yeah, of course. Death and destruction. Better not to risk it. So what are you going to do now?"

"Wait, I suppose. George said he'd call me back."

Kamile shrugged. "Fine, but you're welcome to visit me if you get bored."

Right now Ash wasn't even slightly bored. Anxious over the sudden separation, relieved by Edward's recovery...*extremely* curious about the unknown gateways – but not bored. "Thanks. I might come find you later."

Four

MUTINY

"...So Ash is stuck here for a while until something else happens, I suppose," Kamile explained. She sat at their house's small dining table, feeding Isla. Or trying to, since the baby kept turning her head away from the bottle. Her own bowl of savoury grains was virtually untouched. "She didn't seem too upset about it though, not since she spoke to her husband on the…mobble fone thing. I offered for her to come here, but she said maybe later."

Magdalene studied her older friend for a moment. Kamile wore a scarf around her neck as always, and her usually bubbly expression looked a bit flat. Even her tone had been less cheerful than normal – which Mags figured was a small miracle, considering what she'd gone through. As for herself, she thought Ash sounded fascinating. A girl from another time!? And some of the gateways were actually portals through time?! Amazing!

"Was she wearing funny clothes?" Poli asked. "Like, a big poofy skirt or tight trousers or a painted face?"

Kamile shrugged. "Some long dress thing. Funny-ish, I suppose, although not that strange compared to some current fashions. I'll have to introduce you, and you can decide for yourself. And speaking of introductions…" She looked up at Magdalene expectantly, her mouth curving into a slight smile.

"When are we going to meet this 'friend' of yours?"

Mags felt her cheeks heat. "What friend?"

"The one you've been sneaking off to see," Poli – the big traitor – cut in. "Some boy. Colmar."

"That's not his name," Mags countered, lifting her chin. "And I haven't been sneaking." Or not much, anyway.

"Come on, you can tell us," Kamile probed. "It's just us girls, since Ric is off with Aras chasing down flying trees."

But she couldn't tell them. She didn't want to, because they might disapprove of the age difference and the way he was so *special*. "He's just a boy," she lied instead. "But it might be nothing, OK? Don't hassle me about it, and I'll tell you more when there's something to tell."

Poli looked put out, but Kamile just shrugged. "Sure, honey. No problem."

But then Mags thought Kamile had had a lot of boyfriends, so perhaps she didn't take dating too seriously as a result. She was with Aras now – sort of – but Mags wasn't sure if that was going to last.

But even so, she decided that once the meal was over she would slip away. She wasn't supposed to see him until tomorrow, but surely he wouldn't mind if she had something really important to ask? And he knew ever so much about everything. He was so wise, and so handsome, and…so handsome…

"So I heard something new this morning," Poli announced. "There was a whole houseful of miners on the outskirts of the valley – killed. Dead, and they don't know why."

Magdalene's eyes shot open wide. Now that was scary, and maybe a bit exciting. Mostly scary. "Really!? Where? How?"

Poli lowered her voice dramatically. "Up in the west forest. They say all the dead people were smiling, but there was blood everywhere-"

"That's enough!" Kamile cut in sharply. "There were three men, Poli, and they *do* know why. It was a dispute between the three, and they killed each other. Aras told me this morning. Horrible, yes, but nothing to dwell on, and nothing to be afraid of."

Mags figured the last part was for her, but she saw how Poli blinked, her eyes widening in that way that said she was upset. "But Jean told me that it was a total mystery, and that there was a recording of the men laughing right before they died-"

Mags felt her own eyebrows shoot up again. "Jean from school?"

"Yeah, her dad works as a watchman sometimes, and he said he saw it himself. *He* didn't think they killed each other. And that means there's a killer on the loose! A messy one."

"Enough, Poli!" Kamile snapped. "There's no killer on the loose, and Erastus is safe. Or safe enough, if you don't go through the wrong doorways. Don't go scaring people for no reason."

There was a moment of shocked silence – Kamile *never* shouted – then Poli burst into tears and fled from the table. Kamile sighed. "Sorry, Mags. I'm a little out of sorts today. It's just..." But she didn't finish her sentence, instead stood up with Isla under one arm, then headed out of the room after Poli.

Magdalene just sat for a while, her half-eaten lunch in front of her. She really ought to finish it, but all she could think of was 'killer on the loose!' And perhaps, 'there are doorways that take you through time!' The first one was scary – if it was true, and the second one was thrilling – if it was true.

He would know the answer. She wasn't supposed to visit again until tomorrow, but really...when it was this important, she was sure it wouldn't matter.

Magdalene shoved the last of her bread into her mouth, then stood and slipped from the house.

The Mountain of Glass

Elspeth hummed as she walked towards the place she'd last seen Jon. She'd spoken to Anne at length, and while she had forgotten her original reason for seeking her out, it had been a pleasant conversation. By the Rood, Anne did have a most eventful life, Elspeth mused. But then mayhap her own life was almost as eventful…

She was so intent on her pondering that she did not look up until she'd reached the place where she'd last seen Jon. But he was gone, and she recalled he'd said he was going somewhere. But where?

Elspeth headed for the most obvious place: the fruit orchard where they so often relaxed and spoke together. But a few minutes later when she arrived, he was still nowhere to be seen.

Instead, one of Amaranthus's People stood under a spreading peach tree, studying the branches intently. A youngish, sturdy woman with fair hair, she nonetheless had that sheen of power that showed clearly what she was. Sometimes when she moved, 'twas as if someone else was underneath, someone who might not even be human at all…

But she smiled at Elspeth. "What are you looking for, little one?"

Elspeth wasn't bothered by the possibly different appearance of the woman. Their host, Amaranthus, even wore a couple of different forms. "I seek my friend, Jon." She gave a quick description of him. "Have you seen him?"

The woman nodded. "Yes, I saw him. But he is gone now."

Her heart sank at such a blunt answer. But as it could have several meanings, she persisted. "Gone where?"

"Gone back to where he came from."

Elspeth was stunned. Anne had said as much, that Jon would be returning home, but she did not think 'twould be so soon, and without even a farewell…

Tears pricked her eyes. Surely he had not thought so little of her? "Which way did he go?"

The woman pointed down further into the orchard, towards an area they did not often go. There was merely a rock wall down that end, so it looked to be of little purpose.

Elspeth nodded in thanks – she could not bring herself to speak – and with her head down, rushed towards the wall. She reached it quickly. 'Twas simply the side of the inner Mountain, which while large, was not infinite. The orchard stretched to either side, and up above her, the smooth rock stretched out until it became as transparent as glass, and the blue sky could be seen through it.

But there was more than that. In the quiet glade, where there was nothing and no one except for rock and trees and the occasional sentinel-bug, there was also a shimmering remnant gateway.

Elspeth sucked in a deep breath, and in that moment she knew he was gone. "Oh, *Jon.*"

At that very moment

Jon strolled along under the canopy of fruit trees, his thoughts whirling. It seemed like there was a ticking clock, counting down the moments he had here until he had to go back home.

'Home'. It wasn't a fun place. Not many good memories, although he had a couple of friends. His adoptive mother was there, and somewhere, his birth mother. His birth father too, regrettably, although now *he* was a carrier, and that was also no fun.

And then there were the things that were worse than no fun. The things that were terrible…

He sighed heavily. *That* was why he needed to go back, to put things right, if he even could. Besides, you never could run away from your responsibilities for long. They'd always come back to bite you in the backside.

Jon came out into the area where he often sat with Bets. He'd come over here while Bets was with her sister, then had returned to see if he could find her. She hadn't been there, so back he came. As before, a blonde Person stood under one of the trees, seeming to be talking to it. After a moment of watching her curiously, he asked, "What are you doing?"

"Talking to the tree."

"Er…yes, I thought so." Jon paused. This Person was called-…Simplicity, that was it. He remembered that you had to be very specific about what you wanted, as she didn't read into things at all. Not even a bit. "Why are you talking to the tree?"

"It's connected to an orchard of peach trees in the normal realm, in lower Gallica," she replied, turning to him with a smile. "They're in danger of getting early blight, so I'm determining if I need to resolve it before it spreads."

Jon frowned thoughtfully. "I didn't know you did that kind of thing."

"Yes. I do."

"Oh. That's good."

Simplicity nodded, then focused back on the tree.

Have you seen my friend? Jon wanted to ask, but she looked very absorbed in her work and he didn't want to interrupt.

"Yes," Simplicity said. "I told her where you had gone."

"Oh," Jon said again. It would never cease to disconcert him how the Mountain locals would just pick information out of his head. But they were friendly sorts, unlike certain other Creatures, so he decided not to be bothered. "Thanks."

He paused, debating whether to look for Bets again, then decided it wasn't worth it. They could go around in circles trying to find each other in this place. Instead he sat down under a nearby tree and watched Simplicity tree-talk. Bets would surely show up soon enough, and he had something to tell her.

Before the Rift

Somewhere above the dirt-world, there was another world. This one was shaped differently: made of light, sound and alter-power. It was also where the People lived, along with the Master. It was usually a place of peace and beauty (because why live anywhere ugly if you could help it?) but today…

…Today a battle raged. All across the light-world, the many People who'd listened to Bright were moving. They were violent, capturing and suppressing the others who tried to stand against them, and causing chaos. And no one had even seen it coming…

Bright smiled to himself as he slipped through the innermost halls of the Mountain of Glass, Truthful and Strong on either side of him. They all wore their new two-legged forms, but even so they were never stopped. The few times they came across another Person, the Person would look at them in surprise, then let them pass. No one would counter Bright, no matter what form he wore. Not even with these unexpected new stripes, courtesy of Peaceful.

But no one outside their inner circle had seen this coming. Peaceful certainly hadn't.

Bright pushed aside the niggle of wrongness that came when he thought of her, of what he'd just done. He'd made his choice, and she'd made hers, for better or worse.

Beraht! And Veritas and Geburah. What are you doing here in the heart of the Mountain?

Bright recognised the presence before he even turned the corner. It was Loyalty, one of the weaker People. He stood in front of the door to the Master's inner sanctum, an expression of curious interest on his narrow face as they came into sight. He was tall, long-limbed and pale skinned, with a slight resemblance to Truthful's usual form. He also looked rather plain next to the beauty of the door he guarded – but then his value wasn't in his looks.

"Why are you formed like that?" Loyalty continued aloud now he'd seen them. He still looked curious rather than angry. "With two legs, and two arms with hands. Truthful, your wings are gone, and Bright, your tail is gone. Did you not like your tail?"

"It's temporary," Bright replied, flicking a glance at the other two. "We've come to see the Master."

"He's not here. He's out-"

"In the dirt-world, with his pets. I know. Stand aside, and we will wait for him in his chambers."

Loyalty blinked, uncertainty now showing on his features. *This is not usual.*

After a moment of inspiration, Bright said, "The Master ordered us to wait for him here."

Loyalty's expression of uncertainty cleared, and he nodded, moving aside. Bright and his two companions stepped through the pearlescent door, a moment later emerging in an enormous, light-filled inner room.

Why did you say the Master had ordered us to wait? Truthful asked quietly, ensuring Loyalty couldn't hear. *He did not order us.*

Bright shrugged. He was feeling quite proud of that himself, and he'd known Truthful would be the one to question his clever new trick. *I knew that if we told him we were coming to take the Heart, then he might try to stop us, and we would have to capture or destroy him. So I told him something I thought would give us a better outcome.*

Truthful appeared to be considering this carefully. It was a new concept even to Bright himself; that their words did not need to align with the actuality of the universe. Strange, but with so much potential... *So...you can say what you want, rather than what is true.*

"Yes, but it does not change the truth," Bright replied aloud. "See, the Master isn't meeting us here, no matter what I have said. And now we're alone, and I can take what I want without being challenged."

The other two looked impressed, and Bright could see Truthful in particular was pondering the idea. He wondered if the other Person would be able to perform the same trick. Perhaps not – after all, truth was the heart of Truthful's character.

"I could do it," Truthful suddenly said aloud. He'd known what Bright was thinking, of course. "I could do it as well as you."

His attention caught by such a bold claim, Bright paused halfway across the room, glancing back over his shoulder. *No, you couldn't.*

Yes, I could. There was a pause. *You...have no stripes.*

Bright looked down at his arms, half-expecting to see the borrowed stripes had indeed disappeared. But they were still there, as bold as ever.

"You did it," Strong mused. He looked impressed. "You did

Beraht's trick."

"I think I could be very good at it," Truthful said smugly. "It just takes some thinking."

Bright shook his head with a sneer, turning back to his real focus. The Heart. "You'll have to change your name if you keep up with that. They'll have to call you Not-truthful."

His companion didn't respond, and Bright carried on across the chamber to its centre. He couldn't see the Heart, but he knew it was there. The chamber was vast and round, filled with a bright white light that emanated so strongly from the centre that it blurred out what was held there. But he knew. The Master had held little back from him.

He strode forward on those strangely stable two legs until he could just see the beginnings of the altar that held the Heart. Water splashed under his feet, shining over the glass floor in a perfectly round pool surrounding it. Then he could see it, as big as his head and as black as onyx – then a moment later appearing so light as to be translucent.

The water that came from the Heart's centre also enveloped it, shooting upwards in an everlasting pillar. It would then appear as a pool at the top of the glass city, rippling down through the streets and throughout both the light-world *and* the dirt-world. The Heart was the source of the water of life – and of the light that surrounded them, and the power attached to it.

The Heart was the source of the Master's power. And Bright knew that once he had it, he'd be like the Master. Better than him, even. Ruler over his own kingdom…over this one.

He pushed his clawed hands gently into the pillar of water, then more forcefully, reaching for the Heart. Then finally he took hold of it, feeling it warm and alter-power-filled against his skin, and he felt that power go into him. His usually bright form became more and more intense, filling with light until he glowed as much as the pillar did, then he felt himself growing double, triple, then ten times his usual size.

He sucked in a startled breath, feeling like he could stretch out his mind and touch the universe – all the worlds, from the highest light-world to the newest ones made of roiling fire and rock.

Share, Truthful said from somewhere outside the pillar. Bright could sense his mingled fear and excitement. They were really doing it. They were really taking what they said they'd take, and Truthful had ever longed to be more than just a lieutenant. *You said you would share.*

Share, Strong agreed from somewhere else in the room. He emitted only eagerness without fear, as if any respect he'd had for the Master had gone once they'd stepped into this room. *Share, Beraht!*

I will share, Bright replied, *just once I've...*

Beraht.

Bright couldn't help himself. The moment he heard the Master's voice, so very heavy and strong, he froze with his hands on that precious Heart. It was hard to overcome the habits of a lifetime. But he made himself. He kept pulling the Heart away from the pillar, pulling it away until it was light and beautiful and held safely in his own hands. Then he pressed it to his new form's chest, using all his power to force it into himself. Once the Heart became a part of him, the Master would never have it back.

You're supposed to share! Strong snarled from somewhere in the brightness. *If you take it all, there'll be none for us!*

If I don't do it now, there'll be no time! Bright snapped back. Didn't they know the Master had called for him, and was already looking for them? It was more surprising that they hadn't been found yet, but then perhaps the Master didn't know everything. Or maybe he did know, but was so weakened by the attack on the city as a whole that he was unable to face this challenge.

What are you doing?

The voice seemed to come from all around Bright, and he turned to face the new threat even as he focused on absorbing the Heart. He'd never felt more powerful, and he just had to take his chance NOW... ***"Don't you know?"*** he replied aloud. ***"I'm taking your place. I'm becoming like you, and better."*** Oh, it was working. Even his voice sounded like the Master's now. Magnificent. Everything he deserved.

But then a small shape low on the ground caught Bright's eye. It was a two-leg male, even smaller than Bright's form had been, and it was standing at his feet. The figure was dark against the light, yet it was staring him right in the face.

The Master, Bright realised in shock. A moment later that became exultation. The Master was already small, already losing power, which was no doubt being gained by Bright himself. That knowledge spurred him on, and he took the last of that strength he'd taken from Peaceful to pull the Heart fully into himself. In that moment the Heart's form seemed to collapse into air, and then his new, five-fingered hands were coated in shimmering black.

"I DID IT!" he howled, sending his voice out so that all the light-world would hear it. **"I HAVE TAKEN THE HEART! I HAVE ASCENDED! I HAVE TAKEN THE THRONE! I-"**

Ahem.

This voice was quiet, but still commanded attention. Bright looked down to see the Master pointing towards the pillar of water where the Heart usually rested. There was something there – something black and shimmering, and about the size of his head...

You can't take the Heart, the Master said quietly. *It is mine, and it belongs here. Your power comes from it. From me.*

Bright looked down again at his hands, but the black coating that he'd taken to be power was sinking into his skin, disappearing. A moment later it was gone, and he was much the same as he'd always been, just bigger. But then seconds later that too changed, and he felt himself shrinking back to his previous size.

In desperation he lunged for that small figure, throwing a wave of intense light from his hands, straight for the Master's solemn face. He blasted him with everything he had – everything he'd stolen from Peaceful, and with all his innate light power. *Destroy him!*

For a while the Master glowed intensely as the light struck him. Bright couldn't even see him anymore; just a figure shaped in light. But then the Master stretched out his hand and the light faded. It faded from the Master, leaving him with his usual faint glow, and it faded from Bright, leaving him almost…dim. The Heart glowed ever stronger.

"Your power comes from me," the Master repeated aloud. His voice was still quiet, but unmissable in the otherwise dead silence. "No matter what form you choose to take, you cannot use it against me, Beraht. Nor you, Veritas, nor you, Geburah, nor any that you've convinced to turn against me. You have only what I've gifted you."

He looked so sad, so very sad, that for a moment Bright had an odd feeling. It was like he'd done something he shouldn't have, and he disliked the outcome. But that was quickly overcome by fury and humiliation. He'd felt so strong, so very close to the Master's abilities, but now it seemed like he was much less.

Bright had failed. That overwhelming realisation came along with a wash of absolute dismay – something else he'd never felt before. He'd risked everything. Everything! And had now lost…everything…

"Then I don't want it!" he snarled. "I don't want you, and I don't need you. I never have, and I would rather stand on my own that live under your rule any longer."

"I knew this moment would come, and yet I dreaded it," the Master said sadly. "Then choose, Beraht. Stay with me, and never turn away again, or take your freedom from me. It will not be what you think."

Bright heard him repeat the same thing in his mind, and he knew that statement had gone out through the light-world. It was clearly an offer to all the others who'd chosen to side with Bright. And in that moment, Bright felt some of those People turn away from him; felt the breakages of many thin cords of alter-power that represented their agreement, as they turned back to the Master.

But there were others who stayed connected to Bright, and he felt their own pride, anger and indecision as they rejected the Master's offer…

As for Bright, could he turn back? He pondered it for a mere moment before deciding he could never lower himself to turn back, not with the memory of what he'd done and almost had. No. *No.* He couldn't do it.

"I do not want you," he said again, gritting out the words. "I do not want the water or anything that comes from you, and I will be great on my own. You'll see."

He felt an echo of agreement from the others that had stayed with him, wherever they were in the light-world, and from the two in this room. It seemed that once they'd set themselves against the Master, they'd also lost the desire to turn back.

Good! Bright decided frantically in that moment that he and the other rebels *wanted* to be on their own. They really did. Controlling their own destiny. They'd be strong, powerful. Free.

Then have your freedom.

With those words the Master turned towards the Heart. It

began to glow inside its pillar of water, ribbons of light streaming towards it from every direction. Just then Bright felt the most dreadful feeling; like he was a goblet that was being emptied of liquid, or a pillow that was having the stuffing pulled out. He suddenly felt dry and dreadful and heavy and *dark…*

And he could see the light streaming from his own clawed fingers into the pillar, as intense and *bright* as ever, going and going and *leaving him…*

The most horrible, awful emotion was now besieging him. It was the opposite of courage and confidence and peace, and he didn't yet know its name, but in that moment he gave it one.

Fear.

No. No! he thought frantically. Without his own light, his brightness, who was he?

But then all his light was gone, and the Heart pulsed once inside its pillar, then settled. Just the same as it had always been. Bright thought about rushing towards it, set his mind on going immediately from one place to another. Right…*now!*

But he was trapped in this one location, and his feet were too, too heavy. Why was he so heavy? He couldn't…he couldn't *fly* anymore!

"What have you done to us?" he heard Strong cry from the other side of the room. Was he talking to the Master, or to Bright?

He looked up to see his companion – but oh, Strong now looked so different. His blue skin had become patchy and greyish and his whole form was lacking in life. Even his twisting tusks were hollow and dark in appearance, like something that had been left under the dirt-world's sun for too long.

How could it be? Bright thought in anguish. How could the water have been so very, very important…?

Oh no, now there was something worse happening. It felt like cords were attaching around his limbs, around his neck, fine but strong. It felt like he was about to be taken away somewhere, somewhere he didn't want to go – away from the light-world.

NOOOOO!

Truthful had already fled from the chamber, and casting his mental sight ahead, Bright saw where he'd gone. He'd headed for the Hall of Treasures the Master had created – the ones for those weak two-legs. Bright had taken the knowledge from Peaceful's mind earlier, but hadn't thought he'd need it.

Bright raced after Truthful, forcing his weak, desiccated body to move while it still could. Behind him he could hear Strong's lumbering steps, heavier than they'd ever been before. They were all heading for the same place, and he could sense that others were too. They had to take what they could get now, if they were to have a chance…

Don't take what isn't intended for you. It won't have the desired effect…

Bright freely ignored that advice, and he reached the hall's doorway just as Strong did. But there was someone standing in front of it. *You mustn't go through*, Loyalty began. His eyes were wide and full of something Bright had never seen before…fear, and reproach. Directed at *him*.

That just made Bright furious, and he lifted a hand to blast the lesser being, but Strong got there first. He struck Loyalty so hard that he went *through* the door and disappeared into the space beyond. As if that wasn't enough, he charged after him and found his fallen body – little harmed, of course, since even weak People were hard to damage – and began to strike him over and over again with his fist.

Bright was fascinated at Strong's fury. He'd never seen this before…had never seen Strong act this way before. But if he delayed any further, even by taking his anger out on Loyalty, he would lose his chance to take the treasures.

Delay as you wish, Truthful said from somewhere inside the hall. *It doesn't matter.*

Now that shocked Bright too, because it *did* matter. Clearly it did! Truthful had just told another…not-truth, perhaps so he might gain more himself. Would he make a habit of this? It could become quite confusing if Bright wasn't careful.

It seemed Strong wasn't fooled, because he came away from Loyalty's pummelled body and headed straight for the treasures. They'd all taken the same information from Peaceful's mind, and they knew what to get. Hundreds of tiny flasks or vials, each with a word inscribed on them. Bright couldn't read them, but still he knew what each meant. He grabbed a handful, including one that he knew would gift flight, and then rushed towards the exit again.

But it was too late. The tiny cords that had been ever-winding around his limbs now seemed to have him entirely.

You cannot stay here anymore without the water of life, he heard the Master whisper. *The light-world is for life, not for dead creatures.*

Dead? What was dead? For a moment he was frozen in place, and then…

Suddenly he was slingshotted away.

Gone.

Gone from the light-world, gone from the very feeling of life that was adjoined to it. Bright didn't even know what that meant. All he knew was that he'd been cast out, weak and dry and…somehow, even though he still lived…*dead.*

DRY

The light-world

Amaranthus stood in the same room where he'd had that final conversation with his former second-in-charge. He didn't move, didn't speak. All around him he could hear conversations; hear the chaos and confusion and pain of those loyal People still here with him.

He could also hear the other ones, the ones who'd chosen to turn away. They hurt too, and he felt that pain with them, even though it was pain of their own making.

He'd known the mutiny was coming, and yet, it still hurt so dreadfully when it finally happened. It hurt to have the ones he'd cared for so very much, the ones he'd gifted so very much, turn against him as if he was their enemy.

He hadn't been their enemy, but that was before they tried to kill him and steal the Heart. That was before they decided to target his other children, the ones made of flesh and blood. The ones made to look like *him.*

A ripple of agony shot through Amaranthus's entire body, his regret echoing through the living water, down into the light-world. He could feel his other People mourning with him. They didn't quite understand the full ramifications of what had happened, but they would.

Then he moved backwards, back into the rushing flow of water from the Heart. He pressed against it, feeling its power move through him as he spread his hands out. Water flowed out from each finger, sending alter-power in every direction as he gave his instructions.

Separate the fallen ones, he told the power. *Make a place they cannot leave. Make a prison that will hold them for millennia, until the mortal realm has run its course and they can finally be held to account.*

And as the ground shook and the very fabric of their reality began to split, he added one final command. *No matter what they plot or devise, let them never forget their ultimate failure…and who stands against them.*

⁜

Bright fell for a long time. He tried to halt the fall but was unable to do so, until suddenly he hit ground hard enough to rattle his teeth. Around him tumbled the others, like ripe fruit from an orchard of trees shaken in the wind. Hundreds, perhaps even thousands had fallen, but far less than those still left in the light-world.

He'd landed on hard, dry earth; something entirely unfamiliar. He stood, still wearing that damned two-leg form, and cautiously looked around. It looked like the ugliest, most unaccommodating parts of the dirt-world, but it wasn't, because…well, he just knew it wasn't.

Those dry brown hills and plains stretching into the distance didn't look like any part of the dirt-world he'd ever seen, because that world had *water.* And it sure wasn't the light-world, either. It was a complete desert, and looked as dry and empty as he now felt.

"Where are we?" Strong said as he got to his feet, looking

around him with a scowl. "This isn't the dirt-world, or the light-world."

Ah, he had a brilliant way of stating the obvious. But then wisdom had never been his strength.

Bright waited for Strong to turn in anger at the insult, but when the anger never came, he realised something new. Strong hadn't heard him. He hadn't heard his mind.

Interesting.

"Yes, it is the dirt-world," a small Person argued. "Look over there, at that building. That's the Master's castle for his two-leg pets, right?"

Bright barely had time to register who'd spoken before Strong turned on them, punching them hard in the face. They went flying, and Strong moved to follow them, then began pounding on their fallen figure.

Bright could sense the shock from those around him, but he didn't move to stop it. They had bigger problems than Strong apparently losing his self-control and becoming brutal. But then the Person had said 'the Master'. Surely they deserved a pummelling.

Then Bright squinted up ahead and made out a familiar shape. The small one had been right; there was the castle far in the distance, and he could see a hint of green colour around it. If there were plants, then there must be some life too…

Ignoring the others, he turned and charged towards the castle. Would the Master's pets be in there? Could he have been so very careless?

But while Bright's movements were slow, so slow and heavy and awful compared to usual, when he reached the castle he realised something new. There was still a little life in this place, but it was draining away much as it had drained from him. He could sense it as well as see it, everything cracking and fading, from dirt to plants to even the stone of this place. "The living water's being drawn out," he realised aloud. "The Master has doomed the dirt-world too." He let out a harsh, startled laugh.

But then Truth spoke up. "No. No, he hasn't. He's split it."

This time Bright knew that Truthful spoke the truth. He could still sense the presence of the light-world, as if the living water was somewhere nearby, near enough to smell it, but they'd been separated from it. He could still sense the presence of the dirt-world too. It was close by, still full of its odd, so very physical form of life, but it wasn't here with them. Not anymore.

Somehow, and Bright had no idea *how*, the Master had divided the light-world from the dirt-world, and this desert place from both of them.

Up ahead of them the air held a slight golden shimmer, like a veil from the dry ground right up to higher than the atmosphere went. One of the other castaways stood at the edge of the shimmering veil, poking at it with its small paw. "It seems to be a barrier," it said in wonder.

Another castaway, one called Speed, shook her head and took a few steps back. Then she ran full tilt at the shimmering veil – and landed *splat* as though against an invisible wall, with her six limbs all splayed out. A moment later she slid down to the dry ground, then turned to face the others. "There *is* a barrier!"

They were trapped.

Bright's fist clenched so tightly at his side that his claws punctured his skin. He felt a brief moment of something sharp and unpleasant – pain? – that was quickly gone. He pushed his way through the crowd surrounding, towards the castle doors. The other waterless People had followed him here, just like they'd followed him from the light-world. He pushed through the doors, half-expecting the castle to be empty.

But it wasn't. There was a figure curled up in the corner, small and in a washed-out shade of blue, with its eyes closed. Peaceful.

"She came through with us," Strong grunted from beside Bright. His eyes were small and piggish, and his brow was low and angry. "I thought she'd stay with the Master."

Bright studied the still form for a while, noting how her stripes had reappeared, although faintly. While her colouring certainly was duller than usual, she also didn't look as thin or dry as they did. In fact, she looked almost normal, except that she was here…with them. So he told a not-truth, or perhaps just what he wanted to truth to be. "She's being punished for helping us, for giving me her life force."

Strong looked at him in surprise. "She didn't give it-"

"It doesn't matter," Bright snapped. "She's here, and so are we."

But the two-leg pets weren't here. There also weren't any animals, nor any water. There was nothing living. But they still had those treasures they'd taken from the Master…

There was a long silence. Then Strong asked, "What shall we do, Bright?"

Bright looked down at himself, at his plain, dry, dead-looking form, and felt an overwhelming wash of fury. There was nothing bright about him, not anymore, and in the pit of his being he felt a new name, a new description. "Don't call me Bright anymore."

"Then…what shall we call you?"

Strong sounded genuinely confused, but the former Bright just shook his head. "Never mind that. What we need now…is to find a way back. To take back the water, and to destroy the Master. We need to reclaim our place."

"You said you would share," Truthful snapped from somewhere inside the castle. "You said you would share, but you tried to take the Heart for yourself."

Of course he had. In this moment he saw it clearly: there had been no choice. You couldn't have more than one Master – so only one could use the Heart. Or try to, anyway. But now he knew he needed his lieutenants. There were so many others here with them, and he needed to hold his position, especially now when he was weak.

He held out his hand towards his companion. On his palm was a tiny, unlabelled vial. "This one is for flight. And I *will* share it with just you and Truthful – if you vow to serve me forever."

Strong's eyebrows shot up, but his piggy gaze fixed hungrily on the vial. "I'll vow. I can't stand to be so heavy, so trapped in place. And I've always followed you anyway. What about you, Truthful?"

Truthful turned his black eyes on the former Bright, but his expression was unreadable. "I'll vow," he said finally.

And that, the former Bright thought, was a not-truth. But he still nodded, carefully lifting the cap off the vial, and raising it to his mouth. "Vow accepted."

As for him, he knew what he'd do, and what his new goal was. He'd take back his true form, and take back *everything* from the Master. And the greatest form of revenge? That would be destroying those two-legged dirt people.

He couldn't wait.

On the border between the newly-created realms, in the middle of a great body of saltwater, an island was rising. Its new soil and stone twisted and bubbled around one central point, rising up and up until it was well above the water; until a new mountain had been formed.

It was perfectly shaped, rather like some volcanoes from the normal realm, but unlike them, its heart wasn't made of fire and molten rock. Instead the tiny crater inside the mountain's peak was hollow – the shape of an hourglass, small enough for a two-leg to hold in their hand.

In fact, the only reason the island existed was because of the missing piece, which had been knocked loose during the rending of the realms, and was now somewhere in the new 'normal' realm…

Meanwhile, in the normal realm, a magpie scratched around in some loose leaves under a tree. It hadn't noticed too much of a change in the atmosphere, but then it seldom noticed anything outside of its immediate environment.

Suddenly a tiny, shining black piece of stone *pinged* from thin air to land nearby. The bird cocked its head sideways, then darted to retrieve the stone. Its tiny brain was thinking, *shiny. Take to nest.* And then unexpectedly – with immediate movement across time and space – the magpie was now sitting in its nest, the black stone still in its beak.

It twitched a little in brief confusion, then dropped the stone in amongst the other 'treasures' its nest held.

But then how would a magpie be expected to appreciate the newly created Eternity Stone?

Lunden, 1819 AD

George sat on his brother's bed, his back resting against the headboard. Edward sat next to him, with Olivia on his other side. He gripped both of their hands very tightly, and stared straight forward at the wallpaper on the other side of the very bright room. Not only were the curtains now entirely removed, but all the candles were lit. There'd be a hefty beeswax bill this month.

Not for the first time, George tried to extricate his hand from his brother's tight grip, but Edward just held on tighter. "Eddie," George said finally, a little exasperated. "I need to take a breath of fresh air."

"There's plenty of air in here," Edward countered. "Or open the window if you must."

George glanced meaningfully at Olivia, then when his brother didn't seem to register, moved to whisper into his ear. "I need to use the convenience. By Jove, will you let me go?"

The viscount did release him, but reluctantly. "You will come back, won't you? You won't leave me here?"

Here in the danger of his ornate bedroom, in this lavishly appointed townhouse, surrounded by servants? By heaven, no! And yes, perhaps there was a touch of sarcasm in that thought.

"I'll come back," George promised, although he could hear his own exasperation in his tone. He also saw Olivia's concern in their shared glance as he exited the room. What had Edward so frightened that he couldn't stand to be alone? Deias forbid, had his mind been damaged by the fall?

"As if this wasn't bad enough, now Ashlea is stuck in Erastus," George grumbled aloud as he washed his hands a few minutes later. "Silly chit. Couldn't she have gone straight to the Mountain like we'd agreed, and not detoured into the town?"

But in truth, he could not blame her for making such a choice. She thought she'd seen Anne, and at least she'd been wise enough to stop following through another unknown gateway. They'd done their fair share of following suspicious figures, or taking unnecessary risks. Now if only she could come back with the healing pot, so that Edward might be freed of whatever assailed his mind.

It didn't occur to George that there would be any real delay in her return. There were thousands of gateways, most of which didn't have a doorframe attached, and Amaranthus had always been good enough to keep them connected when necessary. She'd be back.

George paused at the entry back to Edward's room. By Jove, he was becoming weary of that room. It quite hurt one's back to sit in such a position for so long. Was he becoming an old man at the age of twenty-two?

"Georgie?" The plaintive voice from the open doorway showed he'd been spotted.

He sighed. "Here."

He went inside then took a moment to walk around the room, stretching his legs, before turning to his brother. Edward was still pale-faced, with that most impressive bruise on his temple, although perhaps the swelling was going down now. But there were those shadows under his eyes, because he certainly hadn't gone back to sleep since he'd woken over an hour earlier, and the bulging of his blue eyes spoke of some paranoia or concern.

"Come sit with me, Georgie."

George sighed again, but he came to sit at the side of the bed.

"No, *next* to me! You've got to keep me safe."

George paused, staring at his brother. Now that didn't sound encouraging, but he'd had more than his fair share of supernatural dangers or assassins, so he couldn't dismiss it. "Safe from what, Ned?"

But Edward didn't answer.

"The pit," Olivia said finally. Her blonde hair looked limp and dishevelled against her pale face, but she didn't try to pull her hand away from Edward's. "He keeps talking about a pit, George. Whatever can that mean?"

A pit. A pit...

"Ned," George said carefully, "we want to help you. You

know that. And we want to keep you safe. But you must tell us, *what* are we keeping you safe from?"

Edward tucked his chin into his neck and muttered something.

"What?"

"*Dshsshsptts.*"

"What?" Olivia and George asked together.

"Dark spirits! *Things!*" Edward cried out. Then he threw his face into his hands and began sobbing. That was something George hadn't seen him do since they were children, and it was almost more disturbing than what he'd said.

Things. George's mind immediately went to the weird, terrifying and occasionally stinky Creatures he'd been unfortunate enough to meet while time travelling in the Other realm. Some had looked like badly taxidermied animals. Some had looked more like people, but none had looked at all like you'd want to make friends with them.

Oh, they could very much be considered *things,* but how might they have got to Edward? Or was it something else?

After about ten minutes the sobbing finally subsided, and it seemed Edward was ready to talk. "I don't know how I got there," he said quietly. "One moment I was going off for a ride with my friends, and the next my horse was gone, and I was standing in this…this *desert.* I was walking, and I couldn't stop myself, as though my feet were moving without my agreement. Up ahead I could see this vast, dark pit in the earth. Simply colossal! Big enough to fit Hythe Park in at least, and there were people all around it, walking towards it, just as I was. But coming out of the pit…"

He paused, sucking in a deep breath. His eyes looked haunted. "It was like that old Aegyptian mummy exhibit we saw once, Georgie. They were so dry and almost crumbling, but they were moving and alive still. Oh, they were alive, and they were coming towards us. I saw one take a man by the arm, and then it dragged him into the pit, just like that! I couldn't shake the thought that I'd never see him again.

"But I couldn't stop walking. I was walking right into the pit, and then as I reached it and could just about see inside, I felt something take my hand. I looked down and there was this…*thing*. It had too many legs, and it looked up at me and smiled in the most awful way…"

George and Olivia leaned forward, their eyes wide. "And then what happened?" she whispered.

"Well, then I woke up," Edward said in a rather more normal voice. He shuddered, his brow damp with sweat. "By Jove, I never want to see that again. What a nightmare, hmm?" And then he looked down at his knees where they lay covered by the blanket. "A nightmare," he said again to himself. "Just a bad dream…" But a single tear was running down his face.

As for George, he couldn't shake the resemblance of what Edward had seen, to what he himself had experienced in the Other realm. "They smelled bad, didn't they?" he asked quietly. "The things you met. And they looked like they were badly taxidermied, like the otter that old Lord Gottenreit had in his parlour when we were children. But their eyes were so alive, and so malignant."

Edward swallowed. "How do you know that?"

"I'm describing the Creatures I met earlier this year. I told you about them, right before you and Olivia had me thrown into Bethel Insane Asylum." They drew in a gasp at George's reminder, but he continued, "They live in a different realm, separate from this one. It's called the Other, and it's mostly desert. There's no water, and it's the most miserable place you ever saw. But then in contrast, under the ground there's the Mountain of

Glass, which is the most beautiful place you ever saw. Absolutely marvellous! Our friend Amaranthus lives there. I told you about that, do you remember Eddie?"

Eddie nodded. "Yes. And I said it sounded like…dark spirits and celestials. Religious."

George blinked a couple of times. Amaranthus…the Eternal One. But the 'religious' term still didn't sit right. "I don't see what's so religious about it. The Creatures were bloody terrifying – excuse my language, ma'am – and the Mountain was incredible. But it wasn't everything." He paused, thinking of how best to describe it. "There was more. The Mountain isn't Amaranthus's home. Not really. He showed us a little portal to his home, and all I can say is that it seemed to be full of light. Jon – a friend – put his hand through, and it came out shining. And then there were the sleepers…"

Olivia and Edward were still watching him wide eyed, so he continued. "They were like upright, clear-sided coffins, but there were living people inside. People that I knew had…*died* here in the normal realm, but they were alive there. It was as if they'd been given new bodies. And they were sleeping, all waiting to go to this new place, and the capsules were all inscribed with this odd phrase: passage paid."

There was a very long silence. Then Olivia asked, "Are you suggesting that Edward went to Hades, and that these *Creatures* he dreamed about are some sort of dark spirits? Because I know I wished him there once or twice – sorry darling – but he's a good man! Especially now he's got rid of his mistress. He pays his debts. He's polite to his mother, and he even goes to church once in a while. How could that kind of person go to Hades?"

"I don't know," George said awkwardly. In truth the idea concerned him greatly, if he understood this correctly. "But the ones who did go in the capsules – they weren't all good people. A couple of them were murderers! But I think the key is… 'passage paid'."

"Murderers?" Edward's eyes were wide. "I'm not a murderer. By Jupiter, not by a long shot! Well, there was that one time with the – never mind. If a murderer could have their passage paid, then why couldn't I, Georgie? It doesn't make sense!"

Ooh, he really ought to know this one. George knew it was on the tip of his tongue, and it had something to do with Amaranthus who was in fact Deias, creator of all, and who most certainly would know the answer. But he wasn't here, only George was.

Just then a thought sprang to mind. "What doesn't make sense," he said slowly, "is that you would have such an experience, then be brought back, only to be sent right back again. Why bother? For in truth Ned, we thought we'd lost you."

"A second chance!" Olivia said suddenly, picking up on the same idea. "Darling, if it *was* real – and I rather think it a nightmare myself – then now you've got a second chance, do you not?"

Edward's lips were still downturned, but he seemed to be considering this. After some moments he said, "That might be the case, but I'm still bloody terrified. Please…please don't leave me."

George sighed, moving to sit right next to his brother again, and set one arm around his shoulders while Edward's wife again took the other side. "Shall I read to you?"

"No, don't read. Sing."

George shot him a startled glance, then when Olivia didn't seem prepared to do so, he cleared his throat. Then he sang the first words that came to mind: "Rock-a-bye baby, on the tree top…"

Both Olivia and Edward turned to stare at him disbelievingly.

"Er…shall I stop?" If he recalled, this song didn't have such a happy ending.

"No, you may keep going," Edward said loftily. Then he leaned his head on George's shoulder.

Very well then. "Rock-a-bye baby, on the tree top. When the wind blows…"

Snore.

Humph. And he'd just got started, too. But George sent a mental thank you to Amaranthus or whoever had been watching, then just for his own amusement, finished the song.

Erastus, 2598 AD

Magdalene quietly made her way through the backstreets of Erastus until she reached an alley. Crookshank Alley wasn't unusual at first glance. Like the rest of the valley, dry patches of dirt alternated here with lush grass, and it was one of the grassy patches she headed for.

Past the end of the alley was a lovely stone doorway. It stood on its own, doorposts and lintels each carved generations ago and worn by time, but still upright. There was nothing through that gap except a grey fog – another realm.

She paused just outside the doorway, for a moment wondering if she'd misstepped by sneaking out here. But then she thought of *him*, and reminded herself that poor Asher (or whatever her name was) was stuck in Erastus. And all those people killed out in the outskirts…terrible. He would know the answer. So really, she was being selfless by coming back here today.

Oh yes.

Magdalene had barely tapped her fist against the nearest doorpost when the grey mist shimmered. There was a faint golden light, and there he was, leaning against the doorpost and wearing a smile on his handsome face.

Cobalt was tall and gorgeous with warm dark eyes, and long, flowing golden hair that went all the way down to his waist. It should have made him seem feminine, but against his definitely masculine form, it just made him look even more gorgeous. His hair shone like gold in the sun, and seemed to move as if it had a life of its own. She was pretty sure it was alter-power of some kind. He looked somewhere in his twenties, but Magdalene knew he was much, much older…and also that he wasn't quite human.

See why Kamile wouldn't approve?

"Hello, Magdalene. What brings you back today so soon after our last meeting?"

"H-hi, Cobalt," she stuttered. "Um…I hope you don't mind, but I had a few questions. Important ones-"

"I never mind," he cut in smoothly. "You're here about…a killer? You're afraid that they're still out there, and that you're all in danger."

"Yes, that's exactly it!" Mags sighed in relief that he'd cut to the issue so quickly. "And the adults said it was just a bad fight, and that it's over, but I think they're wrong."

"Hmm." Cobalt appeared thoughtful for a moment. "In this matter I'm afraid they're right, dear Magdalene. The three men were under the influence of certain substances, and they fought and killed each other. A truly nasty tale, but one that stops there. There is no killer on the loose."

"Oh." She warred between feeling relief and an odd disappointment, then settled on relief. She knew she shouldn't find bad news interesting…except that sometimes she did. Maybe it was because when bad things were happening to other people, then they weren't happening to *her*. "That's good, I suppose."

Even though she wasn't so happy that Kamile had been right

in this matter, especially after how she'd cut Poli off as she had. "I don't want any more of my friends to die." She'd told him about Coryn, of course. And that led to another point… "What do you know about time travellers?"

"Time travellers?" His thick eyebrows shot up, and his long hair seemed to wave as if in response to her comment. "What manner of time travellers?"

Magdalene shifted in place, then decided her feet hurt, so sat down in front of the doorway. "People who travel through time using some sort of supernatural gateways. Maybe not like this one. They say theirs don't have doorframes, and that only certain people can see them. That's real, right?"

"Oh yes. There are a few of those people. Gifted types, or perhaps just very lucky. But don't tell me *you* want to travel through time, little Magdalene?"

She sure would! "Um…maybe. But that's not why I'm asking. See, there's this girl who came through a doorway or gateway or whatever, over on the other side of the river. Kam- someone says she came from hundreds of years in the past! Then right after she came through, this huge monster came out of another doorway and destroyed her one. So she's stuck here in Erastus, in our time." She shrugged. "You said there were other doorways. I wondered if you could help her."

There was a long silence. "You know I will if I can," Cobalt said finally. "Does this girl have a name?"

"Asher. Or it could be Ashling."

"Ashlea?" he suggested. He'd gone very still amongst that grey fog, and his eyes were fixed on her with sudden intensity. "Is that the name, Magdalene?"

She found herself leaning backwards, startled, but she nodded. "Um…yes, I think so."

Her friend was silent for another few moments. Then he

stepped back from the doorway, disappearing into the mist for a second before reappearing. "Can you bring her here, dear?" he asked carefully.

"Um…"

"I do believe I could help her if only I could speak to her. There are many gateways – doorways too – to all sorts of places here on my side of the barrier. As you know, I cannot come out of my realm, but your kind can come in to me." When Magdalene still didn't answer, he added, "It would be *most* helpful if you could bring her here. Or to another doorway! As long as it's on this side of the river, she should be fine. We could *certainly* help her."

Magdalene had never heard Cobalt speak with such energy, or even for so long. Generally he just listened. "I've never even met her," she said apologetically. "But I could ask?"

His dark eyes blinked rapidly for a moment, his face almost blurring. But then he smiled. "As you like, dear. It seems that this is Ashlea's problem rather than your own, although you are to be commended for your kindness." He reached out a hand towards her, right up to the doorway. His fingers shone lightly. "Would you like to come through yourself, dear? Time travels much differently here than it does on your side, and no one would even notice you were missing."

Magdalene looked wistfully at those shining fingers, then thought of how he'd seemed to vanish for only a second earlier. She stood, then reached out just a little. "How differently?"

"An hour on my side is a mere minute on your own, and there is much you could see here."

Oh, oh, she was *so* tempted! He'd asked her before – almost every time she came, in fact – but she'd always turned him down. She knew Kamile wouldn't approve, and she really did want Kamile's approval. And to be honest, there was an element of fear, or mistrust. She *didn't* know this person. Not right to the core. So could she truly trust him enough to leave Earth behind?

"The scrying pools that show all knowledge," Cobalt murmured. "The river of youth that will wash away all signs of age and injury…"

"Is that the same as the water of life?"

"It has the same source," he answered quickly. "But it is more potent here. Did you see Mama Silver, Magdalene? She's human like you, but she's also more than two hundred years old. She has the wisdom that comes with age, and the good grace that comes from much time spent here, learning on this side of the barrier. Don't you want to be like her one day?"

Mama Silver was the pretty woman with the silver hair and red lips. She'd been here earlier today, and had been so very friendly with Cobalt. Oh yes, Magdalene remembered, and a little dart of jealousy shot through her. That was followed by hope. Could she, boring old Mags, really become as fascinating as *that*? Human, yes. But *special*.

So that was why Magdalene found herself slowly reaching out until her fingers touched the edge of the doorway. Then an inch further….

Then she pulled away, a millisecond before she would have touched Cobalt's fingers. "I'm sorry," she said regretfully. "I can't."

Cobalt seemed to lean forward until he almost filled the doorway, his hand pressed up against an invisible barrier. "You can't, or you won't? Don't you trust me? You've come here so many times, and yet I can feel there's something holding you back. What is it, Magdalene?"

"It's just…" She paused, shaking her head then stepping back again. "I just can't today. Thank you for the help, and I'll…I'll see you next time."

She ducked her head, then turned and ran, feeling ashamed and confused.

He didn't call out after her.

She hadn't touched him. Not quite: he'd been a moment too slow. But she *had* touched the barrier, just for a moment. It had been enough to create a tiny connection, more than what they'd had before with temptation and desire. Those were a force of their own, but without actual contact, ultimately meaningless.

But now she didn't see or sense the tiny, thin thread of alter-power running from her and back to that doorway…

First Ash wandered aimlessly around Erastus, alternately flying and walking while she checked out the area, and waited for a new remnant gateway to miraculously appear, or for George to call back.

But wandering aimlessly didn't work, because she kept finding herself dropping to the ground at unexpected times as she passed doorways, and getting lost, so she tried wandering purposefully. That meant spotting a likely destination somewhere in the town, then heading for it and seeing if it would prompt any far-sight that would help her choose her next step.

The first six stone doorways she passed didn't do anything except make her a little nervous. They tended to have dark or foggy insides, and she knew they *could* be the direct route to somewhere really helpful like the Mountain of Glass, or they *could* be a direct route into the Other realm. The scary, desert-ish parts, not the nice bits.

Or they could lead to the middle of a volcano, or the middle of a riot, or the middle of a rope bridge over a ninety-metre drop…

You get the picture. Basically, she wasn't going through without express permission to do so. That could come through her gift of far-sight (which would appear when it felt like it, not when she wanted it), or through Anne or Amaranthus showing up and directly leading her to the right door. But for now she decided to just…wander aimlessly, mostly.

Ash turned a corner in a back alley and was met with a wall of rock. She realised she'd reached one side of the small valley, this part where the town butted right up against it. This part was rocky, an almost sheer cliff with occasional greenery filling the spaces.

She turned around and headed back into the town exactly the way she'd come. She could hear chatter in the distance: the happy sort interspersed with laughter that said a group of people were enjoying themselves. Maybe they'd have food, she mused. Maybe they'd know where Kamile lived, because Ash was *bored*…

Then she made it around the corner and saw a group of people: about a dozen of them all sitting around two small tables outside a sort of restaurant. There were plasticky umbrellas shading them from the mild sun, and for a moment she just stopped and stared. They were all good-looking, all wore white, and all had silver hair. They also all looked extremely happy.

It was like a convention for sci-fi hippies, Ash thought. They reminded her of something off some movie… And yes, she knew she was being petty and cranky. It was probably lack of food, she consoled herself, because she needed to eat more now she was pregnant. She wasn't *angry* that other people seemed to be having a good time.

Just then, one of them got up and moved away from the table. Not moved – *flew* across the ground, just like she or George would have.

Wow.

Ash was just taking that in when the woman at the end of the table looked up and saw her. It was that lady she'd almost run into earlier, the good-looking one with the red lipstick. Mama, or Joy, or something…?

The woman lifted a hand in greeting. "Hello, sweetheart. Still looking for your friend?"

Ash took a few steps closer, feeling self-conscious until she realised that none of the others were paying her any attention. "Yes, actually. You wouldn't have seen a short redhead anywhere around here?"

Joy patted the empty seat next to her. "Come, sit down and have a drink on me. You can tell me all about your friend, and we'll tell you whatever we know."

"Um…thank you."

Ash sat, because a drink sounded great. And before she knew it she'd been introduced to the whole group and offered a meal, too. The food was good, and the Silvers were friendly, although only Joy actually chatted with her. Ash at first thought they were relatives, but then Joy explained that the hair colour came from power, not from blood connections.

That made Ash immediately think of ye olde Seyen Johannis, AKA the Queen, AKA murderous psycho who wanted to take over the world. *She'd* been pretty and shiny too, until she wasn't anymore.

But *Seyen* hadn't been so nice. Just…nice. It was hard to hate and fear a really nice person, even one like Joy who patted her on the arm every thirty seconds. Or at least it said there was something wrong with Ash, if she was feeling that way.

Unaware of Ash's musing, Joy continued, "The hair colour comes from our exposure to the river of youth, sweetheart." She laughed, a joyous (yes) musical sound. "If one doesn't mind being silver-haired, then it's worth it for the knowledge and power that comes with it."

Ash's lips curved automatically at the edges at that laugh, and she looked away. "River of youth? Is that the same as the water of life?"

"Can't have youth without life, sweetheart." Joy watched her with knowing eyes. "You've had a visit or two yourself, yes? But not for long. I can sense it on you. Just a touch, but not enough to change you like it's changed us. Was that where you were heading today before your doorway was destroyed? For the water?"

"Yes! Yes." Ash was stunned by how much the woman had perceived, and felt a hum of excitement too. "That gateway – or doorway I mean, behind the food truck – it wasn't the only one, was it?"

Joy shook her head, smiling. "Of course not. There are dozens which will all take you to different parts of the river, each lovely in its own way. And here in the valley there are three that I know of. Regrettably two have now been damaged and might take some time to resolve, but there *is* one more."

A doorway that led to the Mountain of Glass. That was undoubtedly what she was saying, and Ash's heartrate picked up in excitement. "Where!? I mean, where is it, please?"

"Why, it's not too far from here. I can show you, if you like."

She liked. Oh yes, she liked.

So ten minutes later, having been fed and watered and cheered up by happy silver company, Ash found herself standing outside a stone archway. It was in an empty space between buildings, with blank walls on three sides and rubble beneath her feet. The archway had carved designs that were worn from age, and through it she could see darkness and perhaps a few glimmers of stars, although that could have just been her imagination.

But she found herself catching her breath and pausing. Even though she'd been eager to come here, now she was hesitant. Darkness wasn't exactly welcoming.

"There's a sort of loneliness about this place, isn't there?" Joy Silver said from behind her. "Perhaps it keeps some people away, and only the truly dedicated find what's on the other side." She shrugged a little sadly. "Food carts are all well and good, but they don't require risk, do they? Or courage. And so the pay-off is proportionately small."

She was referring to the Other entrance that had been destroyed by the black fish-thing, Ash realised. She couldn't disagree with the woman. That entrance was intended to feel inviting, and certainly to appeal to those who were hungry rather than brave. But was Ash really missing something by choosing an easier entrance? The idea startled her.

Now feeling uncertain, Ash rested her hand against her pocket where her mobile phone hung heavy in the thin fabric of her regency jacket. She hadn't had any far-sight, and she relied on that greatly before making any new decisions like this. She *had* agreed that she'd go straight to the Mountain to find Amaranthus. She'd flubbed that, of course, and would be stuck here until she found a way out. Or until the other food cart doorway was fixed. Whichever came first.

But now when she had an option, she was delaying…

"Would you like me to come through with you, sweetheart? I wouldn't mind a power top-up myself."

Six

PAINFULLY FUNNY

"Aras? Ric?" Kamile paused at the edge of the small glade, squinting around curiously. She'd come to find the two as it was time for Ric to return to his classes. She'd left Isla with Poli – a sort of apology for the way she'd snapped earlier – and really, it was nice to go for a walk.

When she'd asked a councilman for Aras's whereabouts, she'd been directed towards this place at the valley's edge. It was an isolated plateau where the trees were still naturally fixed in the ground, and there wasn't any sign of either male. There was, however, a small building. It looked rather like a ranger's hut, and its few windows were opaque, with the usual UV/theft shield preventing her from seeing much inside. She could hear voices from inside, although they were muted.

She had just raised her hand to tap on the doorbell when a voice came from behind her.

"What are you doing?"

Kamile jumped in place, then recognising the voice, turned with rolled eyes. "Aras, don't sneak up on me like that! And I was looking for you, actually. Someone told me you'd be here."

Aras stood only a few feet away; he'd approached her far too silently for such a big man. He studied her dispassionately for a few moments. Behind him a small figure floated amongst the trees, a shimmer of white light left behind by every movement.

She saw it was Ric, wearing anti-gravity wings as he often did, and flying like a small celestial.

"And you couldn't call my link?" Aras asked.

He referred to the small communication device so many wore on their ear and their lip. They were very popular in the cities, although not so much with the Chosen where they'd formerly been living. "You're not wearing a link," she said patiently, resisting the urge to roll her eyes again.

He tapped his front pocket. "Portable. I told you about it last week."

"Oh. I forgot about that." The information must have gone in one ear then out the other.

There was a long silence. "What did you need?" he asked finally.

Feeling a little embarrassed, Kamile took refuge in extreme perkiness. "I was looking for Ric. His teacher said he hadn't arrived at the classroom this afternoon, and asked if I could find him. And you know me, always up for an adventure."

There was a little sarcasm in that last part since this brief walk wasn't exactly exciting, but Aras's eyebrows lowered over his pale eyes. "They shouldn't have come to you. I'm his father."

Even though the Chosen had practised communal parenting, since they'd left, many had clung to the only security they knew – each other. Aras had fallen very quickly into acting possessive about his only son, although certainly not about *her*.

Kamile lost her fake cheer. "Yes, he's no blood of mine, and yet everyone knows he lives with me. With *us*, at least for the time being. I don't think it's that unreasonable they should come to me."

She suddenly felt very low at the reminder of yet another separation. Aras didn't want her for her own sake. He didn't seem to want her for Isla, and he definitely didn't want her as a stepmother for Ric.

She continued, "But I'm sorry for interfering. I'll just go, and you can link the teacher and tell him what's happening. It *is* up to you, after all."

Ric had spotted her by then, but didn't seem to have noticed the argument. He waved from his place several metres above the ground, then began to float closer.

"I didn't think you were interfering," Aras said. "I think…" Then he went silent, his head cocked to the side.

"You think what?" Kamile prompted impatiently.

He raised a hand as if to silence her, his attention fixed on the small building behind her. "Move away right now, Kamile."

Shaken, she did as he asked, moving back into the trees and gesturing for Ric to follow her. "What is it?" she whispered urgently. She couldn't see anything wrong. She could only hear that faint sound of chatter and laughter – increasing laughter, in fact. Someone inside was having a good time.

Aras just shook his head and pulled out a small, black weapon from his pocket. Kamile bet it was illegal, but after what had happened last year, she couldn't blame him for going armed. She carried around a small stun-gun herself, one she'd sort of stolen from an enforcer back in Lile. (He probably would have had her arrested then executed for sedition, so she figured a little theft was OK.)

Then Aras moved forward towards the door and very gently set his hand on the handle…

Just then there was a prolonged burst of laughter, so loud she heard it distinctly even from here. A half second later there was an intense burst of purple light from inside the building. It lit up the opaque windows for a moment, showing the silhouettes of several figures inside, and then *splatter*. There was a sound like heavy rain, and suddenly those same windows were covered in dark spots. The laughter stopped abruptly, and the light died away.

"Fire Lord," Aras muttered under his breath. It seemed even though he'd left the Chosen, their swear words had come along with him.

But Kamile couldn't speak. She could only think about what Poli had said earlier today, and about what the sound and splatter must have been.

Ric looked at her for a moment, and something knowing showed in his eyes. Something that didn't fit a seven-year-old boy. "Bye bye," he said.

The hairs stood up on the back of Kamile's neck, and she didn't need to wait for Aras to check inside the building, then come back out and shake his head. She already knew something terrible had happened.

Then Aras said it anyway. "Get Ric back to the town straight away. There's a killer on the loose."

Half an hour later Kamile was back at her little house and had let Poli know of the rather gruesome happenings in their new town. "I'm sorry I didn't believe you," she said despairingly. "I just couldn't face it, after we thought we'd escaped all of that when we left Lile!"

"I forgive you," Poli said grandly. "After all, you have a lot on your mind."

As did they all. But Kamile didn't take offence. Instead she clung tighter to Isla, who for this moment didn't seem to mind being squeezed like a child's soft toy. "Where is Mags?"

The younger girl looked around curiously. "I don't know. She was just here…"

"Contact her link straight away, please, and tell her we're going into town. There's going to be a meeting."

But even as they left the house, they saw Magdalene's small

figure in the distance. Her dark hair was a little tousled, and her expression looked dark. "I know, you don't have to tell me," she said as they approached.

"You know about the killer?" Poli echoed. "And the town meeting?"

"What? No!" Magdalene shook her head. "I thought I was in trouble for leaving without asking. What killer? You mean there really is one?!"

"Kamile saw it happen herself," Poli announced dramatically. "Every bit, and there was blood everywhere."

"Hold on a second," Kamile cut in. "I certainly didn't see it like that. I didn't even go inside the house, although I could see from outside that there was alter-power involved."

Aras had told her enough, and she'd drawn her own conclusions – as Poli clearly had too. While in theory someone could have been drugged with a laughing agent, to distract them enough to cause damage, Kamile had sensed the power the moment the light had shown. As a halfling, her senses were particularly good. There was no doubt.

But Magdalene's round face had turned pale under her tan. "But…he said there *wasn't* a killer. How can…"

"He?" Kamile queried. "Would this be that boy of yours, Mags?"

"Um…yes." Magdalene's lips tightened, and she ducked her head, frowning. "He said there wasn't one. He *said.*"

Kamile sighed, moving forward and putting her arm around the other girl's shoulder. Although Magdalene wasn't exactly tall for a fourteen-year-old, she was almost level with Kamile's own height. "And here's a reminder that boys don't always tell the truth. Maybe he thought he was right, Mags, or maybe he was trying to sound smart by making up an answer. But never mind that. Come with us to the meeting, and we'll find out what we can do about this."

Not ever being alone in a hut in the forest would be a good start, she privately mused.

"But this boy tells the truth," Magdalene muttered under her breath. "He was supposed to be right."

Kamile just sighed and hugged the girl a little tighter as they walked. Life was full of tiny little heartbreaks, wasn't it? Boys weren't always right, and killers roamed free. And sometimes your government tried to arrest you, and your ex-handfast partner left a poisonous snake in your bed, or your cloistered Compound's leadership cut your throat...

Hmm. Perhaps not *tiny* little heartbreaks.

Kamile thrust those last memories from her mind and focused on what was in front of them. A town meeting, and a rather important one.

After the Rift – 1 BC

Peaceful was floating in a gray fog. She couldn't feel any of her limbs, but she could hear sounds around her, voices, although the words themselves didn't register. Then feeling began to return bit by bit. There was a hard surface pressing against her back...and her front...and her sides. She wriggled and stretched her limbs, trying to push away whatever crowded her in.

Someone! she called out, casting her mental voice as far as she could. *I'm...somewhere! Come get me!*

But no one answered, and her mind remained empty of any voices except her own. Finally it occurred to her that she'd have to free herself from...whatever this place was. So she wriggled and stretched and pushed at whatever hemmed her in, until suddenly with a burst of energy she found herself shooting sideways, straight through the layer trapping her.

Oof. Peaceful hovered for a moment in an unfamiliar open space, blinking at the dim light, before allowing herself to rest tentatively on the ground. Even though she was no longer so tightly trapped, she could see walls close around her, as if she was still in one of the dirt-world's underground cave systems. Not even a nice cavern at that, but a narrow tunnel that quickly curved out of sight. The air was permeated with dust, and when she looked down at herself, she saw her whole body was coloured an odd grey-brown shade.

Hmm. Had she been…*in the wall?!* She shook herself, sending little clouds of dust up into the stagnant air, then turned insubstantial for just long enough for the last of the dust coating her to fall away. *That's better,* she thought in relief. *I ought to be blue, not grey. Now, where is everybody?*

Again no one responded to her mental call, but she did hear those faint voices once more. Not mind-speak, but the sort where you'd use your tongue and vocal cords and so forth. Peaceful focused on their origin and began moving down the tunnel in that direction. The further she went, the rockier the cave walls were, and the clearer the voices became. But *ugh,* she didn't recognise them. They were harsh, sounding somehow damaged, even though she felt like she ought to have recognised them.

"…*Brutal says we're short by at least a hundred. Bring them up from the lower ranks. It doesn't matter.*"

"*What about the Pale One?*"

There was the sound like someone spitting. "*That faithless lie-teller. Let him do what he will, but he cannot come* here *again.*"

"*And what of the enemy's plans?*"

Peaceful paused at the narrow end of the tunnel, just where it opened out into a different space. From here she could see the light brightened from barely-there to a distinct reddish shade, and she could sense the many other minds just around the corner.

But they didn't feel right. It wasn't just those odd, harsh voices saying their odd, meaningless words, but it was something more. Something in this cave around her – something that went beyond the vague ugliness of this place and the vague unpleasantness of the nearby minds.

She couldn't hear the usual cave sounds like distant trickling water, or the echoes of wind or trapped insects as she would expect. Instead she could hear…unhappiness. That was new to her as well, but she identified it at once. It was in the air, thick as the dust from the space she'd awoken, and it seemed to emanate from the very walls around her. She sniffed. Ugh, that was the strangest smell, both sweet and unpleasant all at the same time.

"Where am I?" she asked aloud.

The nearby voices silenced at once. Finally one of them said, *"Who is speaking?"*

"Peaceful," she replied cautiously, thinking this was one of the strangest conversations she'd ever had. She'd never had to introduce herself before, because People would know her at once. "Sometimes I'm called Shulamithe. Who is this?"

There was a long silence, then the sound of heavy footsteps, the kind that had real weight behind them – like a dirt-world creature. Then a figure moved into sight.

Peaceful's eyes widened. The person was shaped like the Master, or like one of those two-legged creatures the Master loved so much, but that was where the resemblance ended. They were facing away from her, and a tangle of long, wild hair fell down their back, knotted throughout with different coloured items, and topped with a spiky, bone-like circlet on their head.

They seemed to be wearing some kind of covering, just as the Master did at times, except these ones were fitting and patterned and…odd. Their skin was odd too, what little she could see of it. Pale, but greyish, and without any form of internal light that she was used to seeing from her companions. It was also lightly speckled, with the occasional stripe…like her.

Then the figure turned, and its one blue and one yellow eye glinted in the dull light. "Shulamithe. And here I thought you'd stay in the death-sleep forever."

For once, hearing her name in the Old Tongue *didn't* bring that usual feeling of peace. Peaceful stared at her old friend in dismay, wondering what had gone so very wrong. Was that a crown he was wearing? It looked horrible. His voice hadn't sounded right either, not nearly as smooth as it ought to be. "Bright?"

"DO NOT CALL ME THAT NAME!"

Peaceful reared back, a little startled, and not-Bright lifted his chin, staring down at her with those still familiar, bi-coloured eyes. They were like always – although nothing else, *nothing else* was the same. "What happened?" she asked quietly. "Why was I in a wall?"

His eyes narrowed. "It seemed as good a place as any for you. You were asleep for millennia, and we kept tripping over you."

"Oh." That sounded reasonable. "What's sleep? What's a millennia?"

There was another silence. "Oh, the world you find yourself in, Shulamithe," he replied finally. "What a surprise it will be. What do you remember from before?"

She tried to focus on her last memory before the dust and greyness, but it was all a blur and a jumble of senseless images. They'd been watching the sunrise…hadn't they? "Nothing of what brought us here."

There were a few seconds of silence, then not-Bright said in his new, raspy voice, "We were betrayed. Our former master stripped us of all of powers without even giving us a chance to defend ourselves, then trapped us in this prison, away from the water of life. Look at us." He raised his arms, showing clawed fingers and dry, cracked skin. And those stripes… "Look what he did to us, Shulamithe. You're here with us too, for your crimes. Are you angry? Are you afraid?"

Peaceful wrinkled her nose. That was a lot of information, but something about it didn't resonate with her. Although it was clear that something truly dreadful had happened, and no doubt it was from lack of water. But what was *she* doing here? "This is truly unexpected. But you know fear – or anger – isn't part of my personality, B- er…what shall I call you?"

Not-Bright turned away, looping his hands together behind his back. "They call me the Tiger," he said casually. "After that dirt-creature. The predator. Because of my stripes, and my power."

Stripes. Predator. Then something he'd said earlier finally registered. *Crimes…what crimes?* "What?"

And then he told her. He told her about how she'd been injured down on the dirt-world, and he'd tried to help her. Then they'd had a disagreement with the Master over…a different matter, and she'd been treated as one of them. Her past loyalty had been forgotten, and she'd been cast down here too, into a world which was much, *much* less hospitable than it had been before.

"You're still wearing the two-leg form," Peaceful pointed out. "And what about your stripes? You only had spots before."

The being-now-called-the Tiger blinked. "A side-effect of being cast down."

"Oh." She studied him again, curious now that her initial shock was fading. She hadn't panicked – really it wasn't in her nature – and all she could think of was that strange thing that

Master had said. *No matter what happens, you'll always listen. And I'll always call you…eventually.*

Hmm. It appeared he'd seen this coming – whatever *this* was. Because she hadn't committed any crimes. She knew at least that much.

"Where are we?" she asked curiously. Past the small space they were in, she couldn't see anything. It was like her senses had been blocked.

"I'll show you."

Peaceful got up and followed him, floating gently when her limbs proved too unsteady to move. They exited the narrow cave intersection they'd been in, moving into another, wider tunnel, then her old friend turned to see what she was doing. For a moment his expression twisted into something unfamiliar, something horrible.

"You can still fly," he said flatly.

"Oh," she said again. "Is that not normal?"

The Tiger paused a moment, then shook his head. "Not for those who've been cast down. Tell me, Shulamithe. Can you still hear your old master?"

Her old master, he'd said. Not his. But Peaceful carefully considered the question, stilling her mind and mentally reaching out for that warm presence, that light at the edge of her senses that was the Master. There was nothing. She frowned. "No."

The Tiger's mouth curved a little at the edges. "Come with me."

She followed him down the tunnel, surrounded by darkness with only a faint orange light, until they came out into an open area and the light became far brighter. They were at the edge of an enormous cavern, but with carvings all the way up the walls, to the very ceiling.

Figures moved around in every direction, and some sat in

front of what seemed like small windows cut into the rock, peering carefully at whatever lay on the other side. Peaceful could see shimmering streamers of different colours connected to the figures, each showing the use of alter-power, but of a sort she'd never seen before.

In the centre of the cavern was a round pool carved into the rock floor, glowing as orange as the burning heart of the dirt-world's sun, and it was the source of all that light. Peaceful could feel the heat coming from it even from here. Arranged around the burning orange pool were a dozen other, smaller pools. Each was a pale yellow rather than orange, and they stank of some strange chemical. There were People crouched around them, stirring their fingers through the liquid and muttering to each other.

People...? A moment later what she was seeing dawned on her. These were People just like not-Bright was a Person. That was to say, not very much at all. So what were they now?

"The scrying pools," the Tiger said casually, gesturing at those yellow circles with a clawed hand. "It's the way we see the outside world from this particular city, as we can no longer access it directly. There are more in the walls, although their vision is more limited. We can influence and control some on the outside, though. I'll set you onto the task shortly."

Peaceful was becoming aware of how much attention she was getting. One by one the former People turned and stared at her, each with familiar faces made unfamiliar by that horrible, dry, painful change. The lack of water, the lack of power. How *terrible*. "Sorry, what? Did you say we can't access the outside world? What world?"

The Tiger rolled his eyes. "The dirt-world, the light-world. Either! Come with me."

He took her by the arm and half-dragged her across the cavern to a small doorway just the right size to fit both of them.

Whoosh! A moment later they were standing somewhere entirely new, on the edge of a great dry desert. It had almost been like her usual way of moving, but not quite. To either side she could see more desert, stretching into the distance.

But unlike the red or yellow deserts of the dirt-world, this one seemed unnatural. It seemed like something had once been alive and full of water, but had been stripped dry, leaving the remnants all around. Although she couldn't see the sun, it appeared to be full daylight, and there were a few leafless husks of trees scattered about. More than that, there were ruins – remnants of what had once been buildings.

Peaceful stretched out her hand, and after a moment of dragging through the too-heavy atmosphere, she stood right upon those ruins, studying them. A mural here, a hint of carving there… "What happened?" she asked again.

But not-Bright/the Tiger didn't reply, and she turned to see a cloud of dust approaching. Two seconds later he stood by her side, an expression of displeasure twisting his new face. "You can still move directly from place to place."

"It was difficult," she allowed. *They* could not, she realised. Just like it seemed they couldn't fly anymore, and like how they were most unattractive to look upon now. "You moved very quickly just now. I have not seen that before."

"We do what we can," he replied tightly. "We still have some power, although not what we had before. What did you ask?"

"What is this?" Peaceful gestured at the ruins in front of her. "It looks like that old outpost where we would sometimes stay on the dirt world, but it's damaged."

Not-Bright/the Tiger studied her with an angled head. "You come out here, and you ask me about ruins? I told you how the realms were split, did I not? How this place was wrenched away from the light-world and the dirt-world, and how *those* two places were also separated. As for where we stand, it is a place that was part of the dirt-world, but no longer." Then he lifted a hand and pointed to one side, somewhere she hadn't yet properly looked.

She followed his gesture. What she'd first taken for the too-bright sunlight was in fact something else entirely. In the distance from where they stood, there was a barrier. It shot right up into the air from the ground, stretching in every direction, and even without her extra senses she knew it was an ultimate barrier. There was no way around it. It shimmered slightly like gold or amber, and she could just make out shapes through it.

"Through there," the Tiger said grimly, "is the dirt-world. They call it Earth now. Simplistic, yes?"

Earth. Peaceful shrugged, but she was fascinated. She made her way right up to the edge of the barrier, noting as she did so that she could see right through. There were cities in the distance, made of some kind of pale stone, and swarming with two-legs. Absolutely swarming with them, all sizes and colours, and draped in strange cloth. "How can there be so many?" she breathed.

"The *humans* breed quickly," he replied with a twisted smile. "They've covered this whole world, and look likely to pack it tighter, unless something else happens."

"But..." There hadn't been many before. Just a few, really. "How long has it been?"

"Days and nights don't pass on this side of the barrier."

"But on the dirt...*Earth* side?" Peaceful persisted curiously. "How long since we were cast out?"

The Tiger shrugged. "Many thousands of Earth days and nights."

Ohhh. Peaceful couldn't fathom such a length of time. Back on the light-world, 'time' hadn't really passed. Things happened, but the essence of the People remained the same. It was only on the dirt-world where life changed so rapidly. Now it was full of 'humans'…

She was quiet for a long while until her old friend said, "Now you know what has been done to us, Shulamithe. You will join in our fight to reclaim what we've lost."

You will, he'd told her. Not *you may.*

She looked again at that horrible, bony, spiky crown on his head, and wondered if he saw himself as some sort of king. But she didn't respond to his statement. It wasn't over, and this wasn't her life. She wouldn't accept it. There had to be something more…

"But first you'll change your name," he continued. "And with that new name comes a new identity. You're not what you used to be. Who are you now?"

Peaceful turned to face him, looking him straight in the eye, and refused to drop her gaze. She could clearly see that he'd changed on the inside. Not just in terms of power or strength, but in his essential character. Now there was pride, and the determination to control without anything controlling *him.*

She'd seen hints of it before, she realised, when they'd been watching the sunrise over the dirt-world. She'd marvelled, but he'd been unhappy, and had despised what had been before them. And there was no doubt in her mind in that moment, that pride was a good part of what had sent them down here. If only she could ask the Master…

"Your name," the Tiger repeated.

Peaceful lifted her chin. She noticed that *he* hadn't given his true name; the one that showed his truest identity on the inside. "I'm still Shulamithe on the inside," she replied evenly. "That has not changed."

Two seconds ticked by. "Then you'll be Shu," he said flatly. "If we have to change, so do you. Now come inside. I've got things for you to do."

And that, she realised ironically, was how she gained a new master of sorts.

Lunden, 1819 AD

"If I can't go to the Mountain of Glass, then I want to go to the River," Edward said plaintively, his shirt half over his head. He'd finally got out of bed and was in the process of clothing himself. "I want to go at once, George."

It was the dozenth time Edward had said such a thing, which rather concerned George. Firstly because he'd agreed eleven times already – once he found a local River source – and secondly because his brother was showing very childlike characteristics. It seemed highly likely that the man's faculties had been damaged. He suggested as much to Olivia, quietly enough that Edward would not hear.

"I thought so too at first," Olivia agreed in a whisper. "But then I recalled that Edward always acts in such a fashion when he is ill. Do you recall that illness he had about a twelve-month ago, before we were married? It was all coddling and possets and woe-is-me. I tell you, at the time I truly considered breaking off our engagement, at least until your mother assured me he was rarely ill."

"What are you saying over there?" the man in question called. He'd begun struggling into his own clothing, eschewing even the help of his valet. He would not wait, he'd said. He must go *now* to the River. Now, before the Creatures came back and stole him away, or before he tripped and landed on his head again. "What are you saying, Livvy?"

"Just that you are rarely ill," his wife called back. She glanced back at George, her pale eyes weary. "But you *can* take us to this River, can you not? It is not merely a story to keep his worries at bay?"

Or mine, her expression seemed to say. And that was the moment that George realised something. He had been truly blessed, and truly gifted by his strange travels, because he *had* been to the River, and he *had* met Amaranthus. He'd taken it for granted, had hoarded that experience to himself and hadn't thought to share it. After all, he could not take others through the gateways, could he?

But there *was* a River. Someone had told him it was spread throughout the entire world, and that one only had to know where to look for ways to access it. If only he knew, then he could take Olivia and Eddie and his mother...and anyone else who would come.

"I will," George answered, and he knew in his heart it was a solemn vow. "Now just a moment, and I'll see what Ashlea knows."

He pulled out his mobile phone that was now running low on battery, and quickly dialled her number. But unlike before, the phone didn't ring. It didn't go straight to voicemail, as it would if her battery was dead. Instead the call just ended.

"Hmm." *That* was rather inconvenient. So George went on to the next option, which he wasn't so fond of. He pulled out a pair of spectacles from his jacket pocket, put them on his face, and set himself to...wait for it...sending a *text message.*

BY...JOVE...WHAT IS HAPPENING... he began laboriously, then realised he was writing all in capital letters. Ashlea had assured him this was the equivalent of shouting, and it just wasn't done! He sighed, carefully deleted the message, then tried again.

Unable to reach you by phone. Please call. Much love, George.

There, that should hit the spot. Now for the slightly harder task – finding a new access point to the River. It couldn't be *that* hard, could it?

The Mountain of Glass

"Oh *Jon*," Elspeth said again, staring at the faint shimmering patch that marked a gateway. It sat just over the rock wall at the edge of the Mountain of Glass, surrounded by some rather pretty fruit trees, and there was no doubt at all that he had left through it.

They'd said he would, she realised desolately, but she'd been hoping 'twould not be for much longer. And she'd been certain he would have bid her farewell…

"If he's left without me, then he would not wish me to follow," Elspeth said aloud, attempting to sound decisive. "Or…if he has left without me, mayhap he *does* wish me to follow," she tried again. "Merely to say farewell."

Yes?

She looked at the gateway once again, dancing from one small foot to the other with agitation. She had never dared to step through one of these gateways without the most explicit instructions to do so. As she'd been told by Ash, Anne *and* George, one might end up in the strangest places. Why, there might be a…a…a pit full of serpents on the other side!

Unlikely, Elspeth allowed. Surely Amaranthus would not allow a gateway directly from the Mountain to such a terrible fate. And why rescue Jon at all, if only to kill him at a later date?

"But mayhap I should just check," she suggested to herself.

No one shouted for her to 'stop, fool!' so she very carefully leaned forward and set one finger through the gateway. There was a tingle of alter-power, the same as she'd felt the other times she'd used such methods of transport, and then she felt air on the other side. Nothing odd, merely air. Neither hot, nor cold, nor particularly damp.

Hmm. But she could not *see* what lay before her, could she?

So 'twas with great trepidation that Elspeth leaned forward, sucked in a deep breath, and pressed just her face against the shimmering space. There was a tingle, then suddenly she was looking out into a scene of deep twilight. She smelled brine, and heard the splashing sound of what surely had to be waves, and mayhap even the sound of mingled voices in the distance. A sharp bark of laughter…

Hmm. 'Twas difficult to make out much even so, Elspeth allowed. 'Twas not quite fully dark, but still she struggled to see what truly lay before her. Water to her left; seeming black and rippling under who-knew-what light. To her right, and before her, the shapes of what might be foliage. But where was the ground?

She leaned forward a little more until her chest was also through the gateway, and pondered a moment on how odd she must look. From this place, she would be a disembodied head. From the Mountain, a be-skirted bottom…

Elspeth giggled to herself, then lost her balance. She trembled in place, one arm flinging forward through the gateway to wave wildly in the darkness, and then caught her balance once more.

Phew, that was close! Imagine if-

"Eek!" Too late. She'd wobbled once again, and both arms were now windmilling through the wrong side of the gateway.

Then with a shriek of dismay, she fell forward into darkness.

Erastus, 2598 AD

I'll come with you, Joy Silver had suggested. And while Ash still thought that the dark archway before her looked terrifying, that offer of companionship was enough to spur her through.

She *had* to go. She had to get to the Mountain, and then get back to George. Besides, she still had the protective medallion in one pocket, the same as she had ever since they'd realised she was pregnant. It had saved both her and George more than once, and felt better than wearing a bulletproof vest. (Or what she imagined wearing a bulletproof vest might feel like. Sturdy?)

"Thank you," Ash told the woman gratefully. Then she took a deep breath, repressing everything inside that said *this is a bad idea!* then stepped through.

Unlike the usual remnant gateways, this one carried with it a chill that ran down her neck and arms as she stepped through, and she shivered even as she tried to make out her new surroundings. She now stood in a place almost the same as what she'd left. There was damaged white stone underfoot, the faint ruins of pillars and rocks to her left and right, and darkness overhead.

Ooh wait, that was new. It looked like she was in a cave, the sort that she'd once been made to explore as part of a school trip, and had tried to convince herself it was fun while really she had been terrified she'd die down there in the dark...

Whew. Ash took a deep breath, blinked a couple of times, then looked around again. Nope, still the same. Rocks, ruins, cave ceiling, darkness. And what she didn't see? The River, or any water at all.

"Joy," she began as she turned to face the archway. But Joy wasn't there either. In fact, neither was the exit. Instead that carved archway was now completely solid: filled with stone as though it was a wall rather than a door.

"Um," she said aloud, feeling her heart sink into her stomach. She poked at the rock a few times as if it would give under her touch, then tried closing her eyes and doing the same. Supernatural gateways were often disguised, and if it was illusion then she might need to convince her mind before her body could move through. But even with her eyes closed, the rock didn't give. Not at all.

"Damn it, damn it, damn it to Hades!" she shouted suddenly. "When will I freaking learn not to trust nice-seeming strangers?!" But Mama Silver *had* seemed so nice!

Yeah, but she'd also ignored all those doubts she'd had about her, Ash realised. Perhaps it hadn't been petty jealousy after all. Perhaps it had been something more intuitive than that.

Her belly twisted and cramped, and suddenly she leaned forward and retched onto the pale stone – the meal she'd been gifted having come right up again. "Urghhh," she moaned, resting her hands on her bent knees. If there was any time for her to have morning sickness, did it have to be right now?

Eeeeeeeeee. Oooooohhhhhh…

Ash's heart just about leapt out of her chest at the faint noises, and she jolted upright. They seemed to be coming from somewhere to her right, somewhere in the rock/ruins. There were gaps down there, gaps where only darkness was visible. And that cold chill she'd had while coming through the door? Still there. Worse, in fact, like it permeated the air surrounding her. Cold to the bone.

She shivered, wrapping her arms around her and wishing desperately that far-sight had jumped in before she'd made such a stupid move.

Up ahead there was the sound of movement, from just out of sight in the cave. It seemed to curve around, perhaps in a tunnel, but who knew? Ash backed away into the now-blocked doorway, but there was nowhere to go. Then a figure came into sight. It was small, squat and almost covered by a hooded cloak, but she could still see its face. It looked like a toad had bred with a very ugly human, and she knew at once what it was.

Creature.

Argh!

Ash sucked in a deep breath, preparing to – what? scream? – but then the thing paused. It cocked its head to the side, looking around as if it couldn't see her. But how could it not? She was right in front of it, barely ten metres away. Was it blind?

The seconds stretched by into minutes, then finally the Creature let out a very humanlike huff. It turned on its heel and disappeared the same way it had come.

Ash's hand was burning, and she realised she'd been clenching her fingers around the protective medallion where it sat in her pocket. She released them a little, wincing at the pain, and stood frozen for a few moments, her heart still pounding.

She was in the Other. There was no doubt of that.

She was in a cave, with no way to go up, or out.

She *might* be invisible, but she wasn't keen on testing that. The Creature could just as easily have been short-sighted. (Her mother would get a similar expression on her face when squinting at the TV sometimes without her glasses, although thankfully a lot less toad-like.)

So it was with extreme reluctance that Ash finally gave up on getting back through that archway, and tiptoed across the cave-ish place after the Creature.

Help!

SEVEN
THE ISLAND OF EXILES

Somewhere dark...

Elspeth's head hurt. It pounded rather like John the blacksmith was striking it over and over with his hammer; which was a most unpleasant thing to imagine. And her back, it burned like she'd been whipped for disobedience, which had happened just the once when she had been a wee child, and mayhap a little too open with her words. And she could feel an odd pressure on her ankle, like someone was holding it and dragging her along the ground.

Elspeth's eyes snapped opened, and in an instant she remembered. She was not back in Iversley, 1556, the bastard sister of the local Countess. Instead she was in some strange new place, and she *was* being dragged along the ground by her ankle. How very alarming! (And uncomfortable!)

"Release me at once!" she hollered, mimicking her aristocratic sister as she kicked out at whoever held her.

Suddenly she was stopped short, and her leg was released to fall heavily onto the ground. It felt like she lay on gravel, and her simple skirts were completely askew. Heedless of her pounding head, she scrambled to a sitting position, straightened her skirts and squinted at her attacker. As her eyes adjusted to the half-dark she could see him quite well. A hulking male figure with short hair, jug-like ears, and a daft expression...

The man stared, and Elspeth stared back, until finally she

grew confused rather than frightened. "Why were you dragging me so?" she asked finally.

The man shrugged. "You was too 'eavy to carry."

He spoke a form of Anglish, which seemed like a miracle. Elspeth now recalled how when she'd met Jon outside the Mountain, they had not been able to communicate at all, for they had spoken different languages. Forsooth, she had not even thought of how this would be a problem; but mayhap 'twas not after all. Moreso since the man seemed stupider and less frightening with every word he spoke.

"And why were you trying to carry me?!" she persisted. "Where am I? Who are you? What happened?"

The man just blinked, and his jaw dropped open a little, thus confirming her original impression that he was a half-wit. "Found you on the ground. You must 'ave taken a hard knock to the 'ead. Taking you to John."

Mayhap it had been a rescue rather than an assault, Elspeth allowed. For it did seem that she had fallen some distance, perchance onto her poor head. As she glanced up behind her, she glimpsed a faint light high in the air – was *that* the gateway? 'Twas high indeed. But 'twas his last comment that truly caught her attention. "Jon? He is here?!"

"Yeah." Then the half-wit raised an arm and pointed off into the distance, whereupon she could see faint red lights like the glow of torches, set amongst what might have been buildings or foliage.

"Verily, this is most excellent tidings! Take me to him at once!" Elspeth ordered, then paused, realising she sounded far too imperious for the situation – or for *her*. Mayhap the knock to her head had made her forget her position. "If you will, please sir."

The man stared at her a little longer with his mouth unappealingly open, then shrugged. He turned and began walking towards the lights, and naturally she followed. As she trotted to keep up across the stony, barren ground, her mind began to swirl with anxious thoughts.

What would Jon say about her arrival? They both knew they were meant to say farewell eventually, although she was most reluctant to do so. Would he be unhappy to see her? It was too late for that now – mayhap she might say that her arrival 'twas an accident, and mayhap he might be *glad* to see her…

But then they reached the cluster of buildings, and there really wasn't time to think any further. The buildings were a series of one-storey huts, built from the local rock, as well as what appeared in the dim light to be debris like driftwood. Without wanting to be unkind, Elspeth found herself scrunching up her nose in dismay. When Jon had said he was a Prince of the Air (whatever *that* might mean; she believed it had something to do with flight) she had not pictured his kingdom being quite so humble.

Then the half-wit pointed at one of the nearer shacks. "'E's in there."

Ah. That wasn't so difficult. Elspeth gave a quick curtsey as thanks, then headed over to that particular shack. She paused outside the rough-hewn door, then knocked carefully. Even so, a piece of wood loosened and fell to the ground. "Oops."

She bent to pick it up, but then the door swung open. Elspeth paused, half-crouched to fix the door, and looked up with wide eyes. The man on the other side of the door raised an eyebrow. He was not very old, mayhap five-and-twenty, and his long, black hair fell over a roughly handsome face.

He was also emphatically not Jon.

"You are not Jon!" Elspeth blurted out in dismay.

"Is that so, darling?" The man raised his eyebrow even

further, which ought to have been impossible. It was near up at his hairline. "Indeed I am John."

"No, you are not!"

"Yes, I am. My name is John. J.O.H.N."

"Not *my* Jon," Elspeth muttered. She stood, noting that she reached this John's chin. *Her* Jon was rather taller, and handsomer too. She sighed in colossal disappointment. "I do beg your pardon, sir. I thought you were someone else."

"Women always say that," this John quipped, then laughed. "Ah well, come in. You're the newest, no doubt. Shipwreck?"

"Pardon?"

"Did you come in by shipwreck," he repeated. "Most people do, since it's an island. But I think there are one or two other entrances."

An island? And not even slightly where she had intended to go! "In truth, I fell from a remnant gateway in the sky and landed on my head," Elspeth explained, stepping away from the door. She could still feel the throbbing, and knew she'd have an egg there soon enough. "But I fear I cannot stay to chat. I must find *my* Jon. Where would he be, please?"

John didn't seem to like that. His eyebrows lowered abruptly, and he scowled at her. "I'm the only John on the island, darling. I'm also the leader of this ragtag band of exiles, so you'll want to be *nice* to me."

Elspeth couldn't help herself; she took another step back. "My apologies if I have caused offence," she said carefully, her mind working furiously. She'd found herself in this situation with over-reaching males more than once back in sixteenth-century Angland, and the answer had always been to deflect, deflect. "An island of exiles, you say? An Anglish one?"

It worked. "What's Anglish?"

"Er…of Angland. The language we speak now."

John's eyebrows shot up again, both of them this time. "I'm not speaking any *Anglish*, darling. You just hear me that way. It's a little quirk from how this island is in the Other realm, as is the sea around it. People come in by accident from those little entrances out in the water, or maybe in the air, as you say. And then we're all here, as one big, happy family."

Mayhap there was a touch of sarcasm in that last sentence, but Elspeth's attention had fixed on his previous sentence. An island…in the Other. 'Twould explain the lack of vegetation, as excepting the Mountain of Glass, the Other seemed to grow nothing at all. But the Other did seem to have something less pleasant: Creatures.

Ohhh. Mayhap her Jon *was* here after all, as he'd spoken of Creatures ruling his homeland. She swallowed. "So, you know each of this island's inhabitants?"

"Indeed I do, darling." John seemed to have relaxed into good humour again, and he leaned against the rickety doorframe. Another piece of wood fell and he stumbled a little, scowled, then leaned against the other side. "But don't say you're still looking for this other Jon. As I said, I'm the only one on the island. I know everyone, and I know you won't do better than me."

Elspeth blinked rapidly. 'Twas these situations where she could not tell the truth, for 'twould bring trouble, but neither did she know the right lies to tell. *No sir, I do not find you appealing at all. You have just the sort of brash, dull-minded personality I find most unattractive.* "Er…"

"There's no escape from this place either," John continued. "The sky gateways are all far too high for anyone to climb back through, and no one's going to risk the Other sea in search of the exits out there. Nope, you're here to stay, darling."

Never! Elspeth wanted to shout, but instead she leaned back and tried to think of what to say. How to be polite but truthful? In this moment, it seemed impossible.

"SKY PIRATES INCOMING!"

The shout from outside the hut caught both of their attention, and suddenly the-wrong-John was pushing past her, looking up towards the darkened sky. "Weapons at the ready!" he hollered. "They won't get us this time!"

Who won't get us? But then Elspeth looked up and saw the most incredible sight. 'Twas a ship in full sail, with masts and sails glowing white as it soared *through the sky* down towards them. There were a few flashes of light, such as might occur when a more modern weapon was fired, and then the ship dropped low, so very low that had she been in the right spot, she might have reached up and touched its bow.

There were shouts from down on the ground, return shots fired mayhap? But then the ghostly ship was soaring away from them, back up into the darkness, becoming smaller and smaller until it resembled a tiny star.

"Ohhh..." Elspeth had been more enthralled than afraid, so now she raced out as if she could reach the ship, if only she ran fast enough. It had left her far behind, but she came to a halt well away from John's hut and stared up at that tiny glowing speck. A flying ship. Who had ever heard of such a marvel?

"We drove them off this time," a familiar male voice said from her left. "But you've got to be careful, darling. A little girl like you would be easy prey for their kind."

By the Rood, he'd followed her! Elspeth barely refrained from stamping her foot. And she was not so very little, thank you very much; merely not *tall*. "I thank you for the warning," she replied tersely. "These...sky pirates, they come to steal from your, er, settlement?"

John slung what appeared to be an old musket over his shoulder, and stood in what he might think was a heroic pose. "They take what they can. But mostly they take people. We have new visitors like you come once a year or so. And sure enough, most of the time the sky pirates will have stolen them away within a month, never to be seen again."

Elspeth quickly made sense of her situation. She'd fallen from a height – she *needed* to find that gateway! – but there was also someone who could fly through the air, mayhap close to her very gateway. "How often do these sky pirates visit you?" Soon, she hoped. This island did not seem very hospitable.

"Every night."

"EVERY NIGHT!" Even Elspeth was startled by her own vehemence. But then she remembered. "But in the Other, day and night does not truly pass. So how can there be a night?"

John blinked, then grinned, revealing several gold-plated teeth. "Fair point, darling. So you know a little about the Other, do you? They come regular as clockwork, and I'd say it's about a day apart each time."

"What do they do with the people they take?"

He shrugged. "Who knows. Eat them, probably, since there's little food to be found here." He stepped forward, setting an arm around her shoulder. "But I'll look after you. Never fear."

Elspeth wasn't so sure about the cannibalism. From the little she'd seen of that ship, it hadn't had a sense of evil about it. Was it possible that she could discern such a thing without true knowledge? Nevertheless, that was how it seemed.

John's arm, however, was heavy and most definitely unwanted. She'd had her share of uninvited attention, mostly back in 1556, but she had not come to any harm due to her noble sister's protection. Even so, she'd perfected the art of avoidance. So now she tried to slide sideways out from under his arm, but his grip tightened.

"It's a dangerous life here," he said low into her ear. "And you don't seem to get it, darling. I'm the authority here, and so you'll do what you're told."

It was a dangerous life anywhere, forsooth! And now a little of Elspeth's seldom seen temper kicked in. She might not be large nor strong nor nobly-born, but she was *not* under this strange John's authority! He hadn't even asked her name, not once. "I'm not your darling!" she snapped, then let her body fall slack. She must have surprised him because he let her fall, so she ducked and scrambled from his grasp.

"Hey!"

The stones underfoot were a little loose, and as she ran, she could see him right behind her in her peripheral vision. Now desperation spurred her along, and she hiked up her full skirts, trying not to stumble.

"Got you!"

A strong hand grabbed hold of her shoulder but she pulled away, feeling the fabric of her loose jerkin give. She was an inch away from falling on her face, but her arms windmilled and this time she kept her balance. She scrambled away, leaving the jerkin behind.

She heard a grunt of pain, and she glanced over her shoulder to see John had fallen down hard on the rocks, with her garb still clutched in one fist.

"My face," he groaned. He did indeed have a bloodied patch above one eyebrow. "You vicious little wench, you hit me in the face!"

"I most certainly did not," she snapped back. "But I will if you do not leave me be! I'd rather go with man-eating sky pirates than with one such as you!"

Then with her store of bravery used up, Elspeth turned and ran as fast as her legs could carry her.

The Tapestry Room, Mountain of Glass

Amaranthus stood by the tapestry, watching a patch of threads carefully. He stood by himself, but he wasn't alone; the presence of this tapestry meant he was *never* alone.

Briefly his hand raised to touch a fine, very long white thread that ran along the entire edge of the tapestry. It was surrounded by black, and from a different point of view it might have seemed black too. But that was an optical illusion. He knew this Person, and he knew exactly where their loyalties lay. He also knew that when he called their name, they'd come running. It was the sort of Person they were.

But then he lowered his hand, and the faint blue image vanished. *Not yet,* he thought. *But soon.*

After the Rift 1 BC

The newly named 'Shu' sat quietly in the middle of chaos for who knew how long. Around her, the ex-People squabbled and swore and looked through a thousand little windows into what they now called the human realm. They were behaving unlike anything she'd ever seen or ever expected. It was as if they had lost their goodness when they'd lost the living water, and she could only sit and take it in.

I'm not like them, she thought. *I'm still* me.

But they didn't know that. The former Bright, her ex-best friend, didn't know that. He'd lost the ability to hear her deepest thoughts, although she did notice that he seemed to hear some of the others' thoughts with direct contact. He controlled them, he manipulated them, and in return they controlled and manipulated each other.

"Shu, you worthless slag!" someone shouted from her left. "What are you doing?"

Slag? What did that even mean? Peaceful turned and stared evenly at them until they quietened. "Acclimatizing," she replied finally. "And what are you doing, Speed?"

Jittering in place, was what Speed was doing. She was thin to the point of wiriness, with her many limbs now looking hard, dull and brittle like they all did, and her large eyes now bulging and flickering from side to side, too fast to follow. "Call me Haste now. And I'm managing the scrying pools and windows."

"What's managing?"

"It's when I tell other people what to do, and then stand over them and tell them they're doing it wrong," Haste answered. She grinned, showing sharp, yellowed teeth. "I don't do it myself, though. It's quite a skill."

"Indeed," Peaceful said a little dryly. "So everyone has changed their names, I see."

Haste shrugged. "Changed ourselves, changed our names to match. *You* have as well."

Perhaps she had. But not on the inside. She changed the subject. "What are the scrying pools for?"

"Here, come have a look." Haste led Peaceful over to the centre of the room, where a ring of yellow pools sat embedded in the floor. Like the other room with the fire-pool, these pools all smelled vile, and each had faint, quick images flickering across their surface.

Peaceful watched for a while, seeing images of the dirt-world but mostly of humans; so, so many humans. She saw entryways into this realm from the human realm – but only one way, for the humans to come in but not for the ex-People to escape. She saw disaster and destruction and pain of a sort she never could have imagined, and she saw that most of the humans were as dry as these ex-People were too. Dry and dead on the inside, lacking the light that came from the living water.

It wasn't the same as alter-power. She saw images of humans doing incredible deeds, some of them glowing with alter-power, but clearly dead, dead, dead on the inside. This terrible thing that had happened to the ex-People? It had touched the humans too. The Master's *pets*.

But some were different. Some had a flicker of inner light, of true power, even if outwardly they looked plain or even ugly. "What is this?" she asked quietly.

"Visions of the future," Haste replied, sounding bored. "Or possible futures. We see what we can, then work to manipulate the outside world. Encourage what we want, stop what we don't."

Haste hadn't understood what she'd meant, Peaceful realised. But she didn't need Haste's explanation about why the light was still showing in some humans, because she already knew what it meant. Her master Amaranthus was still working. He'd have some marvellous plan underway…

But then something new appeared on the surface of the closest pool, and a moment later was echoed across the other pools. It was a burst of light, of life, and for a moment it lit up the entire cavern like a tiny sun. Then Peaceful could see it was like a star falling from the light-world, through the barrier onto the dirt-world. It grew smaller and more intense until it solidified into the image of…a baby. A human infant, small and wrinkled and ugly.

Waaaahhh.

That was the infant, not Peaceful. But then the image vanished, and she was left puzzled.

"Now that, we've been seeing for centuries," Haste said. She'd started jittering high-speed, side to side, her eyeballs practically vibrating. "We don't know where or when, but we know it has to be soon. *He's* going to do something, something significant with a useless human baby, but we don't know what. Not yet."

'He' clearly meaning Amaranthus. A little burst of joy shot through Peaceful at the knowledge. Both worlds were in chaos, but not really. Not at heart, not if the Master hadn't forgotten them. "Interesting," was all she said. Then because her heart felt full, and she feared she wouldn't be able to hide it, she changed the subject again. "But I thought we lost most of our power. Where did these pools come from?"

"You remember the Mas- I mean, the *Enemy* was making gifts for his pets, before the Rift?"

"Sure." Peaceful more than remembered it; she'd been a part of it. She remembered the suggestions she'd made, things that would help the humans not be so helpless.

"We stole some as we were leaving." Peaceful's eyebrows shot up in shock, but Haste continued. "Flight, knowledge, strength, speed. Everything that would help us to live away from the Heart, and away from its water. But after the fiasco with the flight vial – well, we just tipped the knowledge into these pools instead. It seemed safer than drinking directly from the vials."

"And what happened with the flight vial?" Peaceful asked the question because she remembered well how ex-Bright had watched her when he'd seen she could still float. He'd been jealous, so she'd figured he'd lost that ability. And she couldn't see him letting anyone else take it.

Haste's gaze flickered across the cavern to where a broad

blue-grey back was visible in front of a few smaller ex-People. Her voice dropped low. "See those wings?"

Peaceful did a double-take. What she'd thought to be some sort of loose cloth was actually two small, drooping wings, made of the same blueish leathery skin as covered his whole body. Those wings were definitely new, and definitely too small to be of any value for a body that size. Wings, but no actual flight. "That was Strong, wasn't it?" she whispered.

"He's Brutal now," Haste whispered back, practically cowering. "He lost all self-control after the Rift, and you do *not* want to get on his bad side."

Peaceful saw her fear, but didn't take it on herself. Strong, or *Geburah*, had been a friend once. Now Brutal – or *Gerak* in the Old Tongue – was an entirely different being. Just like Bright or the Tiger. "What happened to Truthful?"

Haste grinned, once again showing those yellowed, sharp teeth. "Why don't you ask the Tiger about that? After you've done your work for today. You've been assigned a set of windows."

Peaceful barely held back a sigh. She'd figured out by now that if scrying pools showed possible futures, then the windows showed the present. She'd seen the ex-People reaching out to humans through them, whispering straight into their minds, influencing and manipulating them as much as the humans would allow.

And some of them allowed a *lot*. They didn't know any better, thinking that those voices or suggestions were just their own thoughts. And so many of them had coloured threads of power stretching from the windows to their hearts, linking each of them to one of those here. She could see the alter-power, the life-force, coming bit by bit into this place and into each ex-Person.

It was strange, because the humans she'd known before her long, unnatural sleep would have run a mile from someone like

Haste. But for the few humans who did see into this realm, the ex-People hid their appearances, making themselves seem far more beautiful, far more like their old selves…

Without realising, Peaceful had followed Haste over to the cavern wall, just in front of two dozen tiny holes, each filled with an image of the outside world. A small, barrel-shaped ex-Person sat in front of it, its little hands moving slowly but steadily between images. It was practically covered in threads of power, like a weaver at work at a loom.

Peaceful studied the images curiously, watching the two-legged figures moving around from scene to scene, blurring in and out of sight. But amongst those blurred figures was one that stood out clearly. It was obviously female, with skin as pale as Veritas' had been the last time she saw him.

The female wore her white hair in a long plait down her back, and even from behind, she didn't seem quite like the other humans. She had a glow of alter-power that Peaceful recognised, but it didn't seem like it was from the Master. Then she turned…

Peaceful jolted back a little, startled at the sight of the female's face. Ugh. It wasn't…it didn't look like the other humans.

Haste let out a hoot of laughter at her reaction. "Saw Lilith, did you? She's got a face like a bulldog got hit with a brick, doesn't she?"

"Lilith," Peaceful murmured, a little ashamed of her response. Considering how different all People were, it would be hypocritical for her to be repulsed by a single, odd-looking human. The humans she'd seen varied a lot – but not like *that*. "She's…different."

"She's a half-breed," Haste said bluntly. "The offspring of the White Prince – you'd know him as Veritas or Truthful – and some long-dead human. She doesn't age like the other humans, and she's got a real talent with music, if you know what I mean?"

(Peaceful didn't) "…and she can move in between the human realm and this one. But damnatus, she's ugly as Hades, right?"

"Mmm." But Peaceful was trying to take in everything that had been said. Never mind that the female was unattractive, because frankly, so were all those ex-People around her right now. No, it was finding out that one of her own kind had *bred* with a human? Such a thing made her feel all twitchy and awful inside. It was just wrong, all kinds of wrong. "We weren't made for such a thing," she whispered to herself.

But Haste heard her, because she countered, "We do what we want. Well, all the high-ups do. As for you, you do what you're told." She pointed at the ex-Person sitting in front of them, with all the threads in his hands. "Sit down here, touch the window."

"But I'm in here, Haste," the seated ex-Person objected.

"Then move out the way, damnatus!" Haste snapped. She grabbed him by one arm and flung him aside. "There you go, Shu. Hurry up."

Peaceful glanced at the other apologetically, but he'd already waddled off to another free location, leaving the threads of power open-ended and unused. She carefully seated herself, then gingerly touched a thread. Immediately flashes of images and words came into her head, confirming that the thread was a link to a single human. Now she did sigh. "What do you want, Haste?"

"All of them here, dead," Haste snapped. "But we won't get that right away. One by one we'll bring them if *he* doesn't get them first, and their life force will boost our power enough to break the barrier. And you're going to help."

Dead. That meant like these ex-People here, Peaceful realised. She swallowed, briefly closing her eyes. "But the humans aren't like us," she said quietly. "I can see it already. Their bodies will decay and return to the dirt-world. How can they come here, if they're dead?"

"Their essences, fool! Their will and minds and personalities. Their alter-power, their spark of life! *That's* what feeds us, that's what gives us power even if their fragile bodies have disappeared." She leaned forward into Shu's face, her own expression very ugly. Her breath was worse. "And even if we don't break the barrier? We'll hurt *him,* and that makes it worth it."

"Revenge," Peaceful murmured. She couldn't think of anything that would hurt the Master more than losing his precious two-legs, the ones made to look like him. His true children. She could feel it now; the power in these walls. The feeling of darkness, of wrongness, went farther than just the wickedness of the ex-People. It was all the lives that had been stolen.

And stolen they had been. Now Peaceful knew, she could sense that many, many, *many* humans were trapped in this place, their true selves taken as fuel for the ex-People's revenge. And what made it worse? Based on how much time had already passed, it seemed likely it would be permanent.

Poor, poor humans. Poor Master. Perhaps even the loss of his People wouldn't have been as bad as this.

But of course Haste didn't know what Peaceful had been thinking. "Revenge, exactly!" She prodded a sharp finger into Peaceful's shoulder. "And you want it too, because you're down here with us. Now get to work."

Haste finally moved away, but Peaceful could still feel her eyes on her as she turned to the windows, and began to take the threads, one by one.

Peaceful? Maybe. Depressed, that would be a better name.

But then Peaceful saw something startling through one of the links. A single human, their mind filled with a sense of pain, and their body's connection to their own essence almost snapped.

An 'old' human, she realised. And one that was a mere inch

away from the barrier…

Without even thinking, she acted.

Peaceful dropped the threads, letting them scatter and wither. Perhaps in time they'd vanish and need to be recreated; she didn't care. Instead she vanished and then reappeared above the cavern, right out on the edge of the barrier, where the Other desert met the human realm.

The human was there, stumbling towards the barrier, mere yards away. His body was hideous: oddly lined and withered in that way the ex-People called 'old'. It was nearly worn out, and his essence was almost detached. Once it broke free, his body would decay and return to the earth, and his essence would become part of the cavern walls. Trapped forever; a terrible fate for a sapient being. Peaceful didn't *care* what this human had done or not done!

But the human had a milky film over his eyes. At first she thought it was part of being 'old', but then she realised it was more than that. It was the influence of the ex-People, that same thread that had allowed whispers into his mind and had most likely kept him away from the Master and from any real life.

He didn't know what he was heading into, she realised. He was walking straight towards a true, permanent death, and he had *no idea*.

Just then Peaceful saw that one of the ex-People was already waiting at the barrier for him. It wore a lovely illusion, cloaking it like a garment, and she knew that this human must have known about the Other realm – this prison – to some degree, but he didn't know who he was really dealing with.

The decrepit human reached the barrier and raised one hand towards its shimmering surface. "My beauty," he croaked. "I am here."

"You are here," the ex-Person murmured through that lovely,

illusive mouth. It stretched out one hand, mere inches away from the human. "Come through, and be with me forever."

The phrase translated to *damnatus* in the Old Tongue. Damned forever. Trapped forever.

No!

Fuelled by a fury she never knew she could feel, Peaceful shot towards the two. She knocked the ex-Person aside, and her own fingers touched the human's weak, wrinkled ones just as they breached the barrier. There was a moment where the human's eyes shot wide open, and then suddenly the milky film dropped away and he saw her as she really was. She could feel his shock and his fear and maybe a little joy, and Peaceful put all her strength into pushing him *away* from the barrier, into the human realm.

And then as he stumbled backwards away from that barrier, onto the hard earth of the human world…she fell through with him.

There was a moment where she felt as if she was light as air, as if she'd be sucked back through the barrier. But she was touching the human, and it seemed like he became hollow, and then suddenly she was falling *into* him-

Shu!

Peaceful blinked. Her eyes hurt. They felt dry and uncomfortable, and her lashes seemed to be stuck together. Something hard was under her back, and her whole body hurt. She stretched her limbs, feeling a horrible weakness and aching pain as she did so. *Ugh…*

Then she froze. She stretched once more, carefully this time, each limb separately. But something was horribly wrong. At the end of her lower limbs were these…wiggly little things! She tried to sit up to see them, but it felt as if her body was made of rocks.

Then finally she did it, and she saw herself…

"AAAAAHHHHHH!" She leapt up as if she could shake off the change, but the new, horrible, two-leg human body just went with her. Its frail, wrinkled limbs flailed with her panic, and its *other* extra appendages moved under old, smelly garments. "I'm a male!" she screamed in a hoarse, different-sounding voice. "A male!" *Ohhhhh, how had this happened!?*

"SHU!" someone shouted at her, sounding a long way away. "GET OVER HERE!"

Ooh, she didn't like that voice. In fact, she felt quite-…grumpy. Grumpy, even beyond the fact that she was WEARING THE WRONG BODY! But still she turned towards the voice, and she saw where she was.

There was that ex-Person who'd been wearing the lovely illusion, still in the same place, and looking very displeased. Next to them was another ex-Person, and another, all lined up along the barrier and staring at her with what looked like absolute shock, and another, uglier emotion. And then there was the Tiger…

"Finally," he said. "*Come here.*"

The words came through the barrier with some force, and she knew he'd intended it to be an absolute command, one she couldn't ignore. So rather than test whether she could disobey, she decided to do as he'd said. She walked carefully up to the barrier, each step feeling awkward, like she was manoeuvring a too-bulky puppet. "What?" she snapped in that wrong, male voice. "What is it that you want, oh great leader?"

There was a moment where the assembled ex-People gaped, and the Tiger's one blue and one yellow eye almost seemed to glow. Then he said very softly, "What was that, Shu?"

She suddenly realised what she'd said. "I do apologise," she said with some effort. "I…believe I have taken on the personality of this…form. It appears to be…"

"Suicidal?" someone piped up.

"Bad-tempered," she finished lamely.

"You haven't just taken on the appearance of the form," the Tiger continued, his eyes now truly glowing. "You've taken control. You're wearing it like a suit, even though you seemed to have cleaned it up somewhat. And you've gone through the barrier, Shu. How did you do that?"

Peaceful went very quiet, for the first time the silence in her mind showing its true form. She wasn't alone in that strange form. No, she was sharing it with another consciousness, one that sat quiet and confused at the very back of the body, almost like it was asleep or deeply drowsy.

"I don't know," she replied finally. "It was an accident." She'd wanted to save the human from a permanent death, but she sure wasn't going to tell the Tiger that. She had saved them…sort of. "Maybe because their essence was about to separate from their mortal form."

"Hmmm." There was a long moment where everyone seemed to stare at her, waiting for the Tiger's next words, and then he lifted one hand. "Everyone get out."

Half a moment later the others were gone, and it was just him and her in that weird human suit.

"You've really done it now," the Tiger said, sounding almost gleeful. "Oh, you've really done wrong, Shulamithe. You've stolen the body of one of the two-leg pets. That's worse than anything the rest of us ever did."

Was it? *But I was saving him,* inner-Peaceful argued. She didn't *feel* like she'd done horribly wrong.

Saved me? a very tiny voice said from inside her mind. It sounded like the human.

She released her control just a little and the body stumbled before she held it upright once again. But she knew that lapse was enough for the human to briefly awaken and see through her eyes – to see the barrier as she saw it from this side. To see the Tiger, and she felt his fear and sudden knowledge.

You saved me from that terrible creature, the human whispered. *Saved me.*

A warm glow began inside this strange form, pushing aside the fear and pain just for a moment. *So I did,* she agreed happily. And the ex-People would seem like frightening creatures to this human, wouldn't they? But to the Tiger she said, "I can't take it back. I don't know how to."

He grinned, showing his predator's teeth in that horridly lovely face. He really *had* been more attractive in his four-leg form, Peaceful mused.

"Then don't try," he said. "Wicked Shu, you are going to be my eyes and ears in that realm. You are going to do everything I tell you. Is that clear?"

It was clear that she must *look* like she was obedient. Because in that moment where she'd shown the human the truth, she'd also almost lost her grip on the body. She'd felt how she'd almost been pulled back through the barrier. Oh, what a precarious place she was in! But… "Yes," she replied.

"Good."

There was a moment where they just looked at each other; the two of them on either side of the barrier. Peaceful/Shu wearing the human's body, and ex-Bright in his own twisted form of a two-leg. The form that along with its natural speckles now had faint stripes just like her own… And how had that happened? she wondered with new suspicion.

"But you know it won't be enough," she said finally. "The humans' essence. You could take…oh, thousands. Millions even! It won't break that barrier."

"But it will cause *him* pain," the Tiger retorted. "And it pleases *me.* So it is enough. But there are other ways around the barrier – objects full of alter-power that will overcome even this obstacle."

Peaceful felt her heart beat faster. Was this true? And if so, did she want the Tiger to have them? For all of its horror, the barrier also seemed somehow protective. Protecting the humans, that was; not the ex-People.

"And you will also find me these objects," the Tiger said gently. "One by one, as I order you." He raised a clawed hand, showing a faint purple thread running from one finger. It ran straight to the human body's head, Peaceful saw. A link of power…of control.

She decided in that moment that her answer would always be yes. Yes, she would appear to do as she was told. And yes, she would do *everything* in her power to protect the humans, even as she appeared to follow the Tiger. And yes, she'd start with this one here, by finding a way to free him from this terrible fate. And yes, she would wait for the Master to remember her, to call her back, to let her come home.

After all, she wasn't Wicked Shu. She was Shulamithe, the Peaceful One, and she was *his*.

So Peaceful smiled at her false master with the decrepit human's face, and prepared to do something she'd never imagined she would ever do.

Follow his orders.

A HERO ARISES

Erastus, 2598 AD

The entire town of Erastus seemed to have congregated outside in the central square, all two thousand of them. There was a general sense of unease, but Aras couldn't blame anyone. He felt uneasy himself.

"This was supposed to be a safe place," Kamile said from somewhere down near his chest. She held Isla tightly in her arms, and her large brown eyes looked worried. That wasn't an expression he was used to seeing on her face. "Safer than Lile, safer than the Chosen."

"Nowhere is truly safe," Aras murmured. He stared a little blankly at the large screen currently displaying the councillors, now in quiet conversation rather than giving speeches. What he'd seen kept running through his mind, as well as the possible reasons for it.

He'd seen that kind of violence before; he'd been a soldier. But that kind of…explosive something…usually came from a weapon, not alter-power. And it _had_ been alter-power. Intense laughter, and then sudden death. What would cause such a thing? Twice in one day, too…

"That's not helpful, Aras!" Kamile snapped at him.

"What?"

She stared at him for a moment, then shook her head. "Never mind."

Fine, he wouldn't mind. He turned back to the main screen, his height letting him study it easily over the heads of the surrounding crowd. They'd said that there was danger – of course there was – and that people shouldn't travel alone. They'd said that anyone living in the outer houses should move into the centre of town, and they'd make room until the cause was discovered.

They lived in the outer houses, so they'd be moving. The only problem was, there was nowhere to go. Was the council planning to set up temporary shelter, he wondered, and would it even be helpful?

Aras glanced down again at Kamile, whose attention was now fixed on something one of the girls was saying. He felt himself soften a little. Tent living wouldn't be good for her, or for them, and it wouldn't be fair after everything they'd gone through. But how to fix it?

Out of the corner of his eye he saw a blur of white and silver.

"If only there was a way to fix this today," Joy Silver murmured from down by his side. It felt like she was saying it just for him, and surprisingly he hadn't seen her approach. "Then none of the upheaval would be necessary."

"Do you know something the council doesn't?" Aras asked bluntly. The council was made up of a dozen men and women, mostly older, mostly gifted in some way or another. All accustomed to their unusual environment, and all dedicated to keeping it safe. Safe from the Secular Republic, safe from anything nasty in the Other realm.

Joy shrugged, and he couldn't help noticing every detail of her movement. "No one knows everything. But I *do* know what sent that beast through earlier today. It's sent many things through to us, and I wouldn't be surprised if it was behind the deaths as well."

He looked down at her with new curiosity. "Well?"

"A dark being," she said flatly. "One of great power and great reach. An immortal, unable to come through to this realm itself, but determined to cause destruction. Destroy that being, and you'll save Erastus."

Fey, Creature, who knew? He waited, an eyebrow raised. "How?"

"Find it, and force it through the doorway to this realm. It won't survive the journey."

Aras pondered her words, turning away to gaze at the closest doorway and flexing his prosthetic metal hand thoughtfully. This doorway was smooth and made of slick black volcanic rock, and beyond it was grey fog. *Anything* could be through it. And while his strength was in his…strength, and he had experience of the Other, it wasn't his speciality. He was smart enough to know where he needed help.

"It'll take both power and physical strength," Joy continued in a low voice, leaning closer to him. "I have the first, but not the second. I can *gift* someone else the first – or at least protection – but I can't gain the kind of strength needed. But you already have that."

"You're asking me to go through a doorway, grab some evil immortal, and drag it back out here," Aras said. His voice was even, but he could feel his heart begin to pound faster with excitement and determination. Dangerous? Yes, but he could do it.

"It will die if you do. You saw what happened to that black beast this morning."

"Yes, but I helped it along with a knife," he said sardonically.

She shrugged. "Then help this one too. Or don't. It *is* dangerous, and I'm not offering to do it. The best I can do is narrow down which doorway, and perhaps strengthen the alter-power barriers preventing those beasts from getting through in the first place. Once you're done, of course. I note that the council blocked off the destroyed doorway earlier today, but not the one it had actually entered through. I wonder why that is?"

Joy's last words were a little sarcastic, and Aras's eyebrows shot up. Suddenly he found himself studying that big screen more carefully, with its silent display of the dozen councillors deep in conversation. Who had ordered the doorways blocked in such an ineffective way?

"I'm looking into it," she said very quietly, as if she'd known his thoughts. "But will you do it, Strong-Man? Will you go through the doorway? I can ask around, but I think we'll have better luck with one short, sharp hit. One man, not a whole squad."

"And you're sure this will stop the murders?" he persisted.

She frowned for a moment, then nodded. "I can't see what else is causing them. Wickedness of this type is very, very specific, very powerful. Your report from this morning states that the alter-power looked purple. I only know one who fits such a description; like a signature, if you will."

"Who?"

Joy paused, then checked around her to see that no one was listening. Then she leaned in, standing on her tiptoes to reach his ear, and he tried not to respond to the closeness. "The being," she whispered, "is called the Tiger."

Kamile finishing listening to Poli's intently told story about something that had happened at school the previous day, and turned back to Magdalene. As she'd been since the news came out, she was sullen, her eyebrows in flat, downward lines.

"We'll be OK," Kamile told her with as much certainty as she could manage. "They'll find the…killer." Even saying it aloud sounded terrible. Fire Lord, there was a *killer* out there.

"But he said there was no killer," Magdalene said for the dozenth time. "He *said*."

"So did Aras, so did I just this morning," Kamile countered as patiently as she could. "What makes this friend of yours so perfect that he can't be wrong once in a while?"

"I believe he's wrong," Magdalene said. She looked down, then turned away, her arms wrapped around herself.

Kamile watched her with a frown, but didn't push the subject. She still didn't know who the boy was. Poli didn't either, and that was unusual since the two usually wouldn't stop talking about everything – about boys, school, almost dying back in Lile…

"You know, I've had plenty of relationships that were just for fun," Kamile said, keeping her tone intentionally light. Mags still had her back to her, but she would be listening anyway. "Some of the boys were better than others, but I already knew most of them would never work out. So I was just trying to have a good time, you know?"

"Ew," Poli said, her nose wrinkled. "What's this got to do with a killer?"

So much for her chance to share some wisdom from her own life experience. "It's about something just as important," Kamile replied a little impatiently. "You girls are young, and you might choose to spend time with boys that you know won't be good for you long-term, but you think it won't matter because it's just for fun. So I wanted to say, from experience, that every relationship changes you in some way.

"Even if you can't remember the boy's name later, or even if you secretly think of him as your long-lost love, it changes you. So choose carefully who you spend time with."

The blank look on Poli's face showed that she didn't understand, and Kamile sighed. She wished someone had told her that ten years ago. No, she wished she'd *understood* that ten years ago. Even the fun, light relationships could go in a direction you'd never imagined.

She found herself looking across the crowd for Aras, who was the epitome of a 'fun' relationship turned weird and serious. She spotted him, head and shoulders above most of the others around him, but his attention wasn't on the speaker. Instead he was also leaning down and listening intently to a particular silver-haired, red-lipped woman in white.

Joy Silver was so very close to him, her full lips almost touching his ear, and Kamile could see the tension in his body even from here. They'd make a very attractive couple, she thought reluctantly. She'd always felt like she and Aras were a poor match: he was so tall and strong, and she was small and slim. Almost like a child next to him. Not his type.

There were only two weeks of faithfulness left until their handfast period ran out. And who knew if he was even faithful? He was gone most of the time, and they hadn't been together since Isla was conceived.

Kamile looked down at their daughter, sleeping in her arms with one tiny hand curled in a tight fist. "At least I have you," she whispered. Black and white ponies be damned.

But then she looked up again at Aras, and saw he was moving away through the crowd, away from the city square, and it seemed like Joy was heading in the opposite direction. Surely they weren't going to meet up somewhere?

Suddenly she found herself shoving Isla into Magdalene's arms. "Watch her please," she said with a terse smile of apology. Then pushing aside any sense of embarrassment, she turned and followed Aras.

Kamile might be small, but he was tall enough that she could see his blond head even through the bustling crowd. She followed him out of the square, between the large buildings in this area, then down several winding streets until finally he stopped at the end of a sort of alley; a wide space between two buildings. These ones had been painted in cheerful colours, and the ground between them had the scrubby grass so typical of this dry area.

At the back of the space was a high wall made of red brick, and a small, blue-painted door with a big shiny lock on its handle. It looked like the sort of lock that would test DNA before letting anyone in – high security for a place like this.

She held back, watching and waiting. What was he doing? This wasn't exactly the typical place for a tryst…

"You can come out, Kamile."

Damn. Caught, but pretending she hadn't been, she lifted her chin and sauntered into the alley. "Just being nosy," she said with false cheer. "Gone off to find the killer, have you? And Mama Silver's just being helpful?"

Aras grunted and set his attention to pulling something out of his pocket. He started to fit pieces together, which she recognised as being parts of a weapon. "Something like that."

"Seriously?" Kamile spat out in shock. "You're trying to find the killer?"

He kept slotting pieces together, but he levelled her an even, ice-blue stare. Oh, why did he have to be so attractive? "Of course."

"Oh." There was a moment of awkward silence, and Kamile found herself frowning. "So…you know who it is?"

He grunted again, but this time he turned away a little. She was getting better at interpreting those sounds after their time together, and she took it to mean either 'no, but I'm working on it', or 'yes, but you don't want to know'.

"And you know where they are?"

Another grunt.

"But Aras, that's dangerous!"

Now he stared at her, his eyebrows raised, before starting on the second weapon. It looked like some form of efficiency rifle, but smaller. Those would turn someone to dust. She knew it for a certainty – it was how Coryn had been murdered.

"So…they're dangerous," she persisted. "And you're going after them alone. Or is she coming with you?"

"*She* is just going to put a protective alter-power barrier over the doorway before I go through," Aras muttered. He didn't meet her eye. "We thought it better that I go quietly."

Several moments passed as his words began to make sense in her head. Then her temper rose. "Surely you weren't just going to leave without telling us," she said in a low voice. "Leave for a dangerous task that might get you killed, and leave YOUR CHILDREN with no idea what happened to you. You're going through a *doorway!?* Do you have any idea what's on the other side of those things?"

"No," Aras snapped suddenly. "I don't, because I haven't gone through one before, and neither have you since that 'special' doorway of yours was destroyed a month ago. But now I am going, and I'm going to use what I *do* have for the good of everyone. For you, and for my children who won't have a home to live in if this isn't sorted soon."

Kamile felt her eyes prick with tears. "But what if you don't come back?"

He looked away. "I'll come back."

She didn't believe him. Even if he came back through the doorway, wherever it was, he wouldn't be coming back to *her*. Not really, never again.

"Ready?" A voice came from Kamile's left, and made her leap in surprise. She turned to see Joy standing there, an expression of amused pity on her face. "Sorry, sweetheart. I'm told I move too quietly, but I find myself forgetting. Come to wave off our hero, have you?"

Kamile shrugged, feeling as awkward and inferior as she always did with this woman. "Apparently." Then her temper kicked in. "And it's *your* idea! Where is he going? Who is he going after? What's through the doorway you want to send him through? Where is it, anyway?"

Joy laughed. "Peace, sweetheart. But why don't you ask him those questions? Discretion is best, but there are no secrets between lovers."

She and Aras weren't lovers, Kamile thought sadly, and there was no openness between them, either. She shrunk back a little, abashed. She just shook her head. "The doorway?"

Aras told her.

"Don't do it," Kamile urged again for the dozenth time. That blue-painted door now looked far more sinister. It was a wall that had been created *around* a doorway to keep it from being entered. There was a reason for that! "It'll be a Creature, or a really nasty Fey. We can't fight those with strength, Aras! You're just going in to your death!"

"This isn't a vote," he said flatly. "Your opinion isn't required where you have no experience. I'm going." He turned away from her towards the now-open blue door. Beyond it was a grey haze, and specks of white and orange light. "Are you ready, Joy?"

"As ready as I can be." For once the woman looked solemn. That expression was echoed in the faces of the three other silver-haired people framing the doorway. They'd come on her request, all to help with this one task. "But are *you*, Strong-Man?"

"Always." And damn it if he blushed.

Kamile sucked in a deep breath and wrapped her arms around herself. He was going. He was really going through that little blue door, to chase after some terrible being that probably did exist, but that was probably going to kill him. And he thought that his prosthetic arm, and his natural strength, and some alter-power gift from this woman would save him…

Then he reached the doorway, and paused just outside. She held her breath, waiting for him to turn around, to look at her. But instead he just ducked his head and passed through, disappearing into the haze.

"I can't hold it much longer, Mama," a silver-haired youth said from the other side of the doorway. His bronze hands rested just outside the door frame, and his expression was twisted. "Ahhh!"

Suddenly he was flung backwards, and the door slammed shut.

Kamile screamed. "Aras!"

A moment later she felt a hand on her shoulder. Joy looked down at her sympathetically. "He can't come back the same way, sweetheart. Some doorways are entrance only, and this was one of them. Now either he'll come back a hero from one of the other doorways, or…"

"Or what?" Kamile croaked.

Joy's red lips tightened into a straight line for a brief moment. "Or he won't come back, and we'll have fed the wicked Tiger." She sighed. "It won't be the first time."

Now Kamile did cry. She'd been forced from her home, had almost died, her best friend *had* died, she was infatuated with a man who couldn't care less about her, and now he would probably die too!? It was too much.

She turned her back, but she could see out the corner of her eye that bronze-skinned youth quietly move up to Joy, his feet floating above the ground. "The other girl," he whispered solemnly. "You said she went home."

"I thought she did," Joy whispered back as if Kamile couldn't hear her. "But it's impossible to know. I followed her through the doorway and she was nowhere to be seen."

There was a hum of agreement from the younger Silver. "That could mean anything."

Another Silver moved up quietly, this one a young girl with a broad, freckled face. "Hope for the best, prepare for the worst," she murmured. "But you can't get her back now, even if she *didn't* get through to her river."

This broke through Kamile's desolation, and she turned to the others in shock. "A girl looking for a river?" she blurted out. "Was this girl about your height, pale-skinned with messy dark hair? Wearing a big, really old-fashioned gown like she's out of a history VR session?"

Joy turned to her, wide eyed with surprise. "That's the one. Ashlea. I take it you know her?"

"Sort of." Kamile hardly knew the girl, except for their brief but strong connection via Coryn, and the events of a few months earlier. "What happened to her?"

Joy shrugged, spreading her hands out with palms upwards. "I tried to direct her towards a doorway that would take her to this place she wanted to go. There's one on the other side of town that often directs towards, a...river of life? Youth? I've seen it once or twice, it's a good place to visit, although there are better elsewhere. So she stepped through, and I followed after her, but then she was gone. Some of the doorways move, you see. That was one of them, and I confess my timing wasn't perfect."

"Oh." That made Kamile feel even worse. "Then where did

she go?"

"Impossible to know," the freckled girl piped up. "But don't worry. It's probably not bad. Someone like her, someone flowing with alter-power, they're always OK in the end."

Hopefully that was true. "And someone like Aras?"

"We gave him all the power we could," the third Silver said. This one was an elderly, kindly man with a lined face. "It's all we can do. Now we just have to hope."

Kamile needed more than hope in these circumstances. She needed a miracle, but she didn't know where she could find it. So with one last look at that innocent-looking blue door, she turned and headed back to the town square.

But as she walked past one of the free-standing doorways, this time she definitely saw movement. On the other side she could see a view of the town – was it the same doorway she'd been distracted by earlier? But now there was definitely something else there, something like a shadow and a speck of light that didn't belong.

Kamile stopped and moved closer to the doorway, although made sure not to touch it. "Show yourself!" she said again, even though last time it hadn't worked, had it? But she had to try.

But unlike that morning, the scene through the doorway flickered and swirled like a damaged VR set, and then suddenly the town was replaced with a scene of dramatic contrast. She appeared to be looking through into a sort of dark cave, with complete shadow on one side and flickering orange light from the other side. Then the darkness and light shivered and moved until two small equine forms were visible, with two sets of eyes gleaming faintly in the orange light.

Last time Kamile had met these two in such a way, she'd been a mere child, and they'd been standing in a moonlit meadow, in one of the most beautiful settings she'd ever seen. Was it any wonder she'd been tempted to go through to the Other with them?

But this time there was no such temptation. The cave...or whatever it was...that they stood in seemed to emanate foreboding. Perhaps it had been all her visits to the River, but now the two Fey/Creatures certainly didn't look half as adorable as they had in the past either. She couldn't quite make them out...

"What do you want?" she asked flatly.

"Do we need a reason to visit an old friend?" the white pony asked in a small, rough voice, its too-human eyes glinting with what seemed like malice.

"An old friend who isn't good at listening," the black one added. Its small body was almost entirely hidden in the darkness.

Their voices had seemed sweeter last time, Kamile thought. They'd carried some weight to them, something beautiful and supernatural that was now missing. "You're not my friends," she told them harshly. "I now know that you're Creatures, not Fey, and I have no interest in talking to you ever again. Is that clear?"

She took a step backwards, intending to turn her back and walk away, but the white pony spoke up again. "Brave words for a Halfling with an unnatural child," it hissed.

Kamile froze, caught by surprise, and the black one continued, "Yes, we know about that. We know *all* about you and your little family, Kamile Greenskin, not that it will last. Your kind is never meant to have happiness. Your poor little mixed-blood infant certainly won't, with all the problems that come from such a heritage. Poor, poor wee thing. Didn't we always tell you not to breed?"

The Creatures spoke with such malignance, and it seemed like with every word, they spoke her worst fears into being. She swallowed, her mouth feeling dry. "Isla is normal. She doesn't have any problems." She was even blond like Aras. Adorable. Ordinary.

"And you look so very normal too, in the realm you currently stand in," the white pony whispered. "But what happens when you step through into the Other realm?"

Kamile already knew the answer to that. Her limbs would distort and stretch a little, looking vaguely unnatural, and her skin would turn a light, bright leaf-green colour. She couldn't go far from the Other either, or she'd grow ill – hence the choice to live in Erastus with all its Other doorways. *She* wasn't ordinary.

"Isla is normal," she repeated, as if by saying it, she'd make it true. "I don't believe there's anything wrong with her, and I want you to stop following me!" She had bigger problems right now – like Aras playing hero, and now being beyond her reach. Not that she'd tell these two that.

The two Creatures laughed in unison, a low, jolting hiss of sound. "Bring us the child," the white pony said. "Bring her to us, and we'll leave you be."

Those words seemed to break the haze of fear and confusion that sat over Kamile, and she shuddered in dismay, realising how very close she'd come to the doorway. A mere step away. She quickly moved backwards, shaking her head as she did so. *No. No. No, no, no!* "Isla is never coming near you!" she vowed.

She turned and ran, but she still heard their voices in the distance. *"Then we'll never leave you alone…"*

The statement rang with truth, because how could she stop them? She couldn't even stop her sort-of husband from going through a doorway on his own.

She'd never felt so helpless.

The Island of Exiles

Elspeth huddled in the shelter of a rocky cliff, her knees pulled tight against her chest, and her body pressed as far into the smooth rock as she could manage. She'd heard at least two of the island's inhabitants move past her in the last half-hour, but neither had spotted her.

Mayhap her hiding place would suffice a little longer, but she could not stay indefinitely. She'd need to eat and sleep sooner or later, and of course she simply must return to the Mountain. Oddly enough, she was not particularly frightened, nor hungry, nor tired at present. Mayhap 'twas a sign that all would be well.

She knew not where she was, except that 'twas a dark, rocky island lacking in greenery, and small enough that she could traverse it in an hour.

If only she hadn't fallen through that gateway. If only she knew where she was now…

After several more minutes of complete silence, Elspeth dared to look out from her hiding place. All she could see was the rocky ground sloping down into the black water, with no one in sight. The water was so still, she mused, without even a hint of waves as she would expect from such a place.

But even as she thought that, she noticed gentle ripples running across the water's surface. She followed them with her gaze to their origin, which was a shape in the water, barely visible against the dark surroundings.

It looked not at all human. No, on her oath those were *antlers* coming from its head…

Elspeth froze, all thoughts momentarily having fled from her mind. She could only watch as what had to be a Creature moved closer and closer to shore; closer to *her*. She had seen such things before; things that looked neither fully like animals nor fully like men, and she'd quite happily never see one again. Except now, there was one right in front of her.

She fisted her hands in front of her, lighting them both up with silvery supernatural flame. Just let it attack, she thought fiercely. Ooh, the beast would be most sorry…

But discretion seemed the better part of valor, so she merely sat with her tingling hands at the ready, breathing shallowly as the thing drew closer and closer to shore. And then, as it stood and began wading, it suddenly…stopped. Then as if retracing its steps, it moved backwards, in precisely the same way it had approached.

Elspeth breathed a sigh of relief, but too soon. The Creature had waded backwards for only ten feet when suddenly it began to move forward again in a bizarre repeat of its earlier actions. She sucked in a breath as it reached the same point close to shore that it had before…and then reversed its path once again.

Finally her confusion overcame her fear a little, and she leaned forward to watch as the Creature went backwards…then forwards…then backwards again…then forwards again. Over and over, until she counted fifteen attempts to reach shore, all in the same place, and with precisely the same movements every time.

Hmm. Did the beast even know what it did? she pondered. Feeling baffled, she stroked her chin with one hand, briefly forgetting what she held. But while the silvery flame tingled rather than burned, she did notice one thing that was not at all ordinary.

The flame moved not at all. No, it sat over her fingers as if 'twas frozen in a moment of time, and even when she moved her hands from side to side, the fire didn't flow or flicker with the breeze.

How very odd. For while her flame was most certainly supernatural, 'twas not meant to sit on her hands in such a way. Or it never had before.

But just then Elspeth heard footsteps crunching in the loose gravel along with the sound of voices, and she huddled out of sight again.

"Get out of here, you stinking beast!" a rough female voice shouted. There was a scuffing noise, and then a small splashing sound in the distance.

"You missed," a male voice said. "Throw another rock."

"*You* throw another rock," the female countered. But then further scuffling noises and several splashes sounded close together, suggesting that mayhap they had *both* thrown rocks.

Elspeth was not certain what to think. Were they truly throwing rocks at a *Creature?*

"Dunno why 'e comes back here over 'n over," the female commented. "Same way. Every time. Surely it must know it can't touch the ground here."

"John says that time doesn't pass on the island," the male replied. "So maybe to the beast, it's only tried just the once. Anyway, if it comes back over an' over, then why do you miss with those rocks every single time? Shoulda' had enough practice by now."

There was a sound a lot like a slap – something Elspeth had heard more than a few times herself – and she cringed.

Ooh, they sounded like awful people. Stupid, at least. But still, she wondered, mayhap they would be able to help her.

"Gotta keep moving," the woman said, not sounding at all like she'd been the one slapped. "Find that little girl John's after, or it'll be us who's on the whipping post tonight."

Elspeth instinctively sucked in a breath, tightening her hands into fists. She felt the too-still flame burn a little higher, and she tucked her hands into her belly as if to hide the light. It must have worked, for only moments later she heard the footsteps recede into the distance.

Time doesn't pass on the island? Little girl?! Whipping post?!!

They mustn't find her. She had to escape.

In the darkness

Help help help help help, Ash chanted inside her head as she crept through corridor after corridor in the darkness. It was lit only with a faint orange light that seemed to come from everywhere and nowhere, and that initial sense of desolation she'd felt outside the doorway was also everywhere. If there'd ever been a sign *not* to go into a place, that had been it…

What was this place? she wondered. It was like a maze, a true underground one with rough-hewn tunnels that all looked the same, with so many different ways to go. She'd lost the ugly little Creature some time ago, but she'd also lost that initial entry point.

Amaranthus, she shrieked inside her head. *Why won't you answer me?*

He was a great one for talking quietly into one's mind, so quietly that she'd think it was just her own thoughts at first. That would last until she realised the thoughts were way smarter than she knew herself to be. And even when he hadn't been speaking – as he often didn't – she'd always felt like there'd been a connection there. It was a connection she barely noticed until now, because it was missing.

Even stupid, erratic far-sight wasn't working. Her flight ability was there…kind of…but now seemed pointless. The roof was low and bumpy, no good for flying at all. Not that there was anywhere to fly…

Sorry, Baby Broadbean, she thought desolately. *I am a terrible almost-mother. I'm too stupid to live, and we're both probably going to die down here. It's a good thing you don't have any idea what's going on, because you'd be crying.* Just like she was on the inside. She was too scared to cry on the outside, because she didn't want any more of those terrifying Creatures to hear her. It was a miracle none had already.

Ash remembered the Creatures' origin story well. She'd been told it once wrong, then again right, and both versions had stuck. Once upon a time there was an immortal king – that was Amaranthus – who was really powerful and awesome and all that, but he had some enemies among his own people. His second-in-charge tried to take over, but failed.

As a result, the second-in-charge was kicked out of the amazing, supernatural place they all lived in, along with those who'd risen up with him. And because they were sent away from this amazing, supernatural water they all drank, they died. Kind of. More like immortally, resentfully undead. Like taxidermied animals come to life…kind of.

She'd run into these Creatures more than a few times before. Before, she'd been able to defend herself somewhat. They'd left at her very *words*. But that was out there, and in here? She felt like it was the complete opposite of that beautiful capsule room she'd once visited. It felt like death instead of life – and if there was a time for being dramatic, it was now. *Ugh.* The very walls seemed to cry out in fear and pain…

Ash turned another corner in the horrible location, and suddenly she was in a more open space that she realised was the source of the actual crying. Holes were everywhere, covered with metal bars: in the ground, in the walls, in the ceiling. And from each one, the sound of crying and fear and perhaps the scent of incontinence. It was basically a dungeon, or Hades. Probably the same thing. And it went on, and on, and on into the distance.

"Help us, help us!" someone cried out to her from a nearby cell. It was a woman, her face etched with lines of fear or pain, and her hair straggling down her back. The cell was barely bigger than she was.

The cry was taken up by others in adjoining cells, and then people were sticking their hands out between the bars towards Ash. "Please, help us!"

Well, there went her idea that she was somehow invisible. "I'll help you, but please shush!" Ash whispered loudly. "I don't want to be found!" Or else she'd be in there with them, no doubt.

"You've got to let us out before the Creatures come back," a man cried. "Or we'll lose our chance!"

Double-damn. It *was* the Creatures keeping them in here. "Where's the key?" Ash asked urgently. "Where's the exit?" 'Cos she'd like to know that too!

There was brief moment of silence, then someone said, "You're the one out there! Don't *you* know?"

"I don't even know where we are!" she retorted sharply. "And keep your voice down, will you?"

"We're in one of their cities," the straggly-haired woman whispered. "We all got here through stupidity or just by accident. I came straight into this cell, so I don't know any other way out."

"Speak for yourself," the man in the adjoining cell snapped. "Stupidity, Erin?"

"What else can it be when you follow a 'voice' just because it makes promises, hmm?" she snapped back. "When it tells you that you'll become some sort of god if only you go to this one particular spot, and bring a sacrifice? Because you did that, and I call that bloody stupid!"

"Yeah, well *you* just walked through a stone archway straight into what looked like a field of flowers! In the middle of a city!

And you didn't even question why it was there?!"

Other voices joined in the argument, all accusing and insulting each other for their decisions that had led them to this place, and Ash was an inch away from pulling out her hair in frustration. She turned away from the first two, focusing on their environment and ignoring the sounds. This area with its cells seemed to go on and on, and each cell was as tiny as the last. If they were all the same, Ash estimated there could be as many as a hundred people down here.

All surrounded by rock and dim light, with no exit to be seen. There was graffiti on every wall; words she couldn't make out, but which looked to have been drawn in blood or some other bodily fluid. Every now and then there was a small, low hole set at the very base of the wall. Not big enough to crawl through, but perhaps if you were desperate you might try. But you'd have to risk whatever was on the ground to get to it, Ash thought in distaste. It was probably for sewage, since this whole place smelled very unfresh,

Just then she realised it wasn't just her mind; the whole place had suddenly fallen silent. And there was that rank smell again, sort of like that time she'd found a dead possum in her garden shed back in the Southern Isles.

Someone let out a hiccupping gasp, and all eyes seemed to be fixed on her…or something just behind her. Ash felt the hairs rise on the back of her neck. She slowly began to turn around…

PRISONERS

Ash turned slowly, the hairs still standing up on the back of her neck. But even so, even though she *knew* there was something behind her, she still didn't expect…*this*.

It was something's chest. It looked like a rough old crocodile hide, crossed with a plate of armour. It smelled vile. And then she looked up and saw its face.

Its muzzle was like a crocodile's too. The teeth – curling out from that muzzle in a yellow-brown tangle. The eyes – beady and too many for that face. It huffed out a breath that sent Ash's hair flying back from her face.

She screamed. And not just a little scream, but a big, terrified one that was extremely loud and lasted for a long time. Then the people around her in their cells began to scream in sympathy. It was briefly a harmony of terror – then Ash dashed backwards, but hit her back against one of the walls.

The Creature sniffed, shook its head, and flicked those multiple eyeballs in various directions. "SHUT UP!" it roared.

Everyone fell silent, and Ash was shaking. She was scrambling in her pockets for some kind of weapon, although she knew the one that had worked before. Her words. She needed a name, then she could send this thing away, but somehow that felt so very, very difficult. Even gathering the courage felt almost impossible…

The Creature stomped forward towards her...then moved past her to the nearest cell to grab the occupant. "What's all this shouting about?" it snarled.

There was an awkward silence, filled only by the choking of the man who now had a scaly fist around his neck. Ash could feel everyone's eyes on her; everyone's except the Creatures. Her heart pounding in her ears, she stepped slowly away from the thing. One step, then another. It was like it hadn't even seen her – or perhaps hadn't even heard her scream.

Oh, what *luck* if it was true... Could it be the protective medallion?

The Creature shook the man again, who was really in no state to answer anything. Everyone else seemed to have been cowed into silence. As for Ash, she circled her way around the Creature until she was at its back. It had a thick, short tail rather like a dinosaur, to go with those two big, claw-footed legs. It also had a belt around its waist, with a series of items inside. Her spirits rose. A key?

"You're going to kill him!" the straggly-haired woman cried out. "He can't answer!"

"Then you answer," it snarled back.

The woman's eyes darted to Ash, then back to the purple-faced man, and her face crumpled. "There's someone in here," she blurted out. "Someone you can't see."

"Traitor!" someone else hissed, but the Creature finally dropped the man. He fell to the floor of his cell, sucking in painful gasps, and the Creature turned.

Its beady eyes were narrowed suspiciously – all eight of them – and it sniffed again with those big, scaly nostrils as if it could smell Ash. Maybe it could. She was certain that it couldn't *see* her, since she was right there in front of it.

Ash felt frozen with indecision. Tell it to go, and give up her location if she didn't have that previous ability? Or stay quiet and try to dodge it?

Just then an image flashed in her mind; of the Creature stuck in one of the round floor cells, jammed by its round belly.

This isn't a cartoon! Ash told herself. *Those things don't really happen!* And far-sight would be really useful right now!

But her imagination wasn't listening, because the image popped up again. A moment later it was replaced by an image of her picking those items out of its belt while it couldn't move.

The Creature was moving towards her, and she tried to duck away. Something under her foot gave way, and she let out a cry of dismay. One of the floor cells' bars had broken under her, and she scrambled to pull her foot out, horrified. But at least she hadn't been injured.

But it had seen the floor, even if not her, and it began what seemed like a coughing/snarling fit. "*Intruder,*" it was saying in a much harsher, unfamiliar tone. "*Intruder in the main cell wing.*"

Then it pulled one of those items out of its belt. It looked like a thin, pronged stick, but as it touched it, a murky green light began to shine around the prongs. It also reeked like a mix of sulphur and rot. The Creature spread out its arms, moving slowly in the general direction of where Ash stood, and waving the glowing stick in front of it in wide sweeps.

What to do? She didn't know what that thing was, but she sure didn't want to get jabbed with it. "Creature, go away!" she whispered hoarsely, finally taking that last, vocal step. If it worked, she'd be fine. If it didn't…

The Creature's beady eyes lit up, and it turned to fix on almost exactly where she was standing. It had heard *that*, and it hadn't gone anywhere!

Uh oh.

It swore in that harsh, horrible language, and then it moved faster than Ash thought such a large beast could. She shrieked, ducking aside and feeling something burning hot move right in front of her face. She fell, feeling the hard ground under her palms, then scrambled backwards in the world's most awkward position, like a crab impression.

The Creature was stomping after her with sweep after sweep of that burning stick, stomp after stomp. So close! Ash shrieked again, unable to help herself, and then the wall was at her back…

"Argh!" One moment the Creature was a mere arm's length away; the next it was suddenly much shorter. Its lower half had disappeared into the ground, its tail bent upwards and squished against its back. It was stuck inside that round hole from the broken bars, and it was swearing and struggling like crazy. Its *arms* were even stuck…how did that happen?! It also looked really stupid, Ash thought with panicked humour.

The Creature thrashed its head and snapped those tangled, twisted teeth, and Ash took back that assessment. Scary, but stuck.

She cautiously got to her feet. The Creature *had* fallen into the hole, just like that mental image had shown. Its weapon had gone flying, the light now having vanished from its prongs, but the other items were still there. Still accessible.

"Far-sight?" she murmured to herself. But that was supposed to be more like videos, not single screen-shots!

Ah well, she'd take what she could get. Ash crept towards the Creature, ducking under its thrashing jaws, and grabbed for the closest item. It was a small boxlike shape, seemingly made of old metal, and its purpose wasn't at all clear. The Creature swore again, now seeing what she was doing, but she felt emboldened.

She ducked around and went for the other side, grabbing for any other items she could reach. Finally she'd cleared out its belt, and now had half a dozen objects which she shoved in her Regency-era jacket's pockets before running towards the nearest cell.

The people inside had gone crazy once they'd seen what she was doing, all clinging to the bars and begging for her help. Talk about pressure! But Ash focused on what she was doing and tested item after item on the nearest set of bars. Finally when she pressed the square box-like item against the bars, they vanished. The woman inside fell out with a babbling cry of thanks, then turned and ran down one of the halls, vanishing from sight.

"Huh." Did *she* know where she was going?

But Ash kept going, working as fast as she could, until every last cell was open. Many of the prisoners copied the first, scattering in every direction, but several of them remained behind, looking towards her anxiously.

"You'll get us out, right?" the straggly-haired woman said urgently. "You've got some power, because the Creature couldn't see you. Still can't! But if we don't get out of here now, we're dead. The others will be coming even now. So what do we do?"

"What do we do?" The others took up the cry. "What do we do?"

Gaaahh! The pressure was enough to make Ash's eyes twitch. She thought again of those brief images; of how far-sight had come *just* enough, but not that much. Could there be more?

Amaranthus, she tried again, still feeling that barrier. But was there now a hint of awareness, a hint that perhaps he was there, somewhere close?

"Give me a minute!" she whispered, looking around desperately. More halls, more corridors. She'd been lost in the past, but far-sight or some other rescue had always come along just in time.

Amaranthus, HELP!

Reman Palestine, 31 AD

Peaceful sat huddled at the side of the road just inside the gates of a small human settlement, her borrowed body aching from an old injury that had twisted its legs into uselessness, and from hunger. A most unpleasant sensation, but one she'd grown accustomed to in the last thirty or so years she'd been in the human realm.

Just then another human male – a 'man' – walked in through the gates, the long robes he wore of a sufficient quality to indicate he had funds. As he walked, the half-dozen wounded, crippled or sick humans lined up near the gates all cried out towards him, stretching their hands up and begging for aid, for coin.

Coin. A thing that was useless in itself, but that could be exchanged for much more useful goods. Peaceful never would have imagined that she'd care about such a thing, let alone desperately desire it. Out of habit she stretched her own hand upwards, letting out a soft sound that was the best this mute body could manage. But the man just curled his lip and threw a couple of tiny copper-coloured discs into the dirt to her left. Several of the more mobile beggars leapt for them, but Peaceful couldn't do more than move a few inches.

She huffed out a discouraged sigh, then settled back into her place. She'd have to wait until the sun began to set, she decided, then perhaps she could crawl into the city, and maybe even find some discarded fruit or bread…if the other humans didn't chase her off.

She'd found all humans to be capable of the most terrible behaviour; as bad as ex-Bright at his very worst. Selfish, vicious, cruel. And to think, they'd been created to be part of the Master's world.

Well, *that* certainly wouldn't be happening, she thought grimly. Her twisted legs panged with that same ache, and she suppressed a groan, rubbing one hand over the most damaged part as if to soothe it through her filthy robes. It didn't work.

Had she thought the new, barren Other realm was bad? The human realm was just as twisted, but unlike the Other, every living being here needed constant sustenance. Constant water, warmth, shelter, and food. And not just any food. Oh no. Peaceful had found that out the hard way, when a previous body had been desperate enough to eat the long grass growing around a tree.

The body had suffered in pain, then had brought it back up. Then to make matters worse, the well-fed 'owner' of the land she'd been on had chased her away. *No beggars on* my *land.*

She'd wanted to tell him that his life was a mere breeze, and of the fate that awaited most humans, to eternally power the repugnant Creature cities. That he couldn't truly own anything, let alone land, because he'd take nothing with him when he went, not even that rather portly form. Definitely not that rather portly form.

But she'd said nothing, because it was so very, very rare for a human to ever listen to her, unless they were her host. In which case…about half and half. Then when the body inevitably wore out, even with her best efforts to keep it running, she'd see the life-force and everything that made up that person go flowing out. Either down into the ground to languish with the others, or…elsewhere.

It was the elsewhere that gave her hope, even amongst all this mess. Just a little hope…

BOOM. The sound vibrated through the ground and through Peaceful's borrowed body, making her jolt in surprise.

BOOM. Then the second sound hit, and this time her fingers tingled from the force of it. She sucked in a deep breath, looking around frantically for its source.

"What are you doing, Adah?" the neighbouring beggar asked

curiously. "Were you stung by a bee?"

Didn't you hear that? she wanted to ask, but of course she couldn't. This body – Adah – didn't speak. Instead she craned her neck to see what was coming – because that deep, ground-shaking noise kept coming over and over, like the steps of a giant.

And it was then that Peaceful realised it wasn't a physical sound, because none of the humans here could hear it. No, it was a supernatural sound, the sort that only someone with ears like her own could hear…

Suddenly the host's mind stirred from her sleep. Adah was a woman in her late fifties, one who'd lost everything and had no prospects whatsoever in this world. A most miserable case. *What is it, Shulamithe? What's coming?*

Hush, Peaceful told her. *You rest.* She added some forcefulness to that command, and she felt the other person she shared the mind with fall back into slumber, while Peaceful herself focused on the road up ahead.

BOOM.

BOOM.

BOOM.

What could possibly be coming that would have such an impact?

But then her physical ears finally caught up with what she'd heard supernaturally. This time she could hear a crowd approaching, and after some minutes had passed, they finally reached the gates of the town and came into sight.

At first glance there didn't seem to be anything unusual about them, beyond the sheer number of people who'd come to this little, two-hundred-person town. The crowd had to be fifty-strong, mostly men, but she could also see women and children in there too. They were all crowding in around someone in the centre…

Peaceful had raised her cupped hand out of habit (and because the body really did need to eat something) but now she lowered it, her jaw dropping. She'd seen something more importance than mere food.

The man in the centre of the crowd looked much the same as the ones around him. Brown skin, dusty simple robes, a good-sized beard. But she could see through that physical form into what was inside him. And unlike most of the other humans, who like ex-Bright and the other Creatures completely lacked even a hint of living water, this man was overflowing with it.

It was like the River of Life was bubbling up from inside of him, filling him to his fingers and toes under that plain robe, and then spilling out to all those around him. It looked like light to Peaceful, even though she knew no one else would see it. No one else had heard the steps either, although they'd must have sensed them in some way too, to show the excitement that they had.

It was Amaranthus. Her master.

Oh, she hadn't seen him in *so long*…

Suddenly Peaceful's hands curled into fists, and her breath came shallow and fast. What was he doing here amongst the ragged two-legs? She'd known he'd always loved them, but they were now so, so far short from what they'd been in the beginning. They were tainted, toxic, and miserable.

But what was worse, was that she could see he wasn't just disguising himself as a human like she was; just wearing a human suit, borrowed from a near-dead human. No, he'd done more than that, and she knew in that moment what the many visions of that baby had been, down in ex-Bright's city when she'd first woken.

The lightning-bolt baby had been born, and had become this man.

Amaranthus, a human. But *why?*

"Miracle man," she heard someone to her left mutter. Then

they shouted it again, "MIRACLE MAN!"

Then suddenly all the beggars were shouting it, and then it seemed the whole town rushed over to join the crowd. All Peaceful could see from where she sat were knobbly ankles and the backs of people's robes as they clambered to see him, to talk to him.

They'd had miracle workers to visit before a couple of times. They'd been men or women flowing with alter-power, usually identifiable as from the River, but a couple of times having that dark dryness that gave their true origins as from the ex-People. Sometimes they'd been able to transform objects, or heal people, or even change the weather.

But they'd been human. *Human!*

Adah's mind stirred again. *Miracle man?* she queried.

Hush, Peaceful told her out of habit. *Sleep.*

No! Adah argued. *There's a miracle man! He could heal me properly, not like you did! You've got to get to him!*

That bold statement was enough for Peaceful to shake out of her stunned stupor, and to focus on the mental conversation. It was one of the few times she could actually talk, in the twelve months since she'd moved into this near-dead body. *So what if he can heal you?*

She felt Adah's confusion. *But you are my friend, Shulamithe. Why would you not want me healed?* Then there was anger. *You want me to stay sick so you can keep using my body!*

Not at all! Peaceful argued. *I want you to be safe, Adah. You need to be honest with yourself. Even if you were well, you're still past your youth. Your husband and children are dead, and there's no one to care for you. You don't even have friends! You'd be better just to sleep, to pass the time away until it's...time. Then maybe...*

Maybe when I'm dead, I could go to a better place? Adah sounded scornful. *You know nothing, Creature. Humans want to* live, *even if it's only for a while, and even if it's a flawed life. The hope of something better in the future doesn't mean that we must not live* now.

I'm not a Creature, Peaceful said reflexively, rejecting the now common word for ex-People. Other humans called them dark spirits, or even daemons. *I'm trying to help you. It's all I ever wanted. How can you want to live in such misery?* She'd shown Adah her own memories of the light world, and had assured her that the Master intended the humans to pass onto that place.

Intended. It wasn't the same as ensuring it *would* happen.

Adah sounded mulish. *That's not your choice to make. Now get up and find that miracle worker, or I'll do it.*

It was an empty threat, since Peaceful held full control over this body. Adah herself had been on the edge of death after a particularly nasty illness, made worse by malnutrition and the cold. But Peaceful couldn't reject such a strongly worded request from someone she didn't dislike. Besides, she herself grew tired of the shared pain.

During their conversation she'd almost stopped hearing the repeated beat of the master's footsteps, noticeable only through her supernatural senses. But now she felt something else instead; a warmth emanating from in front of her. She looked up to see the Miracle Man standing there, looking down at her.

"Do you want to be healed?" he asked, his audible voice as ordinary as any of the others beside him. But his eyes – his eyes were the same as they'd always been, and the remarkable kindness within them made her both cringe at having been separated from him, and want to embrace him.

Peaceful did neither. Instead she just stared at him mutely while in the back of her mind, the real Adah shouted a resounding *yes, yes!* She wanted to agree, but even after thirty years in this mortal realm, with time dragging her down every single hour, minute and second of the day, she couldn't come to terms with the new state of the world.

Sure, Adah might be healed. Peaceful *wanted* her to be healed. But what was the point of giving her a few decent years in this realm, when her eternity would likely be spent down in the walls of those terrible cities? If the Master loved his pets so very much, then why would he let the vast majority of them end up imprisoned in such a way?

Why was he *here*?

"Adah can't speak," one of the other beggars said helpfully. "Not since she was sick a few years back."

"I see," the Miracle Man said. Then he leaned forward and pressed a hand firmly against Adah/Peaceful's forehead. Then as she felt a gentle warmth run through her, he whispered, "Sickness isn't the only imprisonment, and I came to set the prisoners free." Then as Peaceful mused on that shocking, relevant comment, she heard his mental whisper, *And I'd find a new host if I were you. This one doesn't need you any longer.*

Then as he moved away to the next person, Peaceful was left there in a thrilled, stunned daze. She could feel Adah, the real Adah, had moved forward almost to the front of her mind. She was about to be pushed out, because it was true – Adah didn't need her any longer.

"How are you feeling?" one of the neighbouring beggars asked excitedly.

Then someone – Adah or Peaceful, she didn't know – opened those long-unused lips and said in a husky voice, "Good. Just…good. But…who *was* that?"

"The Miracle Man?" the other beggar replied with the confidence of someone who'd met him two minutes earlier. "Haven't you heard? That's Yeshua of Nazarith."

Peaceful heard the name translate in her mind as *He shall save,* and in that moment all of her minor worries and pains and fears vanished, and she once again carried that peace she was always supposed to have.

He shall save.

There was an answer to the hideous state of this world, and it had just arrived in the form of a human male.

Lunden, 1819 AD

Edward paced anxiously back and forth across his small bedroom, his arms wrapped around himself. He'd been in bed, swaddled up in the covers and seated between his wife and his brother, but it hadn't made him feel safe. Not truly.

And now George had gone off somewhere, looking for an entrance to this 'river' that supposedly would help his situation, but he hadn't been back in, oh, *minutes*.

Even Livvy had abandoned him. She said it was to go to the powder-room, but Edward wasn't so sure.

"Please, please," Edward murmured to himself, pushing aside those horribly vivid memories of the pit, and the dry, terrible creatures that had been about to take him inside. As much as he tried to reassure himself it had been merely a nightmare brought about by pain, in his heart of hearts he didn't believe it. "Please George," he muttered. "Please, Livvy." Then he added just for good luck, "Please, Amaranthus. Don't forget me. Don't leave me for the dry beasts."

Perhaps he ought to go out himself, he mused. Where was a particularly holy place? Westmunster Cathedral? Or perhaps even that little place down the road where everyone dressed plainly.

Perhaps *that* would be a holy place, and he'd be able to finally find security.

As Edward veered close to a tall bookshelf, he felt something wet soak right in through his stockings. "Ugh!" Temporarily forgetting his fear, he felt his face screw up with irritation. "Who spilled something and didn't clean it up?"

The puddle of liquid looked almost golden on the polished wooden floor, and a new fear came into play. They hadn't spilled the *brandy* had they, then attempted to hide their crime by sitting the decanter upright again? By Jupiter, he'd spent a pretty penny on that earlier in the year. It was an excellent vintage, and practically worth its weight in gold.

Edward carefully got onto his hands and knees, leaning down and almost putting his nose in the liquid. He sniffed. It didn't smell like brandy. Not like anything, in fact.

He looked up at the bookshelf, trying to see where it might have spilled from, and was rewarded with a splash right in the forehead. He blinked, startled, then sputtered as a trickle of liquid ran generously right into his eyes. "Argh!"

Oddly enough, his eyes didn't burn. Not brandy, then. Instead they felt warm and a little tingly, and the light in the room suddenly seemed bright. He stood, and then he could see exactly where the liquid was coming from. There was a good-sized book on the shelf, crammed in between a biography and an art history tome, and a thin trickle of shining liquid was running steadily from the base of the book onto the ground. Whereupon he'd stood in it, and got it in his eyes, and so forth.

"How curious," Edward murmured aloud. It was a newish copy of the Good Book, which naturally he'd never picked up. One didn't *need* to pick it up, he'd always thought. It was enough to simply have it in one's vicinity. "Why has somebody poured water over my bookshelf?"

He picked it up, naturally, and opened it. And once he did so, the whole world changed.

It was the oddest thing, Edward would think later to himself. While he knew that he still stood in his bedroom, holding that dripping wet tome, at the same time he saw the walls around him shimmer and vanish, replaced by a green haze. It appeared to be lush trees and grass, but whenever he turned to try to focus on the scenery, it seemed to move.

And his feet were wet yet again, like he was standing in a puddle, or perhaps he'd wandered into a stream without realising. He looked down at his stockings, and saw both wooden floorboards *and* thick, lush grass underfoot.

There was a faint sound like water running, or perhaps like the murmur of speech, but he couldn't truly make out who it was. Was there someone standing in the distance?

"Good day?" Edward ventured. Later, he'd think how he ought to have been more surprised or amazed by his clearly supernatural surroundings. But in that moment, he could only focus on the distant figure.

Then the wavering figure seemed to sharpen in his vision until it was a short, brown-skinned old man with a bald head and bright black eyes. No, that was wrong. It was a tall, younger man with actual hair, but those same dark eyes…

No, wrong again. The figure shimmered and solidified until it was fairer and bearded and somewhat stern in expression. It looked like Edward's father, who'd died of an illness a mere two years earlier.

He caught his breath, but then the man began running towards him, and it wasn't his father at all. It was someone else, someone he'd never met, but was certain that he ought to have known. Edward opened his mouth to say something, but then the man had thrown his arms around him in a tight, tight hug.

"Edward! Oh Edward, I'm so happy that you're here!"

Edward blinked, pulling away just enough to study that face one more time. He still couldn't focus on their features, but those eyes were unchanging. They looked so very wise, so very deep, so very kind. "I beg your pardon," he said blankly. "Are we acquainted?"

"No," the man replied, then leaned in for another tight hug. "Not for a long time."

"Oh." Now Edward wasn't accustomed to enthusiastic embraces from father figures. His own father, the previous Viscount Morley, had merely given him a tight-lipped nod of approval once in a while. But he found this wasn't at all unpleasant. In fact, he found that he was feeling…better…than he had in a very, very long time.

The way this not-quite-human was acting, was as if he already knew Edward, and cared for him. It broke down any walls that would have been between them, walls of politeness and expected behaviour, and of course the rather odd supernatural nature of where they were.

"I've been waiting for you," the man continued. "Waiting for you to come find me. You're stubborn, just like your father. He wouldn't talk to me either, not until he knew his time was almost up. Oh, how he regretted the delay! But you, my son, you very nearly had a shortened lifespan, did you not?"

Edward pulled away, his own eyes widening and fixing on the other man's. "You know about that?"

"Edward, I *saved* you from that. I pulled you back at the last moment, made sure your life-force stayed connected to your body. If you'd truly died then, you would have been lost forever."

"Oh," he said again. Suddenly he felt as though he wanted to cry, and indeed a drip of liquid was running down one cheek. "So that all was real. I suppose I knew it was. And you must be the Eternal One."

The man slipped one arm through Edward's and began walking, pulling him alongside as they strode through what felt like ankle-deep water. It was getting deeper with every step, in fact. "That is one of my names, yes. But you may call me Amaranthus."

This, *this* was the Amaranthus that George had spoken about, Edward realised. Little George, the less popular brother, was somehow the favourite of an incredibly powerful being.

I have no favourites, a quiet voice spoke into his mind, and he knew it was Amaranthus. *I only have mine, and not mine. And you, my dear Edward...*

"Am I yours?" he blurted out. "I want to be. I want to be *here* after I die. I don't want to go back to that place. I want to be safe! But how can I be? What do I need to do?"

He'd given up his mistress, but he couldn't take back that he'd had one in the first place. He could start attending Sunday services again, but even that didn't feel like enough. Why, he might even start reading the Good Book! But would it be enough to make him safe? To bring him *here*?

No.

Edward stopped still in what was now knee-deep water. "No?" he wailed. "Then what do you need? Tell me, and I vow I'll do it!"

Amaranthus set his hands over Edward's, and looked him right in the eye. His dark eyes grew deeper and more complex with every passing moment, and Edward found he couldn't look away. *Do you know that you are welcome with me, Edward?*

Well, yes, that at least was obvious.

I've been watching your life's thread since you were conceived. Time does not limit me. I've seen your ups and downs, your wickedness and your kindness. I've seen everything, *Edward.*

Everything? Edward swallowed, thinking of something particularly awful he'd done as a boy. Something he tried not to even think about.

Even that.

Well. It was over then, wasn't it? he concluded. There was no way he could ever be safe, because he didn't deserve to be-

"Passage paid," Amaranthus cut in aloud. "You can't earn your way here, Edward. It's a gift. You just have to accept it."

Edward was silent for a moment. He could see the man's sincerity in his every expression, but could it really be that easy?

Yes. Accept it first, then become a better person. Let's not overcomplicate things.

"Oh." And then even though it seemed far, far too small and low and humble for the enormity of what had been done for him, Edward said it. "Thank you."

"Oh Edward. You are most, *most* welcome."

"Edward?" George strode into his brother's quiet bedroom, his mind buzzing with ideas. How to find a branch of the River – did the River have branches? Or was that trees? And if there were, would any be local, and how would he find them? If only Anne or Amaranthus was here, then they would be fine, for they might answer any questions needed.

But at first glance the lushly appointed room appeared empty. "Edward?" George called again.

"Here."

George spotted the man crouched on the floor by one of the walls, with his face practically pressed into a bookshelf. He appeared to be kneeling in some kind of liquid. A feeling of dread overtook George. Perhaps his brother had truly gone mad, the poor soul, if he was no longer even continent. "Whatever are you doing, Ned?"

Edward looked up at him, and his face seemed bright, clean and happy…and somewhat wet, also. Had he fallen in the liquid? "Come see for yourself."

Oh *dear*. That level of happiness and innocence on Edward's world-weary features was most certainly not normal. Mad, indeed. Pushing aside the crushing sense of disappointment, George carefully knelt down beside his brother. "We'll just help you up, shall we?"

"*We* shall not do anything of the sort," Edward snapped, rolling his eyes. "Look at it, Georgie, and for once don't be so stubborn."

I'm not at all stubborn, George thought defensively, but even so he did as he was asked. Had to help humour the poor soul, didn't one? Now if only Ashlea could come back with that healing balm! "What am I looking at- argh!" He looked up, and suddenly something was in his eyes, as if he'd stepped under a tiny waterfall. There was a moment where George felt the alter-power, where he *knew* that something was about to happen, and then the scene around him changed.

It took about half a second for him to recognise the hazy green, the shimmering of water like diamonds, the smell of pure life. (No, not manure, better than that.) He knew that he was now at the River, which was either directly in the Mountain of Glass, or a sort of realm of its own that came directly from the Mountain. He also recognised a small, redheaded figure in a green tunic. "Anne!" he exclaimed, trying to put his shock into words.

"I know, right?" For a moment she flickered, then she was standing right in front of him. She'd also sounded rather like Ashlea in that moment. "'Tis an odd place for a River entry, but the best ones always are in odd places."

"I was looking for a way in," Edward commented from somewhere to George's left. "And there it was."

"If you look, you'll find," Anne said cheerfully.

Indeed they had. George shook his head again, still feeling utterly baffled, and utterly pleased. It seemed his musings had been answered far faster than he'd expected. "But in a *book*, Anne?"

"Not just a book, *the* Book. So yes."

As simple as that. "You might have told me earlier, so I needn't have rushed around like a madman," George muttered good-naturedly. "I suppose there's another way to bring Ashlea home, too. She went to the Mountain to get the healing balm for poor Edward here, although perhaps that's a moot point now he's at the River. But somehow she went to Erastus instead, and…well, perhaps you might have heard of her predicament?"

Anne's expression grew sombre. "That the doorway in Erastus was blocked? Or that she went through another doorway into a Creature city?"

George felt the blood drain from his face as her words sank in. "WHAT!?"

"That the doorway in Erastus was-"

"No, no, the other part!" Suddenly it didn't matter that they'd miraculously found an entrance to the River leaking from a book of all places. Even Edward's head injury didn't matter anymore. It was all about Ashlea. "Where is she, Anne? We must bring her here at once!"

"In the Creatures' territory," Anne replied gravely. Her usually animated oval face was pale and solemn. "She went straight in without even realising. She thought she was using another entrance to the Mountain."

"Well who told her *that*?" George exploded. He thought of his poor, gentle (or perhaps not so gentle) wife, who was *with child*, being amongst those dreadful beings. Had they harmed her? Killed her? "And why did you not help, Anne of Covington? You seem to show up when it suits you, hmm, but not in time to save my *wife!?*"

Anne raised an eyebrow and stared at him for a long while, and George could feel Edward doing the same. Finally his shoulders slumped. "I will allow that Ashlea is not always the most circumspect of women," he said apologetically. "But Anne…a CREATURE CITY!?"

"Something like Hades, is it?" Edward mused thoughtfully.

George hadn't quite made that connection, but now he did. If Amaranthus was Deias, and if those dreadful Creatures were practically dark spirits, then yes, their home was Hades. He moaned. "Oh, Deias. Ashlea is in HADES! Baby Broadbean is in Hades!" Poor child, only the size of a legume, and yet to even see daylight. Would it even see daylight?

"Come now, your trouble is not yet finished," Anne said briskly. She stepped up towards him and set her hand on his shoulder. "She's not entirely unprotected, and you are here for a reason. Will you go to retrieve her?"

"Of course!" He settled. "So it's…safe, then?"

Anne rolled her eyes. "Of course 'tis not *safe*, George. It's *Hades*."

George blinked. "But…will you not go with me?"

She paused, then inclined her head to one side. "Follow me." She led him a little way along the riverside, towards a rock wall from which streams of water ran down. It was covered with thick green moss, and he didn't recall seeing it the last time he was here. "Amaranthus doesn't go to the Creature cities, George. And neither do his People."

"But…" George felt his lip tremble. "Why not?"

"Because he went once, very briefly and memorably some two thousand years ago, and left an exit that any human can use," she replied simply. "A hidden door that is accessible from anywhere inside, if only one is looking for it. And trust me, Ash *will* be looking for it. I can send you to her, but I cannot go through myself."

"Send me," George replied quickly. "Anytime."

"Very well." She set her hands on his back as if to push him right into that rock wall.

"Wait!" He glanced at her over his shoulder, suddenly nervous. "Do the Creatures know about this exit? Will it be easy to find?"

Now Anne laughed; turning her pale, solemn features into the usual pretty girl that he knew. "By the Rood, indeed they do know about it. It drives them mad! But they cannot block it off. All they can do is try to hide it. But once inside, you shall find it, George. I shall send you with two pieces of advice."

"Yes?"

"One – there are many entries into those cities, but they're one-way. They're gates that are blocked off to prevent the Creatures' escape, but the barrier also affects humans." Anne handed him what looked like a bracelet. "This will enable a single human to return through one of those one-way gates, including this one."

"That isn't very much use when there's two of us!"

"There is still the hidden door," Anne said serenely. "Whether you find a use for the bracelet is up to you."

"Fine," George said grudgingly. "And the second piece?"

She handed him a small, baton-like device. George took it, staring at it for some moments. "What does it do?"

"'Tis a baton," Anne replied cheerily. "One wields it with force, striking one's opponent."

He glanced up at her sharply, eyebrows raised in disbelief. "Anne, I'm going into the hive of both realms' most terrible, immortal beings, and you're giving me a *stick*?" It was barely longer than his hand!

"'Tis a *baton*, not a stick. And if the Creatures are so very dreadful, then you shall have to hit them very hard, shan't you?"

"Or run very fast," he muttered. He turned back towards the rock wall, swallowing. For Ashlea. This was all for her, and for Baby Broadbean. He thought again of the times they'd run across Creatures, and of how they were most apt at disguising themselves. How would he even *know* if he'd found his wife? "What if…what if they wear an illusion again?"

"They can't disguise their true selves when you are in their territory," Anne said quietly. "You recall how those first Creatures you met outside the silver door to the Mountain of Glass were in their real forms. But the ones who later disguised themselves as myself and my sister were attempting to trick you into walking through a doorway in the normal realm. 'Tis their most favourite trick, but it shall not work on you this time."

He nodded, relieved, but his heart was still pounding with terrified anticipation. It would be alright. It *had* to be alright. "Send me through."

"Very well."

He felt a sharp shove on his shoulder blades, and then suddenly he was surrounded by darkness.

The Lunden Townhouse

Edward shook his head, bringing himself out of the River-haze and fully back into his room. No, it was true. George had wandered away with the redheaded chit, and he'd not only vanished from the supernatural River location, but he'd also vanished from this place too. And from what Edward had overheard, not a moment too soon. "Good luck," he murmured under his breath.

"Edward?" He looked up to see Olivia standing in the open doorway, her pretty, pale face shadowed with the same fear and weariness that had burdened him these last few hours. Behind her he could see a maid holding a tray full of silverware. "Have you spilled something? Where is your brother?"

"An excellent question." Edward stood, now feeling full of energy, and quickly made his way to the door. He retrieved the tray from the startled maid, gave her a nod of thanks, then pulled his wife inside and closed the door. "Let me show you something…"

THE SKY PIRATES

Jerushalom, Reman Palestine, 33 AD

Peaceful had been following the Miracle Man, Yeshua of Nazarith, for two years now. If any of the Creatures were to ask, she'd say that she was collecting information, but the truth was that she just couldn't stay away.

First in Adah's body, but now Adah didn't need Peaceful any longer, she'd had to move to a new host, a young boy called Jehu. He'd been barely ten years old, orphaned, and about to die of a disease that the humans didn't even have a name for.

Well, now he was quite alive, and Peaceful rather suspected that if she was to leave him, he'd be just fine – if not a bit cheeky, like he was now. But they'd become good friends in these two years, and especially in the last few months, he'd barely slept at all. That meant she had to share the mind with him *all* the time. Even now, when they were in the packed city of Jerushalom, waiting for the outcome of a trial for blasphemy, of all things.

What's happening? Jehu prodded. *I can't see.*

If you can't see, then I can't see either, Peaceful reminded him. *We're sharing the same eyes.* The trial was taking place in a small, open-air court, which could fit a maximum of sixty people – and she/Jehu wasn't one of them. They waited with the crowds in the surrounding streets, trying to hear what was going on.

But don't you have extra senses? the boy persisted. *You can sense the Messiah's impending success! Has he blasted that foreign dog's court to splinters yet?*

'He' being the Miracle Man, of course. Or as many of the locals had taken to calling him, the 'Messiah'. They thought he was here to free their nation of the oppressive Reman rule that left armed soldiers in every town and bled the money from their nation's coffers. That, and the puppet king that the Remans had installed when they'd conquered this land.

The locals had very high expectations for their Messiah. Peaceful couldn't blame them, especially as many of them had concluded he was the long-awaited son of Deias. Yes, the humans had their own prophecies too, and many of them would rest their hopes on them. *Life might be dreadful now under Reman rule, but one day, we'll be free. One day, our Deias will save us.*

And out of everyone, Jehu knew exactly who Yeshua was, because he'd seen what Peaceful saw. So his expectations were even higher than most of the thousands of others who followed Yeshua as he walked – on two feet – or occasionally sailed around the region.

The Master had chosen to live like a human, Peaceful had observed, except for the occasional miracle (hence the name). That made it so much harder to understand why he'd allowed himself to be captured by his enemies, and brought to trial like a common criminal. Hence their current situation…

But in response to Jehu's question, she replied, *I don't sense any power being used. I don't think he's even speaking.*

Then a rumble of sound began from the nearby court, and Peaceful's ears pricked up. She leaned forward as much as possible, pushing against the surrounding crowds.

"…crime has he committed?"

Ooh, Pilate, the Reman governor, was shouting now! *See, even the Remans can see the stupidity of the claims against him*, she said scornfully to Jehu.

He did claim to be Deias, Jehu pointed out. *We know that he is, but they're being stubborn and won't believe it.*

'They' being the local religious leaders in this case. While their entire purpose for being revolved around the master, unfortunately when he'd shown up in person, they hadn't recognised him. *Whose side are you on?* Peaceful asked, a little amused. *Now Pilate will let him go…*

But the noise had arisen again, shouts loud enough that the words were clear even from here. *"Crucify him! Crucify him!"*

A chill ran down her spine. They must be talking about someone else. There were always any number of criminals to be tried by the Remans, because under Reman law, the locals couldn't condemn anyone to death. But only the Remans could crucify anyone – which was a particularly disgusting, violent, slow death.

It won't happen, Jehu said confidently upon hearing the same thing. *The Messiah must be planning something really dramatic, really amazing, right at the last minute. It'll be incredible.*

You're right, Peaceful agreed, thinking that it was impossible anything else should happen. The Master would have a plan. He always did.

The hours passed and the news spread that Yeshua of Nazarith had been sentenced to death, and she still couldn't really believe it. She trailed behind with the crowds, some weeping, as he was led out through the city by Reman soldiers, then was forced to drag a wooden cross up a nearby hill to the place of execution.

He'd been badly beaten, and some beast had pressed a crown of thorns into his head. Blood ran down his now misshapen face, and if Peaceful hadn't already known who he was…well, she wouldn't have known who he was.

Why is he letting them do that? Jehu raged in the back of her mind. *Why does he let himself be dishonoured like that?! He needs to show them who he is!*

He'll have a reason, Peaceful countered, but she couldn't shake her own anxiety, her own disquiet at what she was watching. It was so opposite to her own nature that she knew the feelings must come from the boy. Right?

But then the soldiers hammered the crosses into the earth…then hammered the Master onto the cross. On either side was another common criminal. Then they put up a sign over his head reading, *King of the Iudeans* – the local people who'd either loved him or hated him.

Ohhh, this looked bad. Peaceful couldn't even watch from the moment they'd begun. She wanted to block her ears from hearing the cries of the wounded, or the jeers of the crowd, or the tears of those who'd supported him. She was crying – no, *Jehu* was crying, she corrected herself. This couldn't be the end! The Master told her he'd come to free prisoners, not to become a prisoner of death himself.

He wouldn't die.

He *couldn't* die.

Hours later, the sun was setting and the crowd had dispersed, leaving behind only a few distraught followers and the soldiers guarding the execution site. The three hung today were still alive, because it could take days to die. *Days.*

They were clearly in so much pain, and there was no dignity in such a death. Even if the Master didn't die, Peaceful told herself, why would he degrade himself so? There was no answer.

But even as Peaceful thought that, she saw him suck in a deep breath, and his face twisted with agony at the effort. Then he spoke: a bare whisper, only just audible. "Forgive them...they don't know what they're doing."

Oh, oh, now she/Jehu was crying again. But *the Master* didn't know what he was doing! she told herself fiercely. He'd never once come down to the Creature cities, although he must surely be aware of what they were doing to his precious humans every single time their bodies could no longer sustain them. Why would he put himself through this? What point was he proving?

Clouds had been gathering as the sun lowered towards the horizon, but as if reflecting her mood, the sky abruptly went dark. There might have been a clap of thunder – or it might have been the impact of a phenomenal amount of alter-power suddenly being released from one human form. The atmosphere suddenly felt as heavy as lead, and the usual faint tingle that signified the presence of the Master had vanished.

In that moment Peaceful knew, just *knew* that the Master had left that body. She looked around, trying to find an open entryway to the light-world or some sign of his plan, but all she saw were the remnants of glowing life-force vanishing into the dry ground.

No. NO! It couldn't be, because that was what happened to...dead humans...

In Peaceful's mind, Jehu was entirely silent, but she felt his shock and dismay at her realisation. She slumped to the ground, barely taking it in as the Reman soldiers who were guarding the condemned men moved up to the first cross.

It's Passover tomorrow, Jehu pointed out dully. *They'll have to kill them now, because they can't have an execution taking place over a holy day.*

"This one's dead already," she heard one of the soldiers say to the other. "For the supposed son of their god, he didn't last long, did he?"

"Are you sure he's dead?"

There was a pause, then a nasty, squelching sound. "Yep. Blood mixed with water. Dead alright."

A figure approached from Peaceful's left. In her peripheral vision she saw long, colourful robes bordered in the kind of stitching that took real money. "Ew," a woman's voice said. "That's disgusting." But she didn't sound disgusted at all, instead almost amused.

Peaceful looked up to see an unfamiliar woman wearing the clothes and jewellery of a wealthy matron. She had the olive skin and strong features typical of this region, and her veil was worn in such a way to ornament her beauty rather than hide it. "Have you no respect?"

The woman smiled at her and touched a hand to her – Jehu's – head, and finally Peaceful saw through the rather excellent illusion. Underneath was a much more familiar face, this one very pale, with yellow eyes and a distinctive underbite.

Lilith the Halfling. Ex-Veritas's immortal offspring – and as Peaceful well knew, also the person through whom the Tiger usually communicated, as she could freely move in both realms. As before, Lilith had easily recognised Peaceful, no matter what body she wore.

"Respect for who?" Lilith answered lightly, her voice far more musical and lovely than her true form. "Two thieves and a liar? Or should I say, three thieves. The liar also stole so much from the Creatures when he stole their power before the Rift, Shu. Now it appears he's given it back, if inadvertently." She let out a sigh, her mouth twisting a little. "I suppose the barrier will be coming down any moment now, with that level of life-force being funnelled into the city walls. I wonder how the normal realm will handle the Creatures retaking their true place?"

Not well at all, Peaceful would assume. In fact, if that was true, it would be absolute chaos. An absolute disaster; destruction on every level, worse almost than the Rift itself.

Perhaps Lilith thought the same way, because her true face wore an expression of dissatisfaction. Perhaps like Peaceful, Lilith would lose her value once the others could all freely travel into the normal realm.

But that didn't sit right with Peaceful, and she made her borrowed body sit up straight. Standing was still too hard; not when the Master's now-empty human body was still nailed to that cross up there. "Surely the Mas...the *enemy* didn't put his full self into that body," she pointed out. "Who knows what could happen?"

"Mm." Lilith fussed with the edge of her linen robe, then flicked her fingers through the air almost dismissively. The movement made a lovely sound, almost like a faint ringing of bells, and Peaceful felt her host's body tingle a little in response. It was a purely physical response to Lilith's alter-power gift, and on top of everything, it just irritated her.

"Must you do that, Lilith? You know this host body is too young to give you any real power."

Lilith worked in a similar way to the Creatures, by creating threads of power between herself and humans, but her links were made through physical touch, or through stirring the senses. Her musical gift could affect women and children, but was far more effective on men – the stronger they were, the more they could be manipulated. That was partly why Peaceful preferred not to use men as host bodies, when possible. They were too easily influenced in such ways.

"Habit," Lilith said with a shrug. "You should go to the Tiger now. He wants everyone to see his victory."

Ohhhh. That was the last thing Peaceful wanted to do, but she forced herself to nod briefly. "Of course he would. But if I go, it might be some time before I can find another body to use out here." They had to come to the edge of the barrier – or so she presumed. She hadn't once returned to the Other realm since she'd accidentally left over thirty years earlier.

"They've started keeping live humans down in the cities too," Lilith said dismissively. "For entertainment. Some of them get sent back out, either with or without their memories. I'm sure you could piggyback on one of those." She smirked. "Or just walk right in with your little boy there. You *may* get to walk out again."

They were keeping *live* humans too? Peaceful couldn't keep the sneer of disgust off her face, and she felt Jehu's strong opinion too – and perhaps a touch of fear. *I won't take you with me,* she told him firmly. *This is where you and I part.*

Will I be alright?

Would he? The Master had just been murdered. Or his human form had, at least, as Peaceful expected some part of him still remained on the light-world. A being as vast and powerful as Amaranthus couldn't be condensed to one physical form, surely. The body still hung within viewing distance, if she was brave enough to look up, and a vast deal of his power had gone straight to the Creature cities. So would Jehu be alright? She didn't know.

You will not die when I leave you, Peaceful told him instead. *You're well enough to support yourself, and you are a clever boy. Go into the nearest city and seek employment.*

She felt his uncertainty, and to her left, Lilith still waited, rather like a spider with a small bug just outside its web. "You leave first," Peaceful told her. "Then I'll follow."

Lilith narrowed her eyes, but then shrugged. A moment later there was a sweet sound like a bell being rung somewhere in the distance, and she'd vanished. She moved as fast as a Creature in the Other, when she cared to do so.

With an aching heart, Peaceful turned her back on the scene

of execution. She could still hear the wailing of mourners, and the groans of the last condemned man who was yet to die. She trudged down towards the city of Jerushalom, and when she was within sight of the gates, she stopped. *Be brave.*

I will, Jehu said meekly.

She didn't tell him she'd been talking to herself. But then she began to release her hold on his body, like she was stepping back further and further until she could no longer feel his limbs, and his mind's voice was a mere whisper, and then suddenly-

SPROING.

Suddenly like an arrow being released, she felt herself pulled at great speed straight from the normal realm and into the Other. And there was the barrier, shining golden and impenetrable and brighter even than normal, and then-

…Then she was through.

The Island of Exiles

Elspeth crept along in the half-dark, her heart pounding and her full skirts caught up in her fists to stop them dragging on the ground. Her head still ached from her initial landing – z'wounds, but she would have quite an egg there by morn – if she lived that long.

She'd waited for what felt like hours in that same hiding place, which was enough for the Creature and the rock-throwers to come back twice more. Then at last she'd gathered enough courage to keep moving. She'd made her way past that same cluster of ramshackle houses; in worse condition even than the roughly built village houses of Iversley, 1556 AD.

She could hear the shouts and laughter of the inhabitants.

There appeared to be six or seven of them, and what ruffians! Their leader appeared to be of the same type, sadly.

Elspeth had prepared herself to use her new, silver fire to defend herself, but had not been forced to do so, as she had passed by unseen. Now she made her way to the centre of the island where it rose into a peak, and began climbing. Pausing for a deep breath, she took stock of her surroundings again.

Around her she could dimly see the form of the island, almost circular, but with regular sections ebbing and flowing and creating small bays and points. Rather like an upside-down spinning top. The locals had created floating bridges from some of these points; made of driftwood and all-sorts, half-sunken in the water and disappearing a little off into the darkness. Mayhap they were intended for fishing, Elspeth mused. Who knew?

She climbed further. The island's peak seemed to grow narrower and narrower, until she was clinging to its smooth rocky sides and silently lamenting her choice to come up here. But on the other hand, she could already see its value. From up here, the gateways shone like faint stars in the darkness: half a dozen of them spread either far out at sea, or high up in the air.

She spotted the one that must be her own entrance point, and reached out a hand longingly. A moment later she wavered and almost slipped, desperately grabbing back onto her rocky shelf. "Who do I think I am?" she muttered desolately. "King Kung?" 'Twas something she had heard her sister say once. She understood that it referred to a legend of an enormous bear who was in the habit of climbing tall towers…right up until it fell off and died.

Gulp.

"She's up there!" A faint voice floated to her on the faint breeze. "I can see her, John!"

They'd found her! "Saints' bones!" Elspeth cursed, then spared a moment of guilt for any saints who might be listening. It appeared she'd soon be testing her silver flame on these humans – and she could not decide whether she wanted it to work or not. She pictured Amaranthus in the tapestry room, moving from thread to thread, each one touching the mind and life of an individual person. Did he see her even now?

Amaranthus, she thought desperately. *I do seem to have made an error here. Would you please, sir, see your way to-*

Suddenly a bright light filled her eyes, so intensely that it seemed as though a star had fallen. She heard bubbling laughter, felt something tight around her hands and arms, and then-

"Oof!"

Elspeth landed on something soft, then bounced a little. Her vision was still filled with flickering lights from that odd abduction, and she flailed her now-free limbs until she struck something fluffy.

"Ouch!" a small, high-pitched voice said from nearby. It sounded like a child. "Jolly, she hit me in the nose."

"A big strong lass like that," a different, equally high voice chided. "Your poor, wee self."

Elspeth lay suddenly still. Were they mocking her? For she knew well that while she was not as tiny as her sister, neither was she above average height for her own time.

Now in the corner of her eye she could see two small, round forms. They looked like a child's soft toys come to life, or like oversized kittens. Big eyes, small paws, round bellies, animated faces that were neither human nor animal. One was yellow and had big round ears; the other was blue, with ears that were long and floppy like a rabbit's.

Any fear Elspeth felt vanished. All she wanted to do was…hug these things, tight around their fluffy bellies. She wanted to put one in her leather pouch – if only she'd had one – and carry it around with her. She wanted to say *'awwwww!'*.

"Ooh, she's seen us, Jolly," the rabbit-eared one chided the round-eared one. Or at least that was what it sounded like it said. "Are you wearing your illusion?"

The round-eared one, who appeared to be 'Jolly', looked displeased. "Of course I am…oh." A moment later the fluffy, toy-like figure shimmered and was replaced by an equally miniature boyish figure with long, curly blond hair. It wore a wide-brimmed hat and a long red jacket, and carried a very small sword in one hand. "Avast ye blaggards!" it announced. "Will this do?"

Elspeth could not help herself. She sat up and giggled.

"Ah, good day, milady," the now-red-coated Jolly said politely. "I trust you have recovered from your unexpected rescue?" His voice was the same, but now came out of the cherubic face of a human child.

Behind him, the second fluffy creature had changed into a similarly small human form, but this one wore a scarf around its head and a slightly anxious expression. "You're not afraid of us, are you?"

She considered them both, comparing them with the forms they'd both briefly worn. It appeared that her chance to use her silver fire on the island's ruffians had now passed – and she minded not at all. "You are People, are you not? From the Mountain of Glass."

"Yes, we are!" Jolly answered in delight. "How did you know?"

She shrugged, then struggled to her feet. 'Twas difficult because she was standing on what seemed to be a vat of jelly set into the deck of what was clearly a wooden ship. Everything glowed luminescent, making her surroundings as clear as day. A large net lay to one side; mayhap that which had caught her. Standing, she could see both these two reached only to mid-chest.

"'Twas not so difficult once I thought about it," she explained. "I saw your true forms, you see. I had been wondering for some time why the Creatures seemed bestial, but the People merely look like humans. Then I heard someone say that *only* humans look like Amaranthus, which follows that his original People do not…?

"'Twas most confusing at first, until I saw once or twice that the People of the Mountain's appearances do change, at least a little. So either you are Creatures, somehow hiding your stench and hideousness, or you are in fact the People. Verily I do prefer the second possibility."

She nodded emphatically, feeling rather pleased with herself for drawing such clever conclusions. She recalled Amaranthus once saying that she and her sister had an innate gift for seeing through illusion – although it seemed a weak gift, if she'd missed seeing the People's true forms all this time.

The two exchanged startled glances, then turned back to Elspeth. "Indeed you are correct, milady," Jolly said. "We are People of the Mountain of Glass, but we are also…*cough cough…the sky pirates.*"

There was an expectant pause, and Elspeth's eyebrows shot up. They both looked so very earnest, and so very adorable. "In truth? You do not look so very…piratical. And why do you call me 'milady'? I am no lady at all."

"It's because pirates always call women milady," the second, quieter one said anxiously. "We'd understood that humans like this. They find it, erm…"

"Charming," Jolly finished. He set his sword into his scabbard, then took off his hat. "So what were you doing on the Island of Exiles, miss…what is your name?"

They had a round of introductions, by which Elspeth was able to explain her story, and to hear that of these two. She also persuaded them to release their illusion, and entertained herself by watching them intently. They looked so…so…*sweet!*

It had become clear through her time on the Mountain that what she thought she saw, was not necessarily what was truly there. Jolly was the round-eared one, who also appeared to be the leader. The other was called Sweet, and she thought he matched his name perfectly.

Awww.

"So Amaranthus sends you to rescue those stranded on the island," Elspeth said slowly, pondering the concept.

"It's because humans aren't afraid of us," Sweet explained shyly. "Not in our human disguise, although the suspicious ones might be of our true form."

Only the very foolish suspicious ones, in her opinion. And 'twas a good choice for Amaranthus – who would be afraid of these two? "But you only come down for the barest moment in your ship," she pointed out. "Do you not know that the exiles fear you? One told me that the sky pirates would *eat* me if they caught me."

"Did you believe them?" Jolly asked.

"No, but others might. Mayhap if you were to land upon the island, come out and speak with people, then they might believe you and come with you." Elspeth threw her hands in the air. "There is nothing down there! Naught at all to keep a person there!"

"We can't," Sweet said, just as Jolly said, "They want to stay."

"Pardon?!"

The two had a battle of expressive glances, which Jolly seemed to win. He said triumphantly, "Most of those ones down on the island, they want to be there. They have no place in their societies, because they are *bad* people. Some of them have been there for a long, long, long...*long* time." He scratched one small paw over his furry forehead, shrugging. "It's true."

"No time passes on the island," Sweet continued earnestly. "And the island exists neither in the human realm nor truly in the Other realm. There are no Creatures on it at all, and neither can we People ourselves touch it. Nor will most gifts from the Mountain work there. It's the nature of the place, you see."

Elspeth screwed up her nose, glancing over the low barrier to the land below. All around was darkness, and she could just make out the faint shape of the island in the distance with its orangeish, firefly-like glowing torches. There were tiny pale stars all around them as they soared through the night, and every now and then they would come close enough to see that 'twas not a star at all, but a gateway in the air.

"Where did this island come from?" she asked. "And why are there so many gateways all around it?"

The two People exchanged sheepish glances. "Well...the island's origin is a long story," Jolly replied, "but the gateways were our fault. Sort of. When the island came to be, we kept coming to visit it out of curiosity, although we didn't touch it. Others came too, but mostly just us. And then..."

"And then we realised that all these remnant gateways were being created every time we visited, and they were sucking humans out of their own realm and depositing them on the island, where no time passes," Sweet finished. "So Amaranthus gave us the task of returning the humans to their homes. See, it's not just because we're...unintimidating. We're fixing our mistake, too."

"But more and more humans keep coming through the gateways," Jolly added quickly, "and a few of them are as stubborn as those below! So very, very stubborn, and they don't want to go home!"

Indeed, he had said that more than once, Elspeth thought wryly. They also hadn't answered her question of how the island had come to be.

"The Eternity Stone!" Jolly blurted out. "It came out of the light-world's bedrock during the Rift, and left this odd little island in the Other sea that we can't touch!"

Elspeth blinked at him for a few moments. The information was most helpful, and quite reminiscent of her earlier conversation with Amaranthus...but had he been reading her mind to know what she'd been wondering?

"No. Alright, yes! Does it matter?"

He looked so earnest in that moment, and just a little irritated too, that it only made him looked cuter. She couldn't possibly be offended by someone so adorable.

Hmmm. But would *that* thought offend *him*? "It matters not," Elspeth replied thoughtfully, her attention moving back to that same conversation about the origins of the Eternity Stone, and how Amaranthus had told her to look out for opportunities, or some such thing. "By the Rood," she breathed. "'Tis as though he foresaw this very meeting!"

The two People exchanged another glance. "I expect he did," Sweet said. "But your thoughts are moving too fast to follow. We can see that you've heard of the Stone, or maybe you've even used it. But...are you thinking that if the Stone was to touch this island, then there wouldn't be missing bedrock any longer...?"

"And then the island would disappear, and the nasty humans would all have to swim," Jolly finished excitedly. "They'd beg us to save them!"

"Er…" In truth, 'twas not at all what Elspeth had been thinking.

"I really don't think they would beg, Jolly," Sweet countered.

"I'm sure they would. *I* would, if I was them and about to drown." Jolly turned to Elspeth. "You would beg for help, wouldn't you, miss?"

"Ahhh…"

But the wee Person had returned to his cheerful argument, and so she was left to ponder this unexpected happenstance. Her clumsy mistake had brought her here, to this place that existed both outside of the normal realm and the Other realm, and to these two odd folk who had a rather wonderful manner of traveling.

If the Eternity Stone was returned to its origin, she mused, then surely it would cease to exist, and would no longer be in danger of misuse by villains. And if she had paid sufficient heed to the tapestry earlier, she knew where to find the Stone too… "Good sirs," she cut in, "do you know the whereabouts of the Stone at this very moment?"

They both fell silent and turned to stare at her expectantly.

"We're currently outside of time," Jolly said politely, "so no. But if I was to rudely read your mind…not that I *am*, of course, but if I was to do so…then I'd say that *you* know where the Stone can be found." An excited gleam lit up his eyes.

Next to him, Sweet wore much the same expression. "And you can call us back when you find it, you know. All you have to do is say the code phrase, and we'll be there with our ship in full sail!"

Elspeth knew any number of places where the Stone might be found, but she only knew one place where the sky pirates' ship mightn't be a terrifying sight to the locals. 'Twould take some courage for her to go there alone in search of a villain, but in that moment she resolved that she would do so. "Erastus," she said decisively. "Late June, in the latter end of the twenty-sixth century..."

The Other Realm, 33 AD

Peaceful found herself in a tunnel with stone in every direction. The air was heavy with alter-power, and she felt the same sorrow weighing down on her that she'd had the last time she was here – the sorrow of being surrounded by so many stolen lives. But this time it was heavier, deeper.

Odd, since she could now feel that she was no longer weighed down by gravity herself; now back in her own true form, hovering just above the ground. The rock itself seemed to hold a slight grey-gold glow, and she stretched out a fin towards it...

Just then there was a *whoosh* of air as a small Creature rushed past in that odd sprint they did, and she quickly dropped her fin. But it didn't seem to notice her at all – it didn't even acknowledge her, in spite of her years away.

Then another Creature rushed past, then another. Not just the small ones. Finally Peaceful turned away from the wall, moving slowly down the tunnel in the opposite direction they were all going. Apart from the first few, she didn't see many down here at all. The Creature city seemed to be abandoned. She stretched out her senses in every direction, not even appreciating that she could do so in her true form, and quickly located them. There was a whole mass of Creatures, all outside the city. All lined up along the barrier...

The barrier. Her heart ached, and she looked once again at the wicked rock with its slight glow, the prison of a million life-forces.

A million and one, now.

But was the Master truly down here with the humans? *Truly?*

She reached up again for the rock, unable to take her eyes off it. She'd never touched it when she was last here, as she'd had an idea of what was around her, and hadn't wanted to share in the suffering.

But this time when she made contact, she could feel the Master there, just like he was standing on the other side of a glass wall. But he wasn't his usual self. The light was there, but it was fainter than usual, and seemed covered with something dark, something ugly. Something that should have been impossible.

Master, Peaceful whispered in utter dismay, *have you been…tainted?*

At first there was no reply, but then she heard his voice in her mind, very small and very weak. *Yes, Shulamithe. I have done more than just taken on human flesh. In this moment, with my human form's death, I also took on all the toxicity that they've been bathed in.*

She couldn't help but cringe back. *All?*

Yes. All.

But why!? Why would he do that, Peaceful wondered frantically. What could he possibly gain? Or had he just lost…had he just been too weak to do what he'd hoped; having for once overestimated his abilities? That should have been impossible too. She didn't think Amaranthus *could* overestimate his abilities.

There was another long silence, one where she heard whispers from around him, from the many human spirits within the walls, like the sound of wind moving quietly through trees.

I already told you, the Master said, his voice seeming to come from all around her. *I'm here to free the prisoners. All of them. See for yourself.*

But he *was* a prisoner, Peaceful thought. And even though she didn't understand it, even though it was the worst thing she'd ever seen, she turned slowly and looked around her. Her alter-power senses spread further in this environment, and she saw all the Creatures lined up against the barrier, which shimmered and moved and looked thinner, weaker than she'd ever seen it.

And there was ex-Bright, the Tiger, pacing back and forth as though his mere movement would break the last thin threads, and with his savage face alight with his impending freedom. He again wore that horrid crown which Peaceful now knew to be made of bones and sinew; a symbol of his mastery over this realm. The Creatures more quietly called it the Death Crown – death being that hideous thing that brought all the humans down into this place. Death being what had happened to *them*…sort of.

Ex-Bright, the Tiger, King of Death and the Creatures. Keeper of a new name only he himself knew. *"How close we are!"* he roared. *"How soon we will be free to retake our places, and to take our revenge! Victory is ours!"*

"VICTORY!" she heard the Creatures cheer. *"VICTORY!"*

Around her, Peaceful could see the faint shimmers and hear the sighs and groans of new humans brought down here. They died so fast, those beings, and with each death she saw the walls of the Creature city grow heavier and denser, and saw the barrier between the realms grow thinner. In the normal realm, the sun rose and set three times, and she was only just aware of it, as the time passed differently here.

Free the prisoners? Peaceful thought in sudden horror. The Master hadn't meant…the *Creatures*, had he?

In that moment she was certain she heard a chuckle, even though she wasn't touching the walls at all, and she felt a faint warmth across her skin. *Don't forget who you are,* the Master told her, and his voice sounded strong once more. *And don't forget who I AM.*

With those last words, suddenly the world around her lit up

as bright as the heart of the light-world, as bright as the heart of a star; even brighter than Bright had been in the height of his glory. She closed her eyes, feeling herself thrown backwards as incredible warmth and power streamed through her with as much force as the initial creation of this small universe, and suddenly all she could hear was…

…joy. Music and laughter and cries of joy, all far beyond anything she'd ever heard before, even before the Rift.

Then Peaceful opened her eyes, and with those special senses she saw an amazing thing. The walls – the walls so full of sorrow and incalculable life-forces – they were emptying out! The sounds she heard were all of those humans escaping through the most colossal gap above her – the rocky roof of the city had been torn open, and above her was an entrance directly to the light-world.

Not the Mountain of Glass where Amaranthus had made his temporary home, but the true light-world. She could see shining forms of humans rushing into it, becoming solid and bright as they entered, then too bright to see. She could hear the cheers of the People welcoming them….

Me too! she thought, and she reached up towards that brightness. She could feel the warmth reach out to envelop her, but then as she would have moved through the gateway, something held her back. She could sense the Master still down here.

Am I not to go? she whispered, even though joy filled her. He'd freed the prisoners! The right ones, too! *Ex-Bright said I am being punished. I thought he lied. Did he speak truly?*

But in that moment Peaceful knew, just *knew* the Master's heart. As sometimes happened, their feelings would overlap until they were closer than even mental communication, and she knew exactly what he wanted. She was welcome back in the light-world, so very welcome, and she'd been away so very long.

She saw in that moment too exactly what had sent her here; exactly what Bright had done, and it was too much for her to really take in. But if she wanted to stay away just a little longer, to continue wearing those human suits, she could make an incredible difference…

I will never again come down into this realm, Amaranthus whispered to her. *Never. But this door I've created, this exit for the trapped humans, shall remain until the end of time. Will you help them find the door, precious Shulamithe? Or will you come home now? The choice is yours.*

It really was her choice, Peaceful knew. The Master had never once forced her to do anything. She'd always followed him freely, because his was a mind more complex and wonderful than she could fathom. Whatever his plans were, they must be for good. And because she'd caught a hint of his plans while they'd merged minds, she knew what choice to make. *I'll find the live ones,* she decided, thinking of those trapped humans Lilith had mentioned.

And then, when the time was perfect, she'd go home. But who knew what good she could do in the meantime?

Reman Palestine, 33 AD

Lilith stood at the barrier to the Other, something inside her trembling with unease. To any passing human (of which there were none) she'd look like a woman alone, standing in the middle of a rocky desert. But she saw the shining barrier that stretched from the ground to the heavens, and she saw the party going on the other side – the *Other* side.

Oh, and there was the Tiger, of whom she was terrified as were all intelligent beings. He'd been pacing back and forth in front of what must be all of the Creatures in this area, practically snarling with excitement as the barrier seemed to grow thinner and thinner from all the power taken from the Deias-man.

Stupid Amaranthus, some of the Creatures had whispered amongst themselves, not that they'd dared to say the name. *Put himself into human form, then died. What a fool.*

But she'd thought, just quietly, that a being as ancient and powerful as the Eternal One surely…surely would never be truly foolish. Was there something they didn't know?

And now those quiet ponderings seemed to have been from a deeper wisdom, because Lilith hadn't stepped through the barrier when she'd been called. She'd delayed a little, and now it was clear that something was wrong. Something was about to happen….

The gateway to the light-world burst open so suddenly that it sent her flying backwards, even on this side of the barrier. She could barely make out what was happening on the Other side, but she knew one thing. It wasn't good.

The Creatures were whimpering, and the barrier in front of her was now brighter and stronger than ever, its temporary thinness having reverted to something even worse than what they'd had before.

And he was there, the Eternal One; moving up through the ground in a form almost too bright to look at. She'd never seen him before like this, since she'd been born after the Rift and had apparently missed all sorts of glories, but she couldn't take her eyes off him. Had he always been so massive?

She squinted as the manlike being of light leaned down over the fallen Tiger, dwarfing him, and then reached out one hand to remove the Tiger's death-crown. The crown shimmered then reappeared on the being's hand, looking rather like an odd, dark tattoo. It was a part of him now, Lilith realised.

Then the Eternal One turned and looked towards the barrier,

towards where she stood. He began to walk closer…

She threw herself to the ground as that brightness approached, wondering if she'd be burned to ash. For a moment it seemed like she would, but then suddenly the light seemed to go out. She lay there still on the hard ground, blinking against the sudden dimness, then realised that the being had vanished, that was all.

She heard groaning from the Other side. "Where did he go?" one brave (or stupid) Creature muttered.

Good question, actually. Where did a being of absolute light and power go, when it returned to the physical realm from where it had just been killed three days earlier? Lilith had some idea, and she didn't want to be anywhere near the Other realm right now. Not when the Tiger had faced a worse humiliation than she'd ever thought possible.

Not long after, Lilith stood almost invisibly at the edge of a graveyard, watching as a group of snivelling women approached the place that the now-deceased Miracle Man had been left. A tomb in the rock, with an enormous boulder in front of it. But now the boulder had been rolled away…

Lilith swallowed, but she couldn't take her eyes off the scene. There was something here…*someone,* more like…

Deceased? Not anymore.

She saw him before the women did, and she turned on her heel, fleeing with all the power she could muster. She'd go to the other side of the normal realm if she could – to the cold lands to the north or the burning lands to the south, anywhere to get away from this place. She certainly wouldn't be going back to the Other realm; not for two thousand years if she could avoid it.

Because one thing was clear. Yeshua of Nazarith, AKA

Amaranthus in human form, had never intended to stay dead. And with his resurrection, the world had changed forever.

Time to run.

Eleven

THE TRUTH
ABOUT SILVERS

Somewhere above the Island of Exiles

The ship moved smoothly through the air, its every mast, sail and railing shining faintly with whatever had made it resemble a shooting star. As for Elspeth, she was pondering what Amaranthus had told her about the origins of the Eternity Stone – and wondering if she was mad to consider seeking it out herself.

"Erastus ahoy," Jolly announced suddenly, interrupting her musings. "It's not far at all, see?" He pointed to a distant gateway in the sky, one which they appeared to be approaching at great speed.

"Erastus," Elspeth muttered. "I do recall my sister speaking of that place, but I have never imagined I would visit that particular future town. I suppose now is the time to do so." But she could feel her resolve weakening with every passing moment.

"Future town what?" Sweet asked. He sat in her arms like a large fluffy toy, and she occasionally brushed her hand over his oh-so-silky ears.

She looked at him surprise – was he mocking her? – then realised how odd her question must seem. If they were in this place, mayhap a full millennium from the year she'd been born, then 'twas not the future at all. 'Twas the present – *this* place's present. "Pay me no heed. I was merely thinking aloud."

But Sweet set his small paw on her hand, and his large silvery eyes briefly flickered blue. "You have travelled a long way," he murmured thoughtfully. "For a two-leg, anyway. But you have further still to go."

Elspeth glanced at him curiously, but Jolly spoke up from where he appeared to be steering the ship. (In truth she suspected he steered not at all; rather that the ship went where its course had been set. Nevertheless, it pleased him to be thought captain, with or without his large hat.) "Don't call them two-legs, Sweet," he scolded. "It's rude."

"But you've got two legs as well," Elspeth commented.

Sweet shrugged, then ducked his fluffy head into her hand. "Is jus' a name," he said in a muffled voice. "Sowwy."

"So will it be Erastus or not?" Jolly pressed impatiently. "Because we don't have long to decide whether you wish to be heroic or not, and it will be a *long* time by your standards before we run into you again like this. Erastus to be a hero…or back to the Mountain of Glass, like a girlish blaggard."

Sweet scolded him, but Elspeth sighed, unoffended. 'Twas merely his manner, she now saw. "Erastus will do very well, and I thank you. If all goes as intended, I shall call you again-"

"Good!" Jolly cut in quickly. Then in a moment he'd grabbed Sweet by one paw, yanking him away from Elspeth, then also grabbed her hand and lifted her to her feet. There was surprising strength in that tiny, fluffy frame. "One gift from the Mountain for your travels, Betsy. Choose what you want."

Elspeth was still shaken from the sudden upheaval. "Pardon…?"

"Choose a gift to help you through this challenge," Sweet piped up. "Strength to lift a boulder. Knowledge to see all secrets.

The ability to move from place to place without crossing space in between…"

"*Ohhh.*" They meant a gift from the Mountain – how utterly wonderful! For a moment her mind fluttered frantically between her many options. She might even fly like Anne, or be stronger than even the largest Person, or have speed enough to outrace any pursuer… But then she thought of Jon. "Language," she blurted out. "Is there some means by which I can speak any language?"

"All-tongues," Jolly said decisively. He slapped something into her hand. "Drink up, quick!"

Elspeth drank, the tiny bottle barely giving a sip of pepperminty flavour before emptying.

She felt a tug at her hand. "It will allow you to speak and understand all languages, even those from the non-human worlds," Sweet told her. "Better than anything human-made, yes?"

Awww, he was so *sweet!* "Yes," she began to say, but then she felt Jolly's small, furry hand grab her other wrist.

"Hurry up!" he ordered, dragging her to the edge of the ship, to where the balcony vanished and its sheer side was exposed. He was practically vibrating with excitement; his little black nose twitching. Up ahead a bright gateway was growing closer and closer, looking as though 'twas filled with pure light. "We're about to pass the Erastus gateway in three…two…"

"Pardon!?" Elspeth gasped, but she'd already felt a hard shove from behind.

"Good luck!" she heard Sweet call after her. She could have sworn Jolly said something like 'Avast!' but then she was through the gateway, into the light.

Erastus 2598 AD

Kamile hurried back to Erastus's crowded town square, her arms wrapped tightly around herself, and her mind filled with images of Aras vanishing into that fog. Worse still, all the things that might be happening to him even now…

Her eyes were stinging with tears, and she ducked her head as she reached the place where she'd left Isla and the girls. They were waiting just where she'd left them, and as she approached, Poli looked at her reproachfully, a wriggling infant crying in her arms. "Where did you go, Kamile? Isla's crying, and you can't just run off like that! Anything could have happened to you!"

She'd been scolded by a fourteen-year-old, but she had no energy to dispute. "You're right, I'm sorry. I shouldn't have done that." She took Isla, lifting the baby to her shoulder and leaning forward so her hair covered her face. The baby cried, she cried; it was all the same, really.

She could see Poli moving closer from under her curtain of brown hair. Her expression was concerned, as was Magdalene's from where she stood further way. "Kamile? What's the matter?"

Kamile sniffed, blinking until she could see a little better. "Oh, it's just Aras. He's gone off to be a hero, and might never come b*aaccck*…" And then she dissolved into tears again.

"What? Where did he go?"

Kamile took another deep breath. *Sigh.* "I'm sorry," she said again. "I don't want to burden you two. You're so young, and you've got enough to worry about."

"But we're your family!" Poli argued intently. "Whatever the problem is, we need to know too!"

So she told them.

"Let me get this straight," Poli said two minutes later. "Aras has gone off through some secret doorway, without even knowing what's on the other side, to face some terrible Creature. He was gifted some kind of protection from one of the locals, and is planning to drag it through to Erastus where it can be killed. That's the plan?"

Kamile shrugged. "More or less." It didn't sound any better when Poli repeated it.

Poli screwed up her nose. "Which local would suggest that kind of thing?"

"It was Joy Silver, and a few of the other Silvers. Four of them, and they all thought it was a good idea."

There were a few seconds of silence where both Poli and Magdalene stared at her wide-eyed. Then Poli exploded. "Mama Silver? Are you *crazy?* Don't you know who she is?"

Through the doorway

Passing through the doorway had felt like being blasted with hot and cold air all at once; like the hairs stood up violently all over Aras's body and then tried to flee before settling down again.

His heart was pounding so hard he could hear it, but his hands were still and ready at his sides. One on the sabre; his other, prosthetic hand on the pistol. All around him was grey cloud, so thick he couldn't see anything at all except flashes of faint light over his arms, rather like lightning. It tingled, and it seemed to be what the Silvers had gifted him with.

But finally the cloud faded and the tingling reduced, even though his heart was still pounding double-time. Then at last he could see what was around him – what was through this doorway that could either be his making, or his destruction.

He now stood in dim light amidst stony rubble. It was mostly white like much of that in Erastus, with hints of what might have been beautiful carvings once upon a time. Most of it was so worn it was unrecognizable, and merely crunched underfoot.

Besides the rubble, the earth was dry, rocky, and dark. It stretched off into the dark horizon, scattered with odd shapes that surely must be more ruins like these. He appeared to be in a desert, and there were no stars. It was cold, although not freezing, and there was no wind. No smell to the air. Nothing, really.

Just the Other, Aras thought to himself. He'd been here before, or at least in places like it when he'd been a knight of the Chosen. So now he focused on what he already knew. *Stand quietly, take in your surroundings. Remember your plan. Go unseen, focus…*

Crunch.

There was the faintest sound from somewhere off to his left, and he spun around to face the new threat, smoothly drawing his pistol as he did so. He squinted, trying to make out something. Anything. Then in the distance, behind a pillar, he caught a glimpse of a pale form.

He waited for the enemy to show itself, or to attack. Either way he'd be ready. His stomach was drawn tight with nerves, tenser than he ever remembered being. His skin tingled once more, and the hair stood up again on the back of his neck and down his natural arm. But the other arm, the one holding the pistol…it lowered.

Aras stared at the silvery prosthetic in dismay as it spread its metallic fingers, releasing the weapon to fall with a clang on the stony ground.

He hadn't done that! There seemed to be a purplish sort of haze over the metal, he noted a mere moment before a shaft of pain struck his belly. He snapped forward, bending over in agony as terrible pain rippled and spread through his abdomen and chest. It was too intense for him to even reach for any other weapon with his natural hand. He went to groan, to react in some way, but all that came from his mouth was *"Ah ha ha ha ha-"*

He was laughing? Why was he laughing when he was *dying*? And so easily too. He hadn't thought it would be so quick…

The Tiger, he realised through the pain. It must be nearby. It was working on him even from a distance!

And so even as the convulsions of laughter became agonising, even as he could see the blood seeping through the cloth of his shirt, and as he could see the pale figure approach in his peripheral vision…he rested his natural hand on his sabre's hilt, and gave everything he had to holding himself together for just five…more…seconds…

Erastus

Peaceful sat at the edge of the crowd, unseen and uncaring. She wore the form of a youngish woman: average height, average build, average weight. The smooth facial features were average too, but wore a serenity that came from the host's complete lack of empathy rather than any real peace.

For someone like her, someone who'd borrowed (or rescued) near-dead humans for two-and-a-half thousand years, such emotionlessness was very odd. This person *seemed* peaceful, but in truth they were ruthless and uncaring.

Like now. In the centre of the square, one of the councillors expounded on how they would face this new challenge that was decimating their population. How they'd protect their people, how they'd find and destroy what was causing it. Chaos, perhaps they'd even close all the doorways until this was resolved!

Peaceful barely held back a sigh. Humans. So earnest, and so clueless.

Centuries earlier, some other earnest, clueless humans had been searching for the cure to their mortality. They'd experimented with alter-power, but had inadvertently created all these doorways instead. Some led straight from one place in the normal realm to another, and were safe enough.

But many of the doorways led straight to the Other, both Mountain and desert, and some were so incredibly dangerous that it would have made her shudder…if she'd been the sort to do so. Her host most certainly wasn't that sort.

But anyway, the humans had foolishly settled in this place now called Erastus, and now they were surprised that some of their own were being injured? Although from the description of the injuries, Peaceful wasn't sure what exactly had caused them. Not a Creature.

The laughter reminded her of a Halfling, Lilith, who she fortunately hadn't seen in decades. Lilith had had a gift with music and sound that could draw all kinds of emotion from people, and which she'd often used to control and manipulate others. But the rest of it; such bloody injuries and even death? No, it didn't fit with what Peaceful knew of that person. Not at all.

As her eyes skimmed the crowd she spotted a trio of familiar figures. Three females: a brunette and a redhead who were not yet women, and a smaller, lean brunette holding a tiny baby. She didn't know the first two except through connection with the last one, and even through the haze of apathy from this host body, she felt her heart soften.

Kamile. That was the last body she'd worn before this current one, and it had to be one of her favourites just from the girl's temperament and kind heart. It had definitely been a rescue, too. Even now the girl wore the signs of her almost-death: a scarf tied jauntily around her neck contrasted with her clearly distressed face, and also hid what Peaceful knew to be a vicious scar.

Just behind Peaceful's consciousness, the host's essence stirred. They saw what Peaceful was looking at, and a wave of hatred and derision rolled throughout their body. *Worthless half-breed. You should have left that one to die, Creature! Instead of bringing her away from the Other, all the way out here, to flaunt her mixed-breed infant and to proselytize young girls-*

Shulamithe. The mental command worked immediately, sending the host's essence back to sleep, and Peaceful followed up by erecting mental barriers, shutting them away, hopefully permanently. *And I'm not a Creature*, she added silently.

Chaos, out of all the bodies she'd worn, this was one of the worst. Not at all repentant of its crimes, and not grateful for the second chance at life. It actually *wanted* to go back to the Other! It *wanted* to meet the Tiger, even though Peaceful had clearly shown it through images and memories exactly how that would turn out. It was convinced that it alone would be the exception.

Now Peaceful did sigh, and the host's mouth sighed with her. Unfortunately the host had actually been one of those to almost murder Kamile, so she wouldn't have bothered rescuing it, if she'd had any other choice. But after she'd left Kamile's body, she had to go *somewhere,* or she'd have been zapped right back to the Other.

But what was her dear Kamile so upset about?

Peaceful checked her illusion was in place, still making the host look a little different from its true appearance, then quietly got up and moved through the crowd closer to those three girls. Close enough she could hear their discussion, and hear exactly what was making Kamile cry, and the redheaded girl hop up and down in agitation.

Oh…chaos.

The Creature City

"You can't come with me," Ash said finally. "I can't hide you from the Creatures in this way. I don't have any magical powers!" Not any that would help right now, anyway. "Just wait here, *hide*, and I swear I'll come back as soon as I find a way out!"

"But back in the cells?" the straggly-haired woman queried (her actual name was Erin, but first impressions last). "We just got out of there!" Beside her, the other half-dozen remaining escapees looked equally as unhappy.

"And you're free to go running off in every direction like most of the others did," Ash said yet again, feeling her eye start to twitch. She wasn't up to being anyone's rescuer. Not today, not here. "Maybe you'll get out, or maybe you won't. But the Creatures think you're already down here! If they come and find you here, apparently never freed, then surely they'll leave you and go for the others, yes?"

"I don't know," one of the other men said dubiously. "Creatures aren't always that rational. Sometimes they just come and get people, and they're never seen again."

Ash's heart sank down into her stomach. That sounded like what you'd expect from such hideous, horrible beings. They'd managed to stuff the crocodilian jailer into that one tiny cell, but who knew how long that would last? "Fine, follow me if you must, just don't make noise," she said finally.

As if that would save any of them if they were found. *She'd* be OK with her medallion – but the others?

Nevertheless, she crept along through the winding hallways, catching her breath every time she turned a corner and found the new hall was empty. Hades, what luck. Oh Hades, she had to stop thinking 'Hades'! It was no longer a useable swear word, she decided. She'd just have to fall back on good…old… *"Poop!"*

She'd turned the new corner into a large open space rather than another corridor, and it was *not* empty. Quite the opposite, in fact. Even in the dim light she could clearly see dozens of Creatures in various stages of activity, spaced around the open area. They were staring through creepy-looking, glowing holes in the walls, staring at creepy-looking, glowing holes in the floor, staring…oh, who cared what they were doing? They were *Creatures!*

Nearly frozen with fear, Ash held out her arm to block the others from moving closer, and frantically made 'go back!' motions. She didn't think they'd been seen yet, but even now one of the closer Creatures was meandering in her direction – if a thing with six legs and jittering eyeballs could meander. Ugh, she could *smell* them from here too; like a pack of hounds had eaten rotten meat and cabbage, then broken wind…

She glanced over her shoulder to see that the other escapees had got the idea. The last of them was vanishing into a narrow side passage. Perfect. She glanced back into the cavern, driven by either horror or fascination, and something caught her eye. Right across the other side of the room, almost hidden in darkness, was an enormous chair. A throne, really, only faintly visible to her in this light. There seemed to be shapes like…bones…all around it, but it was the thing *on* the throne that caught her horrified gaze.

It was a Creature. A more humanlike one, with two arms and two legs and perhaps even some form of clothing. She could just make out the shape of long, shaggy hair and what might be pointed ears, and faint stripes over the exposed patches of skin. But the eyes, oh, the eyes! They burned in the dim light: one blue, one yellow…

Gulp. She'd definitely seen that Creature before, Ash thought hysterically. That was one of those who'd confronted her outside the silver door, the very first time she'd come into the Other with George. They'd managed to get hold of their enemy, Janeus, and had barely escaped being murdered by his two children with the help of the same protective medallion she even now carried.

But then the 'children' had fled, and these...*Creatures* had arrived. And this one here, it still occasionally showed up in her nightmares...

Time to go, she decided. She turned her back on the scene and fled after the others into the second corridor.

But as Ash turned the corner she was stunned to see a stone wall, and not a soul in sight. Had she gone the wrong way? She turned 360 degrees as if she'd find something she'd missed, and her elbow brushed the rock. Then suddenly it felt like someone grabbed her by the shoulders and pulled her upwards.

Whoosh.

"Eeek!"

One moment George was hurtling face-first into a rock wall, pushed from behind by a surprisingly strong Anne, and the next he stood amongst ruins, in semi-darkness. He did not take in much more than that, since he'd seen something more pressing: just beside him was a large fallen figure.

And crouched over that figure was a small Creature. It looked like a taxidermied beaver crossed with a piglet, and it squinted up at George with malicious black eyes. "Oi, don't I know you?"

George didn't pause. His brain took 'fallen figure' and 'Creature' and promptly reacted with 'violence!'. *Whack.* Somehow his hand had operated faster than his mind, and he'd hit the blasted thing on the head with that baton Anne had gifted him. There was a bright flash of light, a sound rather like thunder, and the beaver-pig went flying off into the darkness like it had been shot from a cannon. There was a faint sound like 'ow' in the very far distance, and then it was just George and the fallen body.

"By Jupiter," he murmured, taking a moment to admire his new super-baton. "It might not look like much, but it certainly packs a wallop! Now, as for you, sir…"

He bent down over the figure. It was a fair-haired man, as pale as death and with a wide red sash tied around his middle. He also seemed to have a metal arm lying to one side. The other arm was spread out, with his hand loosely clutched around what appeared to be a sort of sword or knife, its shining blade clean and unmarked. His eyes were open just a crack.

"I say, I do believe I know you," George said in an unexpected repeat of the Creature's words. "The Decimator!" He prodded him gingerly on his metal arm, half afraid the man would suddenly leap up and react badly to having a stranger leaning over him. A most impressively strong man, this one. Huge! When standing, anyway.

"We met a few months ago," he continued. "With, erm, Coryn? There was some Creature attempting to take over the normal realm, and a sort of flask, and a volcano, and people shooting…*ugh*."

The 'ugh' came about because the metal arm which George had been gently prodding suddenly came off. It landed with a clang on the stony ground, leaving behind a stump not even hidden by clothing.

"Oops. Er…Alan, was it? No, *Aras*. That's it. I hope you don't mind, but…" Then George noticed the second rather unpleasant thing. Aras wasn't wearing a sash at all. No, it was a large amount of blood, as if he'd been gutted.

George sucked in a horrified breath, then urgently took off his jacket and pressed it against the man's belly. It felt soft, not at all like the belly of an enormous muscular sort should. "Don't die," he urged. "Please don't die." He couldn't be dying if his eyes were open, surely?

Just then a childhood memory came to mind; the time he'd come across a deceased squirrel on his estate. *Its* eyes had been bulging wide open, and it had been as dead as a doornail. The comparison made George gulp, and he set two fingers against Aras's neck. He felt a weak pulse. Very, very weak.

"George?"

The soft voice calling his name, combined with the horrid surroundings, made him leap a mile in the air. He turned, his baton held before him threateningly, then saw who'd spoken. "Ashlea!?"

"George?"

"Ashlea!"

"George!" Finally it sank in that yes, that young man currently half-crouched – in Hades – with his hands covered in blood *was* Ash's husband, and the sight of his dear, familiar, anxious face made her want to cry. She ran over towards him. "What are you doing here?"

A series of expressions crossed his face, something like confusion/irritation/fear/relief.

"Ashlea Jane O'Reilly Seymour. I leave you for one hour, *one hour* to go to the Mountain of Glass, and the next thing you're in *Hades*?!"

"Sorry," Ash blurted out, and threw herself into his arms. They hugged for a very long time, and the mingled fear and relief just about made her laugh. "You're in Hades too," she pointed out somewhere in the vicinity of his neckcloth. "Why?"

George pulled back a little. "Anne sent me to get you. Edward's fine – we'll discuss that later – but Anne says the People don't come down here. There's some sort of hidden exit, a door that Amaranthus set for humans to escape from these cities. Anne said it should be easily findable if we're looking for it."

"Oh, wonderful!" Ash looked back over her shoulder for the other escapees, but didn't see anyone else. "There are at least a hundred other people somewhere around here. I stole the key to their cells from this big crocodile Creature, but they all took off in different directions, and I don't know how long they'll last here in the Creatures' own territory. The protective medallion keeps me from being seen or properly heard, but there's nothing to help *them*. Even worse, it didn't work when I tried to tell the Creatures to go away. Maybe because…well, there's nowhere for them to go."

In unison they both looked down to the fallen figure they were practically standing on. It only took Ash a few seconds to recognise the man, even with the missing arm and blood everywhere. "Is he dead?"

George shook his head. "Not yet, but I don't think it'll be long." There was a pause, then he quickly added, "I found him like this! I think a Creature attacked him."

"I know *you* didn't hurt him," Ash retorted. She swallowed. Then she carefully pulled the medallion out from her pocket and reached down towards Aras.

George grabbed her wrist. "What are you doing? Ashlea, that's keeping you and our child alive down here, in what must be the worst place in existence. You can't give that up for a…for a dying acquaintance!"

She looked up and met his blue eyes earnestly. She could feel her own pricking with tears. "But George, I don't think Aras has met Amaranthus. Not even once. I don't think he's even been to the River! If *he* dies down here..." She breathed in a sob. "He'll stay. That's how it works. And I can't have that on my conscience. I don't think you can either."

George breathed out a long, sighing breath, then muttered something under his breath. "Fine," he agreed grudgingly, and she reached down to press the medallion against Aras's skin. Protection transferred. "How's your far-sight?"

"Um..." Not present most of the time? Separated, just like she couldn't sense Amaranthus at all down here? "...Alright, I suppose."

"Good. There's that, at least. Now, tell me where you came in, and I can send you straight back out." George held up his wrist, displaying a slender red bracelet that she'd never seen before. "This can send one person back through any one-way doorway. I understand that most of those leading in here are one-way."

"Yes! Yes, they are." Ash looked around frantically, trying to remember where she'd come in. It had been below ground, but nearby she could see what looked like an old archway. There was solid stone behind it. Her eyebrows pricked up. "I don't know why you think I'd ever leave without you, George, but I *think* that might be one."

"Perfect!" George grabbed her hand and pulled her to her feet, slapping the bracelet on her wrist as he did so. "Now come along."

"George...George!" Ash dug in her feet just as she reached the nearby stone door, pressing one hand against the surrounding archway to prevent herself from being pushed through. "I can't just leave you here!"

He leaned in, his usually cheerful visage more solemn than she'd ever seen it. "And I cannot leave my pregnant wife down here. Not for anything. And if you can't do it for me," he cut across her objections, "then do it for Baby Broadbean, who doesn't have a choice."

In that moment Ash realised he was right. She felt her face crumple, but she nodded. "You come straight back to me, you understand?"

"Of course!"

For a moment they stood so close, her hand around the back of his head, their eyes intent on each other. Then George leaned in and kissed her roughly on the mouth. "All will be well," he reassured her.

Ash nodded, then tightening her lips so she wouldn't cry, turned back to the stone-blocked doorway. This bracelet thing better work, or this was all for nothing. She set her bracelet-clad wrist in front of her, over the stone, then sharply leaned in. *Go through,* she told herself.

George watched as his wife prepared to step through the stone doorway. She'd be taking herself and their child to freedom, and leaving him here. It was right, he knew that for a certainty, but by Deias he'd never felt so alone.

She glanced at him, just once, and then closed her eyes and stepped forward.

Smack. Right into the solid stone wall. "OW!"

"Ashlea!" He stepped forward, dismayed. "What happened?"

"It doesn't work!" she snapped, lifting a hand to rub her reddened nose. "It's still stone! Are you sure it was the real Anne who gave you this thing?"

"Of course!" George retorted. His brief moment of relief at not being alone was rapidly replaced by horror that she was still *here.* "Are you sure this is a real way out?"

"I think so." Ashlea stepped back, studying it again. "I mean…it's not the one I came in by, but I'd swear it's the same type. It *feels* like the same type. It must be, right?"

"Give me the bracelet, and I'll test it."

She handed it over, and no sooner had George set his hand against the stone than it began to soften and go through. "Argh!" He pulled his hand back through, baffled. "It does work. Then what's the problem?" Oh Deias, he was so aware of their location, even of their sudden lack of protection. If any Creature came along, they'd be helpless. Except for his super-baton, of course.

"I don't know," she began, then suddenly her eyes widened. "Oh, Hades. I mean- *argh!* George, I'm pregnant!"

"Yes, what of it?" A moment passed and then understanding dawned. "*Ohhh.* There's two of you, and the bracelet only admits one."

Well. That was a fine predicament. But there was always a solution…

George glanced again at the fallen Decimator, and then at his wife. "Do you have any paper in those pockets of yours?"

"Uh…yes, actually. Why?"

"Because I've got a ballpoint pen," he replied, whisking out his fifth-favourite object from the twenty-first century. "And I really think we ought to write a good, old-fashioned note."

Three minutes later, the bracelet was gone, and so was Aras. George and Ashlea stood amongst the now-empty ruins. The stone archway they'd pushed Aras through was once again solid, looking almost the same except for the slight smear of blood left as they'd pushed him through. George held her hand tightly, feeling the hard outline of the medallion pressed between their palms.

"I hope he survives without the medallion," Ashlea murmured.

George hoped so too. He hoped *they* survived *with* the medallion. *Hidden Door, where are you?* "I'm certain he'll be fine."

She looked up at him hopefully. "Really?"

Well, no, but that was what one said in these situations, was it not? False hope was better than no hope, and so forth.

But just then a dreadful smell came to his nostrils. He sniffed, then made a face. Oh dear. He understood that pregnant women had a tendency to flatulence, but that was just *foul*.

"George!" Ashlea hissed, pointing at something up ahead.

A moment later he saw the same little beaver-hoggish Creature he'd batoned earlier. It was shuffling along, its ugly head now at an odd angle, and was muttering to itself. It didn't seem to have seen them.

"Oh, thank Deias," he whispered. "I thought that smell was *you*."

She gave him a glare as foul as the Creature's stench, but then they both froze in silence and watched as it hobbled along in front of them towards the bloodied archway. It paused briefly, then with a *crack* straightened its neck before carrying on. "Dunno where 'e came from," it muttered. "Right outa nowhere. Should tell the Tiger, but 'e'll just shoot the messenger, won't 'e. And I've been hit enough for one day."

George raised his eyebrows.

"It shouldn't be able to hear us," Ashlea whispered. "The others couldn't – except when I tried to send one away by speaking its name."

Hmm. It must be the medallion's special ability for Creature cities, George pondered. For earlier, when they'd first come across the Creatures in the open desert of the Other, they'd certainly been seen. And this particular Creature? He'd vow he'd met it once before, and had almost died as a result. "Let's test it," he suggested.

So when the beaver-hog shuffled closer, he stepped forward without releasing Ashlea and raised the baton in his free hand. It didn't respond, didn't even look up. But by Jove, it was still a Creature, and they had a score to settle.

Whack.

"Good heavens," Ashlea murmured as they watched the Creature go sailing once again into the far distance. "That's more than a home run! What have you got there?"

"Oh, it's merely another object of power from the Mountain," George replied modestly. "I do believe there must be an entire room full of them somewhere. Like an appliance store! One MacGuffin for every possible need."

"What's a MacGuffin?"

"Look it up on Oogle," George told her loftily. "It's a modern thing."

Ashlea smiled up at him, getting the joke. But then he had taken to some technology with a passion, and the internet was one of his favourite inventions (along with tasers, mobile phones, kaleidoscopes, locomotives and ballpoint pens). "Is the baton better than a taser?"

He pondered the question. Which was better down here, in this Creature city where they had to set out in search of a mysterious exit, and rescue as many people as possible on the way? A taser would have failed on its first use, if it hadn't run out of battery. "I do believe it *is* better than a taser," he agreed finally.

And that was saying something.

Erastus

"What do you mean, the Silvers don't exist?" Kamile echoed in dismay. "I saw them, Poli. Three of them just now along with Joy Silver, and there have to be a dozen all around Erastus. Are you saying they're some kind of illusion?"

"No illusion," Poli replied. Her grey eyes were wide, and her freckles stood out boldly on her pale face. She was practically jiggling with panic. "Jean's dad says they're extensions of Mama Silver. They're like…sentries, so she can be in all sorts of places at once." She lowered her voice, looking around them nervously. Even though they were in the middle of the crowd, there didn't seem to be anyone watching. "Jean's dad says no one trusts Mama Silver. She keeps trying to get on the council, but there are too many things that go wrong around her, and they don't know where she gets all of her power. They want to make her leave, or even charge her with something, but they can't get any solid proof she's done anything wrong."

Kamile felt her heart sink into the pit of her stomach. She'd trusted Joy, she'd trusted her with sending Aras through that doorway even as she'd fought it, because *all* the Silvers had agreed. She'd felt outnumbered. But if she really hadn't been… "That's a big claim," she said quietly. "How do people know this?"

Poli's mouth opened and closed a few times. "I don't know," she said finally. "But Jean's dad says *everyone* knows the truth about the Silvers. I would have said something earlier, but there was so much going on…"

"I'll have to meet Jean's dad some time," Kamile murmured. Oh, Fire Lord. Could it be true? What did it mean for Aras?

Magdalene had been watching them with wide, haunted eyes. "I think it's true," she whispered.

Kamile looked up sharply. "Do you know something, Mags? Because now's the time to tell it."

Magdalene licked her lips. "I don't like Mama Silver." But that was all she said.

"It seems to me that most women don't," Kamile countered wryly. Because of course her own reaction had also been dislike, and she'd put it down to petty jealousy. "And most men do. But that's not enough reason to think her some kind of…supernatural villain. Has she done something, Mags?"

"No…not really…" Magdalene looked up at Kamile defiantly, then ducked her head again.

"Is it something to do with that boy?" Poli piped in suddenly. "The one you've been keeping secret, Mags?"

Magdalene shot her a glare, then finally nodded. "I know she's been talking to Cobalt too, and…he said there was no killer."

Cobalt. The mysterious boy finally had a name. "But Mags…" Kamile furrowed her brow, trying to make sense of it when the context was so, so important. "What's so very bad about being wrong?"

But the younger girl would only look at her feet. *"Mumble mumble."*

"What?"

"She said he's through a doorway!" Poli shouted. "Mags, I can't *believe* you fell for something like that!"

Magdalene's eyes shimmered with unshed tears. "But he was so nice, Poli! So handsome! And he listened to me, and he never made me feel stupid. But then today he told me there was no killer, but there clearly is!"

"And did this Cobalt try to get you to come through the doorway to him?" Poli challenged.

"Yes…but I didn't!"

"Wait, wait!" Kamile shouted. She stepped between the two

girls, Isla squalling in her arms, and a headache blooming in her temples. "Magdalene. Are you saying that you've been talking to some…person through one of these stone doorways, someone who Joy Silver also talks to, and he tried to get you to go through to him?"

Magdalene shrugged a shoulder, wide-eyed. "Well…he can't come through to me, so sure. But today Mama Silver came to Crookshank Alley to talk with him! I didn't hear them what they were saying, but it looked like they were friends. Then later he said that if I went through a doorway too, I'd become like her one day. You know, beautiful." She ducked her head, her cheeks turning red.

A doorway in an otherwise ordinary place. Promises of beauty and friendship. Sounded familiar, hmm? Right then everything Kamile already knew and had guessed and remembered about the Chosen and the Fey/Creatures, all clicked into place. Liars and deceivers, always and forever more. "Fire Lord." And Aras. Poor Aras. "Poli, please go get Jean's dad at once. Can you do that?"

"Yes, of course-"

"And Magdalene…" Kamile paused, looking at the girl who was her own height, but oh so much younger. She felt a wash of affection and sympathy run through her. It was normal for a girl with no father to seek out male affection, especially the older, secure-seeming type. She'd done it herself. So she leaned forward and kissed her on the cheek, passing over the baby as she did so. "Hold Isla. And no going through any doorways!"

Then she turned and ran full-tilt towards where she'd last seen Aras.

THE HIDDEN DOOR

Kamile ran back towards the alley with the secret doorway, her heart pounding with fear and adrenaline. But when she arrived there, all was quiet. The Silvers were nowhere to be seen. She took a step closer, and then she could see everything.

Aras was sprawled face up, just outside the doorway. His metal arm was missing, and his grey tunic top was soaked red from mid-chest downwards.

Kamile let out a cry of horror and ran towards him. She crouched down and patted his face, looking for a response, then when there wasn't one, checked the pulse on his neck with shaking fingers. But she couldn't tell if there was a pulse, or if it was her own panic. She pressed her hands against his belly as if she could heal him by her will alone, muttering prayers in between stuttering sobs. "Please, please, not Aras! Not him too."

If only she had some unusual abilities! But even though she was a Halfling – half human and half Creature/Fey – the best she could do was identify when alter-power was in use. And even then, not always. She didn't even have a communication link to contact anyone!

Kamile noticed a small, ragged piece of parchment tucked into his jacket, half soaked red. She barely spared it a glance except to see it had some kind of ancient-style code scrawled on it. A threat, maybe? She shoved the thing into her pocket in case it was useful later, then realised that Aras had a communication link in his pocket that the council had given to him.

She frantically checked all available pockets before finally finding it inside his blood-soaked inner pocket. She pulled it out, then tapped at it a few times to make sure it was active. "Help! Please send a medic right away!" She gave her location, then repeated the request a few times before sending it to everyone on his contact list. Then she began to take off her own outer tunic, planning to use it as a bandage. It wasn't much, but it would be better than nothing. It had to be, because there was nothing else-

"It won't do, you know."

The quiet voice made Kamile jolt, and she glared up at the newcomer through teary eyes. "And you've got a better idea, do you?"

The other woman shrugged. She was rather bland-looking, not plain, just nothing that would draw attention. She even wore a plain brown tunic and cloak almost like one of the Chosen would. "Yes."

And then suddenly she changed. One moment she was ordinary, unfamiliar; the next she was ten years older with grey-streaked brown hair, familiar serene features, and eyes that flickered rapidly from blue to gold to blue again. She also had a rather decisive blaster wound in her forehead.

"Starbright?" Kamile choked out, horrified. She thought the former leader of the Chosen had died back in the same place where she herself had been returned to life. Aras had told her so, since she'd been unconscious through most of it.

Those unfriendly eyes softened, for a moment shining bright gold. "Don't be silly, dear Kamile. You know me."

She didn't know the voice, or the face, or even the eyes. But she did recognise something. "Shulamithe?!"

"Yes, it's me." The nonhuman wearing Starbright's body came and knelt next to Aras, setting one hand on his chest, and Kamile let her. "He's still alive, but not for long. I can save him."

Kamile knew at once what that meant. Shulamithe would inhabit Aras's body, would keep him alive and perhaps let him heal just a little, while his spirit slept somewhere in the background. She'd done the same to Kamile, and had saved her life in the meantime. But as for the body Shu wore now? It would live or die depending on its strength. But Kamile didn't care. "Do it, please."

The immortal didn't wait. Starbright's body closed its eyes, its hand resting on Aras's chest, and then there was a brief moment where Kamile felt a fluctuation of alter-power like a warm breath across her skin. Then Starbright's body fell sideways to lie limply across the ground, and Aras took a deep breath. His eyes fluttered open…and they were bright blue, not their usual light, almost cold blue.

"Done, dear Kamile," Shulamithe said in Aras's deep voice. "He'll live – at least for now."

Kamile began to weep again, taking Aras's cool hand and leaning over his body. If even this immortal couldn't guarantee he was saved, then could he ever be?

Peaceful just lay there on the hard ground, adjusting herself to this new, rather large body. Perhaps it was usually strong, but now it felt broken and weak, and there was a lot of pain clustered around its belly and the stump of its missing arm.

She focussed her attention on supporting those areas, doing her best to heal them. It wouldn't work straight away, but maybe after a few hours…

She saw that Kamile was still crying. "How long does he have?" she wept. "You can tell me. Please, Shu."

The question seemed odd, and Peaceful realised she was seeing it through the new host's extremely logical brain. "I don't know how long he has," she replied simply. "I don't see the future. It could be fifty years, or it could be ten minutes. Only Amaranthus knows that kind of information."

"Oh." Kamile's tears reduced to sniffles, and she studied Peaceful thoughtfully before glancing briefly to the side, to where the old host body lay.

"Is it dead?" Peaceful asked dispassionately.

Kamile nodded, then looked away again, obviously unnerved.

"Ahh." Peaceful breathed in, closing the host's eyes briefly as she accepted this truth. Nothing lasted forever, and she'd always known that the former Elder Starbright didn't have much time left. "She has made her choice, over and over. And now again."

The Halfling watched as Peaceful manoeuvred the large body to a sitting position. It was hard, regardless of the belly wound, because of the missing arm. She'd have to do something about that.

"Why did you help her? Starbright, I mean," Kamile asked as she studied her intently, and Peaceful knew she was watching *her*, not the host. "When you rescued me, you said it was because I deserved a second chance. But surely she didn't deserve one!"

Peaceful wiggled her new, large fingers and rolled those enormous shoulders. "No," she agreed. "But I don't always choose the deserving. I choose whoever is there, and what *they* do next is up to them. Some of the worst people, when they repent of their crimes, have become some of the best, perhaps in part because of their desire to make up for their pasts."

There was a silence where Peaceful could see Kamile's dismay, even as the girl tried to press her tunic against Aras's wound. Peaceful let her. Even though she could do quite a bit of healing simply by inhabiting the body, it never hurt to have a bandage or two.

"But I did find out some interesting things while I borrowed her body," Peaceful continued as she glanced over at the corpse. "Why the Chosen tried to kill you, why the Creatures tried to kill you. Not just because you were leaving them, dear. But because of who you would become."

Kamile looked up at her, startled. "We're talking about the same people, right? The ones who put venomous snakes in my bed, and then cut my throat? Those ones?"

"Mm. It's because the Creatures have limited access to the future. And when they see people who are destined to improve the world in large or small ways, they try to stop it before it happens." Peaceful took the tunic bandage gently away from Kamile, then took a moment to wipe her small hands free of blood. The belly wound was almost sealed now. "So the Creatures saw you in their scrying pools when you were only a girl. They saw you would lead so many to the River; lead them towards Amaranthus. Like a mother, but for many who weren't even your own children. And they tried to stop you over and over."

"Me?" Kamile shook her head in confusion. "But I'm not... I just have Isla now."

"Really?"

There was a brief silence. Then Kamile said, "Well... I suppose I could count Ric, that's Aras's son, but I don't know how long he'll be staying with me. And then there's Poli and Mags. I mean, I *do* like kids...." She sighed, shaking her head as she seemed to accept it. "How?"

"They tried to stop you first by convincing you not to breed –

which worked for a while – and then by having a black border snake put in your bed when it clearly *wasn't* working. But someone decided that was too slow, and that's when you were kidnapped."

The girl's lips tightened, and Peaceful could almost see her mind working through her expressions. Her gifts were limited while wearing these forms, so she had to rely on things like body language.

"That's very useful information," Kamile said finally. "I really, *truly* wanted to know that. But now, I mean, right now, I need to know something else. Who attacked Aras? Who's the one doing all of this? Is it this 'Tiger' that Joy Silver told him about, and does that Creature even exist?"

Peaceful's mind began whirring a mile a minute, and she felt her eyes glow. Who would blame the Tiger for something like this? Sure, he was capable of it, but he tended to think a lot *bigger*. "Let's ask your baby-daddy."

"What?"

Peaceful sighed. "Just an old joke. I'll ask Aras."

The Creature City

Ash and George had been wandering purposefully around the ruins under the shelter of the enormous cavern, carefully holding hands so that the medallion stayed touching both of them at once. George held the super-baton in his free hand, and she still had the bunch of odds and ends she'd taken from the Creature jailer. She knew at least one was a key, but the rest could be anything.

Finally they found an entrance back into the labyrinthine Creature city. As unpleasant as it felt, they both knew it was the right place to go. "This hidden door can't be so hard to find," Ash murmured to George hopefully. "Otherwise why would Anne mention it? Why would Amaranthus *bother* putting it down here, if it's so difficult?"

"Jolly good," he said in that way that meant he wasn't listening at all. His thick eyebrows were low over his eyes, and he was staring intently at every inch of their surroundings as if the door would suddenly reveal itself by a handle or a small, convenient sign.

"Or maybe it's hidden too well," she murmured, suddenly feeling desolate. "After all, those people were down in the cells for who knew how long. If they'd seen any kind of exit, they'd have taken it, right? Or maybe the people who did see the exit took it, and that's why they weren't there to help the others. Is that good or bad?"

"Hush!" George said abruptly, confirming that he hadn't been listening at all. But because she wasn't unreasonable, and because they were in *Hades*, she hushed.

In the silence she heard a sound, like someone moving just out of sight...

They crept around the corner and saw a Creature. It was right in the middle of the corridor, large and hairless, and with legs to spare. It had legs for arms, legs for legs, legs hanging off its back and scratching its head... It was using a couple of those legs to hold a struggling woman up against a graffitied wall, and another couple to press an older man against the ground. The grounded man whimpered as his face went flat into the rock, and he writhed in place, trapped horribly and clearly very aware of it.

"Where are the others?" the Creature was asking the bedraggled woman in a bored tone. Without waiting for her to respond, it lifted her and gave her another whack against the wall.

The woman just cried, and Ash felt George's hand tighten on

hers. Glancing at him, she saw his thick eyebrows had set into 'angry' position. *Are you sure,* she wanted to ask. *This thing isn't like the little furry one you hit earlier.*

But it wasn't the time or place to ask, and so she could only watch as he lifted his baton and drew slowly closer. He stood behind the Creature for a while, as if trying to work out exactly where would be most effective to strike, but then shrugged.

Whack. There was a flash of light, the Creature shrieked, and its long, belegged back arched inwards in a rather disgusting fashion. Ash gasped, the other woman dropped to the ground, and the man scuttled away from the Creature on all fours, his expression desperate. Then *whack,* George got the Creature again, but on the head this time. It went flying against the opposite wall, upside-down like a bundle of sticks with feet on the ends. "Take that!" he hollered.

This all happened within about three seconds, and Ash could only watch dumbfounded as the woman (who probably had a real name, but she'd never know it) muttered something unintelligible, slapped a hand against the wall's disgusting red graffiti...and vanished into thin air.

And then the man, who looked to be older than Ash's father and very, very worn out, crawled towards that same patch of wall, moving as if using the last of his strength. He stretched out one hand towards where the woman had vanished, and cried out something Ash couldn't quite make out. He shook his head, stretched closer, and tried again. And this time it must have worked – because he vanished.

"George!" she hissed. "They must have found the hidden door!"

"But where?!" he whispered back. "I don't see anything! Surely it's not the sewage grate?"

"No, they weren't anywhere near that!" They'd been closer to that spot on the wall with the graffiti…there. No, *there.* Argh, *everywhere* had graffiti, Ash thought in dismay. It looked like it had been scrawled in blood in a hundred different languages, with several words spread around a rough 't' shape.

Even as she was thinking that, the text seemed to swim and change until it was in Anglish. Crude Anglish, but definitely readable.

Yeshua paid my passage.

What…?

And just as she was thinking, *Hey, what's* that *doing down here?* they had company. Four more Creatures-type company.

"INTRUDERS!" the tangled leggy Creature shouted from its place on the ground. "Hidden intruders!"

"The doorway," Ash tried to tell George. "I think it's something to do with the text on the walls!"

But his eyes were bugging out as he looked from new Creature to new Creature, probably trying to work out whose head would be the easiest to baton. (If Ash had a vote, it would be for the shortest Creature with the big bald head. Now that was almost like having a target right in front of them.)

She dug her fingernails into his hand around the medallion, finally getting his attention. "The hidden door!" she hissed, pointing with her free hand. "It's on the wall, George! See the cross?"

His eyes widened as they focused on where she was pointing. "But…surely that's too easy?"

"I don't exactly have a better idea, do you? And it sure looked like those two were using it!"

"But we have to get past the Creatures! The medallion means they can't see or hear us – but can they feel us?"

"They'll still be in here," one of the newer Creatures chittered through its enormous, insect-like mandibles. "I can *smell* them."

That answered that question. But then three out of four Creatures pulled out weird utensils in various frightening shapes, and they lit up green, blue, and purple. They looked like evil and awkward lightsabers, but she'd bet it'd pay not to touch them.

Ash and George exchanged desperate glances, then he lunged sideways, dragging her with him. She had no choice but to follow, and really, now wasn't the time to insist on equal rights. *You don't go first, sir. We go together!* Or perhaps not.

So she followed him, stepping in exaggerated slow motion around the swinging light-utensils and accidentally stomping on a Creature's foot for half a moment. She squeaked, its eyes lit up and she stumbled, almost letting go of George's hand. She was sticky with fear-induced sweat, forcing herself to move as slowly and carefully as he was, and for a brief, crazy moment was reminded of a scene from her favourite action movie where the hero had to cross a room covered with laser beams. The hero had made it, but had slipped slightly and lost his half of his snazzy bow tie to the lasers…

Ssss. A purple blade swung a mere inch away from her nose, and she couldn't help but whimper, especially when she saw a hair flutter away from where it had come loose from her up-do.

Then she felt the wall at her back and realised they'd reached it. They'd reached the mystery doorway. She grinned desperately at George, then slapped her free hand against the wall without letting go of his hand or the medallion. So close. Somewhere around here was an invisible exit, and she was going to find it…

Then suddenly a *green light came sweeping down between them, and their grip was severed. Something struck Ash in the head, and-*

She ducked abruptly to one side, whimpering as the green weapon barely missed her. Thank you, far-sight! And not a moment too soon.

"Get through the door!" George hissed in her ear.

"I can't find it," she tried to say, but then her hand slipped from his grasp and everything was back at high speed. She was crouched on the ground in front of the dark red-brown graffiti, the words *YESHUA PAID MY PASSAGE* written so very clearly. The medallion was just out of arm's reach in front of her, and George was now hanging upside-down in the grasp of one of the bigger Creatures.

"You conniving little turd," it snarled.

But then in rapid motion George whacked its arm with his super-baton, and it went flying away in a bright flash of light. George tumbled to the ground, but Ash couldn't focus on that because something was coming towards her. She shrieked and backed up, desperate to find the door, but still only feeling solid rock behind her. There was nowhere to go, even though she was touching the text. What was she missing?

But then in an abrupt moment of clarity, she remembered the two escapees had been saying something. And what could it possibly be except... "George!" she shouted suddenly. "YESHUA PAID MY PASSAGE!"

Suddenly Ash felt open air behind her; warmth and incredible light moving to envelop her. She'd found the door...but she was about to leave her husband behind.

So with everything she had, with a last desperate push, she shoved the medallion and sent it skidding across the rocky ground towards George. She saw him reach for it, then suddenly she was hurtling through open air, surrounded by light.

If George could have ordered his thoughts in those few chaotic seconds, they would have gone something like this:

Oh good, Ashlea's gone.

Oh good, I've got the medallion.

Oh dear, I think they're going to kill me.

Eeek. Eeek. Just dodged that one! Got in a good blow there, and now diving for the hidden door (are we terribly certain it's an actual exit because it looks like a rock wall to me) and oh dear, they're flinging their weapons around freely now, most likely because they can't see me. But I can't find the door so what am I missing?

Oh that's right "YESHUA PAID MY PASSAGE!" *ahhh…I'm about to make it-*

OUCH!

But then somehow he was pulled away from the chaos and surrounded by the whitest light, and the most intensely beautiful sound, and what felt like air…

For a brief moment George was as light as the air itself, like a delicate soap bubble. Time seemed to slow in that moment of incredible ecstasy, and he looked around to see he was in a vertical tunnel. The walls were shining like the sun, yet somehow he could see text scrawled over every inch of them. *Passage paid. Passage paid. Passage paid. Passage paid…*

Ah, this again? But where was the passage to? Below him was something bright. Above him…well. As he wondered that, he looked up and saw the universe had opened up over his head. It shouldn't be possible, but whatever was up there was even brighter than the tunnel itself. He could just make out buildings, and what looked like many people moving around. Oh, and coming from it was the most beautiful sound…

George reached up towards that place of ultimate light, desperate to see what it contained. Why, he'd give his very soul for such a thing.

Just then he heard a chuckle. *Not yet.*

Then suddenly, just as suddenly as he'd come through the hidden door, gravity reclaimed him. His whole body now seemed to be made of lead, and he plummeted down the tunnel, down-down-down…

"Argggh!" he tried to say. *I'm falling!* But just as he comprehended that, he fell into water. He felt himself go far under the surface, felt bubbles all around him tingling in his clothes and hair and unmentionables as if he was swimming in champagne, and then a moment later he broke the surface.

George sucked in a deep breath, flailing his arms about for a few seconds before realising that a) he was quite alright, and b) his feet were touching the ground. He stood, waving his arms a little to keep his balance in the waist-deep current, and looked around. It appeared he was in some kind of lake, if a lake had current. Perhaps an enormous river, then, except that he couldn't see its banks.

It was vast and beautiful and as still as glass, and it seemed to contain every colour as if it reflected rainbows. Other people were scattered about, all floating like he was, and as he watched another fell *plop* from an invisible entryway, then landed with a splash in the water.

"George! Over here!"

A distant shape waved an arm, and he just about burst with relief as he recognised his wife. "Ashlea!" He flailed through the water, trying to swim or wade, then decided it was easier to go with the slight current like she was. It was taking him towards her, and after a few moments they finally drew close enough to touch.

He grabbed her hand, and then they were in each other's arms, floating and hugging and sobbing. Then finally he stopped sobbing and looked down at her, all wet and smiling. Then he realised *she* was crying also, so perhaps he might continue to do so.

More hugging, more crying. But they were happy tears. Those were something he hadn't had any experience of until now.

"That place of light was so wonderful, Ashlea! I want to go there, but I think I'd have to leave this world behind," he babbled tearfully. "So we should wait, yes? And go together."

"Mm. Let's." His wife sounded rather relaxed considering what they'd just survived; more like she'd had an excellent meal followed by an excellent nap. She didn't comment on his out-of-context speech – it was clear she knew exactly what he was talking about. "But who would have guessed the hidden door was actually a phrase?"

"Took us long enough," George agreed, still weeping. "But why Yeshua, do you think? Why not Amaranthus or the Eternal One or the Unfading One or Deias or-"

She put her finger over his mouth. It tasted rather like lemonade.

"I'm dreadfully sorry," he said, mumbling around her lemonade finger. Then because he couldn't help himself, he licked it, making her giggle. "Mm. This water truly is excellent, is it not?"

"George…" But Ashlea only sighed, sounding so very, very content. "Mm. Yeshua had to be the code word, don't you see? Because while Amaranthus has a thousand names, all those mean different things to different people, depending on what you've been told about him. But he was only born into human form once, and that was as Yeshua of Nazarith. Deias – I mean – oh, whatever. Even *I've* heard of Yeshua, but only now am I beginning to understand what he really did.

"Amaranthus died, George. He died as Yeshua, then went down into that Creature city, and somehow he made a way that anyone can escape true death, just by acknowledging what he did all that time ago. And I think…" Her face scrunched up just a little, but it was adorable. "I think this must be the most important realisation I've ever had in my entire life. It makes everything else look small. Everything."

"Everything!" George choked out in agreement, then realised he was sobbing again. Happy tears that blended in with the odd sparkling water, but still. "I can't seem to stop crying," he said again. "Perhaps it's something in the water." It hadn't made *her* cry as much, he noted. Just very, very placid.

"Mm. It's the water of life."

"Really? Are you quite certain?"

Ashlea leaned back, kicking her feet out of the water and splashing about. A cascade of rainbow drops fell in every direction, making George feel like he'd burst with happiness. "How can it not be?" she said simply.

"But I can't stop crying! I'm just so very *happy...*"

Now she laughed, and her laughter made him laugh too. Then she laughed some more, so he laughed some more, and so forth. It was a very lovely laughing session, and he told her so.

"George, I think you're high."

"No, I'm floating," he corrected her happily. "Floating on water and alter-power, and happiness from our narrow escape from Hades. HADES! And without even a scratch!" He stretched out his legs, waving his booted feet out of the water, and floated on his back.

"George...look at your left foot."

He looked, and he saw that not only was a chunk of his boot missing with seared marks around the removed piece, his littlest toe had also changed shape. "By Jove," he said in surprise. "They cut off my poor little pinky toe!"

"Your poor little toe," Ashlea echoed. "I guess you didn't get the medallion after all."

"Medallion?" George spared a moment of brief regret, realising it'd been left alone on the ground...in Hades. "Oh, well. Never fear. I do believe my pinky is healed already! And I didn't even feel it. D'you think I'll need a prosthetic?"

Ashlea burst out laughing, and after a moment he laughed too. He didn't care about his toe, or his boot, or anything at all except being here in this moment. "Ashlea my dearest, darling, most perfect love, I do believe there is nothing wrong with the world, here or anywhere. I don't care if we never get out of this place. We can be here for ever and ever and- what?"

Ashlea mouthed something that looked like 'otter-all', but he couldn't hear her over the sudden roar of something in his ears. "Say it again louder, darling. I didn't catch that."

She leaned forward, her figure feeling solid and delightfully wifely in his arms as she leaned right into his ear and shouted, "WATERFALL!"

Oh-

Erastus

Kamile watched as Shu, wearing Aras's body like a suit, went quiet. His/her eyes flashed gold-blue-gold-blue, and then his low brows furrowed. "He's asleep."

"What?"

"His true self is sleeping," Shu replied matter-of-factly through Aras's mouth. "Like yours did when you were terribly injured. It may be some time before he awakes."

Kamile had been holding it together so well, especially seeing 'Aras' sitting up, but the reminder that he wasn't actually conscious at all was too much. She felt her face crumple again.

"Come on," Shu/Aras told her kindly. She/he sat next to Kamile, putting Aras's only remaining arm around her shoulders. "It's alright. Just give it time."

"But we might not have time," Kamile sobbed. "There's some

crazed killer around, and there's almost certainly a lying Silver, and even though our handfast year is almost up, I might never get to tell him some important things that I've been thinking. Maybe he'll never wake up!"

Starbright hadn't woken after Shu left her. Look at her lying there, all dead and gross and…ugh. Kamile turned her back. "And I don't know how we're supposed to explain *that* to the authorities."

Shu/Aras didn't respond to that last comment. "What would you have told him?" she/he rumbled. "You can say it now. I'll tell him if he wakes up."

"Oh." Kamile furrowed her brow, briefly tossing up her pride versus this opportunity, and finally decided that her pride would have to give in this time. "I suppose I would have said…that I don't *want* the handfast to end. We haven't even had a proper handfast! It was more like an awkward hook-up when he was in love with my best friend, and then he settled into being the provider, but we don't have any real relationship. But I want to!"

Kamile half-smiled, realising that she was admitting the full truth, then continued, "I've been infatuated with him ever since I first saw him. I remembering thinking, Fire Lord, what a man! But then his eyes had slid right by me, and landed on girls like Coryn." She shrugged. "I can't blame him, just like I can't blame him for wanting to make a real choice now, rather than just stay with me, when he was tricked into handfasting with me all that time ago.

"And now…now I really think I do love him, and I want to get to know him and not just through handfasting. I want to do it properly like people do around here, and I think…I won't have the chance." Kamile finished her spiel on a deep sigh, shrugging her shoulders and curling into Aras's big, quickly warming body. "He always makes me feel safe," she murmured.

There was a brief silence. "He thought you weren't interested," Shu/Aras rumbled. "He thought you were just helping out a friend, and that you played around with men anyway. He thought you didn't really care about him. You're so often flippant. How could he have known?"

"I'm flippant because I don't want people to know I care!" Kamile shot back. "Because then when he doesn't choose to stay with me when the handfast is over, I won't be so humiliated. It's easier that way."

There was another long silence. Then she/he said, "A bit of encouragement. That's all it would take, and he'd stay with you. Marry you, if that's what you wanted. He just needed to know that he was wanted."

Kamile laughed into the neckline of Aras's grey tunic. "You're making this stuff up, Shu. That's not at all true. I'm not even his type! He likes…leggy blondes with great cheekbones, not skinny little brunettes who occasionally turn green."

She felt a hand cup her cheek and turn her face up to Shu/Aras's. "*He* likes pretty girls of all sizes, with big hearts and great senses of humour," she/he said solemnly. "A shared history and occasional honesty helps too."

Kamile stared into that handsome, familiar face, and then realised something. His eyes…they were light blue. She felt herself go cold then hot with shock and embarrassment. "Aras? Is that you?"

He opened his mouth to speak, then suddenly his expression was creased with pain. "Ahh!"

Kamile pulled away and realised several things. One: Aras was once again running his own body, and he was apparently uncomfortable, and two: the council and medics had come. Lots of them. Oh dear. And what about Starbright's body…?

But then there was another surprise as that woman's fallen

form stirred and lurched into an upright position. A moment later the hole in the forehead vanished, and the hair and features once again melded into that plain, forgettable figure. "I may have forgotten to mention that he woke up when we started talking," Shu said from inside Starbright's body. "And he'll be alright now the medics are here, although no fighting monsters for a few weeks, I'd say."

Kamile was torn between excitement, relief and panic. Oh Fire Lord, he'd heard *everything*. But at least they didn't have to explain away a corpse. "I thought Starbright was dead!"

Shu/Starbright shrugged, looking a little embarrassed. "Mm…yes, actually. But I can run bodies for a short while once their essence has left. I've probably got an hour or two before I have to find an alternative."

Kamile drew back a little, wrinkling her nose. Oddly enough, that felt more disgusting than anything else they'd come across today. "But the killer!" she cried suddenly. "Aras, who was it?"

He blinked, then looked down at his one remaining arm, flexing his fingers. There was something fine and white on his sleeve. "I don't know, but I think we can find out."

An hour had passed since Aras's return through the gateway, and everything had changed. Now he sat in the middle of the town's medical centre, surrounded by medics and watchmen and the councillors themselves. Kamile was to his right, her small hand tight in his with Isla tucked in her other arm, and Poli, Magdalene and Ric were being cared for in a nearby room.

His gut felt like it was full of glass, but it could have been worse. He could be dead. And underneath that pain of a split abdomen was a quiet, persistent happiness. Kamile loved him.

Him. Huh.

To his left, two medics were arguing over the best way to attach his new temporary prosthetic arm. It wasn't much – it looked like a wrench crossed with a hook, truthfully – but at least it couldn't be controlled by random Creatures. And in front of him was the same watchman who'd been so quick to listen when he'd told about the hair samples he'd managed to grasp.

The watchman was short and solid, with greying hair, dark brown skin, and an intent manner. He also held a recording link, since apparently the first three times Aras had told the story hadn't been taken down. "So you went through the blocked-off doorway on Joy Silver's advice," he repeated. "She informed you that she'd given you some kind of protection-"

"And the other Silvers said so too," Kamile cut in.

The watchman looked at Aras, who nodded. "That's what they said."

"Multiple Silvers made the same assurance," the man said clearly into the recorder. "Then she sent you through with a sabre and an efficiency pistol. I won't ask if you have a license for that."

"Good." Because he didn't.

"And on the other side, you found yourself…"

"In the Other realm," Aras finished. "Desert. Dark. Ruins. Cold. Just the usual. But I wasn't alone. There was someone else there, someone who I could barely see since they moved too fast, but they were dressed in something pale. Then I could sense alter-power being used and I lost control of my prosthetic, and there was this agonizing pain. It felt like my guts were exploding, except I couldn't stop laughing. I could see them approaching from my left, so I pulled the sabre and swung."

The room had silenced, and even the medics seemed to be watching him with horrified fascination. "And then what?" someone asked.

Aras shrugged, feeling that same frustration and disappointment. "Then who knows. I woke up outside the doorway, with no weapons and no arm, and with Kamile crying over me. I know I'm lucky to be alive."

"Hmm." The watchman noted down something on his tablet. "And there was another woman at the scene, although she seems to have disappeared. A…"

"Jane Deer," Aras repeated, using the regular term for an unnamed female. He and Kamile had agreed not to mention Shu/Starbright's involvement, since it raised too many questions. "I don't know her, although I'd swear she saved my life. I would have bled out otherwise."

"Unknown helper," the watchman repeated. "Lucky."

"Try miraculous," Kamile muttered under her breath. "That was too bloody close."

"And who are you, miss? The wife?"

She looked hesitant, so Aras spoke up, turning his hand so it covered hers. "Yes. My wife, Kamile."

He could see her smile even then. "And you, Mister Watchman?" she asked cheekily. "We haven't been introduced."

"Hendriks Asa. My daughter Jean goes to school with your redhead in the other room."

Kamile's eyebrows shot up. "Oh, *you're* Jean's dad! I'm so glad to meet you!" She smiled up at Aras. "Poli's always saying how Jean's dad says this or that, especially when it comes to that Joy Silver. It sounds like you know what you're talking about." Her face fell. "Look, it sounds like you're wanting to pin this on her, but she actually didn't go through that doorway that I saw. She was there for several minutes after Aras went through, and it sounds like he was attacked right away…"

"Mm."

Just then the medics managed to attach Aras's new prosthetic

– he knew it had taken because of the sharp bite of pain, and the sudden feeling of having a few extra fingers.

"The hair fragments you brought through," Hendriks said. "That's matched a DNA sample we have on file – only it's not Joy Silver's."

Aras felt his shoulders slump. His feelings about that woman were so mixed, but he hadn't shared Kamile's conviction that she was a monster. He'd be cautious, but they needed proof.

"But then that doesn't mean much, since it wouldn't be very hard to tamper with the original samples so they didn't match," the watchman continued. "Except for this. Whoever that DNA belongs to is somewhere in Erastus…and we can track them."

That was better than nothing, Aras figured.

"Oh wait," Kamile said suddenly, jolting upright. "There was this thing tucked into Aras's jacket when I found him. I thought it might be some sort of curse, perhaps." She reached into a pocket and pulled out a crumpled brown thing, smeared with red. "It has some sort of code on it, see? Or maybe another language? But it looks ancient."

They all leaned in, Aras himself feeling very curious even though he knew that was his own blood marking the item. It did indeed look ancient, its edges ragged and the whole thing brown, like synth-paper that had been in the sun for many years. But the faded grey symbols on it – they looked a little familiar.

"I've seen something like this," he said thoughtfully. "On an ancient building when I was on military duty. Some of the old civilisations used to engrave text on stone or metal, and some of it would last centuries. Do any of you have a translator?"

Hendriks called for one, then leaned forward curiously. "If it wasn't for the text on it, then I'd say it was probably just the Other prematurely aging things," he commented. "But…hmm, it really does feel odd, doesn't it? Not at all like anything I've touched before. Maybe it *is* a clue."

In short order a translator was found, and the odd paper was scanned.

"It's actual mid-age Anglish text," Hendriks said thoughtfully as the results came up. "So from the late 1900s to the early twenty-first century, with that odd handwritten alphabet they used back then. So of course it can't have anything to do with what happened today – oh, and here's our translation." But then his expression changed and he went silent, and a few moments after that, he flicked a button, and the translator's output showed in holographic form.

"Joy Silver tricked me into going through a doorway to Hades," Aras read aloud, feeling curiously numb. *"Don't follow unless you have power from the Mountain of Glass, because you'll probably die. George and Ash O'Reilly-Seymour.* Anyone heard of those people?"

"I have," Kamile replied in a small voice. She'd gone pale, and her brown eyes were very wide. "Ash is the time-traveller I mentioned earlier today, the one who was stranded, and Joy Silver *did* send her through a doorway, even though Joy told me she'd lost her. Maybe…maybe that paper *is* old, but I think this is from today. Ash probably just doesn't write in any other language. I don't know who George is. Maybe her husband; I think she said they'd been separated."

"A time-traveller?" Hendriks asked, his eyebrows shooting up.

"Yes, her and others,' Kamile said emphatically. "It's a long story, but I swear it's true."

Aras believed her, because he'd been there for part of that story. But when no one else challenged the idea, he let out a deep breath. The last of his doubt over the Silver's culpability evaporated, although he found himself oddly disappointed. "There's your evidence."

"But what about Ash?" Kamile asked, her face twisted in worried lines.

The others exchanged grim glances. "Wish her luck," Aras said finally. "She's going to need it."

LAUGHTER

"WATERFALL!" Ash screamed in George's ear, tightening her arms around his neck. If he was weepy with happiness, then she felt like she could burst with it. Even the fact that they were seconds away from possible doom felt thrilling. And so she released him, closing her eyes and stretching her arms out, and thought, *FLY…*

Splash. A moment later she found herself sitting in ankle-deep water, at the edge of a completely different river. This one was smaller, and while one bank was hidden by hazy cloud, the other was just within arm's reach. Ash shook her head, startled. The water of life high seemed to be fading, and she could finally see where they were.

"George, do you recognise those trees?"

He'd landed a few feet away from her, and was now sitting with his knees sticking out of the water. His pupils didn't seem to line up. "Yes, my darling?"

He was still on an alter-power high, Ash realised. "Those trees over there, just off the bank. The dry-looking pines. Don't they look like part of Erastus?" When he didn't respond immediately, she poked him in the shoulder. "Hey. Snap out of it."

George blinked a couple of times, and his eyes finally focused. "Pardon? Erastus?"

"Yes! At least I think so." Ash struggled to her feet, feeling strangely reluctant to leave the water. The River wasn't as supernaturally beautiful here as it had been before they'd come over the waterfall, but it still felt peaceful, and was just the right temperature. But even so, as she stumbled ashore with water running from her sodden clothes in rivulets over her shoes, she felt a new sense of hope and excitement.

Her husband was a few steps behind her. "I say, Ashlea. What are you wearing?"

She looked down at herself and realised in surprise that she wasn't wearing the jeans and 21st century top she'd begun the day in. Nor was she wearing the Regency dress (and corset) she'd gone to Hades in. Instead she was now wearing a form-fitting white tunic that opened out over her hips, and a loose pair of trousers in the same colour. They flared out from the waist and stopped somewhere below her knee. It almost felt bridal – and it was now dry. Handy. "Huh."

She studied George. He was now wearing a similar outfit, perhaps the male version, and she recognised that clothing style too. "Erastus," she said decisively, remembering that she'd seen this type of clothing before during this time period. It was their version of jeans and a t-shirt, but maybe a bit classier.

They couldn't head back, so they began to walk away from the river, towards the trees. But they'd taken barely ten steps when suddenly the River melted away to nothing, and they were standing in an entirely forested area. The tall, thin trees stretched upwards with sun streaming through, there was little undergrowth, and Ash could see some familiar buildings not far in the distance.

"Another hidden entrance," George murmured, looking around him. "And that wasn't the Mountain of Glass, although it felt like it."

Ash paced around the area, studying it from all angles, then recognised a familiar barrier. "George, this is the Mountain entrance that was destroyed earlier today! The one with the food cart. See, you can just spot the remnants of it. And see over *there,* they've tried to block it off."

Or *had* blocked it off. Her inability to access it had been the whole reason she'd taken that other stone doorway in the first place, even against her better judgement.

His eyebrows shot up. "I say. Have we come out the back?"

Ash laughed, although she felt a little hysterical. "If only I'd known, I would have just circled around!"

"Except I didn't see an entrance to the Mountain in there, did you?" George pointed out reasonably.

"Well, no, but it doesn't mean there wasn't one there!"

He paused. "Do you want to go back in now? There's no urgency to go anywhere. Edward is fine now. We can stay for a bit, or we can go looking for a way back to that hall of doors. Whatever you'd prefer."

Ash considered the question. "I think I'd like to stay for a bit," she decided finally. "I ran into Kamile briefly earlier – do you remember her? She was the pregnant Halfling who was possessed for a bit."

"The one with the throat wound?"

"That's the one." As if there could be more than one possessed, pregnant Halfling. "Anyway, I saw her, and she thinks that this is the last entrance to what she called the River, and that it's gone. So at the very least I need to find her to let her know that she can sneak in the back way."

"Good plan." George took her hand, squeezing it, and began studying the area around him thoughtfully. "I say, do you still have all those thingymajigs from Hades? The keys and whatnot."

"Lost them in the waterfall," Ash replied cheerfully,

completely uncaring. "Do you still have your super-baton?"

His eyes widened, and a moment later he pulled the deceptively small object out of his pocket. "Voila! Ah well, at least if we don't have the protective medallion anymore, we've still got this."

Ash suffered a brief pang of regret at the loss of the medallion, then shrugged. They'd just have to live like they had before – which was if a sword, arrow, rock or ball of fire came flying at them, they'd dodge it.

"Oh, and there's one other reason we might want to stay here for a bit," George said, suddenly sounding concerned. "To see if we can find our old friend Alan the Decimator."

"Aras!"

"Yes, that's the one. By Jove, I hope he's alright."

Aras, who'd been shoved out of a one-way evil doorway into who-knew-where, and who very well could be dead already. Ash felt her heart sink. How could she have forgotten him? "What a mess," she murmured. "Amaranthus, if you're listening, can you please make sense of all of this?"

The Tapestry Room, Mountain of Glass

Of course I'm listening, Amaranthus thought patiently. *I'm always listening.* He'd be dismayed by Ash's lack of confidence if not for the fact that he already knew she'd say that, and therefore wasn't surprised by it. He was also very difficult to offend.

He pulled his finger away from the white thread where it crisscrossed with so many others, humming to himself. How very unpleasant it must have felt to these two being down in the Creature-run areas of the Other. Down there, most of the Mountain gifts didn't work. Even Ash hadn't been able to use far-sight, except when she inadvertently passed one of the hidden doors. There were several in every room, and it drove the Creatures mad that they couldn't remove them.

So Ash and George had escaped, as he knew they would, and they'd freed ninety-two others in the meantime, including Mr Aras Morison. But even though they'd left the Creature-run areas, the challenge wasn't quite over yet.

Amaranthus traced his finger back to that fine white thread that symbolised Ash, and which was now tightly woven in with George Seymour's one. Both of those were about to run into *another* white thread, one that had gone on quite an unexpected journey.

He smiled.

Erastus

Magdalene sat in a corner of the council offices that had been designated the 'kids' area, even though she was way too old to be a kid. There were also up to thirty others, all who had homes on the outskirts or the current danger zone – actual kids, children, and some older ones who were helping to look after the younger. Isla was now asleep in the babies' room, and Poli seemed perfectly happy to play with some three-year-olds.

The adults were elsewhere, dealing with the important things, of which her misbehaviour wasn't one. Kamile and Aras weren't angry at her for messing with the doorways, Magdalene had realised. They weren't even disappointed. They were too busy for that.

But Mags herself? She just couldn't stop thinking about Cobalt, and about how he'd looked at her with his warm dark eyes and had promised her there was no killer. And sure, boys could be wrong! Beautiful, immortal men could probably be wrong too. But Cobalt…she'd put her security in him, her trust in that idea that he *was* perfect…except for those eyebrows. She'd even gone against her friends, and had sneaked away to see him, just because she'd thought he was perfect.

But he wasn't perfect, and Poli and Kamile didn't understand how hurt she was. Her heart hurt so much, and the worst part was that she didn't even know the truth. Was he somehow bad, and lying to her? Or had he just made a mistake?

So Mags quietly stood and moved to slip from the room. Poli looked up and saw her – Poli was an observant sort who always seemed to notice things at just the wrong moment – but Mags forced a smile. "I'm going to see Kamile and Aras."

"OK."

But then when she reached the other room where those two were, it was super busy. Aras was sitting in a chair, looking very important even though he was bandaged up and not wearing a shirt, and one arm was now a weird, metal thing with pincers for fingers. Kamile didn't seem to mind any of that because she was wrapped around him like…like they were in love or something. And that wasn't bad, but it was weird too.

And there were all these council people and watchmen, all crowded around and talking very loudly about trackers and DNA and 'we'll narrow it down to a twenty-foot radius', whatever *that* meant.

Kamile looked up and saw her standing in the doorway, and smiled. She looked tired. "Hi, Mags. Are you OK?"

She didn't want to tell the truth in front of all of these people, so she shrugged. "I'm alright. I was just…coming to see if you were."

"We'll be better once this person is caught, and Erastus is back to what it should be. But yes, we're OK."

Kamile turned and smiled at Aras in such a sappy way that Mags almost felt embarrassed for her. But then he smiled back! Maybe it was because he'd almost died, she wondered. Because she and Poli had always figured that Aras and Kamile would split eventually. Kamile had talked about 'one year', which should have been up pretty soon.

"Well…that's good. I'll see you later, after…everything." And then Mags ducked her head and moved to leave.

But that was when she saw something just inside the door, on someone's seat. It was a small black pistol. Not a stunner or a paragun, because it didn't have any gel pellets or the bright light that stunners always had. No, it looked more serious than that.

Mags glanced up to see if anyone was watching, but they were all caught up in their so-serious conversation about 'repeat offenders'. And so she slid over, picked up the pistol and tucked it inside her loose jacket. After a few seconds of tense waiting, she realised no one even noticed that she'd done it. Perfect. Then she slipped out of the room, with just one place on her mind.

She had to see him. She had to know the truth.

Peaceful waited quietly just outside the council offices. She was far enough away from the entrance to be unnoticed, yet close enough to hear some of what was happening, and she'd done her best to blend in with the crowd of people moving in and out.

She knew she really ought to find another human host, maybe someone in a coma or who'd been near-fatally injured. If she didn't find one soon, she'd begin to lose control of the current body, and would promptly find herself back in the Other. Back with the Creatures.

Ugh.

But even though Peaceful knew the risk, she couldn't help but linger. She had to know what was going on, that Kamile and the others would be okay. Besides, it didn't sit right for her to just leave when there was potentially such danger around this usually peaceable town, and when she herself had far more knowledge of alter-power than most in this place. Something about all of this nagged at her, like a hangnail or a jagged tooth that just needed to be fixed.

She'd stay just a few minutes longer, she decided. Who knew? Maybe she could find the culprit herself, and there would be her new host. Two problems solved at once.

Maybe.

But when several minutes went by with no apparent outcome, she slipped on a cloak of alter-powered unnoticeability, then quietly stepped into the building.

"I was thinking, we *have* lived extraordinary lives, have we not? Even though Dr Walker claimed once upon a time that we were ordinary enough to be stolen away and forgotten, we haven't proven to be that at all." George paused thoughtfully as they walked through the pine forest, his arm tucked securely through his wife's. They'd chosen to walk around the edges of the forest, skirting the town, as if to make sense of their thoughts, rather than just heading straight home.

"Or perhaps it's our circumstances that have made us so," he continued. "Perhaps if we'd stayed in our own times, if we'd followed the usual paths set for us, mediocrity would have been our experience. And I'm so dreadfully, dreadfully glad that it hasn't been."

There was a silence from Ashlea, and he looked down to see her expression was intent, with her nose wrinkled in that way that suggested she was thinking deeply.

"Well, those were my deep musings from all that time spent in the water of life," he continued when it seemed she wouldn't speak. "There was something about that water, about being saturated with it after so long in that terrible place, that made me feel like I see the world in a whole new way. I feel like I understand things now. Or perhaps not quite understand, but definitely grasp the edges of some new revelation. Do you see?"

"Hmm."

George persisted. "What did *you* come to realise in the water, Ashlea?"

She shook her head, seeming to come back to the present. "Oh. All sorts of things, I suppose. But I was just thinking that this is a lot like when we first met."

"Really? How so?"

"Well…we're in an unfamiliar forest. Kind of unfamiliar. And we're stuck away from home, but there's the hope that we'll get home soon enough." She shrugged, smiling up at him. "All we need is Anne screaming about witchcraft, and it'll be practically identical."

Anne rarely screamed about witchcraft anymore. George almost missed it. "And we'd need you to pepper-spray me in the face," he pointed out. "And if it's all the same to you, I'd rather you didn't. Once was enough."

"I do like to be memorable."

By Jove, he wouldn't be forgetting *that* memory! "And another thing. There's no horrendous, alter-power-using witch woman attempting to control or kill us here. So that's a notable difference."

"Hmm."

That didn't sound very decisive, so George shot a glance at Ashlea in shock, almost walking into a tree branch as he did so. "What's this 'hmm'?"

"I was just wondering…would you ever hit a lady?"

Now George *did* walk into a tree. He stopped still, almost letting go of her arm. "What sort of question is that?"

Ashlea shrugged, then reached forward to pick a piece of greenery off his new white jacket. "Back when we first met, if you'd known that Seyen Johannis was what she was, would you have hit her with that super-baton of yours? Taken her out if you'd had the chance?"

He was struck dumb for several moments. It was a truly problematic question. He now knew exactly what sort of vile, dangerous person 'the Queen' had been, but it was so terribly difficult to turn against one's upbringing. One did not strike a woman. And a beautiful one? That would be even more difficult.

"Because," Ashlea continued, "I think you'll have to get past that. And when the time comes, there'll be just a moment you'll need to take advantage of. And you'll need to-"

"Hit a lady?" George choked.

"Yeah. More or less."

He didn't know how he would have responded to that, because suddenly a small figure came flying out of the woods, straight towards them.

Two minutes earlier

When Jolly had pushed Elspeth from the ship into that gateway, for a moment she felt as though she had fallen into the sun. 'Twas so very, very bright, but then a mere moment after that, she

281

landed heavily on her hands and knees on dry, grass-covered earth. "Oof!"

It had not hurt so terribly, she allowed as she climbed to her feet, but the shock had been unpleasant. She sighed, dusting pine needles off her palms and full skirts, then looked around.

She stood in a cluster of tall pine trees, the sort with long, skinny trunks and short branches spiking in every direction, and the bulk of their foliage up far, far higher. Above her the sky was blue with streaky white clouds, and she caught a glimpse of something sailing past in a gap in the canopy.

She blinked, then shook her head. No, that simply could not have been a flying tree! She must have imagined it.

"Erastus," Elspeth said aloud, testing the word on her tongue. It immediately translated in her mind as *beloved*.

Ooh! How excellent, the all-tongues gift was working already! Now, all she needed to do was find an amiable local, then give a description of the villain who held the Eternity Stone. It could not be so very difficult, she told herself hopefully, or surely Jolly and Sweet would not have left her here?

She looked around again, trying to find a likely direction, but then heard a faint sound. 'Twas like a few musical notes in the distance, or mayhap a child's weak cry. The comparison made her shiver, and she wrapped her arms around herself.

"No," she said aloud. "I am strong and bold, and have many gifts of supernatural origin. I am not afraid of unknown sounds!"

The whistle/call sounded again, and something tingled in her belly, like fear or mayhap the beginnings of laughter. Something pale moved in the distance…

This time the shiver was more intense, and she caught her breath even as her hands lit up with silvery flame. Mayhap not so very brave after all… *Amaranthus, can you hear me? Please send my sister, for I no longer wish to be alone!*

Whoooo.

That was it. Elspeth turned and sprinted in the opposite direction, hitching her skirts up as she did so. She'd not made it more than twenty yards when suddenly she wasn't alone anymore. Two white-clad figures came into sight: a young couple, a few years older and quite a bit taller than she was, and seeming to be deep in conversation. They both looked at her in surprise.

Forsooth, 'twas not Anne. But 'twas enough.

"Elspeth?!" the tall, dark-haired girl exclaimed. "What are you doing here?"

"Ash! George!" Overcome with relief, Elspeth threw herself at them, settling on wrapping her arms around Ash's waist in a tight, desperate hug. "Oh, there's something in the forest! Something unnatural. I'd vow 'tis witchcraft at work!"

There was a shocked pause, then both of them began to laugh. Not just a little, but a lot.

"'Tis no jest!" Elspeth exclaimed in dismay. "Why do you laugh at me, you imbeciles?"

"Sorry, sorry," Ash said finally, wiping a hand across her teary eyes. Yes, she had laughed to *tears.* "But we were just saying how it was like old times, except for Anne shouting about witchcraft. And then you showed up."

"Oh." Elspeth could see small humour in it, and mayhap she felt the urge to laugh too. But only a little. "But it does not change the danger of the moment," she persisted. "We must flee, or find safety. Do you know the way to the Mountain?"

The other two were still giggling, although they appeared to be trying to listen.

"No," Ash said through her laughter, just as George snorted out, "Yes."

"Well? Which is it?"

"Maybe," George stuttered out. "Still looking for friends."

"Oh." Elspeth did not appreciate their lack of solemnity in such a moment. "Well, I trow that together we shall be safe enough, but I would be much more at ease should we leave this location. Come along!" She began to walk, and the other two seemed to follow.

"I went through a gateway at the Mountain," she explained as they did so. "To find Jon, for he had returned home without saying farewell. But 'twas a poor choice, for 'twas not his gateway at all! 'Twas a most odd place, one outside time. But never fear. I was rescued by two small People in a flying ship, who sent me here to seek out the Eternity Stone and return it to its origin."

"That sounds…ridiculous," Ash choked out, then started laughing again.

"Ridiculous," George agreed through another snort of laughter.

Elspeth stopped walking, and confronted them with her hands on her hips. "'I disagree! 'Tis quite a fine challenge, even if I stumbled upon it by accident. And where might you two have been, hmm?"

There was a pause, then they both started laughing together. "HADES!" Ash practically shouted. "BAD GATEWAY!"

Oh, by the Rood. They were acting like fools, Elspeth thought irritably. Then she abruptly realised what they were telling her. They'd been in a Creature city…in Hades itself. She sucked in a horrified breath. "You…you went to *Hades*, but you are now safe again?"

"YES!"

The other two were laughing like lunatics, and it made Elspeth wonder if her own panicked reaction was unfounded. "We might all agree that we should choose our gateways far more carefully," she told them, pouting a little at their foolish behaviour. "But what is wrong with you two? You are acting as though you've eaten the wrong type of mushroom!"

Then something high-pitched was ringing in her ears, and in front of her the two had collapsed into each others' arms, sobbing with laughter. Or just sobbing…? Finally something struck Elspeth as very, very wrong. The sound…it had followed them.

"George," Ash choked out. "Now would be a good time to…hit a lady." Then she fell to the ground, groaning through her frantic laughter, and with her hands clutched around her belly.

Elspeth could feel her whole body shaking in sudden trembling pain, and a brief sound forced its way past her terrified lips. "Ha. *Haaa…*"

In her peripheral vision she saw something moving. Something flickering, but she couldn't fix her eyes on it. Something pale…

Oh Amaranthus, oh help! She stretched out her fingers and again called upon her gift of cleansing fire, and a moment later felt it roar down from her fingertips to her shoulders and then down her body. The tense fear and shaking left, and suddenly all she felt was the warm tingle of her gift at work.

Acting quickly, she ran over to George and Ash. She set a hand on each of their shoulders and pushed the flame over them, forcing it to cover their whole bodies. She could not see it here in the daylight, except mayhap as a faint silvery shimmer, but she knew that it worked because they both stopped shaking and laughing.

"Elspeth," George said wide-eyed, suddenly solemn. "What is happening?"

"I do not know." She felt just as wide-eyed, and in spite of her confidence about her gift, she could not shake the fear. Her back was to the woods, and *something* was out there. "'Tis witchcraft at work, or some evil power."

Ash, who'd been crumpled on the ground, had her hands

pressed against the faint curve of her belly. "I couldn't stop laughing. It hurt, but I couldn't stop. And what's this silvery stuff all over us?"

"'Tis my gift!" Elspeth explained. "Cleansing fire."

Ash's eyebrows shot up, then she nodded, still panting. "Really? Wow. You'll have to tell us about that later, but for now, what's attacking us? Because it better not hurt my baby!"

"There's something here," George said urgently, his gaze flickering behind them. "Something in the trees. Do you have far-sight?"

The question was to Ash, who nodded. "I keep seeing the same thing, over and over. But it doesn't make sense! I keep seeing you over and over again, and this other figure in white that moves too fast, from place to place-*ARGH!*"

Just then Elspeth saw something in the corner of her eye, as if someone had come right up behind her. She felt the slightest touch on her back, and there was a flash of purple and a hiss like water hitting a hot cauldron.

She turned, and the other two climbed to their feet, one on either side of her, each holding her fire-covered hands. And there in front of them, on the ground, was a figure writhing in silence. It flamed purple, silver, charcoal and white, rolling around so fast that she could not get a fix on it, and almost without making a sound. And then suddenly it blinked out of sight, only to reappear ten feet to the left, still writhing, then twenty feet further back, before vanishing entirely.

"What in Hades was that?" George exclaimed.

"I don't know," Ash said grimly. "But don't let go of Elspeth, and remember what I said before."

"I remember," he replied dolefully. "Hit a lady."

Elspeth knew not what to make of that, but it must have made sense to him, for they both seemed to hold her hands as if she was a lifeline. The tension among the three was palpable.

But the attacker didn't reappear, and she could no longer hear that odd musical sound. "Is it gone?"

"I don't know," Ash replied. "But we need to get to safety. The town is this way."

Meanwhile in the council offices, a young watchman had been fiddling with the DNA tracking device. A 'beautiful blend of science and alter-power', it could take a sample of hair, skin or saliva, then track the sample's owner down to a twenty-foot radius.

But now, it didn't seem to be working. "I don't get it," the watchman complained, frowning heavily. "It seems to lock in on the suspect, then next it flashes red and has to reroute."

Hendriks looked over the man's shoulder to the holo-screen displayed in his outstretched hand. A circle of red would flash, then vanish, then reappear again somewhere in the same area. "Close enough," he said finally. "Let's go, and see what we find."

Across the room, the big, bandaged blond man tried to get to his feet.

"Are you kidding?" his wife asked in dismay. "You almost died! You can't go out there again!"

"They don't know what they're facing, Kamile. Any help I can give, I'll give."

"I'll have to agree with the wife on this one, Morison," Hendriks interjected. "You're in no condition to fight."

Aras Morison's lips tightened in his pale face. "I can shoot from a distance. I'm an excellent shot even with my natural arm."

Eh, good point. "With that definitely licensed efficiency pistol of yours, hmm?"

Aras's eyes narrowed. "With the very one. Where is it?"

"I left it on the chair," one of the other watchmen said. "Just there." He pointed to a chair near the door that was most definitely empty.

"You left a deadly weapon *on a chair* in a busy building?" Hendriks exclaimed in disbelief.

"Er…yes?"

"Get the video surveillance." Ten seconds later the screen had popped up on the wall in front of them, and Hendriks watched in dismay as a petite teenage girl slipped the efficiency pistol under her jacket and left the room. "Any idea who that is?"

"Yes," Kamile squeaked. Her face had paled. "That's Magdalene, who lives with us."

Hendriks sucked in an unhappy breath, and restrained himself from snapping, 'and that's why you don't let kids into war meetings!' Anger wouldn't help anyone now. Instead he asked, "Any idea where she might have gone?"

She nodded. "Probably Crookshank Alley."

"We'll get her," Aras said flatly. He was now on his feet, and was carefully shrugging into a jacket. He still wore a sabre attached to his hip, the same one they'd retrieved the suspect's hair sample from.

"That's near the edge of town," the watchman with the tracker said. "Hey look, it's near the suspect, too."

The suspect was moving into the city. That wasn't good. "Then I guess we'll be going together," Hendriks said. "Let's move."

Magdalene stood silently in Crookshank Alley square, at the opposite end from Cobalt's carved doorway. It looked as misty and mysterious as ever between those two stone posts, and she had never felt so uncertain. She held the pistol in one hand, tucked out of sight inside her loose trouser pocket, and she couldn't take her eyes off that space. All she needed to do was walk up to the doorway and call his name, just like she always did…

"Hello, miss."

Mags leapt in fright, almost pulling the trigger inside her pocket, then turned to see who'd spoken to her. A few metres behind her was a boy dressed in white. About her age, he was extremely good-looking with bronze skin, silver hair, and a friendly, curious expression.

Silver hair. Mags quickly checked his feet – they rested solidly on the ground.

"Are you alright there, miss?" the boy persisted. "You're out here all alone when the rest of town seems to be in the civic square, and you seem upset. Can I help you with anything?"

She opened her mouth, but didn't know what to say. Poli had said that the Silvers weren't real people; that they were just an extension of Mama Silver. Standing here now, she didn't know what to believe, or what to say.

"Miss?"

"I…I shouldn't have come here," she stuttered out finally. Nodding at the bronze boy, she ducked her head and quickly turned away, heading back down the street. Ten minutes and she'd be back in that safe council building, and no one would even know she'd gone.

But she'd only walked twenty metres away when that same sense of hurt and frustration came over her. She stopped and turned around, heading back around the corner. That was when she saw the boy standing in front of the doorway with his hand against one stone side.

From his left and his right other Silvers were approaching: an old lady and a young girl. Then they walked *into* the boy, their figures blurring for a moment before vanishing as his seemed to grow larger. Mags watched in shock as another, then another Silver did the same, then finally there was just one figure, standing in front of the doorway with their back to her.

The woman had yellowish-white hair trailing down her back in a bedraggled plait, over ragged white clothing. One pale hand rested against the carved doorframe, with delicate fingers blackened as if dipped in coal.

Mama Silver turned and smiled at Magdalene with blood-red lips. "Hello, sweetheart. Have you come to see your friend?"

"Now, I don't want you to think this isn't a safe town," the young watchman told Kamile confidently. "We haven't had this kind of danger in generations. My dad says the last time anything like this happened was fifty years ago, when a group of visitors got it into their heads to go through the blocked off doorways, thinking they'd come out like gods or something.

"Now, doorways are blocked for a reason! We care a lot about the safety of locals, but some visitors just don't listen to common sense. Unfortunately it's not the last time that will happen, but in that case most of 'em got killed. A couple of others came out flaming with alter-power and out of their minds."

"Uh huh," Kamile said distractedly. She'd left Isla with Poli, and now her full attention was fixed on something to her right, something behind those buildings. She could feel it, feel the alter-power waves, feel that something was wrong in the atmosphere. They'd put her in light armour then put her at the back of the group, but even with these dozen men and women, most of them armed and prepared to take on the worst, she still felt something was wrong. Something over *there*.

"They carved up a few buildings, killed a couple of people. One of 'em's responsible for those flying trees you still see every now and then. We had to shoot them in the end, of course. The people, I mean, not the trees. Sad. But it was for everyone's good, my dad says."

"I've got a reading," the watchman with the tracker said brusquely. "To the left, towards the edge of the forest."

The bulk of the group followed him, turning left, but Kamile stopped in her tracks. She couldn't hear or see anything, but she *felt* it. "Over this way!" she called. "Aras, there's something over there!"

Was he watching? She didn't know, but she felt a new sense of urgency. And then without waiting to see if anyone followed, she turned and ran.

⛧

"Morison, your girl's taken off," one of the younger watchmen told Aras. He sounded aggrieved. "Took off into the town, see?"

Aras glanced over to see Kamile vanishing around the corner, her dark brown hair streaming behind her. "Give me your weapon."

"What?"

Aras didn't pause, instead he slipped his hand quickly into the other man's holster and drew his stunner. It wasn't an efficiency pistol, but it would do. "We've got a problem," he said. "She's a Halfling. If she says it's over there, then it's over there." Besides, he still had his own sense of right and wrong, and it worked most of the time.

Then cautious of his aching everything, he made his way after Kamile.

Magdalene felt the pistol slip from her hands to fall on the ground. Then as if her legs were moving without her permission, she found herself walking over to the stone doorway, over to this frightening version of Mama Silver. And while the woman's face was lovely and smiling, her eyes had changed. Now they were yellow like a dog's, and too wide.

Mama Silver smiled at her, then glanced to the doorway. "Cobie, come say hello to your friend."

Then the grey mist behind the doorway rippled, and he was standing there. And in spite of her fear, Mags found herself catching her breath. Even if Mama Silver looked like a mess, Cobalt was as gorgeous as ever. His hair waved down to his hips like it was coated in gold leaf, and his dark eyes were so warm and kind. "Hello, Magdalene."

"Cobalt," she stammered. With him so close, it was like there was a tug on her heart, almost a pain. Had she been wrong to distrust him? After all, anyone could make a mistake…

Then he stretched out his hand to the edge of the doorway just like he always did, and this time she felt herself reaching up to meet his touch. She lifted her hand up to the edge of the barrier, then finally through it, until she felt the tips of those fingers touch her own.

There was a moment of fear and anticipation, when he just smiled down at her. But then his hand closed around her wrist, and his skin felt wrong, bristly. And then his gorgeous form wavered and suddenly someone else entirely was holding her. He was still smiling, but no longer gorgeous. And the bristles? That was the least of it.

Magdalene screamed.

Fourteen

SHOOT-OUT

They'd reached the edge of the town, but it seemed too quiet. It reminded Ash of one of those thriller movies where if everything was silent, it was for a very bad reason. She was no longer holding Elspeth and George's hands, and Elspeth's odd fiery gift had gone out, but they were all highly tense.

"Even the slightest hint of a music note," George said in a low voice from beside her. "Even the slightest urge to laugh…"

"Trust me, I'm not laughing," Ash retorted. The complete opposite. Unlike her time in the Creature city, now far-sight was coming fast and often. Usually it would show her the far-reaching consequences of her immediate actions (wouldn't we all like to know that?) but now it wasn't making sense.

She just kept seeing George, over and over in all these different places. Not looking evil or illusive or anything weird. Just him, in that white suit, with his messy fair hair and something in his hand that she couldn't see. And then there was a second scene, *one full of chaos and confusion, where Ash stuck out her foot and something went flying…*

"The Eternity Stone!" she blurted out, suddenly realising exactly what she'd seen.

"What?" the other two said in unison. Elspeth looked particularly startled.

"It's here! Someone's got it. The villain's got it. And I'm going to trip them up, and it's going to go flying, and then–"

They heard a scream in the near distance, just out of sight.

The three of them exchanged horrified glances, and Elspeth lifted her chin. "As I said before, we must get that Stone," she vowed. "I shall use my cleansing flame."

"I'll use my super-baton," George added. "Ashlea. You should stay here, for the baby's sake."

Ashlea, don't go into town, let me drive you. For the baby's sake. Ashlea, don't climb that wall, what about the baby? Ashlea, don't go to Hades. For the baby's sake.

Not unreasonable, but still… "George, I'm the only one with far-sight! And we've only got about thirty seconds!"

His handsome face looked oh so very pained, but finally he nodded. "Stay at the back, will you?"

"Fine!" she replied, although she had no intention of doing such a thing. How could she trip the villain and get the Eternity Stone if she was at the back?

Then there was another scream and the sound of weapons firing. Even from here they could see the lights flashing above a nearby building.

"Mags!" Kamile screamed across that quiet alley.

The girl was at the other end, right outside a doorway with her hand halfway through, and some horrible hairy Creature holding her wrist from the other side. In the half-second she glimpsed it, all she could see were big bristly eyebrows, and *hair*. And then in front of that, beside Magdalene, was a figure in white with a long, scraggly pale plait…

But then there was a flash of light like a stunner had gone off, and the Creature jolted backwards, clutching its hand. Magdalene fell away, crying, and the pale figure vanished. Suddenly Aras was beside Kamile, shouting, "Get away, Mags! As far as you can!" Then to Kamile he said urgently, "The other one is the killer. That's who attacked me!"

Fire Lord. And they were here *alone*?

Ah, but they weren't alone. Suddenly there were armed watchmen everywhere, and councillors with their bright alter-power lights, and they were firing upon that doorway as if it was the entrance to Hades. Mags had crawled away, and the ancient stone lintel lit up rainbow-coloured and finally cracked, falling and blocking the top half of the door.

"That's not the one!" Kamile shouted over the din, even though she *knew* that whatever that thing had been, it sure as Hades wasn't friendly. "There's another one! Don't let them get away!"

Finally she made her way to where Magdalene was huddled crying, and she wrapped her arms around the girl. "Let's get out of here!" she whispered urgently.

"He was a monster," Mags wept. "His hair...his eyes..."

And what could Kamile say to that? "A Creature, Mags. They like to play nasty games, and I'm *so sorry* you were caught up in one."

"I knew better," Mags said. "I knew from the start it was a bad idea, that there was something hidden from me, and that's why I never went through the doorway even when he asked. But I kept going back, because he was beautiful, and I was *stupid-*"

"And sometimes we let ourselves get caught up, even when we do know better," Kamile said briskly. She pulled Mags behind a tree, then slid along the wall towards the alley's exit. The whole place was still being lit up with bright orange, yellow and purple flashes of weaponry and alter-power. "I'm just glad that you're safe. And you won't make that mistake again. Real boys next time, yes?"

"No boys!" Magdalene declared. She was still shaking. "No boys ever again!"

Kamile paused. Hopefully that decision wouldn't last, because boys had their good points. Just look at Aras. "Until you're eighteen," she tried. "And we'll shoot them for you first to make sure they're not Creatures in disguise, OK?"

Magdalene laughed just like she was supposed to. But then she laughed, and laughed, and bent forward clutching her stomach. And Kamile was laughing with her, but it *hurt*.

And all around them the weapon fire seemed to have died back, although there was a ringing in her ears like loud music. *Ahahahahaha…*

They thought they'd trapped her with their alter-power barriers and their modern weapons. They thought that just because they'd blasted the stone sides of that one doorway and had broken it, that they'd capture her too.

They were wrong.

Lilith leaned back against the fallen archway, taking the merest moment to regather her thoughts. She hadn't survived this many centuries just to be taken in by a group of suited-up, armed mortals. At full strength, she could have captured them with a song. She could have used her alter-powered voice to wrap binding cords of alter-power around them, to make them laugh as they turned their weapons on each other, or to make them her enthralled slaves until death parted them.

The stronger they were, the more *masculine* they were, the

easier it was to bind them. The more fun it was, too.

Of course, having crowds of slaves just tended to draw attention, and Lilith now preferred to blend in, to work behind the scenes if possible. But then she'd found the Eternity Stone, and all her existing alter-power links had broken the moment she'd used it. Then she'd tried to use her enthralling gift to bind someone new to herself, to drain their energy slowly, and instead they'd just died, and she'd ended up with a phenomenal power boost.

It had been messy. Very, very messy, and not at all subtle. She'd known at once that she'd have to stop using the Stone or else give up her usual ways of working. But then she'd figured that if she'd already made the mess here in Erastus, she may as well get the most out of it. Drain as many people as she could, then go to the other side of the world and start again.

But she'd somehow failed to kill the Strong Man, even though she could have sworn he was dead and that she'd taken all the life-force he had to give. But here he was along with the councilmen and the town watch, having cornered her in an alley with their DNA tracking devices, thinking they could finally take her out.

Lilith sneered at their weak efforts, and set off again. As a Halfling, the Stone she held so tightly in one hand couldn't send her across time, but it sure could send her across space. She kept moving, kept using the Stone to go from place to place faster than they could follow, and she kept brushing her fingers over them one by one, hearing the faint, lovely music created by that motion, and sending them into convulsions of laughter. So strong that soon enough they'd collapse…

Lilith felt a smile curve her still-red lips, forcing her illusion to cover her with the latest lovely face she'd chosen even as she moved so very, very quickly. *Laugh, my friends,* she told them in a voice like the sound of bells. *Laugh until you die…because you will.*

And then she saw three new figures approach the far end of the alley, behind all the chaos. One, the tall, dark-haired girl she'd sent straight down to the Creature city as tribute to the Tiger for its continued 'friendship'. Somehow she'd made it back to the normal realm. Two, some fair-haired young man with a stupid look on his face. (All males were stupid, Lilith thought, that was why they were easy targets.) And three, that little girl, the one who'd burned her earlier today…

This time she'd be ready. So she focused on a spot right behind the man and away from the small fire-wielding girl, then she squeezed her hand around the Eternity Stone…and jumped.

They arrived to a scene of absolute chaos. Ash could feel the power in the air, tingling over her skin like hot and cold wind currents. All around them people were laughing, collapsing in piles. She could see blood coming from someone's mouth…

Far-sight kept showing her the same two things over and over, her heart was pounding in her chest, and she kept thinking *when, when?* And then suddenly-

The villain was in front of George, just to her left, and Ash acted. She threw herself to the ground, throwing out one leg to the side in her best break-dancing impression, and by some miracle, struck at just the right moment. She felt something hit her ankle, and then the woman in white went flying head over heels. As if in slow motion, Ash saw something small and dark go flying from the woman's hand to land in front of George.

"THE ETERNITY STONE!" she screamed. "GET IT, GEORGE!"

Then slowly, too slowly he was reaching down, and the woman in white was reaching for it too, but then oh thank Deias

Elspeth had got in with a blast of whatever that silvery stuff was. It sent the woman screaming backwards, rolling on the ground, but George was unharmed. And he had the Stone...

"What do I do with it?" he shouted at her.

"Look for the right moment!" Ash shouted back. She didn't know why they were shouting; it was loud but not that loud, and it just seemed the thing to do. "Hit the lady, George!"

And then she stepped back because really, she didn't have any weapons whatsoever, and the person struggling to their feet was looking increasingly scary. Pale as milk, with that off-white plait, but with a face that kept changing. One version was classically lovely with blood-red lips, but the other version had met a frying pan or two in its day. It wasn't really the colouring, Ash mused, but perhaps the big lower jaw full of unhappily jagged teeth, or the extremely displeased expression?

But now the scary woman had her eyes on Ash, and she reached out with both hands outspread. "I might have lost the Stone," she shouted as if to Ash alone, "but I have not lost my power!"

In that moment, as Ash remembered she *could fly and probably ought to flee,* a high, sweet musical note sounded, and a wave of power washed over her like the shockwave from a bomb. Suddenly her skin felt like it was crawling with ants, right from her scalp to her little toes, and she felt herself jerk out a burst of convulsive laughter. "Ah ha ha ha ha-"

Oh Deias oh Deias oh Deias, help!

She could see George in the background, his expression horrified, and that damned baton in one hand. He seemed to be flickering from place to place, but she was *hurting-*

"Damn it, George!" she ground out. "Just *hit her!*"

Thirty seconds earlier

I've got the Eternity Stone, George thought in absolute shock. He looked down at the little object in his palm. Yes, it still resembled a tiny black hourglass, complete with a short string of coloured beads on one end. It looked like a cheap keyring from Ashlea's time, but could it really be the Stone? The anti-ageing, time and space-travelling Stone? The one people had repeatedly killed for, and so forth?

Oh, Hades. What did *he* have the Stone for?!

"What do I do with it?" he shouted in dismay.

"Look for the right moment!" Ash shouted back from her place ten feet away. "Hit the lady, George!"

By Jove, that sounded *terrible.* But the lady was certainly a villain, there was no doubt about that. From the glimpses George caught of her, she was wild-eyed and snarling, even though she did have rather lovely white skin and beautiful red lips. Oh, she was *very* attractive. He just wanted to smile at her, really, and have her smile back.

Villain villain villain, he scolded himself. Then he squeezed the Stone and thought, *the right place,* and suddenly he was standing two feet behind her, with the baton in one hand, and her long whitish plait just about hitting him in the face. *Hit her hit her hit her. Just do it.*

But she's a lady, his inner self argued. *One does not hit a lady.*

They do when she's a murderous villain!

But then damn it, he'd missed his chance because she'd stepped away, and all around him people were collapsing in pain even as their surroundings lit up with alter-power and silvery fire. The woman was shouting something about power, and it occurred to George that he'd acted too slowly.

He had a time travel device. Right. George focused on a time twenty seconds earlier, before he'd started delaying, and whisked himself there. Then he could see his *other* self just in front of him, with the lady villain just in from of *him*.

Second chance. *Step forward and hit the lady*, he ordered himself. *Do it for everything that is right!*

But then the lady turned a little, and she was smiling so beautifully, and George felt it touch his heart and make it beat double-time. Then *argh*, she changed and she had a face like a bulldog he'd once owned! He was shaken from his odd fugue, but again he was too late. She'd moved; he'd lost his chance.

One last time! This time George used the Stone to skip back in time fifteen seconds, and to move just over *there*. And this time he raised the baton, and-

"Damn it, George!" he heard Ashlea shout. "Just *hit her*!"

Well, sorry dearest wife, but it wasn't that easy! Heavens above, he *really* should not be the one with the Stone. And why couldn't the lady be ugly *all* the time? It was a strange fact of the universe that pretty people were harder to hit than terrifyingly ugly ones. In fact, some faces seemed to beg for a punch, while others begged for a kiss…

Back ten seconds.

"Damn it, George!" he heard Ashlea shout. "Just *hit her*!"

Everyone was laughing, even him just a little now, and as if in slow motion he finally turned and saw his wife collapsed on the ground. She was groaning and clutching her belly – why was she doing that, he wondered dully – and there was a sudden burst of red on her white tunic-

Oh, *schnit*, as Ashlea would say.

Back in time another ten seconds. "Damn it, George!" he heard Ashlea shout again, like a broken recording. "Just *hit her*!"

This time he thought of her bloodied belly and Baby Broadbean, and he set his jaw.

Whack. There was a flash of bright light, then the woman went flying backwards to hit the broken doorway with an audible crack, then fell still. Suddenly everything was silent, except for the sound of groans. George rushed over to his wife's side, shoving his hands on the front of her tunic. It was still white. Had he been too slow?

"Ah, George, that tickles!"

"You're not hurt?"

Ashlea sat up, then glared at him. He could see Elspeth sitting behind her, an almost matching scowl on her face. "It hurt like Hades for a bit," Ashlea said, "but not anymore. You took your time."

"She was a lady! It's *hard* to hit a lady!"

Ashlea raised her eyebrows, then sighed. She patted him on the arm. "Fine. I probably shouldn't complain about my husband being so reluctant to commit violence, but really, I think if you'd been any longer there could have been some real damage!"

There would have been. He still saw that blood in his mind's eye, and he closed his fingers tight around Eternity Stone. *Never,* he swore to himself.

"Someone really ought to do something about that person," he said finally, forcing himself to breathe evenly. "And it really oughtn't to be me."

✣

"*Ugh.* Ow." Kamile forced herself to a sitting position, rubbing at her aching stomach. It felt like the severe cramps she'd had once after eating some street food in Lile City (never again!). But from what she remembered about the blood she'd seen on Aras, if a few more seconds had passed, it would have been much worse.

Next to her, Aras was shaking his head, pushing himself up on his new prosthetic arm. Its metal fingers stuck in the ground briefly, and he stared at it, looking baffled. There was blood rimming his lips, as though he'd coughed it up.

"Aras!"

He coughed, then shook his head. "I'm OK. Where is that thing?"

The *thing*, AKA the murderer. Kamile looked up to see the pale figure still slumped over by the broken doorway. "Knocked out or dead, hopefully."

All around them people were stirring, getting up, although Kamile spotted one or two figures who might have some trouble moving. And where was Magdalene?

She spotted the girl not far away, near the exit to the alley. Her face was pale and her eyes too wide, and her expression held a weariness that made her look older than she ought to. "Kam," she started to say.

"She's getting up!" someone shouted.

Then suddenly there was chaos again; everyone was moving to go for their weapons, and some unfamiliar girl had her hands on fire, but Kamile didn't have any weapon at all. But to her right she could see the *flash flash flash* of a rapid stream of bright light. And then the villain was screaming as something seemed to strike her, and then next thing she'd vanished through that gap of the broken doorway.

Gone.

Then Kamile realised who had been shooting – and *what* she'd been shooting with. "Mags! Put that thing down!"

Magdalene looked at her with a scowl, but lowered the

efficiency pistol she'd stolen from the council building earlier. "She was going to hurt people," she said. "I couldn't let her hurt people."

"Shame your girl didn't have better aim," Hendriks said some time later, his tone too casual for the topic of conversation. "I'd swear she hit the perp at least once with the efficiency pistol, but the perp isn't dust, is she? So she mustn't have hit her full-on."

Mags *had* hit the villain, whose DNA declared her to be one Lienor Danica, now also known as Joy 'Mama' Silver. Hendriks explained how Lienor had lived in Erastus some thirty years earlier, and had been tied to a string of disappearances at the time, mostly young men. They'd managed to mark her DNA, but then she'd vanished herself.

No one had made the connection with Mama Silver, mostly because so much time had passed, and because the two looked nothing alike. But it was clear that the DNA on record for Mama Silver had to be a fake, or they'd have caught her immediately.

"You said Lienor claimed to be a Halfling," Aras rumbled, his voice deeper than normal now his throat had been damaged too. He'd heal, Kamile knew, so that was all that mattered. "Halflings react differently than other people."

"Yes, but efficiency rifles or pistols turn people into *ash*," Kamile argued. Then she sighed, thinking again of Coryn. It would have been a quick death, at least. "And Coryn was mixed-blood too. That woman must be dead, because what kind of Halfling is so powerful that she could withstand that kind of weapon? Let alone everything else that was thrown at her. I could *swear* I saw her on fire at one point…"

"She's the first Halfling."

All three of them looked across the room to see who'd spoken. Kamile immediately recognised Shulamithe as she stood in the doorway, still wearing that tidier version of Starbright's body, and with an expression of guilt across her face. "I'm so sorry, Kamile," she said, and her voice sounded strained. "I was waiting here. I wanted to help, but then I thought I'd just look for another host…but then you'd all left, all to face Lilith. That's who it really was. Not Lienor Danica. That's just one of her aliases."

Aras glanced briefly at Kamile, and his raised eyebrow seemed to say what she was thinking. *What about the need for secrecy?*

"Who's this?" Hendriks asked. "A friend of yours?"

"Yes," Kamile said quickly. She rose, moving over to where Shu/Starbright still stood. "I thought you had to leave," she said in a hushed whisper.

"I do. I'm really pushing it by still being here, but I stayed here for you – and I saw the DNA samples that had been left out when you all rushed off. I recognised the name at once, because I've known Lilith for a long time. Oh, centuries. Longer, even. And while she didn't used to use her power fatally like she did here, she's absolutely ruthless. Stronger than you, Kamile. Stronger than even your man here." She nodded towards Aras, who was listening avidly from nearby. "You could have died, all of you. It must have been divine intervention that you didn't."

"Lucky we were here then, hmm?" a fair-haired young man said from nearby. He stood hand in hand with Ash, the time traveller who'd somehow got a change of clothes, and who'd somehow managed to escape from a dodgy doorway. In the post-battle chaos he'd been briefly introduced as Ash's husband George, but he didn't look at all concerned over their recent trauma. Both he and Ash wore slightly rumpled-looking white tunics. "Safety in numbers, and whatnot."

Shu turned towards him, and her eyes briefly glimmered blue and yellow as she studied him, then Ash next to him, then a petite, dark-haired girl that Kamile had earlier seen throwing around some sort of supernatural fire. In spite of her earlier bravery, that last girl was now shuffling from one foot to another as if she couldn't wait to escape.

"Ah," Shu said, her whole posture relaxing. "Safety in numbers, when those numbers have gifts straight from the Mountain of Glass."

"Mountain of Glass?" Hendriks said, now looking quite interested. "And are these 'gifts' widely available? Can I see your registration, young man?"

George's thick eyebrows shot up. "Er…"

"He saved my life today," Aras cut in, his voice hoarse. "Him and his wife there, on the other side of that doorway Joy Silver sent me through. They're safe." He paused. "Don't know about ID, though."

"Hmm," Hendriks mused. "So we've got an unknown friend of Miss Kamile's," – he nodded towards Shu – "…and George and Ashlea Seymour, no ID but in possession of some unusually powerful weapons and abilities." Hendriks shrugged. "Ah, well. This isn't the Secular Republic, and we don't require everyone to have all the right paperwork before we'll let them stay. But the usual rules apply."

They'd been taught these when they'd first arrived. No violence. No consorting with malignant forces. And do what you want with the doorways or your own power, as long as it didn't cause trouble. Easy enough to follow, probably.

"Oh, we didn't say anything about staying," George began, but Ash elbowed him neatly in the side then grinned at Hendriks, then Kamile.

"We pass through occasionally," Ash explained in that odd, clipped accent of hers. "We won't cause any trouble."

"And what about your little friend there?" Hendriks asked.

"That was some firepower you were wielding earlier, Miss. Will you be sharing your skills?"

The petite dark-haired girl's eyes widened. "By the Rood, you saw that? No one *ever* seems to see that but myself! That is to say…I regret that I cannot share the gift, and, er, we have somewhere we must go…" She had a perfect local accent, Kamile noticed, but an odd way of arranging her words.

"We do?" George asked curiously.

"We do," Ash and the girl said in unison. Then Ash muttered something that sounded like, *"Schma schmeternity schmone, remember?"*

"Ah," George agreed. "Of course. That…thing. Well, good day to you all, and try to avoid being eviscerated before we see you next."

Then with that cheery goodbye, they set off. Hendriks threw his hands up as if giving in, and Kamile gave the trio a wave as they quickly left. She didn't know what they were up to, but it seemed as much about avoiding questions as it was about going anywhere particular.

Hendriks turned to Shu, who seemed to be growing paler by the moment. "And what about you, ma'am? Anywhere you need to be before you answer any questions? Or is there anything else important you'd like to tell us about this, er, Lilith?"

Shu sat abruptly on a nearby chair. She was blinking rapidly, but her voice was even as she said, "Lilith is…was…a power-leech, just like most Creatures. She's one of the few Halflings who can live in both the Other realm and this one, but she threw in her lot with the Creatures a long time ago. When I knew her, she'd target people, usually men, and create power links with them usually through the sound of her voice, or perhaps touch…

"I never quite understood it. But they'd be weakened throughout their lives, and she'd be stronger." She shrugged.

"Until now. But what I can tell you is that I saw the end of your battle. With those last strikes, I saw her power burn up like an old candlewick. She might not be dead, but she'll be weak."

Kamile looked at Aras, then Hendriks in horror. "Surely she couldn't come back from that!" She turned to Shu. "Are you saying we're still in danger?"

"You're always in danger," Shu replied. "All humans are, all the time, until death takes them to a new place. You just forget about this reality of your lives. But as for Lilith, the object that she had helping her is now gone. If I know her, she'll be more concerned about protecting her own skin than getting any revenge. So block up the doorways you know to be unsafe, put up one of those DNA scanner guards in case of her return…and just live your lives. Even if she's still out there, the worst of the danger for you is over…"

Shu fell silent, and after several moments Hendriks leaned forward to tap her on the knee. "Are you alright, ma'am?"

Shu turned slowly towards him. Then Kamile watched as she let out a sigh, her complexion changed to an ashy grey…and she collapsed onto the floor.

The watchman exclaimed in shock, and Kamile even saw Aras jolt in surprise next to her. But she wasn't surprised. Instead she was curiously numb as a medic was called, and the body was turned over to reveal a fatal wound on the forehead, and a very different face than the woman had had before.

"Definitely dead," the medic said not long later. She wore an expression of puzzlement, shaking her head as if things didn't make sense…which of course, Kamile thought, they didn't. "She must have been using some form of illusion to change her identity, you say? And perhaps something to stave off this injury." The medic looked up at Kamile. "Any next of kin?"

Kamile shook her head, leaning into Aras' side. "I didn't

know her well. If it's all the same to you, I'd like to go home. It's been a long day."

"Of course."

Hendriks watched as the mismatched couple left, the very petite girl and the tall, now one-armed man. They were leaning on each other, and just before they moved out of sight he heard her murmur, "I think we'll be seeing her again, don't you?"

Hendriks turned back to the body of the woman who'd been so very mysterious and helpful, right before she'd dropped dead. Not just slightly dead – but very, very dead. In his experience, bodies didn't turn that colour until they'd been deceased for several hours.

But something inside him told him not to worry about it. And really, he had more important concerns at the moment. "Arrange for the usual memorial," he told the medic, who also occasionally doubled as the town's mortician. "Double it up with Bob's, if you need to."

"Yes, sir." The medic removed the body, muttering the whole time about weird deaths.

If she hadn't wanted to deal with weirdness, Hendriks thought, she shouldn't have moved to Erastus. Just a few hours earlier, they'd identified the 'black fish' that had seemingly destroyed one of the River doorways. It had been Bob Novik, a drifter who'd robbed a local store several weeks earlier, then had fled into one of the doorways…not the River one. They'd only identified him because he'd still had the stolen goods somewhere in there. His DNA had been changed almost unrecognisably.

He'd been a fool, Hendriks knew, but one who didn't get the chance to be foolish twice. Besides, Aras Morison probably didn't need to know he'd killed an actual person rather than some kind of Other beast.

To a nearby watchman Hendriks said, "Get those doorways blocked immediately, and get those DNA scanner guards updated. We won't allow this kind of problem back here." Not in his town. Not when there were *children* here.

"Yes sir." The watchman paused. "All of the doorways, sir?"

Hendriks thought of the two doorways he knew of that both led somewhere wonderful, and were both currently shut off. "No. If we block too many, they'll just pop up somewhere else, like after last year's shut-down. Just block the ones we've had trouble with."

Once all this mess was sorted, he decided, he knew his next project.

Reopen the River doorways, the sooner the better.

Ash, George and Elspeth made their way across the busy town, heading towards the back entrance to the nearest Mountain of Glass gateway. Ash was arm-in-arm with George. They both still wore the white clothing which they'd picked up in their escape from Hades. Surprisingly, it was in pretty good shape.

Elspeth bounced along next to them, seeming as buoyant if she had drunk three cups of coffee. "Oh, what a day it has been!" she exclaimed, beaming at them. "And to think it began with merely taking the wrong gateway."

"It didn't *start* there," Ash argued, feeling a little defensive. "It started with a kaleidoscope and a picnic lunch, and Anne showing up to say Edward was nearly dead. Then we went to Angland again, then I came to Erastus, then I took the wrong gateway. Doorway. Whatever. Either way, I ended up in Hades."

She hunched her shoulders a little. Now they'd got past the initial, phenomenal relief of their escape and the recent battle, and ignoring the fact they'd saved Aras's life plus all those people down in the cells, she couldn't help but think she'd been an idiot. "I will never, ever, ever take an unmarked gateway ever again."

"You didn't know it was dangerous," George soothed her. "Lesson learned, hmm?"

"Actually," Ash countered, "I did know." She'd been thinking about this pretty much as soon as she'd had the mental space to do so, and she'd realised a few things. "I've got some alter-power gifts which other people will never have. But even when they didn't work, I still had my own gut feeling, which I ignored."

She rubbed her belly uneasily, frowning. "I was uncomfortable with Joy Silver from the moment I met her. I should have just listened to that feeling and kept my distance. I certainly shouldn't have eaten with her, or followed her anywhere just because she was pretty and friendly and I felt petty for disliking her. Now I realise that all those people were illusion, I wonder if the food had anything to do with my gifts not working properly."

"Most likely," George said from beside her.

"Hey! Aren't you meant to be on my side?"

"I'm on whatever side stops you from being in such danger ever again," he countered diplomatically. "But do you not recall how back when we first met, back in Iversley in – oh, I forget the year – I went out of my head from drinking tainted water. I very nearly walked off a fourth-storey balcony." He shuddered.

"True," Ash agreed, feeling a bit better. She now remembered that she'd thrown up after she'd gone through the Hades doorway. That had probably reversed any effects from the food. "So no more eating or drinking things from strangers, no more ignoring gut feelings about people, and no more taking unknown gateways. Sounds good?"

"Amen to that," George said enthusiastically. "We'll just keep to our own special gateways, right darling? And no going through alone."

"Never again," Ash agreed adamantly. Imagine if she was trapped away from George, or away from the baby after it was born. "Never ever. We go together, or not at all." And in her mind, that was a solemn vow.

"Verily, I'd been referring to my own foolishness earlier," Elspeth said. Her excited tone had deflated a little, perhaps after hearing Ash's lengthy monologue. "But it seems that even accidents can be turned to something of real value." She pointed at George. "You now have the Eternity Stone…and more importantly, we have a means to put it back where it belongs."

"Oh yeah!" Ash brightened. "You were saying that before, but you never got to explain. So, how do we do that?"

By this point they'd made it across town, to a lightly forested area near the shelter of a hillside. Elspeth stopped walking, then gestured for them to move aside. Then she cleared her throat and said loudly, "Avast, ye blaggards!"

"I beg your pardon?" George cut in, sounding offended. "We're hardly blaggards. Compared to some of the folk we've met, we're practically saints!"

"'Tis the code phrase," Elspeth said in a small voice. "And I have not yet finished."

"Oh. Carry on, then."

Elspeth cleared her throat again. "Avast ye blaggards," she said in a quieter voice. "Sky pirates ahoy, ahoy, ahoy."

There was a silence, then Ash and George exchanged glances…and burst out laughing.

"Are you sure that's the phrase?" Ash asked through snorting giggles. "It sounds kind of…" Ridiculous? Like the jingle off an old pirate-themed TV show?

"It most certainly is the phrase," Elspeth said earnestly. She set her small hands on her hips, looking rather like her sister in that moment. "I memorised it with great care. Ahoy, ahoy, ahoy-"

But just then a strong breeze swept through the glade they stood in. Suddenly a spotlight was in Ash's eyes, too bright to see anything, and there was the sound of bubbling laughter...

Fifteen

THE PRODIGAL RETURNS

Less than an hour after Kamile and Aras had returned to their small home on the outskirts of the town, life seemed to be back to normal. Aras was cooking something in the kitchen from a seated position (AKA, using the auto-rehydrator for very easy meals) while Kamile fed laundry through the machine, one item at a time.

There was something pleasant about the routine of seeing clothing go in dirty and wrinkled, then a few seconds later come out smooth and bright. Isla was asleep in the nearby bassinet, the whole drama having gone over her head, and Ric was using a colouring-screen on the floor in front of her.

Kamile hummed as she took a pile of now-clean clothing to the bedroom. She stepped around Ric, thinking of how in spite of the day's *ridiculous* difficulties, it had ended wonderfully well. Aras was alive and upright…and he loved her. The children were well, and surely-

Just then a faint creak sounded from behind her, and the hair on her arms stood on end. She slowly turned to see the wooden drawers on the room's old-fashioned side table begin to move out, all by themselves. This seemed very familiar…and very ominous.

"Aras!" she shouted just as the bedroom drawers themselves fell onto the floor, revealing two sets of gleaming eyes in the darkness within. She couldn't see them yet, but she knew exactly who it was – the two little pony Creatures who'd for years tainted her view of herself.

"You can't get rid of us," one of them hissed. Its low form came to the edge of the drawer, then it rose up onto its hind legs to reveal something that wasn't at all human, nor pony-like. Something she'd never seen before.

She couldn't help herself. She screamed and threw her washing pile at the thing, almost tripping over Ric at the same time, who hadn't moved at all.

Next thing she heard Aras come thundering in from the other room, and she barely glanced at him except to point at the drawers. He raised a weapon, and the closest Creature stumbled backwards almost comically fast.

But too slow. *BANG* – and the pony-thing flipped onto its back, almost squashing its twin. Then *BANG-BANG* two more shots and the two of them vanished into the darkness. Mere seconds passed, and the back of the set of drawers returned to simple wood. The entry to the Other was gone.

Kamile was shaking, and Aras moved towards her, putting an arm around her shoulder. "You alright?"

She nodded, then shook her head and buried her face in his chest. "You're injured," she cried into his shirt, "and you still dealt with them. But aren't they immortal?"

"Yes, but they still don't like the gun," he replied simply, and she didn't point out that his weapon was almost certainly illegal. Oh, well. "Why were they here? You didn't call them, did you?"

"No! No, I saw them earlier today through a doorway in the town. They were harassing me just like they used to, talking about...about Isla being unnatural, but so much was happening that I forgot." Kamile felt her face crumple. "I can't believe I forgot their threats! And...I don't know how to make them go away."

"I just shoot first," Aras said. "It always works." He scowled suddenly. "Maybe only on the little ones."

Kamile suddenly remembered how back at the Chosen Compound last year, the two Creatures – or Fey, as she'd thought at the time – had been frightened of this man. She'd wondered why, but she now had her answer. *Just shoot first.* "So they used to come to you, too?"

He nodded. "They tried. They'd say things that might sound true, but if I'd lived that way, I'd have been quite a different person. Like…the mighty should rule the weak, and it was right that I should have what I want, because others will give way to me. Things like that. Once I realised what they were doing, I started my current method. What did they say to you?"

She summarised their instructions, adding, "But now I know they were trying to divert me from my real destiny. I'm happy to avoid them, but I don't know how to. I mean…how did they even get in here?! It's not like there's a conduit. Even your old Fey-made arm is gone now."

Aras shrugged. "You don't give evil things a moment of your time. Don't engage with them, because they can't come out to you. Not really. But for them to be here…"

Don't engage, he'd said, and in that moment it seemed so obvious that Kamile almost felt silly. If she hadn't stopped to argue, they couldn't have chased her. Not really. They couldn't even have come out of the drawers properly…she hoped.

"A conduit," she murmured again, stepping away from him and looking around the room. That was when she saw Ric, still sitting quietly on the ground with his colouring-screen, and almost hidden behind his father. She'd forgotten he was even there. "Ric! Oh my goodness, are you alright? You weren't scared, were you?"

Ric's eyes were wide, but he looked down at his screen. "The horsies knocked. Should I have said don't come in?"

Aras bent down towards the screen as if to pick it up, then made an unhappy grunt of pain at the movement. "Kamile. Look at this picture."

She bent down beside Ric, and it only took a few moments to identify the childish image of two smiling ponies, with a long line connecting them to a humanoid shape. Her breath caught in her throat. "What's this, Ric?" she asked gently.

He didn't answer, but she didn't need him to. She'd long been concerned about his unusual knowledge regarding the Other realm. It looked like she'd found their conduit – and it was this little boy in front of her.

"How about we take a visit to that River of yours?" Aras suggested suddenly. "You kept asking before, but now I think it's important. We don't have to wait for the doorway to reopen. We can find a way, right?"

That sounded so unlike Aras that Kamile could only beam at him. "I know one or two people who might be able to help."

The Other realm

Peaceful stood in her own body for the first time in a very long time, feeling almost out of place without a borrowed human form. She'd left her last host body abruptly and quite by accident, but it couldn't be helped. She couldn't have borne leaving that town without sharing her knowledge. But now she was down here a new resolution filled her, and she felt more *Shulamithe* than she had in many years.

"News?" the Tiger said coldly from his place on his throne, grotesquely built out of things that were usually better left buried. "News that brings Wicked Shu all the way back down here, rather than stumbling around in an already dead host body. Must be interesting."

She ignored that slur. *I am not wicked, because the Master says I am not.* "You should know that the Halfling Lilith was severely injured in the border town of Erastus," she replied neutrally. "If she's still alive, then she's lost most of her own power, and is unlikely to ever have the same strength again. I believe she's somewhere in this realm. Perhaps she even went to her father, the White Prince."

That last part had been a guess, but speaking the current name for Veritas or Truthful had the exact effect on the Tiger that she'd expected. His blue/yellow eyes narrowed, but his voice remained cold, as always. "The half-breed is not here, so she must have gone to her vicious sire to beg for aid. He'll most likely kill her."

And that was the reason why even though the White Prince was nearly as strong as the Tiger, he'd never rule this realm, Peaceful thought. Regardless of who Truthful had been once, he no longer played well with others. "Then she may come here, seeking refuge."

The Tiger shrugged. "Then we may kill her instead. Or not; for like you, she has her uses. So few can travel in both realms."

"She held the Eternity Stone," Peaceful continued. "Now it is in the hands of the enemy. I understand they plan to return it to its point of origin, which will destroy many remnant gateways, and the Island of Exiles."

The last part pleased him, she could tell, although he pretended it didn't. "Then let them return it to its rightful place. The Stone has been of little use to us who cannot even touch it, and the Island of Exiles is a place that we cannot even speak into, let alone set foot. So let it go. But all that better not be why you called upon me. Give me more interesting news, Wicked Shu. Surprise me."

He thought he couldn't be surprised, she knew. And she had to put all her effort into keeping her expression neutral. No smirking. "I do have more interesting news," she continued gravely. "Important news. It relates to that time twenty-five hundred years ago, when the enemy had himself born into human form. You recall Yeshua of Nazarith."

Peaceful felt the increased tension all around her; felt the sudden attention from every single Creature within hearing distance. If the Tiger was touchy about the former Truthful, then he was *extremely* touchy about this new subject.

"I recall him," he gritted out. "This better be important."

"Oh, it is," she said earnestly. "Because after he was killed and his essence came down here, into these walls, we all thought you'd won. We thought that Amaranthus had massively misjudged and failed," – and here she heard a furious hiss that she'd actually *used* that name – "…and that now the barrier would be broken, and you would rule both realms, as you always wanted.

"But then he went and resurrected himself, and created all those exits from every single room here in these cities, and all those humans escaped. The ones who'd been trapped inside the walls for so many years. They all escaped with him to the light-world, leaving only a stubborn few behind, and vastly reducing your power."

"*YES!*" the Tiger shouted suddenly, rising to his feet. Swirls of purple-orange power rose up around him like leaf litter caught in the wind, and his eyes glowed like tiny suns. Those stripes on his arms stood out now, just as they did whenever he showed his power. "YES, I remember! You'd better have an exceptional reason for reminding me of this occasion, Shu, or I will make you suffer, whether you have special access to the human realm or not!"

But Peaceful didn't tremble, because she knew something he didn't. "I have a very good reason," she said calmly. "An excellent one. See, all those years ago when the Master came down here and humiliated you, and created an option for freedom for his precious two-legs both dead and alive, he also spoke to *me.*"

And now everyone was silent. The Tiger was silent. The Creatures who were pretending to check the scrying pools and the viewing windows were silent. Peaceful thought even the humans whose essence still remained in the walls were silent, too.

"He told me what you did to me before the Rift," Peaceful continued. "He told me how you stole my alter-power, almost destroying me, so that you'd have more power to attack him and try to steal the Heart. That's why you have stripes, ex-Beraht. Not for any other reason."

He stood from his throne and began moving towards her, his clawed fingers curled at his sides, but she held her ground and quietly continued. "And he said that I could come with him back to the light-world, and regain my place if I wanted. Or, I could stay down here and spy for him. Pretend to work for you, but follow his orders when he gave them." She lifted her chin, meeting his bi-coloured eyes. "I saw your wickedness, and I chose the second. I am Shulamithe, the Peaceful One, and I follow one master, ex-Beraht. One, and only one."

The Tiger lunged at her, screaming in rage, and she closed her eyes. She could see something bright from the corner of her eye, could hear a faint sound like beautiful music. She felt herself begin to change and fade just as he ran at her…right *through her.* And then she felt herself pulled away from the Creature city, away from the darkness and the dryness and the despair, until she was surrounded by light…

In the sky, near the Island of Exiles

George closed his eyes as the ship picked up speed, digging his fingers into the faintly glowing wooden balustrades on either side. "Are you quite certain this is safe?" he asked, not for the first time.

"It's flown by Amaranthus's People!" Ashlea practically shouted. *She* looked quite comfortable, he noted, sitting in an actual chair on this blasted contraption, rather than hanging onto the sides like he was. "It's probably safe enough. Anyway, I thought you liked technology, George?"

Locomotives and all manner of mechanical wonders that were run by people who knew what they were doing, yes. Supernatural flying ships driven by childlike People pretending to be pirates, not so much. The one with the captain's hat might have a sword, George thought wryly, but he wasn't fooling anyone. "Mm. If you say so." He swallowed, then changed the subject. "So…the Eternity Stone. What happens when we dispose of it?"

The non-hat wearing Person, who Ashlea had proclaimed 'adorable!' when she thought he couldn't hear, answered. "A sort of healing, Mister George. The Eternity Stone was created as the two realms were split, leaving an island which is part of neither, and which is now inhabited by…foolish people." He scrunched up his tiny nose. "Returning it should fix the problem."

"People?" Ashlea echoed. She looked over the ship's rail with interest, but of course there was nothing to see except stars and a lot of darkness. "Where?"

"On the isle, living in hovels made of driftwood," Elspeth said from her place across deck. She didn't look at all unnerved by their height or speed, George noted, and she was likely the only one who couldn't fly. "They were rough folk, and unkind, for all that one of them was called John. I think not all Jons are alike, do you not agree?"

"Er…"

"But I do not know what they would have eaten," Elspeth continued. "There seemed to be nothing alive on the whole isle, barring themselves."

"They probably didn't eat anything at all," the captain-hat-wearing Person said. "They won't need to eat, as no time passes. And my name is Jolly, not 'the one with the hat'."

That last part was definitely directed at George, and he felt his cheeks heat. The People had a tendency to read minds once in a while, which he found disconcerting, even if they were good-tempered. Or jolly, in this case. "My apologies, Mister Jolly. And er…what happens to *them*, after the Stone is returned?"

"Good question!" Jolly exclaimed excitedly. "Sweet and I have a bet going, want to hear it?" Then without waiting for an answer, he continued rapidly, "He thinks that they'll all be returned suddenly to their own times through the same gateways they came in by. Ping! Like stones from a catapult. But me, I think differently. I think they'll all come rushing up to us, waving their hands and begging for help, instead of shooting at us like they always do. And then…"

"You'll let them drown?" George ventured.

"No!" Jolly sounded outraged. "We shall rescue them, of course, and be highly gracious about their ongoing poor behaviour. It would be about time, for some of them."

Hmm. "And how long *have* some of them been here?" he asked, thinking it could have been months the way they were talking. Perhaps even *years*.

"We estimate between twelve years to eight centuries," Sweet replied earnestly. "For the worst offenders."

"Eight hundred *years*!" George exploded.

Just then Jolly rose to his feet, his round face alight with excitement.

"Exit coming up, you two! Now who's got the Stone?"

"I do," Ashlea called.

George had given it to her soon after the altercation in which he discovered that hitting a lady (or any female) was not one of his skills. His wife, on the other hand, seemed to have little difficulty striking either male or female should the need arise.

"But I want Elspeth to do it," Ashlea said as she climbed to her feet. "It seems only fair, since this was all her idea."

"Ooh, yes please," Elspeth said with an expression of delight. "What must I do to return it?"

"Come over here and take the Stone," Jolly instructed, "And when I tell you, you need to drop it just in the right place- *ooh*."

That last comment was because as Ashlea had stretched out her hand to pass Elspeth the Stone, the ship had drawn to a sudden halt and the tiny little black shape had slipped from her hand, bounced across the glowing deck, and off the side of the ship to vanish into the darkness.

George's jaw dropped, and Elspeth and the two People's eyes bugged even wider than they already were.

There were a few moments of stunned silence, broken by Ashlea's quite unladylike swear word. "Sorry," she muttered. "I didn't have a good grip on it. So…what now?"

"Wait," Elspeth said. She rushed up to the side of the ship, standing on her tiptoes to look over the edge. "I'd vow it landed, for I saw a speck of light on the isle."

"It did land," Jolly added from where he stood next to her. "Ooh. Look at *that*."

Next thing they were all looking over the edge. Below them, in the darkness, George could just make out the black shape of what must be the island, scattered with orange-red lights as though from torches. But the top of the island, which was shaped in a cone like a volcano, was now glowing white.

"It's shrinking," Sweet whispered. "Look Jolly, the peak is shrinking!"

George couldn't tell, for he had never seen the place before in his life. But as he squinted more closely at it, he thought that perhaps they were right.

"Lower the ladders!" Jolly announced excitedly, waving his miniature sword. "Raise the flags! Turn on the lights!"

With each order he spoke, George could feel the ship lurch under them, saw lights suddenly go on, and saw flags open up above them.

"This is it," Jolly declared. "Finally they'll come, those last stubborn ones. Finally!"

Ashlea sidled up next to George as the two others rushed around, doing what they no doubt thought was very important. "I don't know about that," she murmured. "I can see people now, not far below us, and they seem to be attacking the ship, don't you think?"

If by 'attacking' she meant hurling projectiles that came nowhere near it, then they most certainly were attacking. But the black water lapping all around the island was definitely drawing in closer, and the orange-red torches were going out one by one. Then the island was just a flat circle the size of Ashlea's lounge room back in the twenty-first century, crowded with dark figures...

"By Jove," he murmured in dismay. "What if they *do* drown?"

"They won't drown," Ashlea said. But she didn't sound so convinced.

"They're not coming," Jolly said to Sweet, sounding dismayed. "Why aren't they coming?"

"Because we just came by an hour ago, and there's no one

new on the island," Sweet replied. "These are the stubborn ones. Stubborn, Jolly."

"But...but..."

Below them the dark circle was still shrinking, and George was an inch away from testing his flying skills and seeing if he could rescue any of the dozen or so crowded down there, when suddenly...

"Ooh, did you see that?" Ashlea exclaimed. "One of them went flying- oh, there goes another one."

And another, and another. One by one, each of the swearing, stubborn exiles below was somehow picked up off the rapidly shrinking ground and flung through the air to vanish into various bright spots that had to be remnant gateways. And then the last person, standing on that last tiny patch of ground, looked up and shook their fist at the ship...before being rapidly sucked away and vanishing too. Now beneath the ship there was just black water, roiling and moving like any ocean in darkness.

"Is that it?" Ashlea murmured to George. "The Stone's gone, just like that, and if Elspeth is right, then all the remnant gateways are gone with it."

"It's a good thing that Amaranthus created special gateways for us to use," he replied thoughtfully, his eyes still on that black water. Then he turned to fix his attention on her; on her dear face half shaded by the almost-darkness. "And really, when one considers how the Stone has been used, one must think it couldn't have happened any later."

"I'll have to agree with that one."

In the background the two People had been debating something as the ship once again began moving and picked up speed.

"*Awwwww,*" Jolly moaned. "I lost the bet!"

"You underestimated the innate rebelliousness and stubborn

self-will of many humans," Sweet said simply. "While I expect they have more time in their own homes to change their minds – yes, you lost the bet."

"Well, what now? I can't be a pirate captain anymore!"

"There'll be another assignment," Sweet assured him. "And besides, what about the party?"

Jolly seemed to brighten. "Oh yeah, the party!" Then he turned to the three humans. "Where are we going to drop you three? Because we've got somewhere to be."

"The Mountain of Glass, if you will," Elspeth said politely.

George looked at Ashlea and raised his eyebrows. "Angland or the Southern Isles...? We were interrupted from both locations."

"Let's go with the middle ground," Ashlea suggested. "Erastus, then decide from there."

"Erastus it is!" Jolly said cheerfully. "My, what a popular destination! Now get ready..."

"You'd almost think he's about to push us out," George joked to Ashlea. "How do they get this thing to st*oooo-*"

The Other realm

Goodbye, Creature cities, Peaceful thought as the light filled her vision. *Goodbye, false master. Goodbye, barren lands.*

But then she felt the change of atmosphere, like suddenly being dunked in the water of life, and she heard cheering all around her. She opened her eyes to find herself in the light-world, at the base of a massive shining city. She could hear the water flowing down its sides, and smell the scent of life, and her friends were everywhere...

…barring a few, but she'd said goodbye to those in her heart a long time ago.

"Welcome home!" People were shouting happily all around her, both her own kind and many now-immortal humans. "Welcome home, Shulamithe!"

And then as Peaceful felt her heart fill with joy, she looked across and saw him. Her true Master, Amaranthus. The one she'd seen and heard only briefly since she'd gone away, but the one to whom she'd been loyal ever since the beginning.

He was looking right at her and smiling. And quietly, just for her, he said, *Well done, Shulamithe. And welcome home.*

Elspeth heard the distant cheering as she made her way back across the Mountain of Glass's magnificent garden. Somewhere there must be a marvellous celebration, but she did not mind that she was missing it. No, her attention was fixed somewhere else – on the tall, handsome boy currently sitting under their favourite peach tree.

"Where have you been?" Jon asked, his eyebrows furrowed. "I went looking, and finally had to get your sister. I couldn't find you anywhere."

Elspeth was stunned speechless. She opened and closed her mouth a few times, then realised 'twould look most unattractive and clamped it shut.

He got to his feet and walked over to her. She barely reached his shoulder, but she didn't notice as he was looking down at her so intently. "I have to go home, Bets, and soon. It's…well, I can't say, but I have to go. But I didn't want to go without saying goodbye."

Ah, so he *was* going. Elspeth closed her eyes briefly, then opened them to stare him straight in the face. "Simplicity said you'd gone back to where you came from."

He frowned. "You mean the Hall of Treasures? I went back to talk to Amaranthus about something, then when I returned, you'd gone. Where did you go?"

There was a long silence where Elspeth decided that Simplicity *really*, truly needed to answer questions more thoroughly…and that she herself ought to listen more carefully and not leap to conclusions. Then finally she replied, "Oh, here and there. When do you leave?"

"Um…" He looked uncomfortable. "Now."

"Oh." Elspeth felt her eyes pricking with tears, and she ducked her head, unable to meet his gaze. "Then I wish you luck, my friend. You do not need any…" Company? "…assistance?"

"Amaranthus has that covered. There are a few people back home that will help with what needs helping with… I think." Jon sighed. "Bets…"

"Yes?" She looked up at him hopefully. Forsooth, any declarations of love would not go amiss.

"Thank you. You've been a good friend." And then he leaned forward as if he wanted to – dare she think it – embrace her, but then stopped and scrubbed a hand through his hair as if that was what he had intended all along. "So, I guess that's goodbye."

"Goodbye," Elspeth echoed. And then when he turned and left? She actually did cry.

"You humans are so emotional," a female voice said from somewhere to her left. Elspeth looked up to see the same Person who'd sent her on that wild goose chase some time earlier. She looked like the same sturdy, placid woman as when Elspeth had last seen her, but when she moved, there seemed to be someone quite different hidden beneath that ordinary form… "Don't worry. No separation is permanent."

"Oh?" Elspeth could not help herself. She felt her eyes narrowing as she looked at the Person. "And how long might this separation be, prithee tell me?"

"Somewhere between three hundred years and one thousand."

One thousand…!

No, Elspeth decided suddenly. That would simply not do! Even if she was immortal herself, she simply would *not* go for that long without seeing Jon again! So with that in mind, she turned and marched for the Hall of Treasures, or the tapestry room, or wherever Amaranthus might be.

They needed to talk.

Epilogue

The River, Erastus entry
Four months later

I'm a beachball with legs, Ash thought happily, *but that's OK.*

She was floating on her back in the shimmering water, limbs outstretched like an unwieldy starfish, and feeling utterly weightless for the first time in six months. To her left George was playing 'fetch' with some of the smaller children including Ric, who was the son of Aras and… Ash didn't actually know who the mother was, but that hardly mattered.

Ric seemed far more childlike and innocent these last few times they'd met, but then Kamile said they'd visited the River quite a few times since the entrance was reopened. The River did tend to change people.

Just look at Anne. Even the thought of her old friend made Ash's face scrunch up in vague irritation, and she ducked her head underwater to clear away the feeling. Ash and George had finally had a very clear conversation about exactly why Anne had changed so much, and Ash was still coming to terms with it. Her problem wasn't the fact that Anne had been burned at the stake and was now immortal, Ash told herself irritably, it was the way she'd kept it a secret for so long!

Ash paused, still underwater, then let out an abrupt laugh that turned into a mass of bubbles. OK, she thought with some humour. Her problem *was* that Anne had been burned as a heretic, et cetera. And while Anne could have mentioned it earlier, Ash realised she'd been far too self-absorbed to notice on her own.

Ash broke the surface of the water, smoothing her hair back off her face then looking around. Lesson learned: pay more attention to other people. She decided to start with Kamile, who was sitting in the shallows nearby with her baby Isla, who'd grown to the 'fat and cute' stage over the last four months.

Kamile was chatting with Aras, who Ash thought was looking a lot healthier than when he'd been shoved backwards through a doorway, soaked in blood. Not hard to beat, but even so. His new prosthetic arm was almost a perfect match for his natural one, too.

Look at those guns. Ash paused a moment to study his musculature, then realised what she was doing and rolled back onto her back, looking away. *No perving at friends' husbands, even when said husbands are total beefcakes*, she told herself.

Further along in the water she could see a bunch of young teens, including a couple of friends of Kamile's, Poli and Magdalene. Magdalene was looking happier too, without those dark shadows under her eyes that she'd had for such a long time.

Getting tricked by a Creature. Been there, done that, Ash thought wryly. Fingers crossed…never again.

Just then George saw her looking in his direction. He stood, trying to wade across to her, then raised his arms and flew up out of the water before coming to rest by her side. "There," he said, sounding rather proud of himself. "Couldn't have done that in Regency Angland *or* the twenty-first century Southern Isles, could I?"

Ash found herself smiling. "And I couldn't go swimming in Regency Angland," she pointed out. "Remember how your sister-in-law started asking when I'd be behaving appropriately for my 'interesting condition'?" Apparently in George's time, pregnant women didn't allow themselves to be seen in public once their bellies were too big to hide under a corset.

Yes, a corset. For pregnant women. *Good grief.* And that was a culture that was too embarrassed to even use the word 'pregnant'…

George put his arm around her in the water, then briefly swamped both of them before letting go. "Oops. Sorry. And considering *her* interesting condition, she was probably thinking of herself too," he pointed out. "But we're here, and she's there."

"Mmm." Ash thought how Olivia might be less of an ice queen these days with how often she and Edward now visited their part of the River, but Ash and Olivia would never see eye to eye. But now that Ash and George had decided to spend most of their time in Erastus, that personality clash was no longer an issue. "We're here, having our strange and interesting life." She lay back in the water, thinking. "You asked me earlier why is it that we've been able to do so much, and to see so much, when others can't."

"And risk so much," George pointed out. "I can't count the number of times we've almost been killed, imprisoned or merely driven mad."

"Yes. Well." Ash probably could count them, but it would ruin her nice speech. "I was thinking that there's probably an answer to that, but I don't know what it is."

"I do."

"Oh, really."

"Yes, really," George mimicked gently. "Mrs Ashlea Seymour, the reason that we've had such interesting lives is simply this. We're going to change the world."

Ash lay quietly for a moment, with birdsong and laughter filling her ears (and just a little river water) then decided he had to be right. Because really, there could be no other reason.

The Tapestry Room

Amaranthus moved his finger away from that cluster of white threads, a smile of satisfaction on his face. "They're finally getting it."

Of *course* they were going to change the world. They already had, and would again. But then every person was meant to change their own world. Every person did in some way, for better or worse. Just ask their neighbours, or family, or work colleagues. It was inevitable.

But then a few people did seem to get carried away, he acknowledged as his finger traced another fine white thread, all the way to the far end of the tapestry, where it was almost completely black. Fortunately, he could work with overenthusiasm. It was apathy that was harder to manage.

"Jonny boy," he murmured. "Let's see what you can do."

Not quite the end.

Read on for a description of Jon's story, Whiter than Snow
(Across Time & Space book 6)

I felt a real mix of satisfaction and regret coming to the end of this novel. In this case, I say goodbye to some of my favourite characters, Ash and George. While they may make cameos in the final two books of the series, their own stories have now been completed, and they'll live happily ever after in their own time-travelling way.

Instead the final two books focus on Jon, Elspeth and a few new characters in an entirely new setting. It also further develops the Amaranthus/Creature storyline, and does have a definitive ending. Look out for *Whiter than Snow* and *City of Light*, coming soon.

A few people wondered what happened to Anne in this book. I purposely kept her scenes to a minimum – now she's become immortal and is technically 'perfect' she's not half as interesting to write about. She knows too much! Hence her sister taking her place. Elspeth has a lot of Anne's historical quirks, but lacks the arrogance, so is perhaps more likeable and easy to identify with.

As for the book's content – as always, several ideas came from freaky, fascinating dreams that played out like movies. A killer that made people laugh themselves to death. A vast pit in the ground, with these mummified creatures dragging people into it. 'The island of exiles' with evil inhabitants and a supernatural flying ship. A beautiful but villainous golden-haired man through a stone archway.

In that last dream I was like 'ooh, I know he's evil but he's so gorgeous! I'll just chat with him from a distance.' To extend the metaphor – how often do we choose to mess with things we know will hurt us? Or maybe that's just me.

Perhaps those dreams were a little freakier than normal, but there were some really thought-provoking, serious concepts in this book too. So Edward actually *did* die briefly (did you notice?) and I was able to expand on the question of 'if we're more than just dust, what happens to our 'true selves' after our physical bodies fail?' In this case I got to say *exactly* what happens in relation to this universe's afterlife, which was good fun, but also was the basis for some interesting real-life conversations.

The place/historical names in the book were carefully chosen too. As with the whole series, the names are variants on the existing name, either by using the actual historical name, or by amending the name based on its meaning, or by amending the name. In all cases, the intention is that readers recognise who is being referred to. I.e. Angland is obviously England, but refers to the original tribe of the Angles, from whom the name came. Jerushalom refers to Jerusalem, with the second part of the name meaning 'peace' depending on where you find your translation. I like this interpretation.

On a side note, Edward's near-fatal injury was inspired by a nasty accident my sister had recently. It showed me that I can't just go knocking my characters out and thinking they'll be fine, because concussion is serious, people! (I think I'll have to use drugs or stun guns instead.) And yes, while a lot of my storylines are completely fantastical, I still like to build on a realistic framework.

If you enjoyed *The Hidden Door*, please do review it or rate it wherever you purchased it, or at **goodreads.com.** It really helps improve the book's visibility, and gets it out to other readers.

Cheers

**The story continues
in book 6 of 7:**

Time to go home - ready or not.

Jon is an accidental time-traveller. He's lived as a nobleman, as a refugee and most recently, in the supernatural Mountain of Glass. None of those places are home - which is the place he desperately wants to avoid.

But he'll have to return to the world of the distant future. It's a place where people's worth is determined by the Creature they're pledged to, and after a lifetime of being pledgeless (and feeling worthless) he's made some incredibly dangerous choices. Is it any wonder he doesn't want to return to face the consequences?

And Jon isn't the only one out of time. Elspeth of Covington has escaped Tudar Angland of 1556 AD and is determined never to return. So when her best friend (and unrequited love interest) Jon returns to his own home, she takes the opportunity to follow him. Armed with new supernatural abilities gifted by Amaranthus, she now has the chance to protect someone who doesn't know they're in danger. The only problem is that she'll arrive at a time before Jon has ever left, and therefore before he knows who she is...

But what Jon and Elspeth don't know is that a battle is taking place in the Other realm, one between the Creatures themselves. The outcome will determine the fate of that realm, and of their own world too...